I0618966

EMPIRE
OF THE
SON

More Than The Ancients Series – Book 1

JOSIAH STONE

Empire of the Son

Vision Publishing

ISBN 978-1-898824-05-3

10001e

Contents

Contents

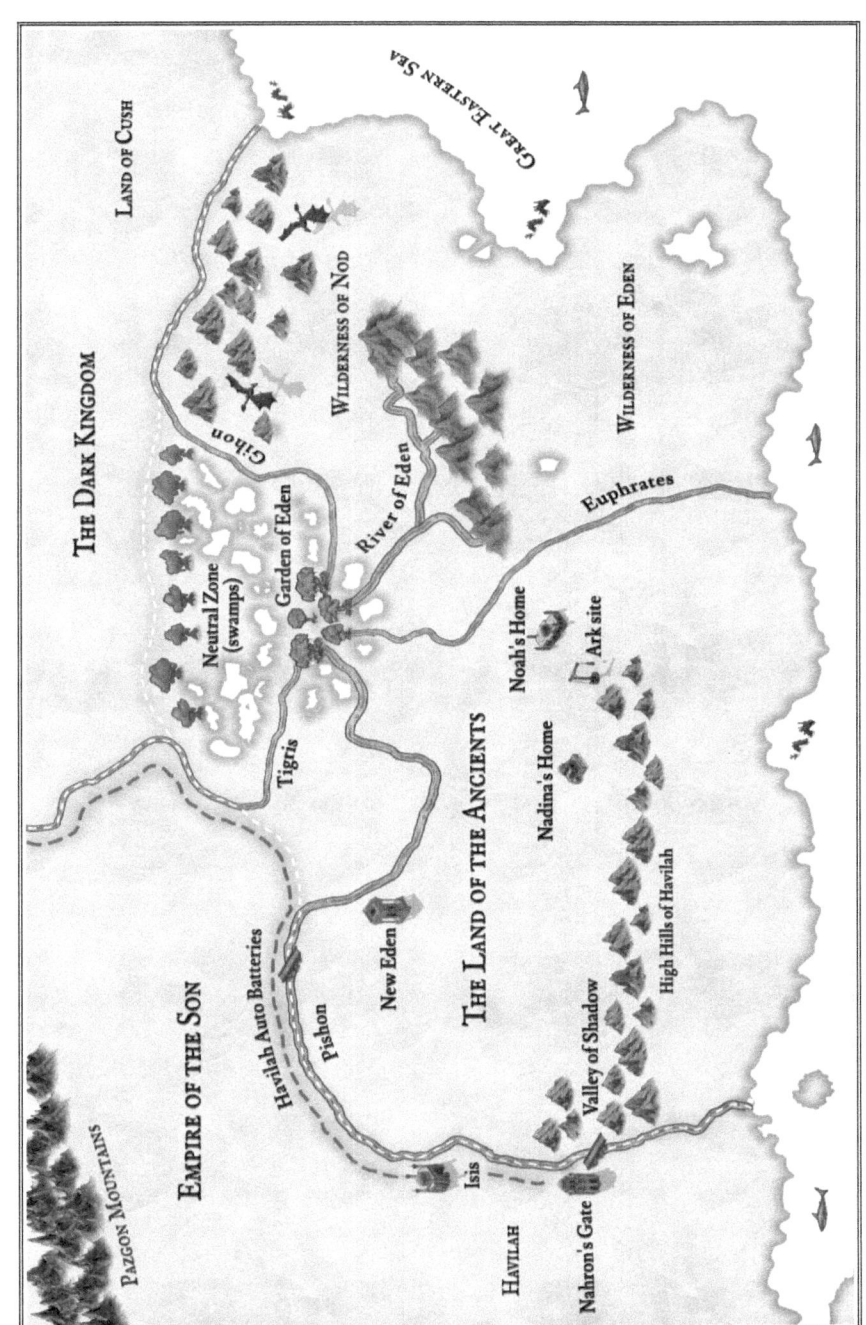

THE DARK KINGDOM

LAND OF CUSH

GREAT EASTERN SEA

Gihon

WILDERNESS OF NOD

WILDERNESS OF EDEN

River of Eden

Euphrates

Neutral Zone (swamps)

Garden of Eden

Noah's Home

Ark site

Nadina's Home

Tigris

EMPIRE OF THE SON

PAZON MOUNTAINS

Havilah Auto Batteries

Pishon

New Eden

THE LAND OF THE ANCIENTS

High Hills of Havilah

Isis

Valley of Shadow

HAVILAH

Nahron's Gate

The thing that has been, it is that which shall be; and that which is done is that which shall be done: and there is no new thing under the sun.

Ecclesiastes 1:9

Chapter 1

The Dream

*W*ater. Water everywhere. An ocean as far as the eye could see. He knew it was deep. How, he did not know, but he was certain it was. He also understood that no matter how far he might travel in any direction, the waters would never end. That was the nature of dreams; you knew things in them, yet you didn't know why.

Then there was the atmosphere over the gently rolling waves.

Peaceful.

This should have made it a happy dream, but something in the dream was wrong, terribly wrong. It was as though the darkened waters were hiding a secret. Something they had subdued and did not want revealed. He understood that. He too had hidden what he'd done. For the sake of order. For the sake of peace. His own peace. Yet the peace in the dream was different. It was as pervasive as the endless oceans of his dream, but instinctively he knew it was not his peace.

The strangest thing was that it wasn't anyone's peace. Because there didn't seem to be anyone alive in the dream to have it

◆◆◆ ⚑ ◆◆◆

The warm rays of the early morning sun soothed away the darkness of the dream. He blinked, unsure which one was now reality. Easing himself up in the bed; he felt vulnerable. This annoyed him. He ruled half the world and yet couldn't order the dream to stop nor have it quietly disposed of. Its persistence had began to wear him down. Recently, it had become an almost daily occurrence. Swinging round, he sat up on the edge of the bed and wearily rested his head in his hands.

Medication hadn't worked. His advisers had been a waste of time. They knew no more than he did, trying to soothe his mind and flatter him with what they assumed he wanted to hear.

Exhausted, he stood up and shuffled to the balcony. The air was fresh. The white marble balustrades inlaid with diamonds sparkled softly. He poured himself a glass of wine, frowning at the horizon. The sun was warm and reassuring, but his heart wasn't. He had to know what the dream meant. He was accustomed to demanding everything. He was the emperor. The irony was that he couldn't demand an explanation of himself that he didn't know how to give.

He mused that some people he'd got rid of may not have known how to give him what he'd demanded of them either. Not that he now cared about their undeserved fates. It was merely interesting to have another perspective on their failures. He loathed people who failed him. As for those who refused to submit to his will, he hated them. Hated them and feared them, although he would never admit the latter. And herein was the problem. The only people likely to be able to interpret his dream were a people who did not submit to his rule.

He watched a group of chirpy birds pecking up crumbs from the previous evening's meal. He envied them. Their lives were so simple – yet so was his. He only had to click his fingers and adoring women and admiring friends attended to his every desire. He knew none of it was real, but then what he declared real became real. That was how he dealt with life. He made it what he wanted. He moulded people to be what he wanted. When he grew tired of them, he discarded them. New actors replaced them, each fulfilling their part.

The trickle of the bird's water fountain caught his attention. The dark heaving waves of the dream flooded back into his mind. He knew that he could not ignore a dream like this. He realised he needed help. The idea was repulsive. Someone he could trust. He wasn't sure what that meant. There had been a time when there were many people he thought he could trust. Some had liked him; one or two might have even loved him. Love was a mistake he no longer made. Not after what had happened with Ariana. No, he would never go down that road again. But trust? There was one person...

Chapter 2

The Emperor's Cousin

*T*almeon was hurriedly escorted into the outer courts of the Great Imperial Palace of the Empire of the Son. The formidable marble columns lining the walkway to the inner courts were intimidating, even to the bravest of souls. The palace's air of grandeur carried with it the message of absolute power. There was no doubt that this was home to a ruler far beyond the reach of his subjects. Everything Talmeon's eye could see was about the unquestionable rule of Nahron. The Great Emperor – as he called himself – who unsurprisingly lived in the Great Palace. Where else? thought Talmeon sarcastically.

Led along the endless mosaic floors, Talmeon recalled how his cousin Nahron had always eyed the capital – the infamous City of Light. Leaving his forefathers' homelands, he had forged a career in the government of the previous ruler of all western lands, Salfar the Great. Nahron had schemed his way from a desk job in the run-down industrial city of Vastar, all the way to a palace bigger than anything ever constructed – except for the Stadium of Honourable Games.

Honourable. Talmeon considered that word for a moment. Honourable was a term that no longer meant anything but was still used as though its meaning held together the very fabric of society. It was true, among the ordinary citizens of the world's single vast continent, and for those who lived under Nahron's rule, there was indeed the façade of honour. There was order and the rule of law, but the nearer the top you went, the more widespread corruption became. By the time you worked in the Great Palace, your life hung by a thread and truth was a commodity that was bought, sold, and even murdered for.

The two Palatine Guards escorting Talmeon in their smart but slightly pretentious blue and red uniforms were silently replaced by Royal Guards. The Royal Guards were dressed only in black, their clothing was, as always, indistinct and utilitarian.

Talmeon caught sight of the Great Doors of Access. Looming at the end of the vast concourse, they were an impressive feat of architectural engineering. Leading to the Hall of Favour, where dignitaries often met their emperor for the first time and sometimes unknowingly enjoyed their last meal. The doors were twenty-four cubits high and twelve cubits wide. Made of the finest cedar wood, they were engraved with all the great victories of Nahron. Of which there were none; yet somehow, they still filled the face of both doors. Talmeon mused that engravings of Nahron stabbing people in the back and poisoning their drinks would be more representative of his cousin's victories. Clearly, these things weren't about to be engraved on anything except perhaps his tomb.

Shortly before reaching the doors, which Talmeon was eager to watch open silently on the very mechanisms he'd designed. The Royal Guards escorting him turned a sharp left. They ushered him through a small opening in a wall. Talmeon's heart raced. Was he going to be murdered? It didn't make sense. Why had they summoned him to the palace? Nahron was brutal and ruthless, but no fool. His known enemies usually died of rare illnesses or simply disappeared. He had never been an enemy of his cousin.

Talmeon desperately tried to focus. He noticed that the guards were unusually respectful. Something was definitely afoot. He concluded that it wasn't his imminent death.

Ushered into an elevator, ascending several floors in seconds; he began to relax. Going up, not down, was a good sign. A walk along a less grand but equally intricately decorated corridor led to another elevator. Where was he going? This time the ascent was exhilarating and much longer than the first. The doors eventually opened. Talmeon gasped.

Gleaming through a glass canopy before him was the whole City of Light. He realised he was in, of all places, the Divine Tower, the very centrepiece of Nahron's majestic palace. A place where no one except his cousin's personal servants and closest advisers ever went. The guards stood still, mutely indicating that Talmeon should stay and wait where they'd stopped.

"Welcome, dear cousin." Nahron strolled through a side door, concealed in a mural of yet another of one of his non-existent battles. Talmeon quickly bowed. Nahron ignored the bow, extended his hand, and then hugged him.

"How are you, how's your family?" Nahron asked. "Your wife and children?" He paused for effect when he mentioned children. It was the customary warning. Talmeon did not fear losing his own life; he'd learned to live with that, but his wife and children, that was another matter. He loved them; their well-being was always on his mind. Nahron's small dark brown eyes smiled at him without remorse; Talmeon bravely met his gaze.

"They are well, my lord, thanks especially to your continuing care and protection." Talmeon emphasised the words, *your continuing*, and thought he imagined it but was sure one of the Royal Guards nearby winced slightly. His words couldn't have been more plain. Talmeon calmly acknowledged that Nahron held the lives of both him and his family in his hands.

At the end of the day, Nahron needed Talmeon and Talmeon needed Nahron. The arrangement had worked well for more than a century; there was no reason to change it.

After a brief tour of the upper glass canopy and pointless comments about well-known landmarks, they were talking freely. It was as though time had taken a step back and they were young again. Talmeon had outlasted almost all his contemporaries in Nahron's service. The understanding between them had been simple; he was family, a scientist, and that was all. He'd politely but firmly turned down every opportunity to advance politically. It was true, as head scientist of the whole realm, his position was powerful and privileged, but his job was technical, not political. Talmeon's technological genius had saved both the empire and Nahron several times. Everyone knew that.

"Walk with me, dear cousin," Nahron spoke ingratiatingly as though Talmeon were the superior of the two.

Talmeon knew Nahron well. It had been years since they'd played together as youths, but he still understood his facial expressions. Nahron was unsettled; something was troubling him. Talmeon thought he knew what it was. The absurdity was that half the empire's upper echelons knew what it was. One of Nahron's closest advisers hadn't been able to resist revealing the secret of his emperor's troubling dreams. After that, it was only a matter of time before the news of it was everywhere. Everywhere, except of course, than on the news. Which would have meant certain death for a very large number of people indeed.

"You look troubled, Your Majesty," Talmeon spoke gently. "Is something concerning you?" Nahron tensed. He wasn't used to such candour. But then he remembered who he was speaking to. Perhaps the only person in the world whom he could really trust.

"Indeed," he answered hesitantly, without an admission of weakness, "I want to tell you about my dream."

Talmeon silently sighed. So that was it? Another dream of grandeur? Nahron had come up with plenty of those over the years. A concerted effort always followed each one to ensure that whatever he had dreamt came to pass. But then why the worried look? Why the trip to the Palace? Talmeon was intrigued. He listened patiently as Nahron recounted his vivid and recurring dream about the endless expanse of water. The sincerity of Nahron's tone and the persistence of the dream left no room for doubt in Talmeon's mind. His officially half-divine cousin was, for the first time in his entire life, having some kind of spiritual experience. And it was profoundly affecting him.

"What does it mean?" Nahron asked, an edge of desperation creeping into his voice.

"At first glance, dear cousin," Talmeon spoke softly but possibly a little too soon, "I have no idea." He paused, looking away and thinking of what it really could mean. He'd already considered the trivial explanations that Nahron's advisers had doubtless fed him. Things like that the completeness of the covering of the water in the dream was symbolic of his cousin's reign and power. However, this didn't fit too well because Nahron was sure he was personally absent from the dream. Then there was the unending expanse of water. Which according to Nahron had some kind of awful finality about it. This also didn't fit well with the idea of him happily ruling the world. Although Talmeon mused that the prospect of Nahron ruling the whole earth did indeed have an awful finality about it.

"My Lord, I really don't know," Talmeon spoke again, "but one thing is certain: the dream is real and must be about something very significant. It would be foolish to ignore it."

Talmeon immediately realised he had implied that Nahron might act foolishly and was about to correct himself when Nahron spoke back.

"Yes, you are right, dear cousin; those thoughts were already mine. To ignore it would be foolish indeed." He paused for a while as though considering something he didn't want to admit. After a while, he spoke up.

"We both know that there is only one place to go and reliably interpret dreams."

Talmeon, still recovering from his earlier mistake, remained politely silent. The official place to interpret dreams was with Nahron's own spiritual advisers. Talmeon wasn't about to contradict that. Failing them, the High Priest Mandarus was supposed to have a direct line to the gods. On the one hand, expecting Mandarus to interpret anything was an absurdity. He was merely a puppet introduced by Nahron. On the other, if Nahron introduced something, genuine or not, it had to be treated as if it were real.

Mandarus had been a provincial waste management administrator. He and Nahron were distantly related. After he'd come to power, Nahron replaced the previous High Priest, whom he had assassinated, with Mandarus. The surprising thing was that despite his background in garbage collection and seeming lack of mental acuity, Mandarus had risen to the role extremely well. He certainly did better at it than garbage collection. Rumour had it that when he'd recently proclaimed solemn three and seven day fasts, he really had fasted. It seemed that Mandarus took his role seriously. Not only politically seriously but spiritually seriously too.

Talmeon was deeply amused at the thought of Mandarus giving any kind of spiritual direction. But then there was one outstanding thing about him. He'd produced the single most beautiful woman to ever grace the face of the earth – Ariana.

How someone like Ariana had been born to Mandarus and his long-dead wife, Talmeon had no idea.

Nahron backed off from whatever he was about to say. They both talked a while longer, slipping in and out of their pasts, family histories, even happy times. The guards were always close. Talmeon thought they were surprised to see their emperor chatting so freely. It was obviously a rare sight, if not one that had stopped happening many years ago.

"Anyway, the reason I have called you here, my dear cousin," Nahron nervously broke through the idle chatter, unable to put off what he wanted to say any longer, "is that I would like you to travel to the Land of the Ancients and find the interpretation of my dream."

A sharp silence hung in the air; even the guards were more alert, although they were not supposed to pay any attention to what was said.

Talmeon was incredulous, "Me, go to the Land of the Ancients!?"

He was barely able to conceal his shock.

"Yes, dear cousin," Nahron spoke with a touch more authority, ensuring Talmeon understood that all the geniality between them didn't extend to his requests becoming optional. "You are going to the Land of the Ancients, and you will find the interpretation of my dream."

Chapter 3

The Land of the Ancients

*T*he Land of the Ancients lay on the eastern side of the High Hills of Havilah, at the edge of the great western plain. There, the mighty river of Eden divided into the Pishon, Gihon, Tigris, and Euphrates. The land bordered the Empire of the Son, their historic ally, and the Dark Kingdom, their mutual enemy. It also extended hundreds of miles east all the way to the Great Eastern Sea.

The previous ruler of the Empire of the Son, Salfar the Great, had got too full of himself. He'd tried to coerce his old allies, the Land of the Ancients, to submit to his new religion. They would not, so he resorted to force. The renowned 12th Legion, fifteen thousand strong, was sent to kill, capture, or, as a last resort, deport everyone there.

Salfar boasted of his upcoming liberation of civilisation from deviant religion. The telecasts showed the famous veteran troops marching into the Valley of Shadow. It was the only way for a large army to cross into the Land of the Ancients from the west.

The disciplined troops with their state-of-the-art weapons were known to be ruthless, even savage. To the 12th, conquer meant nothing more than slaughter. It was considered pointless overkill. Those citizens of the empire in the borderlands of Havilah weren't so sure. They knew that if you went into the Land of the Ancients in peace, to trade, or in harmless ignorance, you came back. If you went with evil intent, one of only two things happened – you either never came back or you joined the Ancients.

The Ancients were the direct descendants of the great Enoch, publicly taken from this world more than six centuries earlier. They maintained the faith of their fathers and claimed true knowledge of the ways of the Creator.

The 12th Legion had entered the Valley of Shadow on the first day of the month of Sunrise. By the next day, they may as well have never existed. No one had the slightest idea what happened to them. No bodies were found, no equipment, not even a bootlace. No last minute garbled message. Nothing. The mist had lifted and they were gone, all fifteen thousand of them. Salfar never recovered from this débâcle. His popularity plummeted. His divine authority dispersed, like the mist in the Valley of Shadow on the sun-kissed morning when his famous legion vanished.

Salfar pathetically attempted to blame their old enemy, the Dark Kingdom, but the idea was absurd. The Dark Kingdom had wiped out the veteran 12th Legion? Leaving not even a single survivor? Deep inside the Land of Ancients – in places where their forces had never been!? News programmes ran ever bolder reports until, in the end, the conclusion was simple. Salfar was a dud and keep out of the Land of the Ancients unless your visit was in peace.

The Land of the Ancients made no statement. They stayed true to their peaceful ways and their friendship with the Empire of the Son. Some from their lands even served as volunteers in the Empire of the Son's military.

This was also the time at which Nahron came to power. Amid the chaos after the revelation that Salfar and his religious leaders had taught nothing but falsehoods, Nahron emerged from obscurity proclaiming restoration. He bought inexpensive off-peak airtime on a popular telecast channel and created a set that resembled the interior of a humble temple. He put his distant cousin, Mandarus, on holiday from his waste management job, in a simple white robe and set him up as high priest. He took Mandarus' daughter, Ariana, and made her look as innocent yet sensual as possible, proclaiming her a pure handmaiden, devoted only to the spiritual well-being of the people. Nahron announced that he was on air with no other ambition except to restore purity. A suitably vague but nonetheless noble cause. He preached about the need for humility and how it was the path to true freedom.

After three days, Nahron was on a multitude of channels, primarily due to Ariana's outstanding green eyes. And also thanks to the telecast executives who knew a ratings improver when they saw one. Soon Nahron was holding rallies in the City of Light's Grand Park. The networks gave him airtime that only the richest moguls could have bought. The people loved him; they loved Ariana and they even loved Mandarus for his mute simplicity. Calls for Nahron's ascendance to power were paid for but, much to his delight, sometimes even genuine. He manoeuvred himself through the chaos of those times to become a custodian of the people. And then their emperor.

The people were moved, overawed. A humble ruler who openly repented of his suitably vague shortcomings. An emperor who built a temple before his own palace. And then there was a simple priest. Someone with no aspirations of grandeur. Moving up from garbage administration, Mandarus was in fact already experiencing grandeur. And above all else, a Chaste Maid, as Ariana had become known. Devoted only to the welfare of the people and the yet to be revealed Son. It seemed as though a return to the great revivals of old had taken place. Naturally, Nahron's increasing wealth confirmed this return to the truth. The reward for his humility was a palace that made the previous emperor's seem like a barn. With the proof of his anointing confirmed by his material blessings, no one could question the divine favour that was on Nahron; the few that did simply disappeared.

Salfar's highest officials, who'd all endorsed their disgraced leader's disastrous venture into the Land of the Ancients, waited in mute terror. They had no credibility left and nowhere to hide. But Nahron was no fool; he had all of Salfar's high-ranking cronies banished to the borders of the empire by the Land of the Ancients. Within one year he ruled the Empire of the Son more autocratically than Salfar could have ever dreamed of. Yet everyone, except those at the very top, believed him to be the kindest and most reluctant humble ruler to have graced the face of the earth.

As for the Land of the Ancients, Nahron had better ideas than Salfar. He too didn't want some crazy preachers from there showing up his hypocrisy. So he stayed off the subject of history altogether. He was so popular in the present that he didn't need appeals to the past to endorse his absolute power. Nahron's plan for the Ancients was simple: don't fight them, undermine them instead.

Nahron banished Salfar's cabinet and governors to the Havilah borderlands. He also promoted many of Salfar's minions to live and work there. The 12th Legion's bereaved families were also among those sent. Their roles were to restore the border regions desecrated by its troops. Of course, the 12th Legion hadn't actually got as far as desecrating anything, because they'd simply disappeared. Even so, it was a brilliant piece of propaganda.

Nahron knew the Ancients wouldn't tyrannise a bunch of disgraced officials. Or their bereaved families. In fact, the Ancients had never been known to oppress anyone. On the contrary, they would

17

evangelise and proselytise them. Then these new low-level cronies, in their eagerness to gain favour with their increasingly divine emperor, would flock to the Ancients' temples on both sides of the border. While hoping to advance their careers, they would inadvertently become an army of spiritual termites.

The plan was simple: corrupt the Ancients. Infiltrate their society and entice their children with glittering career prospects. With wealth, with power – only to do good of course, and with the easy daughters of the old political elite. Modest in public, yet as skilled naked as their parents in political office were fully clothed.

After many decades, Nahron's plan appeared to have worked. The borders between the Land of the Ancients and the Empire of the Son had become blurred. Administratively, it was straightforward. Taxes were levied right up to the western bank of the great Pishon River, but socially you couldn't tell where one area ended and the other began. In time, new temples sprang up, each one more accommodating of the shallow or even non-existent faith of their new attendees. Each one, more glitzy than the previous, and each one less about the Creator and more and more about itself.

As Nahron envisaged, the ladder climbers of the poor and middle classes flocked to these new temples like bees to a honey pot. It was their route to blessings. To promotion in the empire.

Yet all was not lost. In the hinterlands of the Land of the Ancients, there was the family of Methuselah. Never mentioned in the glitzy temples of the border cities. Methuselah's family was different, very different. Prosperous they were, but their openness of heart and life-style was not one the priests of the city elites were interested in emu-lating. They were transparent, and there was absolutely no place for that in a modern temple priest's life.

It was to those distant regions that Talmeon knew he would have to go. Deep into the hinterlands where standard Imperial flying and ground transports didn't work. The energy lines generated by the earth's magnetic field that traversed the globe, powering almost everything that moved, were non-existent there. He would have none of the empire's security apparatus to protect him. Only the sincere entered the hinterlands of the Ancients. The memory of the 12th Legion was not one to be easily erased.

Chapter 4

Nahron's Gate

*T*almeon arrived at Nahron's Gate, a town on the Empire of the Son's eastern border. Named after Nahron's great resettlement program. Initiated after the fall of the previous ruler, Salfar the Great. From there, one could reach the Land of the Ancients by crossing the Valley of Shadow Bridge that spanned the great Pishon River. The river marked the eastern border, cutting right through the town and encircling all the empire's lands of Havilah.

The Valley of Shadow was unusual. It was a verdant valley with steep hills on either side. Those hills ran north and south, parallel to the Pishon. They formed a natural barrier between the Land of the Ancients and the Empire of the Son. A narrow pass near the end of Nahron's Gate suburbs gave access to it. It was on the eastern side of the Pishon. It was called the Valley of Shadow, because its steep, jagged hills cast deep shadows at different times of day. The word shadow had taken on new meaning when the 12th Legion had disappeared there many years ago.

Since then, fewer people from the empire ventured into the Land of the Ancients. At the same time, many of its inhabitants moved to the western bank of the Pishon. The result was that Nahron's Gate was a town that straddled the great river. On the eastern bank, the authorities refrained from levying any Imperial taxes because this was technically the Land of the Ancients. On the far more populous western bank, the empire maintained full administrative control. The result was that the cultures of both sides spilled over into each other. The empire corrupted the Ancients on the eastern bank. The Ancients civilised the western bank. Nevertheless, the empire definitely appeared to have been gaining the upper hand.

The contrast between the atmospheres struck Talmeon. Nahron's Gate was quite different from the infamous City of Light, the Imperial capital. He watched as the crowds milled about on the main concourse outside the government centre and Grand Station. Shops were full. Telescreens filled every bar and cafeteria. But a semblance of dignity remained. By contrast, in the City of Light there was little dignity. People shouted in the streets. They wore indecent clothes and were often drunk or stoned. The better off rarely left their gated communities without protection. The security services administered a rough justice. Even small children freely swore. The streets were full of fortune tellers. An endless variety of idols were always for sale. In some parts of the capital, there seemed to be more women who were prostitutes than not. Wonder cures by various self-proclaimed healers abounded. Lunatic prophets shouted garbled messages on many a street corner.

In Nahron's Gate there was none of that; here there was a natural sense of order. There was dignity too, but it was shallow. Talmeon saw men leaving office buildings. They were scanning groups of women outside. They chose a companion from among them after looking over the alternatives around. It was evident that they weren't meeting their wives or girlfriends after work.

Talmeon decided to take a walk; he felt safe here. His chief body-guard raised some concerns. But, Nahron's Gate was not the kidnapping and extortion town that some others in the south and west were. He browsed the shop's familiar brands and products. Then, a large telescreen outside a nearby bar drew his attention. A somewhat rowdy but cheerful bunch was watching it. The group, mostly men and a few women were engaged in drinking, eating, and laughing at the screen. Curious, Talmeon walked around to face the screen to see what was so amusing. He was none the wiser. A man in white robes was preaching in front of a very large wooden structure. But, the program ended moments later. It had been a documentary about religious quacks and fools. The crowd roared with laughter shouting insults at the screen. The channel switched to a documentary about another preacher. It failed to hold anyone's attention for long.

"Stupid Ancients," shouted someone from the crowd. Talmeon was intrigued. The Ancients were called many things these days. But, they were not usually called stupid, especially by the common people of the eastern lands. The educated elite saw the Ancients' devotion to good works as foolish. Their unique religion had no mercantile gain. The common people of the east, however, usually admired their courage. They also respected their uncompromising faith in the face of the empire's advance.

A particularly well-built, rough-looking man by the telescreen caught Talmeon's eye. He appeared to be the leader of a pack of ruffians who were drinking around him.

"Excuse me, hey you!" Talmeon pointed to the well-muscled man. "Come here."

Talmeon's chief bodyguard rolled his eyes at his three men, ensuring that no one else noticed. "Here we go," he grinned wryly.

Talmeon spoke to the rough-looking man. His tone was polite but firm. The man seemed a little caught off guard. Clearly, he wasn't addressed like that very often. Scowling, he eyed the four bodyguards in their nondescript black attire with their machine pistols swinging lazily on their belts, their thumbs gently caressing the triggers. The sight of them had a civilizing influence on him.

At least thirty of his friends were all around, watching in silence. They waited to see if they would be called to defend their leader. The man didn't get up so Talmeon walked forward, smiled and sat down next to him at the end of his table.

"What can I get you to drink?" he asked. The man relaxed. He smiled back, hoping to gain something from talking to this stranger.

Talmeon made small talk with him for a while. The man introduced himself as Cavilah, a derivative of Havilah from where he probably came. It was a very common name for the area. Cavilah managed to negotiate a round of drinks for his friends but surprisingly refrained from drinking any more himself. Talmeon began to suspect that Cavilah was not quite the brute he outwardly appeared to be.

"How can I help you?" Cavilah displayed a civility that Talmeon thought might be the real him after all. His friends chuckled among themselves. The bodyguards remained standing nearby, evenly positioned around Talmeon. Two facing in and two facing out. No one cared to sit or stand particularly near them.

Talmeon smiled, "I'm on a trip; this is only a stopover; I need to make some enquiries." He paused, "Enquiries from inside the Land of the Ancients." Cavilah's friends roared with laughter. Talmeon was confused. Money-grabbing preachers were one thing, but surely the Ancients deserved respect?

"Enquiries?" Cavilah comically raised his eyebrows. Then he added a little more seriously, "Perhaps I can point you in the right direction? I will do my best, but it does depend..." He trailed off, idly turning a coin between his thumb and fingers, overstating the obvious by staring at it. Talmeon was slow on the uptake, so Cavilah made it easier for him.

"Perhaps... you even need a paid guide?" he heavily emphasised the word paid.

Talmeon looked surprised, "You can guide me into the Land of the Ancients?"

Cavilah's friends quietened down.

"I can even guide you to the Forbidden Gate." Absolute silence fell. Obviously, Cavilah could, and his friends all knew it. Even the bodyguards subtly turned to wait for more.

Talmeon's mind was racing. The Forbidden Gate, he'd heard a lot about it. Despite the prospect of living at least another three hundred years, this could be the only chance of his entire lifetime to see it. The Ancients claimed to know what it was. But as successive generations passed, theories about the Forbidden Gate had abounded. It was the one unchanging constant in a world of ever multiplying religious ideas. The Forbidden Gate's existence was a huge problem for the propaganda of the rulers of both the Empire of the Son and the Dark Kingdom. Tucked away in the Land of the Ancients by the source of the four rivers that fed the earth's one vast continent. It was an enigma that no new religion could even begin to explain.

Salfar the Great had unilaterally declared the Forbidden Gate and the area around it a neutral zone. Prohibiting any of his or Land of the Ancient's citizens from visiting it. The Ancients ignored this meaning-less decree. No one lived there and the Empire had no jurisdiction in their lands anyway. They knew that no earthly borders mattered to this otherworldly phenomenon. It was this lack of response, divine or mundane, from the Ancients that gave Salfar his ill-fated self-confid-ence. It made him believe that one day he would be able to carry out a successful invasion of the Land of the Ancients. He couldn't have been more wrong.

Years later, after Salfar's demise, the new emperor Nahron bribed some of the elders of the Land of the Ancients. The entire area around the Forbidden Gate was flooded, making it even more inaccessible. Wild swamp dragons migrated there from the coast, and the whole place became a death trap.

As with all of the Land of the Ancients, an unexplained flux disrupted communications and energy lines there. The result was that flight across the lands with standard propulsion systems was impossible. The flux ran from the High Hills of Havilah to the Great Eastern Sea and north to the southern borders of the Dark Kingdom. The area around The Forbidden Gate was even more hazardous because both empires constantly attempted incursions through the north western part of this area. Many a dead hero from both sides lay beneath the swamps of the neutral zone.

Talmeon felt distinctly uncomfortable, he decided that any further public conversation about his trip wasn't a good idea.

"Your offer of service is being generously considered," he emphasised the word generous. "We can discuss the finer details a little later." Talmeon changed the subject, "Do your men only have one round of drinks here and then go home to their mummy?"

The silence transformed into laughter. Cavilah's friends liked this strange and somewhat naïve visitor. Soon, thanks to Talmeon, they were all downing a round of the finest ales a city dweller could dream of.

"Tell me about the crazy preacher," Talmeon decided to further lighten the atmosphere.

"What, the one we were watching on the telecast?" Cavilah said, his face lighting up. His friends got ready for another round of mirth as Cavilah launched into the story.

"Fellow citizens of the great Empire of the Son, I give you, 'The crazy preacher from the Land of the Ancients.' An inspiration to us all." He climbed onto a table, sweeping his arms in a grand manner as he spoke. Talmeon was impressed and sure he would have made an excellent preacher. Cavilah's friends settled down as a small crowd began to gather.

"I have a boat," Cavilah announced as the crowd laughed. "In fact, I have a very big boat." Cavilah frowned at the sky, as if to ask, 'Why do I have this boat?' The crowd laughed harder. Even the bodyguards were chuckling. But they stayed alert, their eyes roving. They recognised a relatively safe situation when they saw it; this was going to be fun.

"In fact, my boat is so big that you can get a whole town in it." Cavilah continued his performance. He looked around at the crowd, as though he, the supposed builder, was as surprised as anyone about the boat. The crowd descended into hysterics.

"Without a doubt," he declared, "you have all sinned." The crowd shouted amens in mock approval. "You have all turned from the Creator," this time the amens were not quite so resounding but were instead accompanied by fake crying.

"But," Cavilah paused and looked around with the best halfwit expression he could muster, "if you repent, you can all come for a ride on my boat." The crowd erupted yet again in raucous laughter. Talmeon laughed too. Cavilah had clearly got his performance down to perfection and had done it many times before.

"As you know," he said, his tone softening, "I am Noah, son of Lamech, grandson of the great Methuselah, and father of your hero of the borderlands." His voice rose in triumph as he paused for effect before he said the man's name, "Shem."

At this point murmurs of admiring approval swept the crowd. Evidently, this Shem, although related to Noah, was still held in very high regard.

"And so, I have decided to build a boat, a very big boat in the middle of the Land of the Ancients. High up in the hills and more than 250 miles from the sea and far too big for any nearby river. So if you don't like getting your feet wet, you can join me." Cavilah changed his voice to mimic a female telecast announcer. "First class accommodation may sell out quickly. Please book early to avoid disappointment. If you miss the boat, terms and conditions may not apply."

The laughter returned, the crowd cheered and applauded. Cavilah bowed in all directions, stepped off the table and sat down next to Talmeon.

"So that's it?" asked Talmeon, "he wants donations for his boat?"

"Ah no," sighed Cavilah wearily, "he's a genuine Ancient, he doesn't beg for money for anything. He claims that the Creator spoke to him and told him that all the earth had become wicked and would be destroyed. That only those who take refuge in his boat will be saved. He's been building it for quite a while. To be fair it's quite a magnificent piece of engineering, many people go on special day trips to see it. It's very good business for the local economy."

"But what good is such a huge boat in the middle of the hinterlands?" Talmeon was not really getting the point.

"Don't you get it?" Cavilah laughed, "Apparently, the whole world is going to be flooded."

"The waters will rise..." and he began mock preaching again as though he couldn't stop something coming on himself each time he recounted Noah's message. Cavilah's words carried a strange air of conviction, almost power. Talmeon began to wonder if Cavilah really did have some kind of gift to be a temple preacher.

"The waters will rise," Cavilah repeated, "and cover even the highest hills, the breath of all life on earth will cease, and in every direction all there will be is water, water, nothing but water."

Talmeon finished the end of the last sentence in a strange unison with Cavilah. The remaining few words he rasped out with difficulty as his voice faltered and he went pale.

◆◆◆ ⌐ ◆◆◆

Cavilah's friends sat nearby and were still busy laughing at the retelling of their favourite story. Cavilah wasn't laughing. He'd noticed something earlier when declining the opportunity to be awkward with Talmeon. It was easy to see Talmeon was a high-ranking city official. His authoritative demeanour gave that away. But his bodyguards were something else. Having bodyguards in itself was no big deal. All officials had bodyguards. Yet, Cavilah had noticed what even Talmeon had missed. His bodyguards were not the usual Palatine guards in plain clothes. They were Royal Guards, elite soldiers. Even without their machine pistols and hidden body armour, Cavilah knew they were a formidable force.

Royal Guards did not have the tiny chinstrap scars that all Palatine Guards did. Years of marching in dress uniform left a slight mark under the chin from their helmet's strap buckle. Royal Guards didn't march about in fancy costume. In fact, they didn't have any fancy costumes or march about at all. They rarely appeared in public, and if they did, you wouldn't have known it. They trained rigorously; they practised for every conceivable eventuality. They could operate almost every type of vehicle or flying craft. In an empire of hundreds of millions and a military of millions, there were fewer than two thousand of them. They were the very best of the best. They worked only for the emperor himself.

So, why had the emperor sent a senior and very knowledgeable official, instead of a puppet, to visit the Land of the Ancients? Cavilah pondered over the whole thing. If Talmeon had gone pale at the end of the story of the crazy preacher's boat, then something in it must match what he was looking for. Cavilah decided, based on Talmeon's pale shade, it was far more than trivial. Worse, Talmeon's Royal Guards had become so absorbed in the story that they stopped watching the crowd for a brief time. Men whose professionalism was legendary, had all lost concentration over a story about a crazy preacher's boat!

Cavilah tried to grasp the implications; they were too absurd to contemplate. And then there was the preacher Noah; he was from the family of Methuselah. Cavilah wasn't sure that he'd ever known anyone from that family to go off the rails.

Chapter 5

Evasion

*M*avron had known something wasn't quite right about the girl off to the left. She was definitely observing them. As a Royal Guard commander, Mavron's job was to escort Talmeon through Nahron's Gate. To keep him safe and, where possible, comfortable. At 322 years of age, Mavron Jared Targemah was young, fit, even dashing, yet underneath it all he was ever the professional.

Exactly who and what the VIPs he protected visited was always Mavron's concern. Why was never a question he asked. This time, things were different. He, like his three men who'd worked with him for many years, knew exactly why they were headed to the Land of the Ancients. There were no secrets among a Royal Guard team. They were going there because of Nahron's recurring apocalyptic dream.

The girl had arrived with a crowd of passers-by; she was watching the man called Cavilah's street performance about the crazy preacher's boat. Mavron noticed she laughed in unison with the people she stood near. She nodded her head and looked jokingly around when Cavilah reached his punchlines. She even patted someone on the back and spoke to them, but they didn't speak back to her. She didn't appear to be known by anyone around her, yet she was pretending she was. Mavron was convinced he and his men were being observed. How anyone was on to them so soon after they had arrived on a secret mission, and in an untraceable transport, was of very great concern to him.

At first, Mavron had wanted to hang on to his doubts. It was always the easy route and one he never took. Maybe he was imagining things? He was on a Level 8 mission, a direct and personal order from the emperor himself. There probably weren't more than six or seven people in the whole empire who knew anything about it. He wanted to believe that the girl was merely another lonely heart wanting attention.

He was going to dismiss the whole thing, but there were too many contradictions. For example, where the girl was standing. Not too close and not too far away. Mavron knew that he wouldn't be able to easily reach her if he made a run for her. She was ideally positioned. Several tables were between him, his men and her. Mavron noticed that she frequently looked at a billboard opposite her. The advert was for ale and she wasn't drinking any. She was using its panel as a mirror. Then there was her physique, very well conditioned. She was not modestly dressed like someone from a conservative family nor flaunting her looks like a girl from the aspiring political elites. Her clothing was utilitarian. The girl moved slowly and casually, yet Mavron noticed that she constantly checked all around her. He felt a chill go down his spine; whoever she was, she was a professional.

Mavron looked further afield; nothing appeared out of place. He was happy they were on an open concourse rather than in some hidden back street bar. The girl saw Mavron looking at her; her face held a momentary look of recognition. How was that possible? Mavron felt sick in his stomach. He stayed focused. The girl turned away, smiled, and started chatting frivolously to someone next to her.

Mavron began to think that he recognised her too, but he didn't know where from. He lazily looked away, like a cat before pouncing in a standoff.

The girl was facing away from him now, angled towards a second glass billboard displaying adverts for some distant holiday island. From there he knew she could watch the reflection of his form without having to face him. She appeared to be working her way towards the least dense part of the crowd. Mavron didn't like the fact that he couldn't see her eyes anymore. The moving crowd of drinkers parted for a moment. Mavron looked down; his heart almost stopped. Underneath the girl's black, well-fitting trousers, she was wearing none other than Favicon boots.

Favicon boots were renowned for their durability, exceptional comfort, lightweight, and outstanding grip on all surfaces. They gave the wearer near gazelle-like agility – provided they were fit enough to make use of it. They hid a variety of hi-tech equipment, including sensors, balance aids, stimulants, and even tiny lethal weapons. They were standard issue for all special forces. Most people had no idea they existed, and they were impossible to get hold of without a Level 7 security clearance. Mavron was wearing a pair himself.

He casually reached out his hand to place it on his comrade's shoulder to get his attention. As soon as his hand began moving, the girl, still laughing and chatting as though describing her baby's latest achievements, took off. She reacted so quickly that Mavron was taken completely by surprise.

"Female, fifty-one twenty!" he shouted a coded warning to his fellow guards, looking at them and pointing in the direction of the girl.

"Sir?" one of them frowned.

When Mavron looked back, she was already gone.

Her escape route was well rehearsed; slipping between billboards and groups of people, she stayed out of Mavron and his men's line of sight. Mavron knew a straightforward chase was dangerous. Someone that well trained shouldn't be pursued down obscure alleyways in such a remote town. Even so, he was determined to catch her.

Mavron's fellow guards sprang into action. One positioned himself in front of Talmeon, blocking any line of sight or shooting should the person of interest reappear; they didn't. Mavron himself moved back a little into the crowd; he knew they were not the threat. The other two guards went wide, creating a dispersed target for any assailants and awaited further instructions. Talmeon dutifully dropped a coin on the ground, swiftly kneeling to search for it. He knew exactly what to do in such circumstances when he heard the coded warning.

"Young woman, light blue jacket, blonde hair, pursue!" Mavron spoke to two of his men, again pointing in the direction the girl had gone. They took off running. He carefully scanned the concourse; there didn't appear to be any other threats. The remaining guard discreetly hurried Talmeon away to the nearest government hotel.

◆◆◆ ⌐ ◆◆◆

The girl kept running; she didn't slow at all. As she passed the end of the concourse, the Grand Station's two overweight guards were jolted from their lazy day of poor-quality bribes. They saw a fugitive with a fetching figure and blonde hair dash past. At last, they thought—some excitement! Whoever caught her would surely have the opportunity to take advantage of her regardless of whether she was guilty of anything or not. Could this be their lucky day? Their respective horoscopes had told them both, albeit in different words, that unexpected surprises would come their way before nightfall.

They set off after the girl. It was futile; she ran like a gazelle. One guard soon gave up; the other maintained a lumbering rate on her trail.

Out of nowhere, two men in plain black security attire abruptly ran past the remaining station guard, still struggling to give chase. They ran at what, at least from an overweight station guard's perspective, was an alarming rate. One of the men turned and looked his way.

"You!" he yelled, pointing at the guard, "Code 47."

The station guard stopped running. Struggling to catch his breath, he tried to process what he'd heard. Code 47. Never in his entire life had he heard a Code 47 ordered except in jokes. He glanced up at the rapidly receding two men who'd so effortlessly overtaken him. He'd never seen Royal Guards in the flesh before either, or like most citizens if he had, he hadn't known it. Code 47. He quickly activated his communicator.

"This is Grand Station security officer Finton," he wheezed, barely able to speak. "We have a suspect, unknown concern, female, blonde, light blue jacket, heading on foot into the Sabre district behind Grand Station. I've been advised by pursuers, whom I assume are Royal Guards, that this situation requires a Code 47."

There was quite a long crackling delay.

"Finton, did you say Code 47?" the controller asked.

"Yes, affirmative, Code 47."

"Can you confirm that?"

"No, but I'm convinced," he gasped, finally getting a little of his breath back.

"If you're wrong about this Officer Finton you'll be..."

"Yes, I know," he interrupted, "I will be spending the rest of my career guarding the main entrance to the Grand Station. I'm already doing that. Doubtless you will get confirmation at any moment. I'm assisting the pursuit. Finton out." He always hated calling District Security; they were a bunch of lazy, disinterested layabouts as far as he was concerned.

Local security guards began to run past from nearby offices. Ground transports started appearing. More security personnel piled out of them, all heading down into the cramped alleyways of the Sabre district.

◆◆◆ ☞ ◆◆◆

The girl's pace and stamina were remarkable. Several turns and a few darker and dingier streets later, she rounded a corner. Stopping in a quiet cul-de-sac littered with garbage and surrounded by empty boarded-up buildings, she caught her breath. The Sabre district was one of those places that looked like the very opposite of its name. Somewhere in the distance, a commotion followed her. Eager citizens always loved to catch a thief, although usually only to rob them themselves. Taking stock of her situation, she realised that some of her pursuers were a lot closer than she would have liked. If they were also who she thought they were, then they were probably almost upon her. She began running again, this time straight towards a stone wall only forty cubits away.

The drunk she hadn't seen lying down half asleep in a nearby pile of garbage watched her, bottle in hand. She ran at full speed, straight into a large billboard advertising a circus with wild raptors eating condemned criminals. The poster ripped apart; as soon as she was through, another one exactly the same slid right down in its place. It looked like no one had been there at all. The drunk stared at the wall and then at his bottle.

Gasping for breath, the girl fell into the arms of a surprised man waiting inside a hidden room behind the poster.

"Japheth," she spoke desperately and as quietly as she could, "Royal Guards, they saw me and I think they recognised me."

"Royal Guards! Are you sure, Nadina?"

"Yes, Royal Guards, and they knew I was watching them."

A thousand words could not convey the gravity of the phrase Royal Guards. Royal Guards had unrestricted access to every security facility in the empire. Every tracker, every listening device, every camera, and every drone. It was time to leave and leave immediately. Nadina's blonde wig came off, revealing dark hair that matched her dark, determined eyes. Her own dark brown leather jacket replaced the meek, fashionable light blue one she'd been wearing.

"Did you have everything switched off?" he asked keenly.

"Yes, everything," she replied, "I made no mistakes."

Japheth momentarily held her arm as if to gently lead her out the back. It was always the same; every time he was near her, he touched her without realising it.

"We have to go," he said as though this justified him holding her arm for that brief moment. They ran out the back and into an old battered ground transport.

Mavron liked to be thorough; he could have let the whole thing go. They were being watched, so what? There were spies everywhere these days; Nahron's Gate was near enough the neutral zone to have its fair share. His mission brief was simple: protect his VIP and assist them in any practical way with their journey. All they had to do now was cross the border into the Land of the Ancients a bit sooner than previously planned.

This would have been the right thing to do except that by now Mavron had realised who the girl was. She'd been at the Royal Guard Academy, the only female who ever had.

Someone like that couldn't be ignored. Mavron decided she must be working for a powerful organisation or an individual. Whatever the reason they were being observed, Mavron was convinced it couldn't be a good one. He knew of only one way to find out. Catch the girl. His motto was, no loose ends; it was also why he was still alive.

Talmeon was hastily shown into the Ambassador suite on the top floor of the local government hotel. It was as safe a place as they were likely to find anywhere in the Havilah district. Mavron ordered extra local security personnel to watch Talmeon's suite, closed off the rest of the floor and the one below for good measure. He left his remaining fellow guard at the hotel and set off for the town's District Security headquarters.

Code 47 was Empire of the Son security speak for a citywide lockdown. The town of Nahron's Gate experienced its first major security alert since the Great War. Every exit road was closed, every pathway blocked. No one was allowed in or out of the city limits unless their ID was checked and verified.

Japheth eyed the short queue ahead on the quiet road he'd chosen leading out of town. Ten ground transports were lined up in front of him. All vehicles were being stopped, scanned and checked. Behind him, another seven or eight transports had already joined the queue. He saw something that deeply concerned him. The vehicles were being searched, scanned and their occupants questioned. That in itself wasn't such a big deal; random roadblocks often appeared now and again. What was worrying was that a couple of transports looked like they were incorrectly registered. Their drivers were offering the customary bribes, but these were being uncharacteristically refused.

"The empire sure is looking for someone today," Japheth muttered to Nadina, "they're not even taking bribes." The moment he said it, he realised what was going on. Their silence lasted barely seconds.

"Japheth," the tone of her voice told him everything she was thinking.

"No way," he said.

"Yes," she insisted with a finality that made Japheth realise nothing would change her mind. He knew her well enough; a lack of resolve was not one of her shortcomings.

"Look, there's a kiosk," said Nadina. By the roadside, a few trans-ports further up in the queue, a couple of passengers had left their vehicles and were buying snacks from a sandwich hut. Their respective drivers edged slowly forwards.

"It's my only chance; they saw my face on the concourse. I was probably on half a dozen cameras." Further ahead, two transports were briefly scanned, checked, and waved through. Japheth couldn't help but notice that they both had only male occupants. The checkpoint guards were clearly not looking for males trying to leave the town.

Without thinking, he put his hand on hers, this time without any pretence. Nadina half-closed her eyes, soaking up the warmth of his love. Was this the last time they would see each other? Would this solve the ongoing nightmare? Perhaps it was better this way, thought Nadina. No more fleeting touches, no more avoiding each other at family events. No sin would ever be committed because she would be dead. Japheth would continue his life with his wife and all would be well. She knew this last thought was nonsense. The last thing that made any-thing go well for Japheth was his wife. She had been nothing but a beautiful curse since the day he'd married her. Nadina was somewhat biased, but it wasn't too far from the truth.

Japheth edged the transport two more spaces up the queue and nearer the kiosk. Nadina closed her eyes again, took a deep breath, and opened the door. She wanted to kiss him on the cheek, but she knew you don't kiss someone goodbye when leaving a transport to buy snacks. Everything had to look normal.

"I will come back for you, Nadina," she'd never heard him say her name like that before. "Turn your tracker on as soon as you can."

Cutting through the queue behind the nearest tall vehicle, Nadina crossed the grass verge and headed away from the road. She noticed out the corner of her eye that the occupants of one transport were staring at her. They looked older. Possibly retired security personnel or veterans; otherwise, they would have called her over by now. She tried to look natural and continued walking towards the nearest line of buildings.

Keeping out of sight of the guards at the temporary road block had been her first priority. If they'd seen anyone from a transport leaving the road, then they would have been on to them immediately. Nadina was certain that someone in the transport with its occupants staring at her, would call District Security. Seeing her walking casually while stuffing her face with food wouldn't fit their expectation of a fleeing suspect. They would hesitate for a short time. Then, there would be the time to make a call and give details. District Security would need to check it wasn't a hopeful idiot wanting a reward for a pointless call. This would give her time to reach the buildings without running. Her only regret now was that she'd not kept the blonde wig and bright blue jacket. As soon as she passed out of sight, Nadina ran as fast as she could down the back streets into the slums of Nahron's Gate.

◆◆◆ 🔒 ◆◆◆

Mavron remained in the control room of Nahron's Gate District Security headquarters.

"Nothing conclusive yet, sir," the local security chief said. He wanted to focus on the sides of the town bordering the Land of the Ancients. Mavron corrected him. A well-trained fugitive would avoid fleeing through the affluent tree-lined avenues of the veterans' districts that Nahron had strategically located on the town's east side. They would attempt to go out through the slums on the west. Then, if they encountered problems, they had the possibility of bribing their way out of harm's way.

"Sir?" a supervisor hesitatingly interrupted Mavron studying the town plans. "We have a helpful citizen report; someone walked down a line of vehicles queuing at a road block on the third western sub road. Apparently they left a transport to buy food but then avoided the check point."

A helpful citizen report was often a euphemism for give me money and I will tell you more rubbish, but there were exceptions.

"A woman?" Mavron asked.

"Yes, walking and eating a sandwich, she didn't seem to be in a hurry or unsettled, but she did come out from the line of vehicles. The citizen is a retired commander from the Tigris Battle Group. He said the woman just appeared from further up in the queue and that it seemed suspicious."

Mavron didn't need to hear any more; he began reeling off orders into his communicator. Several flying transports descended towards the third western sub-road from all directions. The whole district was sealed off.

◆◆◆ ◆◆◆

Japheth moved up the queue again, only three transports to go. The transport at the front had a single female driver; she was sent to the side for a more detailed check. The family in the next vehicle were waved through quickly. In it were infants and two adults, most likely grandparents, who were not capable of running off anywhere at speed. The single male driver right in front of him was checked but appeared to have some problem and was sent off to the side. Japheth kept praying; he knew Nadina would be in the slums by now. He had to find a way to help her, but first he had to pass this checkpoint.

The sound of large flying transports became audible in the distance, their resonators giving off the usual deep throbbing hum. Japheth realised this was it. Someone had called District Security from further back in the queue. Hopefully, Nadina was safe by now and the person who'd alerted them had no idea from which vehicle she'd come.

Driving as naturally as possible up to the checkpoint without being waved forward, Japheth smiled at the guard. He maintained a, you know how all these security alerts always come to nothing type expression. He got out of his transport, waving his ID as though he were the most innocent person in the whole world.

Several flying transports approached, including the latest active camouflaging Vandeon troop transporters. They were huge; it was a sight to behold in the usually quiet town of Nahron's Gate. The checkpoint guards and nearby citizens gazed up in wonder. Before the monsters touched down, heavily armed troops began abseiling towards the ground.

Japheth stood behind the awestruck crowd. He casually lifted the barrier pole, which thankfully didn't squeak. The troops abseiling from their transports further down the queue held everyone's attention. He slipped back into his vehicle, slowly moving it forward through the checkpoint. No one noticed as he drove away as quickly as he dared. Skirting all the way around Nahron's Gate, he crossed one of the Pishon's smaller bridges and drove on into the Land of the Ancients.

Passing small hamlets and an old hotel which had become a pick-up point for the by-now famous giant boat tours. He drove behind a run-down café, through a disused junkyard, and parked up. Clambering into a battery-powered recovery vehicle, Japheth hitched up the transport he'd escaped in. Changing its ID broadcaster and plates, he then drove across the Pishon back towards Nahron's Gate.

Battery-powered recovery vehicles were a common sight in border areas. Misinformed tourists frequently drove their transports into the region affected by the flux that covered all the Land of the Ancients. They invariably got stranded as a result. The energy lines that traversed the globe were completely disrupted there. Ordinary transports didn't function much beyond the Pishon. They couldn't draw energy to feed their resonators, the worldwide method of propulsion.

Stranded tourists had to be rescued by recovery vehicles with large backup batteries. These vehicles could drive for many miles without having to cross a single power line to recharge.

Japheth decided that the least attention-grabbing way to re-enter Nahron's Gate was in a recovery vehicle with an old ground transport hitched to the back.

Chapter 6

Capture

*N*adina's basement cell was small, stank, but at least had the luxury of a table and chair. Her capture had been painless. Once she realised she was surrounded, she had given herself up to avoid harm and a needless pursuit. While in hiding, she'd taken time to re-apply her make-up. Then, instead of handing herself in to the first trooper that came by, she waited for an officer.

Nadina knew that by surrendering to an officer, she would be well treated. She assumed that someone of rank would have enough sense to know they'd lose their head if they mistreated her. Activating her homing beacon, she hid it with her micro communicator in her face cream in her makeup bag. She then placed the bag nearby, out of sight.

Nadina gave herself up to a surprised officer. He immediately had her cuffed and scanned; she was clear. Mavron's orders had been strict – no interfering with the suspect at all. Only searched, restrained, and then placed in detention until he arrived. He wanted her in one piece for questioning. Not abused by local security, claiming her injuries were from resisting arrest.

As she was about to be led away, Nadina stepped aside to go back to her hideout.

"Oops, I forgot my makeup bag," she grinned. Every trooper's weapon levelled at her head as another crawled in to retrieve it. He carefully opened it. Unbelievably, she did indeed appear to be intending to retrieve her cosmetics. Her captors kept the bag separate from her. None of them thought to scan it. A brief check inside confirmed it only held lipstick, tweezers, hair bands, and face cream. No one realised she was wearing Favicon boots.

♦♦♦   ⚑   ♦♦♦

Mavron was pleased, if not a little surprised. He'd expected a long search, a hard chase and several casualties. He gave the situation some thought. What would he have done? Heroically evaded capture for several hours, fought a pointless running battle? Or simply handed himself in uninjured? Not thirsty, not hungry, not tired and waiting for a more opportune time to escape? Obviously, the latter.

He spoke by communicator to the officer in charge of the town's security station where the girl was being taken. He reiterated: she was to be secured in a cell, no interrogations, no requests, and definitely no abuse. He'd lost way too many men to that. When he arrived, he would collect her in person and take her to their interrogation room himself.

Mavron made his instructions very clear. He promised great rewards to all involved in the girl's capture and detention.

◆◆◆ 🏳 ◆◆◆

The security station officer very much liked the idea of rewards coming his way.

He'd been told that the prisoner would be taken to their interrogation room. This was on the second floor; but her cell was in the basement. He decided to get a little extra reward. He would show initiative and take her to the interrogation room himself.

The station officer had posted his two most trusted guards outside the prisoner's cell. He wanted to keep things simple by having as few people involved as possible. This way, he could take most of the credit and not dilute any of the rewards. He also wanted a closer look at the attractive detainee. He'd caught a glimpse of her when she'd been brought in. Hustled between fifteen armed troops as if she was a fire-breathing reptile. Ridiculous, he'd thought; she was only a woman.

He unlocked the cell and opened the door. A beautiful young woman stood before him. Smiling warmly, as if waiting for him to escort her on a romantic evening out. Her beauty unnerved him. He tried to compose himself.

"This way," he ordered weakly.

"Is there another way?" she giggled.

The officer fumbled with handcuffs, trying to get them ready to put on his pretty prisoner. She calmly walked right past him. Hers had been removed earlier when she was placed in the cell. Leaving a prisoner handcuffed in a cell seemed pointless overkill. Mavron would have left them on.

"Three big, handsome, strong men like you and I need those as well?" she laughed like she'd seen a price tag on a dress she couldn't quite believe.

The officer was embarrassed. The idea that he needed to cuff a woman on his own, let alone with two of his best guards, was humiliating. He quickly stepped back in front of her. The prisoner followed him, walking as if she were on a catwalk rather than detained in a security station.

One of the guards walking behind received a message on his communicator. He relayed it to the officer, "They'll be here in about ten minutes, sir."

The officer nonchalantly grunted, trying to impress his female captive. He acted as if he answered to no one but himself.

◆◆◆ ⊱ ◆◆◆

Nadina took in all her surroundings, including the idiocy of the officer. An out of town security station, relatively low-grade but still difficult to leave. She said nothing as they walked along a dimly lit corridor and up four flights of stairs. The elevator was not used. Standard procedure was to walk prisoners, not squeeze into confined spaces with them. A lost opportunity, she realised.

The officer paraded her along the first floor of his small station as though he'd captured her all by himself. Nadina made a careful note of every window, adjoining corridor, and nearby offices.

Eventually, they entered an interrogation room on the second floor. Nadina was convinced they had taken a circuitous route just so the officer could show off.

The room had a large panoramic window and was quite pleasant. It was the sort of place where they took prisoners to woo them, rather than force information out of them. The let's-be-reasonable approach, think of your family and look at how nice it is outside. It was not to be confused with the torture cells of the basement. In the capital, an interrogation room and torture cell were one and the same.

The window looked across Nahron's Gate, over the Pishon and towards the border. How Nadina wanted to be home there now. She knew she had to focus. She'd heard some very disturbing rumours about the Empire's plans for the Land of the Ancients. They were anything but good. The rumours were unclear, so she'd gone with Japheth to Nahron's Gate to try and find out more. She had already been on the town's main concourse when she saw Talmeon and his guards. Not realising soon enough that they were Royal Guards, she'd stayed too long. One of them recognised her from the Academy. Being suspicious of her reasons for being there, he'd ordered her captured.

Nadina knew she faced torture, abuse, even prison. She realised the security station was her best chance to escape. It was clearly staffed by amateurs. When the Royal Guard who'd spotted her arrived, she didn't fancy her chances. A simple break for the window was preferable. But the glass was probably toughened. The simplicity of the guards seemed to provide a more obvious way out.

"Aren't you going to interrogate me?" Nadina smiled ruefully at the officer, sauntering past him towards the main window. She stopped, resting her hands apart on a table below the window.

The officer in charge lost all ability to think coherently. He had only ten minutes before some senior official arrived to take his pretty prisoner away. He decided to make full use of that time. As he stumbled forwards, Nadina watched her captor's reflection in the glass. The other two guards, distracted, let their weapons hang loose on their straps. Their fingers far from the triggers.

Nadina waited until the last moment, then jammed her left elbow into the stomach of the officer. Severely winded, he retched for air. Turning, she chopped the side of his neck with her right hand. Pulling him past her, he crashed into the table and window. She used his mass to propel herself towards the guard at the right of the door. She'd noticed earlier that he was the more alert of the two. With one step, she grabbed his right arm above the elbow, twisting him away from her. Throwing her left arm around his neck, she plunged her two middle fingers into his oesophagus. Kicking his legs from under him, he landed heavily on his knees, choking as he fell. Nadina tore his weapon off his shoulder, swinging its butt into the other guard's jaw. He'd remained motionless in shock the whole time. Then back into the head of the winded officer, and then the same again with the still gagging guard. The whole thing took about four and a half seconds, maybe five.

Nadina quickly looked around the room. They had even considerately brought her makeup bag.

"Japheth!" she cried quietly into her micro-communicator, retrieving it from her face cream in her bag.

"I got you," he said, "almost at the gates." Nadina glanced out of the window towards the main gates. A dumpster truck was approaching, the driver swigging a bottle. He was waving drunkenly at the gatehouse guards. Further back down the road there was one very happy waste collector. He'd swapped his old dumpster for a new recovery vehicle, along with a ground transport.

Nadina pulled the jacket off the smaller of the two unconscious guards on the floor. She put it on, along with his cap. Then, she folded her medium-length hair under it, pulling it down firmly. She threw the strap of his weapon over her shoulder, grabbed a spare power clip, and headed for the door. Nadina glanced out of the window. A sleek Tactan command and control transport was parked outside. Even without its active camouflage engaged, she had to look twice to see where its double tail fins ended and the courtyard began. A pilot was strolling away from it. She realised her interrogators had arrived sooner than expected. Peering through a small window to the right, she saw several waste containers at the far end of the building.

"Drive to your left, to the end of the building," she ordered Japheth, "I'll come out."

Before she had a chance to leave, Nadina heard the sound of someone approaching on the stairs. Based on the authoritative commands they were giving, she assumed it was the Royal Guard who'd recognised her earlier.

The man sounded angry: "I said to leave her in her cell," he shouted, storming along the corridor.

Nadina realised she had only seconds. An angry soldier was also a vulnerable one. His anger would shave fragments of a second off his reaction time. She decided to inflame his anger even more. Nadina convincingly cried out as the sound of his footsteps reached the door. She knew that when the commander heard her, it would only confirm in his mind why these amateurish guards had moved her out of her cell in the first place. Sure enough, the commander stormed straight into the interrogation room without checking anything. Glimpsing the bodies of the three men on the floor, he realised his terrible error too late. The butt of the weapon that Nadina had picked up smashed into the back of his head. He was knocked clean out without making even so much as a grunt.

Gently lowering the guard to the floor, Nadina tapped the door closed with her foot. Taking a deep breath, she listened intently to what was going on outside: nothing. It appeared that their brief scuffle had not been loud enough to attract further attention. The earlier shouting had left everyone in the nearby offices feverishly working with their heads down. Rumours had already reached them that a high-ranking official from the capital was visiting. No one wanted to be caught peeping out of their office doors.

Nadina slipped out quietly, closing the interrogation room door behind her. She began to walk as calmly as possible down an adjoining corridor. She remembered it led to the end of the building, and near where the waste was stored. Japheth would hopefully be there. A pile of black storage boxes was stacked against a nearby wall. She picked up two empty ones and carried them in front of her, hiding her face.

It was a strange sight but enough to buy some time. Two civilian staff passed her. They glanced at her, curious. But the uniform: jacket, trousers, military-looking boots and cap put their minds to rest. A female guard carrying boxes to the admin end of the building didn't add up. But everyone knew they had visitors. Staff culture was always to avoid anything that was not their concern.

Nadina reached the end of the corridor, tentatively choosing the last door facing the back of the building. She knocked gently twice, opened the door and walked in, keeping the boxes in front of her face. An overweight officer dozing at his desk stirred. He looked up, bemused to see an unidentified guard with shapely legs carrying two boxes towards him.

"Put them in the corner," he mumbled, closing his eyes again.

"Sure," Nadina whispered quietly and immediately wished she'd said, "Yes sir." She carefully placed them down, slipped past the dozing sloth, deftly opened the window behind him and jumped out.

◆◆◆  ◆◆◆

The officer stirred and awoke, trying to piece together what had just happened. He'd received a delivery of what appeared to be two empty boxes from an unknown guard. When he'd told them to put the boxes in the corner, they had whispered "Sure," not "Yes, sir." Then slipped behind him and jumped out of the window! This wasn't exactly an everyday occurrence, especially at his end of the building.

Suddenly, all the alarms in the complex went off; the officer realised that his career was over – unless he did one thing. He jumped up, shut the window, grabbed his pen and flung papers across his previously tidy desk. The sound of shouting and running footsteps filled the corridor outside. He stood up, pen in one hand, grabbed some papers in the other and looked as suitably surprised as he could. His office door flew open. A guard, weapon in hand, glanced around. He eyed the closed window, the man's surprised expression, the paper and pen in his hands, shouted, "Clear!" and ran out.

◆◆◆   ▷   ◆◆◆

Nadina landed perfectly from the first floor. The soft courtyard surface helped a little; the cushioners in her Favicon boots did the rest. She rolled twice, stood up, dusted herself off and walked calmly towards Japheth's dumpster. Which at that moment was rumbling round the corner of the building as alarms sounded everywhere. She pointed authoritatively at it and motioned for it to go back. Japheth raised his hands as best he thought an exasperated dumpster driver would, and began putting the vehicle into reverse.

No one was paying any attention to the recently arrived Tactan military transport. Japheth tried to think of a way to approach it unnoticed and then how to fly it safely away. He gulped as he saw Nadina, still resplendent in her black uniform, complete with weapon and cap, jogging towards it.

Nadina climbed in the navigator's side of the Tactan, close to the main building, to stay out of sight and leaned across to the pilot's controls. They were slightly newer than what she'd been trained on, but still familiar. She set auto navigation to fly over the next nearest town of Isis. Then changed the flight status from transport to battle mode and overrode the altitude limiter, setting it at 1,000 cubits. Most importantly, she turned off the craft's identifier. Activating the start sequencers, she slipped out and strode towards Japheth's dumpster, sweeping her weapon from side to side.

Nadina climbed into the dumpster, lying flat, dearly wanting to watch what would happen next. The transport's resonators powered up with an intense hum. It rapidly took off, zigzagging into the distance. A horrified silence descended on the station as they realised that all their lives were now in jeopardy. The alarms had stopped. Everyone gazed up at the retreating transport. It vanished as its active camouflage engaged. Moments later, there was a distant bang; smoke appeared on the horizon.

The craft had flown too close to the famous Havilah Auto Batteries. A long line of sophisticated air defences that ran parallel to the border beyond Isis. Anything not sending out Imperial recognition codes, even dragon birds, was routinely shot down.

The station charged back to life; perhaps their hides were saved after all? Leaping into their ground transports, the security personnel raced off towards the distant column of smoke.

Japheth casually drove his dumpster out the gates.

Mavron held an ice pack to the back of his head. He watched the limited recordings from the security station from the time of the escape. A dumpster that collected no rubbish. Interesting.

His suspicions were confirmed when no bodies were found at the crash site of his stolen Tactan. Its processor's records showed that someone had set the flight mode for a quick getaway. But they had disabled the friend-or-foe recognition system. Then they sent it on a suicide route past Isis towards the Havilah Auto Batteries. And no one remembered seeing that particular dumpster driver before, either.

Impressive, thought Mavron. His prisoner had even retained a tracking signal after being captured and scanned. The brave officer, to whom the now escaped prisoner had surrendered, had recently improved his earlier version of events. Enhancing them from a straightforward handing of herself in to a heroic capture. He was now facing a court martial for failing to properly scan her possessions.

Mavron desperately wanted to tie the whole debacle off. He'd assigned two drones to find and track the dumpster. It didn't take them long.

His drone controllers reported that the dumpster had circled the town and was heading towards the Land of the Ancients' border. Mavron assembled a team with two transports. A replacement Tactan, the only spare one in the whole province, and a large Vandeon troop carrier. He chose a suitable ambush point. The last thing he wanted was for his fugitives to disappear into the flux over the Land of the Ancients and become untraceable. The dumpster wasn't the quickest thing on the road. Tracking it was easy; it was heading slowly towards a cluster of hills near the border. The road it was on led to a tunnel. The tunnel ran through a small hill opening into a valley. There was only one exit from the valley: a narrow road. Fools, Mavron thought; it was an ideal ambush spot.

Mavron's Tactan flew nearby, its active camouflage engaged. The much larger Vandeon kept its distance. Both waited until the dumpster trundled into the tunnel, then Mavron's pilot quickly set his Tactan down on top of the hill behind its exit. Two mission controllers sat inside monitoring the whole proceedings. The second transport, the heavily armoured Vandeon, full of well-trained troops, hovered above the tunnel exit. Both teams waited patiently. The ambush spot couldn't have been more perfect. Mavron was pleased; his fugitives wouldn't have time to react, let alone escape. He was still a little disappointed. Surely the prisoner and her accomplice could have done better? Some-thing nagged at him; he wasn't quite sure what it was. The ambush spot was perfect, almost too perfect.

"Everything all right?" he asked the two controllers in his Tactan as they intently watched their scanners.

"Yes sir," they replied, "we can't see anything while they're in the tunnel, but they should be out in a few moments."

Mavron's Tactan pilot looked up towards the pilots in the huge Vandeon hovering with precision above the tunnel exit. They'd already discreetly told him what they intended to do. He was excited. It was going to be a massacre; he loved seeing people unexpectedly dying.

No one in the Tactan thought to look behind them where they'd set down near an overgrown inspection hatch to the tunnel. Why would they? The drones were watching their backs. But who was watching the drones' feeds? The two mission controllers in Mavron's Tactan were supposed to be, but the last place they were looking was at themselves. They were all transfixed by the Vandeon hovering in front of them with all its weaponry pointing down at the tunnel exit.

Mavron found himself clenching and opening his fists. "The dumpster," he asked, "is it out yet?" It was a strange question because the Vandeon pilots would report the moment it emerged.

"Almost, sir," said one of the controllers convincingly. They waited a few more moments in silence. "It's taking a little longer than we thought."

At that moment, Mavron knew his ideal ambush spot was not an ideal ambush spot at all. How could he have been so stupid, falling for such obvious bait? He jumped up, leaning out of the wide sliding side door of his Tactan, frantically looking towards the Vandeon transport. He opened his mouth to order an active mission abort. But something that felt like a hammer hit the side of his neck. Mavron had the sensation of floating. Everything went black.

◆◆◆ ⚑ ◆◆◆

Nadina and Japheth climbed up the disused inspection shaft on the hill above the tunnel, emerging right behind the Tactan. The Royal Guard commander had conveniently opened the Tactan's side door. He was looking towards the Vandeon when Nadina fired her disruptor at him. Disruptors, designed for stunning wild reptiles, were also very effective against people. Anyone struck by their tiny, highly charged plasma bolts was paralysed for a few seconds. The commander fell badly, striking his head on the door frame as he did. The other occupants, not combat trained, were easily stunned and subdued.

Japheth heaved the unconscious commander back inside the Tactan. His head was profusely bleeding. They decided to take him with them. They didn't want anyone to die or to worsen an already complicated situation. Japheth stemmed his bleeding, securing him firmly in a seat.

"Go Nadina!" he shouted.

Nadina was already entering instructions into the navigation system. The idling resonators went to full power. The active camouflage system came online. The Tactan vanished from plain sight. Rising barely two cubits, it shot backwards, turning as it went and raced off into the distance.

The troops in the Vandeon hovering nearby were still eagerly watching the tunnel exit through their gun sights. They'd already decided to fire on the dumpster as soon as it appeared, then claim they were fired on first. They waited and waited. There was no dumpster, no controllers, no Mavron, nothing. They'd no idea what had happened. Calls to the station where their prisoner had first been taken were inconclusive. No one knew anything until they ascended and looked behind them. The missing Tactan's two controllers were wandering, dazed, on the hilltop. Its pilot lay unconscious on the ground. Their visiting Royal Guard commander and prizes were gone.

◆◆◆ ⚑ ◆◆◆

Mavron opened his eyes; everything was still black. His head hurt. He tried to move his hands; they were restrained, his legs too. He felt dizzy even though he was lying down. He tried to piece together what was going on. Slowly it came back to him, the girl, the capture, the escape, the ambush, the... the rest was missing; there was no ambush. Something had gone very wrong.

A door opened, a dim light came on but a blindfold covered his eyes. He heard hushed voices. A female voice came close, a soft hand brushed against his cheek. Whoever it was put a cup or glass of water to his lips. He hesitated; what if it was drugged? Then he realised that he was a prisoner. If they wanted to drug him, they didn't need to politely offer him a drink. He drank the water. It tasted a little strange. It was standard dissolvable painkillers with a stimulant. His head cleared after a few minutes; the pain receded considerably. He was partially unbound and the blindfold was removed, his eyes adjusted to the dim light. Nothing was familiar. Before him stood a man who he assumed was the dumpster driver, although he wasn't sure, and the girl. The one who'd been at the Academy. She was looking back at him; he knew she recognised him. Even with his pounding head, he had to admit she was as beautiful as he remembered from their first meeting.

Other people stood nearby: two women, another man, and an older man. They were all staring at him.

The older man spoke up, "Welcome to the Land of the Ancients, noble servant of the empire."

Even in the poor light, Mavron recognised him. He was the crazy preacher he and his men had seen on the telecast documentary in Nahron's Gate. The one with the boat, the really big boat hundreds of miles from the sea. Great, thought Mavron to himself, I will finally be able to take up sailing again.

Chapter 7

Firefight

The cannons jammed without firing a single round. That was the third weapons system not working on his state of the art Seeker.

Shem decided that continuing to rely on the technology of his Imperial fast attack craft was a bad idea. He would have also liked to have figured out who had sabotaged its systems. But, with five Dark Kingdom Razbar interceptors on his tail, his focus was on staying alive. Five was far above the usual number for a random border encounter. The more he thought about it, the more he realised it was far from a coincidence.

Staying alive meant he had to part company with his Seeker before a missile struck it. A hollow woofing sound filled the air. Shem's Seeker automatically fired its last counter measures. "Counter measures not available," a female voice chimed, eerily calm. The latest round of missiles snaked away, chasing the countermeasures. Seconds later, a sharp intermittent buzzing filled the cockpit; more incoming missiles. With no defences left, Shem knew he had to eject now or die in the blast.

As he reached to pull the ejection lever, the thought struck him. What better way to kill a pilot than to sabotage his ejector seat? Disable the booster rockets on one side of the seat but not the other. Causing it to smash into one side of the cockpit instead of accelerating straight up out of it.

Shem wrenched his canopy manual release lever. The huge glass cover caught the wind, flying straight off. Travelling several hundred cubits, it smashed into the nearest Razbar on his tail. Glass fragments were sucked into its ventilators and the interceptor spectacularly exploded. The four others swerved away, thinking they were under a new attack.

"Come on!" Shem yelled. He liked these kinds of coincidences more than the ones that had afflicted him for the last half an hour. Throwing his Seeker into a stall, he levered himself out of the cockpit and leapt into the air. He free-fell for what felt like way too long before

48

his chute opened. The new missiles above finally reached his Seeker, blowing it to pieces.

His chute deployed properly. Whoever sabotaged his Seeker hadn't expected him to live long enough to use it. After barely ten seconds in the air, he crashed into the top of the dense jungle below. Pulling the harness release lever, he climbed, slid, and fell to the ground. Staggering forward, he fumbled in his left leg pocket for his personal homing beacon. Twisting the top off, he hit the red button. Personal homing beacons were not standard issue. Carrying them on missions was unauthorised. But, like many others, Shem had learned the hard way that standard kit wasn't always enough. He kept running away from where he'd landed.

The foliage where his parachute was entangled erupted in a fireball. The Dark Kingdom isn't taking prisoners today, Shem realised as he was flung through the air by the blast. Dizzy, he noticed his left arm and leg felt different; was he wounded? There was no time to find out. Running as far as he could, he flung open his dispersion net, which opened like a pop-up tent, and dived inside. Hopefully, he would be safe from the enemy's sensors. The floor of the small tent was rapidly turning deep red. Shem struggled to find his emergency spray bandage in his shoulder pouch; all he found was a gaping hole. He could see part of his shoulder socket; blood was pouring from the torn flesh. He turned his head away, trying to hold the wound closed with his right hand; it made little difference. Things were not looking good.

The distinctive throbbing resonators of Dark Kingdom meta bombers filled the air. He couldn't believe it. Surely not all this trouble for one downed pilot? They were going to carpet-bomb the whole area! He staggered out of his dispersion net, vainly trying to refold it and began running as the first meta bombs landed where his chute had been.

Shem's communicator crackled into life.

"Shem?" It was his brother responding to the homing beacon.

"Japheth!" Shem yelled at the top of his voice; he didn't need to explain any further.

"On the way," Japheth shouted back, "twenty minutes. I'll be in the Kestrel." Shem wondered if twenty minutes was anything like enough. The heavy thump of meta bombs was now heading towards him. Clearly, someone had betrayed him, his identity, location, everything. He had no time to speculate. The ground before him began to slope away. Shem decided that blindly leaping down the incline was better than being blown to bits. He ran forward through the foliage, jumped, and found himself free falling.

"I am so not going to die," he spluttered as he fell. Leaves and vines whipped his face. He crashed through layers of branches until he was back on level ground. Without thinking, he was up and stumbling forwards again, still clutching his shoulder. The meta bombs sounded more distant now. Shem heard running water; staggering towards it, he heaved for breath. He felt like he was floating. He collapsed exhausted at the edge of a small stream. He lay under the vast canopy of trees in a hidden valley that had saved his life. The water started to run deep red. He tried to get up but couldn't. Where was Japheth?

The sound of troop transports filled the air. Imperial Vandeons disgorged hundreds of soldiers into the treetops, abseiling to the ground.

"This way," someone shouted. Missile sounds filled the skies, followed by muffled explosions. Air to air missiles? thought Shem. He lay on his back in the shallow water, gazing up at the sky through the trees. Everything was starting to slowly revolve.

"Sir, sir, are you alright, sir?" a soldier leaned over him. Two more, both medics, moved him away from the stream, tending to his wounds. Another came running with a stretcher.

"He's lost too much blood!" one of the medics shouted, "Bring a transfuser!" Shem lay motionless, staring up. The noise of transports blurred as the sky receded into a tunnel. His thoughts seemed to reside outside of his body. Why had the empire expended so many resources to rescue him? Frantic voices cried out but were fading. They were saying something about the emperor. The emperor? Shem's blood soaked the ground, his body succumbing to his wounds. He felt cold.

♦♦♦   ⚑   ♦♦♦

Emzara stumbled against the corridor wall, shaking; a horror gripped her, yet her mind remained clear. She'd felt uncomfortable for the last few days; she knew it was Shem. Having her son serve in the Empire of the Son's Air Force had given her plenty to pray about over the years, but this was different. There was no other way to describe it – she knew Shem was dying at that very moment. Falling to her knees right there in her home, her face pressed to the floor, she began to cry

50

out and intercede for her son. She could see him; he was on his back in an immense pool of blood. The sight was horrendous. She boldly spoke life into his failing body. "Mother," she heard him whisper, "pray for me."

The corridor around her dissolved. A warm breeze brushed her face. The acrid smell of burning metal and rubber filled the air. Ash floated by. Men were shouting in desperation, "We're losing him, the plasma, the transfuser; where is it!"

Emzara heard a voice crying out in prayer; she realised it was her own. Medics were attaching equipment to her son: transfuser lines, a heart starter. His body convulsed as the medics tried to restart his heart. Others desperately sprayed and then bound his profusely bleeding shoulder and leg wounds. She wanted to hold him like she did when he was a child. The crest insignia on the arms of the medics was unfamiliar to her. They didn't look the same as those worn by the men she'd met who her son served with. Then she recognised them from telecasts; they were Royal Guards!

Emzara continued praying and speaking life into her son. Her mind tried to fathom why so many soldiers, even Royal Guards, were devoted to saving him. As if in answer to her question, she saw the multitudes of the neighbouring Dark Kingdom. A sea of lost faces wrapped in bondage to an evil beyond almost all comprehension. Emzara prayed on; now it wasn't just about her son; she knew she was interceding for half of all mankind.

◆◆◆   ⌐   ◆◆◆

Japheth approached the co-ordinates, he couldn't believe his eyes. Missile streaks criss-crossed the skies, plumes of black smoke billowed from the ground. He counted three heavy Imperial Vandeon transports. Numerous circling Seekers, and even two Tactans. Around them, like flies, Razbar interceptors were suicidally launching wave after wave of attack. Some, out of missiles, were using their cannons. The heavy Vandeon transports were firing countermeasures and anti-missile missiles in all directions. The Seekers were constantly engaging the interceptors. As he approached the mêlée, he flew over the fiercely burning wreckage of three huge Dark Kingdom meta bombers.

"By Eden!" Japheth exclaimed, "Another Great War? Where are

you, brother!" He slowed, dropping to treetop level, priming his somewhat limited countermeasures. He double-checked his citizen identity broadcaster was on – he wasn't there to be shot down by his own side. A Vandeon armoured transport nearby began forcibly descending through the tree line. Two others hovered above it. He knew enough of military tactics to know that what they were doing was against all common sense. A burst of static broke the silence as his transport's communicator came alive.

"Civilian transport, vacate this area immediately!"

"Where is pilot Shem!?" Japheth shouted back into the communicator. He flipped a switch by his console. All the empire's encrypted frequencies cleared. He listened to their chatter.

"Civilian transport, I repeat, you are ordered to leave this..." the message crackled to static. Japheth watched in shock as a nearby Tactan spectacularly exploded. Seconds later, one of the Vandeons hovering above the one in the trees took two missile hits to its left side. Billowing black smoke, it began tilting through the trees towards the ground. Somebody yelled over the airwaves, "Heavy Two has gone down!" The third Vandeon took its place, waiting like a sacrificial lamb, protecting the one below, drawing fire for it.

Have they gone utterly and completely mad? thought Japheth, what on earth are they trying to do!?

Another voice broke through the pilots' yelling at one another. This one was calm and authoritative.

"Empire of the Son Tigris sortie, this is Sector Five Control; you are reminded that this is a Level 8 mission. Evacuate pilot Shem alive at all costs."

For a brief moment, Japheth thought he was dreaming. This was about his brother? The empire, no wait, it was a Level 8 mission – the emperor himself had ordered an all-costs rescue of his brother. What in Eden!

Japheth tried to assemble his thoughts and tune them back into what was going on around him. He focused. If this was all about rescuing Shem, it meant that the Vandeons were trying to evacuate his brother. Assuming the crashed Vandeon hadn't landed on him!

Japheth engaged his super thrusters, accelerating straight at the flank of five Razbars. They were targeting the remaining hovering Vandeon. Two Seekers lined up either side of him; his identity beacon told them whose side he was on. He gave their pilots a palms-up. They all fired their cannons together. The Imperial Seekers were out of missiles; Japheth's transport, a converted racer, only had cannons. He emptied half his rounds into the Razbars. Their only aim was to kill whoever was under the Vandeon transports – his brother.

Two of the Razbars spectacularly burst into flames. Moments later, another skewed off up into the sky, then went crashing down into the trees. The remaining two held their course. Firing and tearing up the ground beneath the hovering and descending transports. In the far distance, three more Dark Kingdom meta bombers were approaching.

♦♦♦   ⚑   ♦♦♦

Emzara was looking down on the body of her son. Medics were still trying to restart his heart and staunch his wounds. A mobile transfuser was attached to him, pumping plasma into his body. Three more Royal Guard medics arrived, all with triple gold stars on their lapels. Other soldiers were around him too. They wore the camouflage uniform of Jumpers, elite airborne troops. They were facing out, forming a protective perimeter.

Far behind the group of attendant medics, Emzara saw a disturbance in the foliage. Shimmering and shaking as though a wild animal was running madly through it. Two lines of miniature explosions were racing right towards where her son lay. Emzara's eyes were tightly shut, yet she saw everything in clear detail. Rising up on her knees, she spoke to the fast approaching line of cannon rounds, commanding them to stop. At the last moment, the attendant Royal Guards saw the rounds. Two dived away. A third, caught between them, saw there was no escape. He raised his right hand and touched his fingertips to his forehead.

A true believer, thought Emzara in the midst of all her fervent praying, how unusual.

The rounds came right up to the edge of where the medics were and stopped. Somewhere in the sky, Emzara heard a screeching resonator. It was the third Razbar out of control. Moments later, she heard a distant, muffled thud.

A massive Vandeon was descending right above her son, crushing and splintering branches. The area around Shem darkened under its immense shadow. Soldiers were protecting him from falling debris. They frantically hoisted him up on a stretcher. A large ramp opened from the underbelly of the hovering beast.

More Royal Guards appeared from inside. Emzara watched the lifeless body of her son disappear into the Vandeon, like a coffin into an incinerator. The medics still frantically working on him. She continued praying fervently. Then she heard words that brought relief to her soul.

"Your son will live."

Emzara collapsed, exhausted, onto the floor of her peaceful home. The battlefields on the edge of the neutral zone again, far away. "Thank you, thank you," she whispered.

◆◆◆   ⚑   ◆◆◆

The two remaining Razbars overshot the hovering Vandeons. The Imperial Seekers gave chase. Japheth circled to land, but the Vandeon beneath the tree line began ascending. His transport communicator came to life; the calm familiar voice spoke once more.

"Tigris sortie. We have him, condition critical but stable. Good work! All transports route to HAB, ground troops to sortie point five." Cheering filled the airwaves.

The Empire of the Son craft began moving away towards Havilah in the south west and the Tigris Battle Group HQ beyond. The two Seekers returned; the Razbars they'd been pursuing didn't. None of the remaining enemy transports followed. It was suicide to overfly the infamous Havilah Auto Batteries guarding the empire's eastern border. They turned back north.

Japheth reluctantly turned east, heading home. As much as he wanted to see his brother, he couldn't. Being seen in an Imperial garrison was too risky, especially after the recent events in Nahron's Gate.

The returning Seekers rolled in unison as they passed him. One of the two pilots called him.

"Hey, good work, civvy boy, nice racer!"

Then turned sharply to escort the retreating convoy into the spectacular western sunset. Their resonators glowing deep red as they pushed them to full power.

Chapter 8

Choose Your Tears Carefully

*H*am loved Sashina, and she loved him. They were a perfect match, or so he thought.

Ham had met Sashina a couple of years back. She was among the first tourists to visit the giant sea-going vessel his father and family were building. The news of the huge boat soon hit the Havilah region's airwaves. Tour operators in Nahron's Gate were quick to see its potential. They organised special trips by battery powered ground transports to see it.

Over time, the giant construction had become a money spinner for the local economy. A genuine doomsday attraction was a rare thing indeed. Where else could you go and see an ark, as it was called, being built to save humanity from a coming apocalypse?

The crowds loved it. Even the long ride to the site from the empire's borderlands was an adventure in itself. At dinner parties, it often became a hot topic. Any tale of Imperial citizens venturing into the Land of the Ancients always commanded at least twenty minutes of attention. To top it all, at each day's end, Noah, the main architect, would preach stirring messages to visitors. He warned of a coming catastrophe, the result of mankind's growing selfishness and evil. It was all immensely entertaining.

The crowds came in trickles at first but more recently in droves. Some came just to get angry. Others out of curiosity. Most came for the entertainment. The endless reality shows on the telecasts were getting tedious. A real religious nutjob, building a ship hundreds of miles from the sea and preaching a doomsday message. It was a weekend treat for the whole family. Then there were the standing jokes. Where were all the animals that Noah had claimed would be joining him for the journey? Apparently, it was going to be at least two of every kind. Presently, there were none. The biggest joke was about how many people had booked a place on board other than Noah's immediate family.

At first, the elders of the Land of the Ancients had liked the idea of the Ark. Mainly because they believed it would never be built. A few even pretended to agree with why it was being built. After all, the Emperor Nahron had come to power calling for repentance and a return to the ways of old. So it seemed a good theme to tag along with for a while. It brought more money into the region too, a lot more. However, over time the favour of the elders waned. Nahron's open dislike for what he called "deviant religion" left them nervous. They were sure that, if news of Noah's boat spread, Nahron would be strongly against it. Trade sanctions could follow. Soon they demanded Noah stop the construction. The elders began to call his work an act of heresy – the work of someone not under authority.

Sashina had returned soon after her first visit to the Ark and requested a special private tour. She remembered Ham and hoped to meet him again. These additional tours were free, but Noah's workers took little gifts to facilitate them. Noah turned a blind eye. He hoped that, if people came aboard, their hearts might be touched. He wanted them to move beyond fascination and consider his message.

Sashina met Ham on the upper decks, of all places in his cabin while fitting it out. She was impressed. Ham was decorating his quarters with ornately engraved cedar panels. Each one a work of art in its own right. Adorned with intricate carvings of landscapes, animals, sunsets and even people. The beauty of his craftsmanship was captivating. He displayed a sensitivity she'd not found in other men.

Sashina found him charming and friendly, but he also genuinely listened to her. It was a radical change from the men in her home town of Isis. They only wanted short chats, followed by long periods in bed and then nothing at all.

The two of them talked for a long time that day. Ham began to imagine that the bed he'd just fitted in his cabin would be a place he would share with Sashina. That he'd finally found the wife he was looking for. To say that she was attractive was an understatement. Her figure had immediately caught his attention, slim yet shapely. Her eyes had a gaze that said, "just love me." Her lips were unspeakably appealing. Ham steadied his thoughts; Sashina had come to visit the vessel of her own volition. She'd asked for a special tour and shown an interest in his handiwork. This could only mean one thing. Unlike other tourists, Sashina was interested in why the giant vessel was being built. Surely this indicated that she had a real desire for spiritual things?

Casting his eyes over her, Ham didn't need much convincing.

Sashina had stayed way beyond the time of the last tourist transport back to Nahron's Gate that day. Ham talked to her about his father's message. He discussed the time of the beginning, the perfect garden. Things that were important to him. Sashina had listened and then, to his delight, invited him to visit her home near Isis. His head was spinning. This beautiful woman not only had an interest in him personally, but listened to his views too. He readily accepted the invite, making the long journey to her home that night in his own transport. He met her family.

Sashina's parents were rich, very rich, not that Noah was poor by any means. However, her parents were also influential. Ham imagined how much weight they could give to the message. If they backed it in the borderlands, or even the City of Light, who knew how many people might change their ways? He really liked Sashina; in fact, he found himself thinking about her every waking moment. Ham was in love. Instead of scoffing at him like other women, Sashina showed an interest in him, his family, and their beliefs. It was intoxicating.

In the years that had gone by, Ham's family had steadily lost friends. Even in the Land of the Ancients, people had begun to politely avoid the family of Noah. How many false world endings had been promised by preachers over the centuries? Too many, that was for sure.

By the time of Sashina's second visit, Ham was increasingly isolated. His older brother Shem was busy saving the empire from the Dark Kingdom. Japheth, the oldest of the three, was busy spying on its clandestine activities. Nadina, whom he liked very much, was either with her family or, more recently, secretly working with Japheth. His mother Emzara was a fantastic mother in every way but very busy. She had to stock the vessel for the hundreds or even thousands that might eventually come aboard. No one had any idea how many people would join them or how long the journey would last.

Noah was fully occupied directing and retaining labourers who were helping to build the Ark. Even though they were generously paid, they kept leaving. Their numbers had dwindled to an all time low.

The result of all this was that Ham was lonely, lonely all the time. Sashina seemed like the answer to all his prayers. A fabulously beautiful woman interested in him and his work. His fourth visit was the one where his plans took an unexpected turn.

Sashina's parents were called away to the City of Light for an important event. Ham was visiting for a couple of days. Sashina took him to their picturesque summer home on the forested hills of northern Isis. A more peaceful and romantic spot one could not imagine. The views were breathtaking, the air fresher, and the solitude left nothing to hide. Sashina had taken full advantage of that. Their visit was supposed to last a couple of hours; it lasted seven days. Seven days of passionate lovemaking as Sashina introduced Ham to things he'd only dreamed of.

Every moment was a cascade of passion until the seventh day. Ham returned home to continue helping his father build the Ark. Sashina went with him to stay a few days. One look at the two of them from a hundred cubits away told everyone the nature of their relationship.

For the first few months, Ham tried to deny it, both to himself and others. He planned to sort things out, but every time he visited Sashina, his resolve lasted less and less time. Eventually, he completely gave up. Most of Nahron's Gate and all Isis knew about his relationship with Sashina. His parents were not so naïve as to think it was all hugs, polite kisses, and the odd romantic walk in a garden. Ham loved Sashina. His heart was torn. How could something that felt so good be so wrong?

His mother gently talked to him, "Ham, we all shed tears because of those we love. You can give Sashina the choice to put the Creator first in her life, to marry you and to make her home here with you. If she doesn't, you will shed tears but eventually they will be wiped away. Or you can turn your back on what you know to be right and then one day shed tears that cannot be wiped away. Choose your tears carefully, my son."

That wasn't all. Ham was undermining Noah's message. Recently, when Noah preached his sermons, visitors' voices would cry out, "Where's Ham then?" Someone else would quickly call back in reply, "He's buying wood in Isis." At this point, the whole crowd would burst out laughing. There were no timber merchants in Isis, and the site of Noah's vessel was surrounded by vast trees. The crowds loved a preacher warning them of a coming judgement whose own son fell short of the mark.

Moreover, despite Sashina's interest in Ham's work on the Ark, neither Noah nor Emzara believed she cared for her Creator at all. They thought the Ark fascinated Sashina simply because it was there. Not because she could connect with anything about it spiritually. Noah and Emzara were very concerned. Without a common bond between Ham and Sashina, any marriage would inevitably fail.

Sashina's parents were also not happy. Not because their daughter was sleeping with Ham and not married. About this, they couldn't care less. Sashina's father had at least three mistresses and her mother a new boyfriend almost every month. What they didn't like was being linked to some crazy preacher's son from the Land of the Ancients. They had their careers in the empire to think of. They weren't ready to lose them for anything, least of all true love and religious nutcases.

Ham and Sashina stopped seeing each other. Sashina had a few recreational boyfriends that Ham didn't know of. But she missed his kindness, devotion, and attention. She wanted that for herself. After six months, she went to a temple in Isis and made a special offering for their relationship to be restored. As if in answer to her seed sowing, only a week later, Ham appeared at her family home on the outskirts of Isis. She opened the door and fell into his arms.

Ham declared his love for her. Certainly, the way things had gone was not the order in which he'd imagined they would be, let alone wanted. He knew the way forward was to put things in the right order, not for things to carry on as they were before. Neither did he feel that he could live without her. Right there and then at the door, Ham knelt down. He gave Sashina the most beautifully ornate engraved ring she'd ever seen and asked her to marry him.

Sashina was moved to tears. She bravely accepted despite the cataclysmic repercussions it would have with her family. She'd had many boyfriends. None wanted to marry her. They only wanted to use her perfect body and skip the rest. This first part of Ham's plan went well. He was greatly relieved; finally, everything would be made right. Without thinking, he went inside the house with Sashina and ended up right back where he'd been six months earlier.

Another day and night of passion followed. The following evening, Ham resolved to get back on track. He asked Sashina to move to the Land of the Ancients immediately. They could be legally married there. He explained that he must help his father finish building the Ark. He was sure she would agree – then all his problems would be solved.

"Surely you don't really believe all those things your father says, do you? The temples here in Isis and Nahron's Gate are nice places.

Why don't we go to one of them?"

Ham was lost for words. Seeing his concerned and bereft look, Sashina reached over to kiss him softly. Her lips were warm, soft, and full. Soon, the subject of the end of the world was completely forgotten.

'Nice places,' Ham lay awake later, thinking about what Sashina had said. A temple was a 'nice place' to go. Surely he didn't 'really believe' all that stuff his father said? The words went round and round in his head.

Ham finally realised the true extent of his terrible error. For almost a year he'd been completely deluded. Sashina didn't believe in the coming catastrophe. She was only outwardly interested in anything spiritual. Worst of all, to her, the Creator was a concept, not a person.

Lying next to Sashina, who as usual was sleeping completely naked, Ham gazed at her in the moonlight. What more could any man want? Perhaps given time she would change, maybe have a kind of spiritual awakening? He would love her and take care of her; his kindness would touch her heart and win her soul. For a moment his hopes revived. But how long would that take? How long did he have before the Creator's words to his father came to pass? He considered other options; there were none. Every woman he knew other than in his immediate family circle despised him. Why Sashina loved him he did not know, but she did, and he only wanted to return her affection. Ham was overwhelmed; if only everything could somehow be made simple.

"Oh Lord of the Heavens," he prayed in all sincerity, "please help me, I have been so wrong. Show me what to do." He felt the Creator's presence, His unconditional love. Ham closed his eyes. From the very depths of his heart, he whispered, "Please forgive me," and fell into a deep sleep.

◆◆◆ ⌐ ◆◆◆

Ham woke with a start; it was well before sunrise. He was absolutely sure he'd heard his name being called. The voice had been very clear yet no matter how hard he tried he couldn't recognise who it was. Paradoxically it sounded familiar. He sat up quietly on the edge of the bed so as not to disturb Sashina. Suddenly he felt a strong sense of foreboding. He braced himself, burglars or maybe worse?! His brother Japheth had repeatedly trained him on what to do and what not to do in such a situation. After a few moments Ham realised there was no one else in the house. Sashina's parents were away and the servants had taken a few days off. He relaxed a little, but the feeling wouldn't go away.

Everything was unnaturally still.

"Leave this place," the thought came tangibly to him. He tried to settle a little, to dismiss the notion. He couldn't lie back down and oddly neither could he stand up. Something was holding him until he made his choice.

"Leave this place," the thought came to him again, stronger than the first time. Ham knew this was it. The Creator was speaking to him. Either he left now while Sashina slept, or procrastinated and risked staying indefinitely. His thoughts went to the giant vessel his father was building. He knew that the consequences of staying could not be good.

Ham made a cold, hard decision. If anything about the coming catastrophe was true, then he'd better be on that boat. Sashina could always join him if she wanted to. If it was all a giant mistake, then he would have a lot of apologising to do, or most likely none at all.

Ham collected his things and quietly made his way out. Oddly, the usually squeaky bedroom door didn't squeak at all. He stopped halfway out. He had the thought to look back. He knew he shouldn't, that it wouldn't help, but he did it anyway. Sashina lay naked on the bed; the earliest rays of the sun touched the profile of her body. She was perfect, every curve a work of art. Ham regretted looking. He wanted to get back in the bed, bury his head in her bosom and feel secure and loved. He hesitated, unable to make himself go any further then he saw himself as a child kneeling at an altar. He was praying and giving his heart to the Creator. Ham realised where his final loyalty lay, and it was not on the bed in front of him.

"Goodbye, Sashina," he whispered, tears forming in his eyes. He slipped out.

The air outside was unusually cool. Ham paused for a moment. These strange fluctuations in the weather were getting more common. For a moment, he imagined he heard a distant rumble. He looked up, expecting to see a large transport somewhere in the dim sky, but there was none. Ham began walking. He decided to leave his battery powered transport with Sashina, with a note encouraging her to join him. It was the least that he could do after all that had happened. If she wanted to come to his father's, all she had to do was get in it and drive. The fully charged batteries would take her all the way to his home deep in the Land of the Ancients. Somehow he already knew that she wouldn't follow him.

Ham walked for hours along the forest paths. By late afternoon, he arrived at the centre of Isis. He was exhausted more from emotional distress than from the journey. He wandered through the town in a daze. By now, his heart was aching; he missed Sashina so much, yet he knew he could never go back. He felt like his whole world was ripping apart and he was falling through the middle. He could hardly see where he was going through a constant blur of tears. His bottom lip was sore from biting it so much to try to stop himself from crying. The pain in his heart was unbearable.

Nearby, outside a modest temple, a sacrifice was being held. A priest was repeating the well known words. Ham went over, standing transfixed at the front of a small crowd. The words he'd first heard from his grandfather, the only man who'd ever shown him real affection, rang out. His own father had always been too busy saving the world to give him much attention.

"A sacrifice to save us all, to cover our sins, an innocent life to carry our guilt." The priest sacrificed the lamb and then flamboyantly swung his arm back. Some blood from the priest's knife flicked into the air and landed on the back of Ham's hand. He stared as the single droplet began to run slowly down his skin.

"A sacrifice to save me," he repeated quietly to himself, transfixed by the sight of the blood. He touched the back of his hand to his chest, invisibly staining his black top.

"Oh Creator..." he choked as his voice broke. Ham lost his words in grief as a great warmth enveloped him. Covering his head with his arms, he sank to his knees. The crowd dispersed, waiting for their blessing after the offering. The priest retired to count his money. No one was bothered about a young man crying on the walkway. At least, no one who could be seen.

◆◆◆  ◆◆◆

Ham consoled himself; he knew the Creator loved and understood him. That didn't make the mistakes he'd made any less harmful, but at least he knew the Creator would always have time for him. That He would lead him no matter what kind of mess he got himself into. That was enough. He also knew that Sashina loved him, but also that she would never join him on his father's boat. Why she would not join him if she really loved him, he had absolutely no idea.

Ham decided to return home and focus on the task at hand, the completion of the great vessel. The world was ending, was it not? He wouldn't allow his feelings to get in the way of that. He prayed for strength.

Ham finished the first leg of his journey from Isis to Nahron's Gate. Arriving there, he walked vacantly through the busy streets. He felt nothing at all in response to his prayer. He purchased basic supplies and a disruptor to protect himself from wild animals and reptiles. He couldn't face his family yet, so he decided to trek home. The journey would give him time to adjust.

Ham crossed the Pishon and began walking east through the forested hills of the Valley of Shadow. Fresh tears rolled down his cheeks. He'd made the right choice, so why was he still hurting? His steps were uneven, like his heart, broken. He heard Sashina's voice laughing through the rustling trees. He felt her touch with every leaf that brushed against his skin. He inhaled the scent of her sweet fragrances from every flower. He tasted the memory of her lips from only the air around him. He whispered her name to himself. A thousand voices cried at him to go back, but somehow Ham, son of Noah, kept on walking.

Chapter 9

The Riverbank

*N*adina sat exhausted by the riverbank. The gentle flow of a small tributary of the great Pishon soothed her mind and frayed nerves. She leaned back against a large tree. Its branches lazily sampled the chuckling waters below. The whispering trees and coolness of the lush vegetation all reminded her of the Creator. Each flower, unique. Every leaf, different. Yet, all were in harmony. The stifling conformity of the empire was not there.

Closing her eyes, she recalled the stress of the last few days. It wasn't about the observation mission in Nahron's Gate, nor her capture and then hair-raising escape. It wasn't even about the dire consequences of kidnapping a Royal Guard Commander. No, the stress was all about seeing Japheth. She was, as usual, exasperated.

Nadina decided to try and make sense of everything. It would be futile; it always was, but she tried anyway. She started from the beginning. Her parents were settlers in the Land of the Ancients. They were from the central southern plains, in the heart of the empire.

Nadina had been born in the Land of the Ancients. I'm an Ancient, she laughed to herself. What she really was, she didn't know or care, but thanks to Japheth and Noah's wife Emzara, she was a believer. A true believer, no gimmicks, no hypocrisy. Just a girl who loved her Creator. His peace filled her soul at the very thought, and her mind began to drift into an Eden no longer inhabited.

What it must have been like to meet the Creator every day, as the first couple had done. To talk with Him. To see Him with your own eyes. To be His friend. The thoughts settled her mind and calmed her frayed nerves. Nadina snuggled deeper into her happy daydream. To walk with the Creator among Eden's great trees. To laugh with Him, to embrace Him. And there her daydream ended. Gentle tears began to roll softly down her cheeks because in her dream she realised she was not alone. At her side was Japheth, laughing, talking; he too was embracing his Maker and then later her in a very different way. Nadina's heart was torn. She was drowning in emotion. Struggling to reach the surface, gasping for breath. She wanted to return to the real world. Or maybe this was the real world? Perhaps true happiness was only found in dreams in the real world?

Nadina began to quietly sob. "Oh Maker of the heavens," she hesitated but then let the words fall softly from her lips, "I love him." Something inside her broke; she'd never said that out loud before. She expected to feel horribly condemned but didn't. "I love him, oh how I love him," the words fell ceaselessly from her lips. Her quiet crying wracked her already weary body.

"Forgive me," she pleaded desperately. She was tired of this life, tired of herself. "Forgive me, forgive me for being me!" Eventually, she calmed down and closed her eyes.

Nadina slept for a while and then awoke. The sun had begun to move down to the cool of the day; the sky was dimming. She started over again from the beginning. She wondered if this was how life was, a perpetual puzzle that you could never solve no matter how hard you tried.

Nadina had met Japheth when she was just a girl. The warmth in his smile had immediately captured her heart. His friendship and laughter were always with her like a telecast film, ever running in the back of her mind. He was handsome like his dashing younger brother Shem, but softer, smarter, and quicker. Shem was a hero in every sense of the word, but Japheth was her hero. Her very own hero.

Japheth had not yet been married and she'd innocently imagined that one day soon they would be man and wife. Then her parents were suddenly recalled to the distant City of Light. They chose to fulfil their duties to the empire and its ever more powerful emperor.

Fifteen years passed in the City of Light and much changed in Nadina's life. The capital did not revere the ways of the Ancients. Nadina had done things she'd regretted. She found herself far from the simplicity of her childhood faith. Her outstanding stamina and physical fitness had soon caught the attention of officials. She could run almost at a full sprint for more than half a mile. Her intelligence quota was tested; it was off the scale. She was offered a place at the elite Royal Guard training academy. Nadina passed the gruelling selection tests and became the first woman ever admitted.

For several years, she trained on all the empire's security equipment. She learned every clandestine art and how to survive in the harshest of environments. She had only one terminal flaw; she was strikingly good-looking. Every colleague and instructor wanted her for themselves. Nadina was not happy to oblige. The day before her graduation, she broke an arm and a leg of her combat instructor for trying to take advantage of her. There was uproar and she'd simply walked out of the Academy, never to return. Technically she wasn't a deserter; she'd never graduated. No one knew what to do with her or the public disgrace that would follow if they did. Many were glad they no longer had a woman at the Academy to embarrass them, so she was left alone. Her pay stopped after six months. A generous lump sum was added to make her forget any idea of claiming compensation. Her record simply read, 'Training incomplete.'

Soon after that fateful day, her parents attended an official event at the Great Palace. Nadina had gone with them to be polite. Wandering around the vast grounds, she'd accidentally ended up in the Gardens of Solace. A secluded place of unmatched beauty within the palace grounds. In the middle of it was a white marble statue of the great Enoch being taken up to heaven. Nadina had found comfort there and begun to pray, something she'd not done for a very long time. The beauty all around touched her soul; she remembered the faith of her younger years. The things she'd seen when she first met Japheth. When she'd given her heart to the Creator and learned the ways of the Ancients from Noah's wife, Emzara. She'd found herself praying, giving her hardened heart back into her Maker's gentle hands.

Nadina had felt peace. She'd resolved to attend a temple sacrifice to seal her trust in her forgiveness. She'd never really understood why sacrificing an innocent creature would affirm her cleansing. Offerings, gifts, and crops had their place but not for the covering of sins. Everyone knew that. The empire's corruption had not yet robbed mankind of this truth.

Nadina finished praying and stood up. Before her was a young woman of extraordinary beauty. She had a complexion that was in every way perfect and green eyes flecked with obsidian gems. Her face radiated a serenity and smile that reassured more than a thousand words. Nadina gasped; she was face to face with none other than Ariana, Chaste Maid of the Great Temple of the Son. Words failed her.

Ariana had seen Nadina praying and her tears. Their eyes had met, and she had said the strangest thing before walking away.

"You are my dear sister, forever."

How could she be the sister of Ariana? Ariana, the Chaste Maid of the Temple of the Son, had no sister. She rarely appeared in public and never spoke with citizens. Yet, there she was, or rather had been for that fleeting moment, saying that she was her sister – forever. The rest of the day was a blur. Her overjoyed parents, concealing their delight, announced they were moving back to the Land of the Ancients. In a moment, Nadina's whole life changed. She remembered Japheth and longed to meet him again, hoping he wasn't married. But he was. That was three difficult years ago.

Nadina settled into her old home. She had sweet fellowship with Emzara, Japheth's mother. Once again, she began to spend more and more time at Noah's. She met Shem again, still unmarried and as handsome and charming as ever. After a while, the unspoken assumption was that they would marry. But something didn't fit.

Nadina saw Japheth and his beautiful new wife, Adatenesis. They looked a perfect couple, and Nadina was doing her best to be happy for them. Something deep inside her stirred whenever she saw Japheth, but she pushed it aside. He was married and happily married at that. Everything seemed perfect. Perfect except for her, of course. A while later, something happened that forever changed her perceptions.

Nadina had arrived at Noah's house unannounced early one morning. Walking quietly through the rooms as she often did for fun, she heard an unexpected sound. It was Japheth; he was crying. He was sobbing, really sobbing. Her heart racing, Nadina entered the large living room and walked numbly to where Japheth sat by a window. After several moments of hesitation, she put her hand on his shoulder. He didn't look up, assuming it was a family member who already knew his plight, perhaps his mother or one of his brothers.

"Nothing has changed," he sobbed. "Nothing," he cried. "After all these years it's always the same; she comes, she goes and never stays. Everything is a lie." Nadina had found herself shedding a tear too, even though she had no idea what Japheth was talking about. "I'm so lonely!" he'd sobbed.

The words hit Nadina like a freight transport. The man she loved was sobbing because he was lonely!!!

Emzara appeared at the living room door. Nadina stood up quickly, walking silently on the soft wool carpet towards her. Blushing and wiping her own tears.

"I just walked in," she whispered, "I don't know what's going on, I don't know anything, he doesn't know I'm here, I don't know why he's so..." Fresh tears began to stream down her cheeks. She silently fled, running most of the fifteen miles back to her home.

Nadina had crashed through the door of her parents' mansion later that afternoon, ran up the stairs, collapsed through her quarters' door, and fell against it, sobbing. She'd tried to figure out what was going on. Why was Japheth so deeply hurt? How could he be lonely! He was married, wasn't he? It had to be Adatenesis.

The memory of Japheth's cries never left her; the next time she saw him, he was composed. He'd known nothing of her presence in the room that day.

Nadina remembered it all as if it were yesterday. She put it all down to a terrible marriage choice, but that was only half of it.

The following week had brought the ultimate level of bewilderment to Nadina's life. Just when she thought it was hard but somehow still manageable, things got a whole lot more confusing.

Emzara had come round to apologise for the previous week's episode. She wanted to reassure Nadina and, as often was the case, to simply spend time with her. Emzara loved Nadina; she was like a daughter to her. Her own daughters had married young and moved far away.

They'd had sweet fellowship that day. Emzara hadn't really said what the problem was with Japheth, and Nadina hadn't asked, but it was obvious. Who else could make him say the things he said and weep like that except for his wife?

While they'd been talking, news had come that Methuselah, Noah's aged grandfather, was dying. It was slightly comical because he'd been dying for almost a hundred years. However, apparently he really was dying this time. Naturally, Emzara went immediately to see him, and just as naturally, Nadina went with her.

The room where Methuselah lay had been sparsely populated. Noah was there, Shem absent; engaged in some important mission far away. Japheth was unreachable in Nahron's Gate. Adatenesis was with her family on the other side of the river in Isis. No one was quite sure where Ham was and didn't want to ask. That left only the three of them and a handful of servants.

Nadina had quietly entered the room with Emzara. Methuselah's bed was facing away from the door through which she came in. As soon as she'd taken one step through the door, Methuselah clearly spoke her name.

"Nadina, my child, come here." Everyone was surprised; how did he know she was there? She obediently walked towards him.

"Hello, beloved father," she said, kissing Methuselah's cheek. It was the customary greeting for a respected elder.

"Kneel, my child," he spoke as if it were a divine command, his voice still strong. Nadina knelt. She was not afraid of Methuselah. His enduring goodness and love had been a testimony to the world for 969 years. She was encouraged that he had a blessing for her before he passed on and wondered what he would say. What happened next was certainly not what she was expecting.

"Nadina," Methuselah's voice boomed, "beloved daughter of Noah." As if to reinforce the point, he repeated himself. "Nadina, beloved daughter of my son." His own son Lamech, Noah's father, was already dead. But it was not unusual to refer to grandchildren as sons and daughters. "Child of this family. Faithful wife. Dearest companion (he seemed to want to add a bit more but left it out as though it was too personal). Leader of new peoples." He paused, "Your voice will be heard throughout the lands that have been cleansed."

Nadina was stunned, 'Leader of new peoples?' What in Eden was he on about!

She believed Noah's warnings about the flood. But, it was hard to grasp that all civilisation could be here one day and gone the next. Was Methuselah saying she would be a leader of people after the catastrophe? How could she be a child of the family, a faithful wife, a faithful wife of whom – Shem? Well, at least that part made sense. However, his final words brought the remaining walls of comprehensibility crashing down.

"Sister of the Chaste Maid, beloved of our champion."

'Sister of the Chaste Maid,' the words had reeled around Nadina's head. Did this refer to the time Ariana had met her at the palace and called her sister? She had never told anyone about that. If so, far from clarifying anything, it only confused things even more. How would she become Ariana's sister? Then there was the champion bit. There was only one champion in the family; Shem. He was the champion of so many things it had almost become tedious. If Shem was to be Ariana's beloved, which was absurd anyway. And she was to be Noah's daughter, then who was she going to marry? Noah didn't have any other unmarried sons other than Ham, and everyone knew the path he'd gone down.

It had to be wrong, totally wrong. The last, garbled words of an old man. But, he'd known it was her when she entered the room without seeing her. In fact, as they entered, Emzara had greeted Noah. Yet, Methuselah had still called out Nadina's name.

Nadina had remained kneeling. Methuselah, still with his hand on her head, proclaimed a few more blessings on all present and some not. He looked around, as though he would live for another two or three years after all. Then he withdrew his hand from her head and breathed his last.

The room had stayed quiet for a very long time. Eventually, the servants returned and began their duties. Everyone carried on as if Methuselah had never mentioned Nadina. Nadina looked for the last time at Methuselah's slightly glowing face.

"Goodbye, dear father," she'd whispered and retired to another room.

Emzara dropped her off later that day and gave her a warm hug; their eyes met. Nadina had seen only love in them.

"The Creator is always good," was all she'd said and was gone. The funeral was held shortly afterwards when Shem and Japheth could be there; Ham missed it. The whole thing about Methuselah's final blessing for Nadina was never spoken of.

Now here she was six months later by the Pishon River. They'd captured a Royal Guard Commander; how that would play out no one knew. Japheth told her he was called Mavron. Adatenesis was somewhere in Isis with her son Vindad, child of her first long dead husband. Maybe Methuselah had been partly right about some things but then got mixed up about the rest. Japheth was married, happily or not, so that was the end of that story. There was no way she was going to marry Ham. Everyone now knew he was on another holiday with a rich official's daughter. Although she had to admit she did quite like him in many ways.

Nadina knew she ought to be going home before it got any darker, but she didn't want to move. The area was peaceful, she was tired, and home recently had not been the place where she wanted to be. Her parents, once keen to learn the ways of the Ancients, now prioritised the empire. It turned out that half the reason Nahron had them sent back was to keep him informed about the region.

Nadina stayed where she was, reasoning to herself not to move. She felt uncomfortable. Something nagged at her, but she ignored it. Had she really just escaped from the wrong end of the empire's grip? That was quite an achievement, she laughed to herself. The nagging feeling grew stronger.

Suddenly, Nadina was tense. The atmosphere around her had changed. The river still chuckled along the bank. But, something was very wrong. All her years of training kicked in; the birds had gone silent, the air was unusually still. That meant one thing and one thing alone: real and imminent danger.

Her hand went slowly to the long leather-handled titanium knife in her calf holster. She carefully pulled it out, rising as quietly as possible to her feet. She wished she'd brought her disruptor, but in all her emotional turmoil she'd absent mindedly left it at home. Then she heard it. A silent, almost imperceptible padding sound. She knew all too well that only one creature could be so stealthy yet instil such fear. Every bird for many cubits around had either fled or frozen in terror.

The raptor put its huge head slowly around a nearby tree looking for the prey its nostrils were calling out for. Their eyes met; for a brief moment, the creature sized her up, almost laughing at its puny prize. Then it lunged towards her. Nadina did the only thing anyone had ever done who'd survived a raptor attack without a projectile weapon or disruptor. She ran straight towards it.

◆◆◆　🏳　◆◆◆

How to fight a raptor without a projectile weapon or disruptor was widely known. Unfortunately, most people didn't believe it and ran in the opposite direction and so always died. Nadina was not one of those people. Resolute and level headed, she was never one to hesitate in a crisis. She ran straight at the surprised creature. It expected her, like all its previous prey of mostly animals but also a few people, to make a run for it. She ducked under its huge chin and, with all her strength, locked her right arm around its left arm. Fending off the creature's right arm with her knife, she plunged it up into its armpit, slicing its tendons. It screamed in agony, as its right arm began flailing uncontrollably. Nadina grasped its left arm tightly with her right, pulling herself as close as possible to its chest.

The beast desperately clawed at her with its still usable left hand. Vainly trying to pull her from its only vulnerable spot – against its chest right under its chin.

The creature couldn't get its mouth lined with razor-sharp teeth onto Nadina. Its great strength in its legs, neck, tail and vast jaw was useless as long as she stayed where she was. All it had were its weak arms to fight with. The creature roared wildly, lumbering madly about, but Nadina grimly held on.

"The Creator has a plan for my life!" she yelled at the bewildered creature, "I am to be a daughter of Noah, not your prey!" She drove her knife repeatedly up into the soft skin under its chin.

Blood spewed down, drenching her face. The raptor tried to bite her, its massive array of teeth snapping uselessly together. It began to stagger about, the toll of its haemorrhaging blood catching up with it. Finally, it realised something was wrong, that this easy prey was in fact its doom. It let out a gargled roar and stumbled away through the foliage. But Nadina wouldn't let go. That jaw could slice a crocodile in half in one bite; she needed the raptor almost dead before she let go. Branches whipped across her back as the creature lunged wildly forwards and sideways, trying to free itself. Eventually, it stopped moving and swooned. Moaning and gargling on its own blood, it fell to the ground. Nadina jumped away, turning to face it, holding her knife high.

The creature stared at her and tried to get up but could not. It looked surprised, even hurt by its defeat at the hands of such small prey. It sank back down to the ground, trembling. Nadina watched it die. Such a magnificent creature writhing to such a pointless death, it was a horrible sight. She knew it hadn't always been this way, that there had been a time when reptiles were man's friend. Much had changed since those days. Now, animals and reptiles often devoured each other too.

Nadina stumbled into the river, washed her hair and face, and ran home. Her parents were out, another Imperial appointment no doubt.

Chapter 10

The Forbidden Gate

*T*almeon was impatient; where was Mavron? Why had he gone off on some wild raptor chase after an insignificant girl? Her only crime was to gaze at them in Nahron's Gate and to be a famous drop-out from the Royal Guard Academy. After Mavron's disappearance, Talmeon found out that his team were all Royal Guards. It didn't bother him much. Nahron was a compulsive sneak anyway. It simply meant he had better security than he first thought.

Two days had gone by and no one had a clue where Mavron was. The security station where Mavron went to interrogate the girl eventually updated him. He'd been kidnapped. Talmeon couldn't care less; he'd already decided he would go into the Land of the Ancients with Cavilah as his guide. The three remaining Royal Guards were enough to keep him safe and keep an eye on Cavilah. Talmeon realised that there was more to Cavilah than he had initially thought. He'd told him that he wanted some insight into a recurring and unusual dream. Cavilah advised him to inquire at the dwelling of the world's oldest man, Methuselah. He also explained that this was the same place where the man with the giant boat lived. The one he'd briefly glimpsed on the telecast during his first day in Nahron's Gate.

After a fitful night's sleep, Talmeon wrote a vacuous progress report to his cousin. Soon, he was back in his Vastar Mark IV Executive Transport.

They'd departed mid-morning and were heading out over the High Hills of Havilah. The plan was to fly north along the eastern Imperial border. Then cut east, staying safely inside the northern border of the Land of the Ancients. They would skirt this border until they reached the edge of the Neutral Zone. At that point, they would turn south, deep into the Land of the Ancients. From there on, they would have to rely on their backup batteries. Talmeon hoped these would last long enough to get them all the way to the home of Methuselah.

The idea behind the circuitous route was simple. The longer they stayed out of the flux in the Land of the Ancients, the further they could fly without batteries.

At first, Talmeon's Guards were hesitant to fly an Imperial transport into the Land of the Ancients. As far as they were aware, no Imperial transports had entered there since Salfar's demise. What if they suffered the same fate as the 12th Legion? Cavilah pointed out that they were unarmed and on a peaceful mission. And that if hundreds of tourists could visit the Ark every day using ground transports, without vanishing, then so could they in a flying one. He also reminded them there were many flying transports in the region. Especially around the capital, New Eden. The only difference was that they used engines powered by combustible fuels. Their Vastar flew using resonators.

The Earth's core generated a strong electromagnetic field creating eddies of power that traversed the globe. Mankind had learned how to tap into this abundant power source centuries ago. All ground and air transports with resonators ran off this energy. They drew power into accumulators and then expelled it through resonators. Resonance is a common phenomenon in nature. All matter has a resonant frequency. It occurs when an object vibrates at a natural frequency in response to an oscillating force. Resonator propulsion systems created an opposing force against whatever was next to them, usually air, using this oscillating force. Thereby creating thrust and momentum. The exception was in the Land of the Ancients, where the energy lines were absent. An unknown source, from the High Hills of Havilah to the Great Eastern Sea, disrupted them. It was called the flux. Most believed the disruption was natural, perhaps due to large amounts of metal ore in the rocks. Others believed that it was man-made. Perhaps a clever invention devised by the Ancients to protect their lands. Even something to do with what happened to the 12th Legion. Resonator-powered transports could not operate without energy lines unless they used backup batteries. This was usually for a very short time. Backup batteries were designed to help land flying transports with faulty converters. Not power them for sustained flight. Advanced transports like Talmeon's Vastar were the exception. They had powerful batteries to take them through areas with disrupted energy lines. Nevertheless, they still had significant range limitations.

Talmeon had been impressed with his new Vastar Mark IV ever since he'd left the City of Light. It was state of the art. Its touch panel displays documented everything going on around for miles. It was also very comfortable, which was why he'd ignored Cavilah's advice to take the longer, safer ground route to Methuselah's.

Talmeon sat towards the rear of the main cabin, watching the two Royal Guards in front of him pilot the craft. The third guard was to his right. His job was to navigate the delicate route along the Land of the Ancients' northern border. This meant staying as far from the Dark Kingdom's southern border as possible, while not slipping into the flux. Cavilah was to Talmeon's left. He would be guiding them to the last known settlement of Methuselah's family.

The Vastar's resonators melodically hummed as they sped along almost silently through the air. Talmeon watched the scenery below race by. The Vastar Mark IV had a deep, wrap-around cabin window providing an excellent field of view.

An hour passed; Nahron's Gate and the High Hills of Havilah were far behind them. They were now flying east, comfortably inside the northern border of the Land of the Ancients.

Talmeon found himself thinking about life and death in a way that he hadn't for centuries. He laughed; rumour had it that the deeper you went into the Land of the Ancients, the more your thinking changed. Here he was skirting the border and already wondering what life was all about. He was comforted by the fact that he had many more centuries to live before having to consider such things. Soon they would turn south and head towards Methuselah's. The Havilah auto batteries were far out of range behind them. They now relied on the Vastar's detection systems and active camouflage for protection. The energy lines became disrupted, ceasing earlier than expected. The craft automatically switched to its backup battery supply.

◆◆◆   ⚑   ◆◆◆

After an uneventful ten minutes, a soft beeping sound came from the navigator's control panel.

"We're straying near the Dark Kingdom border," the navigator warned, "move a couple of clicks south." Without Mavron, no single one of the Royal Guards was in charge; they simply had different roles. There was the main pilot, responsible for flying the craft. The co-pilot, a backup because the craft carried VIPs. The navigator – who was essentially there to make sure they were not tracked or shot down.

The large sensor display by the navigator flickered. White dots filled the screen and then disappeared. The process repeated itself several times. Cavilah leaned forward, looking tense. The navigator was bemused.

"The flux is disrupting the display," he intoned, sounding professional, not really knowing what was going on. None of the Royal Guards had ever flown into the flux around the Land of the Ancients before.

"If the flux is disrupting the display, why is it appearing and disappearing?" asked Cavilah. "The flux is constant." The navigator didn't know how to answer that question.

Another chiming sound came from the co-pilot's console.

"Proximity alert, distant contacts," he said flatly. "They're probably inside the Dark Kingdom."

"Probably?" said Cavilah, "so what is their actual distance?" All three Royal Guards turned round and looked at Cavilah.

"Since when are you a trained sensor sweep specialist? Reading too many kids' comics, are we?" accused the main pilot.

Cavilah ignored their comments. "If your sensors can't determine the distance of the contacts, that means they're being fooled." His firm voice and factual statement jolted the men from their complacency. They realised, quite quickly, that whoever Cavilah was, he knew things he shouldn't. If their sensors were being fooled, they were all in trouble. Only, they didn't know how close that trouble was.

Another alert sounded from the main transmission detector. This one was much sharper than the others.

"Transmission alert," the co-pilot said, hesitantly. He was unsure what it meant, being so far into the Land of the Ancients and out of empire transmission range. The navigator glanced at Cavilah as though half expecting an answer. They were Royal Guards. Well trained for every eventuality except those not in any training manual. By now, Cavilah was standing behind the two pilots. They welcomed his presence instead of being irritated by him.

"What does that mean?" the co-pilot asked again. "How can we have a transmission alert in the middle of nowhere and no transmission?"

"It means we're almost dead," said Cavilah. "The transmission occupies the main processor with encoded gibberish, which it tries to decipher. While we wait for the answer, they sneak up on us inside the famous Vastar's blind spot, created by our resonance wake."

The pilot looked at Cavilah with a mixture of shock and concern. Who on earth was this man they'd first met drinking ale outside a bar in Nahron's Gate?

"Tell me," he asked menacingly, "exactly who are you and how do you know..."

"He's right!" the navigator interrupted the pilot as another alarm went off. "We have deflection signatures less than twelve miles behind us in our wake; it's a trap! They're coming up fast; they look like Dark Kingdom Razbars!"

"The Dark Kingdom cannot fly that close to us undetected," gasped the co-pilot, "it's impossible."

"Yes, they can," said Cavilah matter of factly. The pilot wasn't interested in what anyone could or could not do. He wanted to get away from the Razbars, then figure out what exactly was going on. He pushed the Vastar's resonators to their limits to try and outrun the Razbars. Instead of pleasantly humming, the resonators now sounded like they were screeching. The battery indicators began visibly falling.

"You've led us into a trap," he accused Cavilah.

"Four more signatures, missiles!" the navigator yelled before the pilot could say anything else.

"No," the co-pilot joined in, holding back his fear, "no missiles detected. There are no incoming object collision alerts."

"Yes," shouted the navigator, "they're on sensors!"

The pilot drew his disruptor and pointed it at Cavilah's head. Cavilah didn't move; he spoke very calmly.

"Get out of that seat now; otherwise, we're all dead – myself included."

Cavilah's words swirled around the pilot's mind: incoming missiles. He'd explained that the sensor glitches were not the flux. He'd explained where, and how, the hidden craft would come from. He'd explained the purpose of the seemingly pointless transmission. They had at least four missiles heading at them with less than a minute until impact. He knew of no way to lose them. Vastars were not combat armed, they had no armaments or countermeasures. Moreover, only those trained at the Academy could operate the new Vastar Mark IV model. Yet Cavilah knew things about their Vastar that no one should know unless they'd been to the Academy.

The pilot's whole thought process took less than one second; he leapt up from his seat and Cavilah dived into it.

Cavilah shouted at the navigator, "Enter impulse code 31–12."

"31–12?" gasped the navigator, "How the..."

"31–12!" yelled Cavilah. The navigator punched the numbers into his sensor suite. A whirring sound came from the transport's top.

"Setting altitude at 5000," Cavilah shouted to the co-pilot.

"5000!" cried the co-pilot angrily, "Are you insane?"

"Yes, 5000 cubits," Cavilah said firmly, "and do you have an Iridium power surger on board by any chance?"

"No!" shouted the pilot. "By the gods," he muttered to himself. How in Eden did Cavilah know about Iridium power surgers! Next he would be telling them what colour the emperor's favourite underwear was.

The Vaster tilted upwards and began rapidly ascending. Talmeon, already frozen with fear, went pale.

Cavilah brought up the rear view display on the main view screen. No one was surprised he knew how to do that. The navigator was right. Four missile trails were snaking towards them in the distance. Despite the Vastar's exceptional speed, the missiles were gaining on them. Cavilah waited a few seconds. Then he turned the craft south into the Land of the Ancients, deeper into the flux. He manually switched off the backup battery supply. The Vastar fought to maintain altitude. Its resonators sucked the last power from its now-starved converters. It began dropping rapidly. They all felt sick in the pit of their stomachs.

"Missile impact," yelled the navigator, glancing at his display and then diving to the floor. Both pilots leaned forward, covering their heads with their hands. Cavilah ignored them. He and Talmeon watched the missiles as they skewered around outside in all directions, except towards them.

The craft continued to descend rapidly. Its small canards provided only attitude control.

"Get back to your station," roared Cavilah at the navigator.

"Yes, sir," he shot back without realising he'd called Cavilah sir.

"Find the strongest point of disruption on the scanners, a vortex," Cavilah ordered.

The navigator wasn't entirely sure what that meant, so he looked for the most messed up point on his display.

"About fifty clicks southeast."

"Can we make it without resonators?" Cavilah asked.

"We can probably make it most of the way," the pilot was sitting where the co-pilot had been moments earlier.

"How?" demanded Cavilah.

"Because maybe I know at least one thing about this blasted transport that you don't." the pilot muttered and began entering instructions into the canard control systems. The Vastar noticeably slowed in its descent.

"It even glides," muttered Cavilah, "impressive."

"Contacts at high altitude," the navigator warned. They were too far away to be a threat.

"Don't worry," said Cavilah, "only optical tracking works this far into the flux. They can't optically control missiles from that height and distance. The craft behind us will have lost us completely now that our resonators are off. It's a good thing this model can float, glide, or whatever it's doing; the old ones couldn't."

They all wondered if Cavilah had been a Royal Guard himself once, but it was not the time for personal life stories.

"So we fly right into that strong vortex ahead and hide there?" asked the co-pilot.

"No," laughed Cavilah, "we definitely do not fly into that vortex; otherwise, we would never come out."

"What?" asked the pilot. "I thought you told me to head towards it? What do you mean we never come out?" He got nervous; the entire 12th Legion had ventured into the Land of the Ancients and never came out. That had been a long way from where they were now, but he wondered if there was a connection.

Cavilah ignored the questions. "Set down no closer than 100 cubits to it," he warned the pilot. "You understand? Do not fly into it!" Cavilah's tone was very firm.

"We're going to need resonators to reach it," retorted the pilot.

"That's not a problem," said Cavilah, "don't power them up until the last possible moment." At just 60 cubits above the ground, the pilot switched the Vastar's battery supply back on. The resonators powered back up. They raced along for several more minutes, hugging the mist over the swampland below.

Eventually, the pilot turned the Vastar around. He landed it facing away from the vortex to avoid running into it. As they turned, he tried to see through the mist. He wanted to get a glimpse of what Cavilah wanted him to avoid flying into. But it was too thick. They descended and landed heavily. Everyone breathed a sigh of relief; at least they were still in one piece.

Cavilah got out of his seat and unceremoniously pulled the emergency door release. It flew off its hinges with a bang.

"Hey," shouted the pilot, "what are you doing?"

"We can't fly back from here. We don't have enough reserve power after that chase. Even if we take off, they'll find us and shoot us down," Cavilah explained, matter-of-factly. He was standing on some small steps that had folded out, facing the back of the transport. His face was slightly illuminated by something behind them.

The navigator was nearest to the exit; he noticed it was eerily quiet.

"Where exactly are we?" There was only silence. "Where is that light coming from?" He stood up and joined Cavilah to look. The navigator's expression altered from curiosity to absolute shock and amazement.

Both pilots saw his face and rushed out to look too. Talmeon had already guessed where they were.

"What is that, what is that?" murmured the pilot over and over.

"That," said Cavilah, "is the Tree of Life. Eat of it and live for ever."

All three guards gazed in wonder. A large, glowering distortion of light ebbed from something that had the general form of a tree. Its waves looked like a kind of energy. No one could tell exactly what it was because of the light shimmering around it. Even standing a hundred and fifty cubits away, it was huge and utterly captivating.

"So this is the Forbidden Gate," Talmeon had joined them.

"It is indeed," said Cavilah.

"But the way to it is unguarded!" exclaimed the co-pilot. Cavilah snorted. He purposefully looked down at the ground, 80 cubits ahead.

"Tell that to them," he said. The co-pilot's eyes looked down and widened. A curved line of skeletons extended across the ground into the distance. They stretched as far as the eye could see in either direction. The ground was also littered with the overgrown remains of several wrecked transports. Some civilian, others military.

Something had stopped anyone from getting closer than the wreckage and corpses. As if to pre-empt the next round of questions, Cavilah walked very slowly forward. He stopped and stood still, a good thirty cubits back from a couple of skeletons. An angelic being appeared silently from nowhere. It stood forty cubits ahead, holding a sword that pulsed with light. Its form was perfect, like that of a man. Its glowing form showed them that no force on earth could counter this creature's will.

The others drew back in fear, but the creature did not move towards them. After some time, all three Royal Guards and Talmeon had the same question as they eyed the angel and piles of skeletons all around. How could anyone, even for a millionth of a second, dare to entertain any hope of getting past this being? Yet, apparently, multitudes of madmen had actually tried. Judging by the religious paraphernalia strewn along the ground, many of them had been priests or supposed prophets. Whatever their delusions, they were all dead and clearly had been for a very long time. The skeletons were all picked clean. A bird flew overhead and past them, landing on the branches of a tree well inside the line of skeletons. Nothing happened. Cavilah walked back a few steps and the angel faded from sight.

They all stood gazing in wonderment, alternating between looking at the Tree of Life and then at where the angelic being had been.

"Can't you talk to it?" asked the pilot eventually. "The priests of Nahron talk to angelic beings all the time," he stated. Cavilah just laughed.

There was another long silence. Then, the co-pilot continued, "But I thought the Tree of Life was in the inner sanctum of the Great Temple?" Cavilah harrumphed this time.

"And isn't the flaming sword in the possession of Nahron?" Cavilah made a pfff sound with his lips. The navigator was going to ask similar questions but held back. Based on the replies his comrades were getting, he assumed his would be more or less the same.

Talmeon noticed that the whole area behind them was flooded. Obviously, no one visited there on foot any more. Then the thought struck him: if they couldn't fly out and they couldn't walk out, how were they going to get to Methuselah's? Talmeon also observed that Cavilah was more at home here than his Royal Guards. In fact, with

Mavron missing, his team were now following Cavilah, not him.

"So how do we, err, get out?" asked the pilot, looking around, having the same thoughts as Talmeon. As he turned, something caught his eye.

A camera, discreetly placed in a nearby sparse tree, faced away from the Tree of Life.

"Look," he exclaimed, "a camera!" Cavilah harrumphed for the fourth time that afternoon. He then casually turned to it and waved, as if to his grandmother at a school sports tournament. The three Royal Guards soon spotted a variety of cameras around the area. Oddly, none pointed at the Tree of Life, or at where the angelic being had been standing.

♦♦♦   ☡   ♦♦♦

Sindain's cold and malevolent eyes stared at the screen. He'd been urgently called to the City of Light Security HQ. An Imperial Vastar had recently made an emergency landing at the Forbidden Gate. Its markings indicated that it was the emperor's cousin's.

"What's he doing there?" he hissed. The hatred took even his subordinates by surprise. As Head of Nahron's intelligence services, everyone feared Sindain. He was not well known for his compassion. In fact, he probably had no idea what it was. Sindain was watching a live feed from the Forbidden Gate. It was sent via hundreds of miles of secret cable. Any airwave broadcast from there would not work. Nahron had installed it as part of a surveillance system, with the help of well compensated elders from the Land of the Ancients. He could see Cavilah on it. He looked very different from their last meeting. He also saw Talmeon and the three Royal Guards sent under Mavron's command by the emperor. Mavron was conspicuously absent from the images. Sindain's eyes fixed on Cavilah.

"So, I have finally found you, dear brother, after all these years."

♦♦♦   ☡   ♦♦♦

It was true, Cavilah and Sindain were brothers. Things had started out well for them in life. They came from a conservative family, loyal to the Empire of the Son under Salfar's dubious but well provisioned reign. Sindain had worked hard in the regular security service, gradually climbing his way to the position of a district commander. There were the usual compromises. Things had to be overlooked to ensure his career progressed. That was typical for those working under someone like Salfar. All things considered, it was a rewarding job and a commendable career path that he'd chosen.

Then there was the utter débâcle of the 12th Legion. The ensuing collapse of Salfar's government and with it Sindain's career prospects. Nahron had been smart enough not to have Salfar's civil servants and top officials executed. Instead, he'd famously banished them to the Ancients' borderlands. To help rehabilitate the area and repay a debt of the 12th Legion for their aggression. In reality, it was to get them far away from the City of Light while appearing to be doing something morally praiseworthy.

Sindain's position as head of a district's security had been a precarious one. To stay alive, he had to make many compromises. These were not just with how he dealt with political enemies. They were also with the religious leaders who didn't fall for Nahron's fake repentance. It wasn't that they vocally denounced Nahron; they didn't need to. Their genuineness shone a light on his hypocrisy, so they had to go. This was where the real challenges began for Sindain. Cavilah, his brother, was one of the genuine ones. He was a popular temple preacher. Clearly, Sindain wasn't going to have his own brother disappear. But he did have to ask him to mind his step and watch everything he believed in being slowly but surely corrupted.

Somehow, Cavilah survived quite a long time and managed to always steer away from trouble. Then things got worse. Cavilah's son grew up; he was as altruistic as his father. His preaching, and more disastrously for the empire, his exemplary lifestyle caused friction. The empire's gluttonous priests were the antithesis of Cavilah and his son. Even this wouldn't have mattered so much except that Cavilah and his son did too well. They preached powerful messages and were popular. Their broadcasts featured on telecasts far outside the Havilah and Tigris regions.

Disagreements with Sindain during his frequent visits to Nahron's Gate, Cavilah's home, intensified. Sindain wanted Cavilah and his son to take a break, to tone things down, to move to a less conspicuous town. He had orders to sort things out. Cavilah, on the other hand, wanted Sindain to leave his corrupt position and join him. Then Cavilah's son was killed. He had been shockingly young; he hadn't even reached his first century. It was an absolute tragedy. At first, it seemed like a horrible accident, but soon the truth became known. He'd been murdered. Cavilah was reeling with grief. He took comfort in the fact that his son had gone to his Creator with a right heart. But then anger and bitterness welled up in him. He never found out if Sindain or a higher official ordered the murder. Sindain wasn't head of the Intelligence Services then, but had held a very senior position.

Cavilah intensified his efforts. He began to preach fearlessly against the empire. His congregation fled, literally fearing for their lives. Cavilah abandoned his call, angry and disillusioned. Sindain's boss at the time ordered him arrested, but Cavilah slipped away. Rumour had it that he'd gone to the Dark Kingdom, and indeed he had. There he trained in espionage, his gifted ability to communicate proving an added bonus. On paper he was their spy; in reality he needed their training and resources solely to remain alive. Staying in the empire at that time would have meant certain death.

Years later, Cavilah returned to Nahron's Gate. Unrecognisable without his priestly beard and long hair. Careful facial surgery helped him reinvent himself as a gang leader. He ended up looking after many gang members. It was his temple all over again. All the while, to stay alive and provisioned, Cavilah reported to the Dark Kingdom. He often travelled to the City of Light. He knew many a quiet bar and the high society restaurants of the political elite. He soon realised that there was a back door to everything in the empire. On these trips, he became a suave businessman with a bottomless wallet. This kept many unwitting acquaintances engaged in ever more revealing conversations. The sort that kept the Dark Kingdom happy with secrets about the empire's technologies. Cavilah passed on information, believing it would maintain the balance of power and prevent another Great War.

Sindain never could find his brother. Cavilah's voice chords were altered so that he couldn't be tracked by its pattern. The dermal ridges on his fingertips were changed, modifying his fingerprints. He even wore special contact lenses, making his irises unrecognisable to empire scanners. The Empire of the Son would have stopped looking for him but their double agents reported that an unidentified spy was having great success. This enemy within was betraying the empire's secrets through a network of disaffected workers. Rumour had it that this was the missing Cavilah, working in secret co-operation with his high-ranking brother. In reality, nothing could be further from the truth. Sindain was not involved at all.

The problem for Sindain was that he became a suspect because his brother was the prime suspect. To survive, Sindain had almost half the empire's top intelligence agents disposed of. In the process, he made himself head of all Nahron's security services. His ruthless efficiency became legendary. His heart grew calloused, and he was sick of carrying the weight of Cavilah's lack of co-operation and disappearance.

Sindain exercised complete power under Nahron. But his elusive brother was the one thorn in his side. He'd searched high and low for him but in all the wrong places. He never guessed his zealous preacher brother was hiding in plain sight. Frequenting the City of Light's elite districts as an unrecognisable entrepreneur. Gathering information then slipping away and morphing into a gang leader with tattoos. And living, of all places, in Nahron's Gate. The one place Sindain had assumed he would never dare to even look at, let alone live.

Chapter 11

Swamp Dragon

*C*avilah strode up to the Vastar's blown-off cabin door. Jamming his utility knife into a crevice inside its frame, he quickly stepped back. A panel on the Vastar's underside dropped open. A life raft, complete with cover and paddles, fell out, inflating noisily on the ground. All except Cavilah watched in childish fascination. Despite their extensive training, none of the Guards had seen a Vastar's life raft inflate. The pilot thoughtfully observed Cavilah's disinterest. He was busy packing the raft with stores from the transport. He noticed that Cavilah was able to find everything he looked for straight away. The pilot was puzzled. Cavilah had saved their lives yet could have easily betrayed them or fled the scene alone. After observing him for several minutes, the pilot spoke up.

"You're the agent we've all been looking for. You're Sindain's brother, aren't you?"

The silence from the other two Royal Guards was tangible. Talmeon was more relaxed; he looked up thoughtfully, then shrugged his shoulders. Whoever Cavilah was, they both wanted the same information. When they got it, it wouldn't give either side an advantage.

The pilot walked towards Cavilah, who feigned indifference to revelations about himself. After the raft, Cavilah had re-holstered his knife back on his forearm, under his sleeve. The pilot, who had observed where it came from earlier, ignored it and extended his hand.

"Nice to meet you," he said slightly comically, and then more seriously, "and thanks for saving our lives. I thought we were all as good as dead with those missiles."

Cavilah idly slapped the back of his hand. "You're welcome," he replied dryly, unsure how things would pan out.

No one was interested in starting a pointless fight. The three Royal Guards' loyalty to their emperor had started to fracture the moment they saw the Tree. Their beliefs had been completely upended.

"So it's a river cruise then?" grinned the pilot whom Cavilah decided he was beginning to half like. Royal Guards were not normally top of his list of choices of friends.

Cavilah vaguely smiled, huffed, then eyed the pilot sombrely.

"You have no idea. Avoiding a few missiles is going to seem like a happy childhood memory compared to what's ahead."

The pilot and his two companions weren't sure how concerned they should be. Cavilah's confidence throughout the past few hours had reassured them. If he was now saying that what lay ahead would be hard, as if almost being blown out of the sky wasn't, then they knew they had a problem.

"How hard can it be?" asked the navigator respectfully.

"Well, let's see," said Cavilah. "First of all, the empire has seen me." He nodded at the cameras. "So they've doubtless sent a squad to kill me." And as you may already know, Sindain – my dear brother, is not known for his precision. Anyone near his strikes is usually as good as dead too, no matter how important they may be." He turned to look at Talmeon.

"Only an absolute madman would kill the emperor's cousin," objected the co-pilot.

"Accidents happen," replied Cavilah, "and out here they can't be properly investigated." Both pilots and the navigator knew how trigger-happy the empire could be. Talmeon realised he might not be as important as he thought.

"Second," he continued, as though he'd only described an aperitif, "we have the Dark Kingdom. They will want to know why I'm escorting the emperor's cousin and chief scientist into the Land of Ancients. And why am I in a state of the art Imperial transport and not bringing it, along with our VIP, straight into their hands." Talmeon's ego slightly recovered.

This was a sizeable revelation to all. Now that they knew who he was, they realised that Cavilah could have easily betrayed the mission. But he hadn't.

"So we can't stay here." Cavilah ended his second point matter of factly. "Third," he continued, "when it gets dark around here unless you're locked inside the Vastar– which we can't be because as I previously mentioned, company will already be on the way, or are good friends with the angel guarding the tree..."

All four looked round. The angelic being hadn't reappeared, but they knew it would if they stepped back towards the tree.

"When it gets dark around here," he paused for effect, "the last thing you want is to be paddling through this swamp in a bright orange inflatable raft."

He said no more. The imaginations of the guards and Talmeon were left to run their own wild courses.

"So how long do we have?" asked the pilot.

"We need to go now, right now actually," Cavilah replied firmly, "before our friends get here. We have about four hours before sundown. Hopefully, we can make good progress through the swamp before nightfall. Perhaps even to an islet where we will be safer." The use of the word safer, as opposed to safe, wasn't that comforting for them.

"But before we do anything else," Cavilah laughed out loud, "we need to make use of your artistic skills." He motioned at all three Royal Guards; they stared blankly.

"What, they didn't train you to paint?" Cavilah tried to sound as incredulous as he could.

"Oh right," the co-pilot smirked, "I get it." He went to the swamp's edge, cupped a handful of slime, and began smearing it over the raft's orange sidewalls. The other two joined in as Cavilah started doing something with the Vastar's main control processor.

Talmeon collected his few belongings and stood idly by. He wondered why on earth he'd decided against the long journey to Methuselah's on the safe tourist road. Eight hours harmlessly bumping along in a ground transport didn't seem such a bad idea after all. How, by the Trees of Eden, had he managed to get himself into such a mess on a simple fact-finding mission?

Cavilah reviewed their weapons compliment, only three disruptor pistols but better than nothing. He began dragging the life raft towards the water's edge. He paused, looking back at the Tree of Life. It wasn't his first time there. Something about it captured his heart. It symbolised everything that was wrong with the world, and everything that could have been right with it. He lost track of time as those around watched him gazing towards it.

The pilot cleared his throat, "Right, err, we're ready if you are?"

Cavilah snapped out of his dream world. "Ready?" he laughed, pushing the raft into the water, motioning for Talmeon to get in first. Soon all five were inside. It was designed to hold up to eight, albeit squashed, survivors. So, there was plenty of room. Cavilah passed out the four paddles. He said, very seriously, "Paddle slowly and gently. No sudden noises. Talk in whispers. Sound travels easily over water."

"Wow," quipped the navigator flatly, "they pay me a million credits a year, and I didn't know that."

"There's a lot you don't know," added the pilot. He frowned at the paddle, changing which end he was holding, as if he didn't know how to use it. The three guards laughed quietly among themselves. Cavilah couldn't help but smile.

They glided slowly away from the tree, into the thick mist. Cavilah motioned for them to go round the far side of the island they'd landed on, heading east instead of south. They could have objected that this was the wrong direction, but they knew it was pointless. After barely half an hour of quiet paddling, the distant hum of transports filled the sky. Cavilah motioned for them to stop under a large swamp tree.

"Nothing works out here except optics; even infra-red is messed up," he reassured them.

They waited patiently, although none except Cavilah knew exactly what for. In answer to their wondering, there was a distant explosion. The pilot looked knowingly in the direction of the sound. The Dark Kingdom forces, being the closest, must have been the first to arrive. Cavilah had set the Vastar to self-destruct.

"Let's go," Cavilah motioned forwards; they moved on as darkness fell. Cavilah knew Imperial transports with long range batteries would be on their way. He knew they would not dare fly directly across the Land of the Ancients straight from Nahron's Gate. The memory of the 12th was still too strong. They would skirt the northern border like they had done and probably get shot down, just as they'd also nearly been. It would buy him time to lead Talmeon and his men through the swamps. Then, he would take them to the southern forests where the dwellings of Methuselah were.

Cavilah wondered how many had died in the explosion he'd caused. How many had he killed or wounded? He sighed. Life was mad, truly mad. An endless cycle of death and destruction consumed all society. Even the animal kingdom was no better. He knew if the Dark Kingdom's forces had found them first, they would have killed them all, except for Talmeon. Then they would have paraded him in public. Killed him, and then tried to negotiate a deal with Nahron, even though

Talmeon would already be dead.

Cavilah reviewed his new position. Thanks to not handing Talmeon over, he no longer worked for the Dark Kingdom. His brother Sindain now knew where he was and what he looked like. So, he could no longer live openly in the empire. That left only one option, the Land of the Ancients, except that too was now in a precarious position. Recent investigations had brought him across the path of some rumours. Only rumours, but so significant that they couldn't be ignored. Apparently, Nahron had something big planned for the Land of the Ancients. An assistant had overheard something. Cavilah had persuaded them, for a generous fee, to disclose more. Unfortunately, they knew very little. Only that something very big was in the works and it would change the demographics of the whole region.

And then there was the doomsday warning. From a distance, it looked the same as any other, except that this one was inherently different.

The first inconsistency was that heeding the warning required no accompanying donations. This definitely didn't fit the usual pattern. With all doomsday revelations, you had to go to a temple to hear the details. Pay to get in, then make a generous offering, and buy an overpriced record of the impending disaster. Not to mention several copies for your relatives too. This last option was to make sure your loved ones didn't perish in ignorance either.

That was the second inconsistency, perishing in ignorance. Cavilah laughed to himself. All these end of days scenarios were the same. They never had a coherent escape plan. You only paid to learn about them, not avoid them. Then, when they didn't come to pass, the priest who warned you carried on as though he'd never said a thing. Prophecies were tweaked and fresh instalments went on sale.

This perfectly identified all the problems with the Ancient called Noah's prophecy. Because none of them applied at all. It was all nice and clear what to do to survive. He didn't want offerings, and he'd been preaching the exact same message for as long as Cavilah could remember. For some odd reason, Cavilah thought it might actually be true.

As they paddled on into the dusk, Cavilah's mind drifted back to his family. He missed their time together - his wife and son had always been by his side, his truest friends. As the years passed Cavilah had been especially proud to see his son preach with fervour and honesty. They'd gone on mission trips to the empire's western lands, even as far as the pleasure islands of the Great Sea. Later they'd built a modest but successful temple in Pishon's Gate, now renamed Nahron's Gate. Things had gone well. That was at least until Nahron came to power. Their services were too popular and Sindain had his son killed. Perhaps it wasn't Sindain after all, thought Cavilah. It didn't make any difference. It was Sindain's system and even if he didn't set it up, he must have known something or could have prevented it.

Cavilah thought again about the Tree of Life. This last less than glamorous trip had been his third visit, but it always got him thinking. He wished he could have continued as a temple preacher. He wished his son was alive. He wished his marriage hadn't broken. He wished so many things that he lost track of them all, but one wish remained above all others. He wanted to meet the Creator, to be reunited with his son and to leave this wretched world. Paradoxically, he found himself quietly praying for his and the team's survival. The last remnants of the dusk had given way to complete blackness. The low lying mist blotted out the stars and moon. Cavilah couldn't help but notice that the others were all lost in their own thoughts too. He thought he saw the lips of the pilot mouthing a silent prayer. By now they all knew what awaited them in the darkness. Childhood stories of great river dwelling beasts from eastern coastlands left them no doubt. The myths were all true.

◆◆◆ ⚑ ◆◆◆

"Should we stop paddling now that it's dark?" whispered the pilot.

"No," answered Cavilah, understanding his reasoning. "Disturbing the water and the little noise we make is preferable to sitting in one spot with our scent acting like a flaming beacon. We have to keep moving. If we stay still, we die."

"Pistols," he whispered, motioning for each man to hold one, even while paddling.

"Which way now?" asked the navigator as they rounded several huge trees growing out of the water.

"That way," Cavilah pointed south-east, "we must keep moving." His voice was quiet, but they all noticed the strain in it.

Total blackness surrounded them. Fear tried to set in. The paddles were not designed for stealth. They made too much noise, no matter how carefully they were used.

Talmeon had set a tiny red light inside the life raft. It gave just about enough visibility for each man to see Cavilah's hand signals. Talmeon was fiddling with something from the downed transport. The dim red light helped him see. After a few annoying clicks that made everyone nervous Cavilah was about to ask him to stop. Then, there was a slight whirr followed by a convincing final click.

"There we go," whispered Talmeon, sitting back up as everyone wondered what he'd been up to.

Fifteen minutes of no sound except their own paddling was not as reassuring as one might have expected. The swamplands had no night birds because they had no prey. Everywhere was eerily silent.

The illusion of solitude was soon shattered. Somewhere in the middle distance came a loud, deep groaning sound.

Like most people his age, the pilot had decided to give more serious thought to the afterlife when he got older. Glimpses of money begging preachers on telecasts hadn't helped his level of interest. His childhood had been a little different to most other Royal Guards. Like his absent commander Mavron, he'd come from the Havilah borderlands. His family had always lived there. After the fall of Salfar he'd made a name for himself as a capable and trusted security officer. Trust was a rare commodity in any provincial security role. One day Mavron had arrived at his station and met him in a corridor after a minor briefing. Mavron had read his dossier and knew all about him. He offered him the opportunity to train as a Royal Guard. The offer was like winning several lotteries all at once; he'd taken it without hesitation. Shortly before he left for the Academy, he'd paid one last visit to his distant relatives in the borderlands. By accident, he'd encountered none other than the famous Lamech. Lamech, like his father Methuselah and son Noah, was well regarded. Lamech had given him a very strange warning.

"When you have seen the source of life do not forsake the opportunity to give life," he'd said. At the time, it had been gibberish to him. He'd politely acknowledged it and gone on to pursue his dream career.

That was a long time ago; now he'd just seen the source of life, namely the Tree of Life, and that had got him thinking. How was he going to give life? His usual concept of giving life was to take something from someone else's and add it to his own. It was odd, he reflected. He'd also heard the familiar saying that when you entered the Land of the Ancients, you thought differently. Indeed, here he was, a few hours in and already thinking about spiritual things. Something he had not done since his youth. He had an even stranger thought. He wanted to protect the other men on the raft, including the stranger Cavilah. It all made no sense; why protect them? Surely the obvious thing to do was to look after himself? His last thought, although logically faultless, felt flawed in some way. The mist cleared a fraction and a faint moon became visible.

The deep groaning sounded again. This time it was horribly close; whatever its source, it was clearly closing in on them.

"Here we go," Cavilah whispered calmly, "shoot the eyes and stay as quiet as possible." It was a bizarre contradiction. The sound of a disturbance in the water was straight ahead. Cavilah motioned for them to keep going towards it; that way, they wouldn't be attacked from behind.

Panic tried to grip the guards; they resisted it. They were well trained and all knew one thing. Panic in a desperate situation meant almost certain death. The two pilots paddled towards the sound. The navigator pointed his small disruptor pistol forwards, into the gloom. Talmeon knelt in the raft, intently looking ahead, holding the device he had assembled.

"What's that?" Cavilah asked him quietly. He knew Talmeon was no amateur with technology, so whatever he'd made would doubtless help them.

"A shocking present from the empire, to the whateverasaurus," he quipped. The co-pilot next to him chuckled, humour in the face of danger. He admired courage wherever he found it. Suddenly, a sloshing sound erupted to their right. Two lines of ripples, accentuated by the faint moonlight, were heading straight for their raft.

Cavilah was aghast. "Shoot the water," he yelled, pointing at the fast approaching ripples. The panic in his voice told the guards and Talmeon that this was not what he had been expecting.

The main pilot took stock of the situation. Whatever was underwater would shred their flimsy raft. Then, the great beast lumbering towards them would pick them out of the water, one by one, like appetisers. In a moment, he saw his whole life pass before him. He saw the good he had done, but also everything he'd done wrong. He'd known there were quite a few things, but surely not that many! In a moment, he realised that the sum total of his life was nothing except a huge minus score. He decided to change it.

In an instant, the pilot threw his paddle to the raft's floor. Then, he dived into the water, toward the hidden creatures beneath, now only a few cubits away. He reasoned that this would buy time for his companions. They could then shoot the creatures before they shredded the raft and give them a slim chance against the behemoth that was almost upon them. He thrashed about to gain attention, waiting for the bites that would render him a corpse in seconds.

The other two guards realised what had happened. They'd lived for hundreds of years in a society full of scheming, lying, murder, and every imaginable vice. Even their religious leaders were just smooth-talking conmen. Yet, here was a man giving his life for them. It shook them to the core. They too had felt this new inexplicable desire to help, even at risk to themselves.

"What's he doing!" screamed the co-pilot although he knew full well. He fired blindly past his companion at the two lines of ripples. The behemoth appeared out of the moonlight, its towering form looming above them.

"Throw it!" yelled Cavilah at Talmeon. In the gloom, a huge head with gleaming eyes and a massive form lumbered through the water towards them. It let out a bellowing cry that shook the whole area. Talmeon frantically threw his device. It landed with a harmless splosh in the water in front of the behemoth. Floating and beeping with a little red flashing light, it looked like a small toy. Nothing happened.

"Did you arm it!" screamed Cavilah. Talmeon stared in shock. All he had to do to arm it was squeeze it, but when Cavilah had yelled 'throw it,' he'd lobbed it without thinking, not arming it. The behemoth looked at the pretty red light floating in the water right below its huge mouth. The two giant eels in the water and almost upon the brave pilot noticed the flashing red light too. They altered course for it. The behemoth swiftly took the device into its mouth, looking very pleased with itself.

Everyone waited to see what would happen next. Even the eels paused, realising their new prize was in the mouth of the oversized behemoth. The beast moved its jaw a little. There was a loud click, followed by the same whirring sound Cavilah and the guards had heard earlier. The behemoth looked as though it was surprised. The eels circled it, deciding if the shiny object was worth such a suicidal confrontation.

"Get him out of the water now!" Cavilah yelled at the two remaining guards. They reached towards the pilot in the water while Cavilah frantically paddled. The commotion reminded the eels and the behemoth why they'd come there in the first place. The behemoth let out another bellowing cry. The device rolled off its tongue and fell out of its mouth. It fell towards the water as the whirring sound reached its final pitch. The guards leaned desperately into the water. They knew that if they were touching it when the device hit the surface, it meant certain death. With all their strength, they flung the pilot out of the water and back into the raft. There was a blinding blue flash. Everything in the water for at least forty cubits around was killed instantly. The rubber-sided life raft bobbed about on the water as though nothing had happened. The pilot was coughing, spluttering, and spitting out swamp water.

"Paddle!" ordered Cavilah. The navigator tossed Talmeon a paddle. They both paddled hard and fast. Cavilah and the co-pilot tended to the pilot. He was none the worse for wear, although it took a while for him to convince himself that he wasn't dead.

A small islet appeared before them through the mist. Without orders from Cavilah, the co-pilot and Talmeon made straight for it. Soon, they were all out of the water and under the upturned raft, waiting for morning. It was the safest place to be. One by one, they fell asleep from exhaustion. The pilot was the last; he couldn't stop praying as an inexplicable euphoria settled over him.

Chapter 12

The Gift of Contrition

*T*he Empire of the Son's five transports sent to the Forbidden Gate never made it. They were all shot down along the Land of the Ancients' northern border. Nahron was pleased; it was the perfect excuse he'd been patiently waiting for. He needed to have an apparent vulnerability to the Dark Kingdom. Something that would make his gesture of peace and deference plausible. Of course, having four Seekers and a Tactan shot down was militarily insignificant. Experts had quickly found out what went wrong and how to fix it if the empire faced the same situation again.

Nahron was also advised that the spy Cavilah had been seen with Talmeon at the Forbidden Gate. That Mavron was missing and no longer in the company of Talmeon and his remaining guards. Moreover, that Talmeon and his guards were in an uncertain situation. They didn't appear to be Cavilah's hostages. They couldn't all be defectors, so Cavilah must have killed Mavron. Deceived the others, and was about to hand them over to the Dark Kingdom.

The prospect of Talmeon falling into the hands of his enemy was too much to bear. There was only one way out of this dilemma. Nahron ordered the activation of his master plan to defeat the Dark Kingdom once and for all. Codenamed Contrition.

◆◆◆ ⚑ ◆◆◆

Nahron studied Shem's career; it was nothing but outstanding. He'd joined the empire's Air Force at an early age, heroically defending its borders against countless incursions.

Shem was held in the highest regard by many in the military, but he'd always been careful to stay out of politics. His popularity should have killed him long ago, but two things had kept him alive. His unswerving commitment to his duty and unique family background. He was from the Land of the Ancients. He steadfastly held to their ways and beliefs. For Nahron, he was the perfect icon, a true believer with no

96

political ambition.

The emperor had confirmed Shem as the key participant in operation Contrition. At the time, he was midway through a routine patrol that was going badly wrong. He had to be rescued by a huge task force after being betrayed by one of an ever increasing number of jealous pilots. After losing almost half his blood, he was hospitalised in the Royal Guard medical facility. Shem's wounds, although serious, were treatable. Thanks to the empire's expert medical knowledge, he was making a rapid recovery.

Nahron considered that even if his plan failed, at least Shem would be dead. He would be free from the last popular Ancient tainting his empire. But, he didn't want Shem to fail. In a strange way, he had absolute faith that he would succeed. Even Nahron couldn't help but admire Shem. He was resolute, brave, and single minded. Nahron could identify with that last quality.

The only difference between the two of them was, of course, motive. For Shem, everything was for justice, for his Creator and for those he loved. For Nahron, who didn't love anybody, it was all for himself.

◆◆◆   ⟣   ◆◆◆

Shem studied the mission brief from the comfort of his bed in the luxurious Royal Guard medical facility.

He'd seen the moral collapse of society over the years but had stayed on in his position in the Imperial Air Force. He knew the battle against the Dark Kingdom was a worthy cause from any perspective. Everyone, from the most ignorant thug to the most miseducated intellectual, knew what being overrun by the Dark Kingdom would mean.

The mission was risky, even by his standards. In fact, it was outrageously dangerous, yet the more he went over it, the more he was convinced it would work. Shem already knew every detail. He'd been a potential candidate for it for more than a year, training for the mission many times. The fact that it was suddenly going ahead was a surprise, but he was pleased. The world would finally be free from the monstrous evils of the Dark Kingdom. The days of its tyranny would finally end. The Empire of the Son would impose its civilising rule on those poor wretches.

And, closer to Shem's heart, the human sacrifices that Be'elzar, the absolute ruler of the Kingdom, loved to hold would finally cease. Those near enough to the Dark Kingdom's borders could pick up its telecasts. Watching in horror and disbelief, victims being sacrificed by Be'elzar's priests. Their madness spared no one. Terrified men, sobbing women, and squealing children all suffered the same fate. All in the name of the serpent, their supposed ruler of the world.

Shem felt a holy rage, a fire, a determination. Yes, he would complete the mission. He would make it succeed. Even if the Empire of the Son was corrupt. Even if, as his father had foretold, the world was ending soon in a great catastrophe. He would free those in the northern lands. Give them access to his father's warnings through the unrestricted airwaves of the Empire of the Son. In the Dark Kingdom, no one knew what was going on. Every broadcast from the empire was jammed. Their own programmes were an absurd disgorgement of banal propaganda.

Shem was declared fit for the mission and later that very same day reported for duty. Standing in a hangar by his sparkling new Vastar Mark IV, Shem eyed his team. The usual two pilots and a navigator, all Royal Guards, and finally the odd one out. An idol of a contrite humanoid figure bending down on one knee, made entirely of obsidian. Held out in its hands was an ornate box, Nahron's gift of contrition.

The mission was audacious. Shem knew his presence was the master key. As a famous hero of the borderlands, sending him into the Dark Kingdom was a huge statement in itself. He was not going there as a suicide assassin or as an expendable puppet on a bomb rigged transport. He was going there in an act of contrition – which would bring down the whole Dark Kingdom.

There was a brief audience with Sindain, who pointlessly reemphasised the mission's importance. Then their transport was powered up. It was the same as Talmeon's Vastar. Standard issue for ambassadors and innocuous enough for any Dark Kingdom visit. This one had a few tweaks to its active camouflage to ensure it wouldn't suffer the same fate as Talmeon's.

A diplomatic request was sent to the Dark Kingdom, or rather the Kingdom of Light as they called themselves. It read:

"From his glorious and humble majesty, the divine

Emperor Nahron. Everlasting ruler of the Empire of the Son. Who requests noble acceptance from you, O great Be'elzar, ruler of the mighty Kingdom of Light, of a gift. A gift of humble contrition. For the cessation of hostilities between our great lands."

Nahron had called Be'elzar great. He could occasionally bring himself to call people great if he was about to get rid of them. Then there was the bit about the mighty Kingdom of Light. This was the part Nahron really wanted to make sure they got. 'Mighty' after shooting down four Seekers and a Tactan in a way they previously would have struggled to do. The last words were chosen carefully. The use of the word 'contrition' said it all. Nahron was requesting that the Dark Kingdom stop flexing its military muscle. If Be'elzar didn't believe the main statement, he would have no doubt when he read who was to present it: Shem. This was the killer blow. Shem, hero of the Empire of the Son's Tigris Battle Group and of the borderlands. If Be'elzar had uncertainties before hearing about Shem's involvement, he wouldn't have any afterwards.

Be'elzar willingly accepted the offer, unable to believe there wasn't some catch. Ragzan, head of Be'elzar's security, warned against accepting any gift. Especially under circumstances as unusual as these. However, Sindain's predictions were correct. Be'elzar couldn't resist anything that appealed to his pride.

The mission was set for later that evening. With so many uncertainties about Talmeon, Sindain wanted to act quickly. No one knew what had become of him since he'd last been seen at the Forbidden Gate. Moreover, Sindain knew Be'elzar would be gloating after downing five Imperial transports. He wanted to catch him in his overconfidence.

The empire's diplomatic request was accepted without delay.

◆◆◆ ⌘ ◆◆◆

They lifted off, flying away from the setting sun. Shem was mission commander. He sat behind the senior pilot and co-pilot in the Vastar's broad forward control cabin. The interior was dim, lit only by displays and soft lighting because they were flying at night. To his right was the navigator. As with all diplomatic transports, this was often a euphemism for survival specialist. The navigator's job was to minimise them being tracked and to track anything of interest. On this mission, however, there was to be no hiding. The transport had the latest camouflage technology, newer than in Talmeon's downed Vastar. But they had strict orders not to switch it on except in an emergency.

After travelling east for an hour, they turned north, heading into the gloom. In the transport's hold, they carried their gift, the downfall of Be'elzar and of all the evil that he represented. The Gift of Contrition.

Guided across the border by the Kingdom's traffic controllers, they settled into the long journey north. Their destination, the City of Be'elzar, capital of the Dark Kingdom and home to all that was vile in the world.

Their transit was only authorised for night hours. This was to prevent them taking images of the lands below. The Dark Kingdom didn't want them taking pictures of their numerous internment camps for propaganda purposes. The whole land was one vast sprawl of poverty and oppression. None of the country estates and villas that proliferated in the Empire of the Son were found there. Only the City of Be'elzar itself had luxury housing in an isolated district. The navigator looked at the ground below through his infra-red scanners.

"There's another concentration of people," he exclaimed, "that's the seventh camp already."

Shem listened in mute acceptance. It looked as though the whole Dark Kingdom was indeed one vast prison. The mission had to succeed; he decided that there was no way he would allow it to fail. His thoughts wandered to the Ark his father had almost finished building. Shem never doubted his father's integrity in claiming that the Creator had spoken to him. The whole world seemed further away from their Maker than ever. There was evil like that of the Dark Kingdom, unrestrained and brutal. Then there was the evil of the Empire of the Son. Hidden, but where everyone still sought nothing except their own gain. An evil where sacrifices and temple attendance flourished but where no one's heart was true.

Shem hoped this mission would change at least some of that. That it would break the incomparable suffering in the Dark Kingdom. And, when that depravity was exposed, the population of the Empire of the

Son would see it and come to their senses. They would realise what humanity could end up as without following their Creator. Maybe even repent and avert the coming apocalypse.

Several hours later, they were approaching the outer limits of the City. Their sensors showed innumerable multitudes crammed into haphazardly built city blocks. Lights flickered below, yet it was dark at the height at which they were flying. Smog from pollution layered the sky, blocking out the stars. Venting stacks rose high into the air, sporadically letting out bursts of flame. Constantly burning the fumes sucked up from the streets below. Compared to the parks, green spaces, and tower blocks of the empire, they were in another world.

The Dark Kingdom traffic controllers guided them downwards. They descended, slowing as they flew above an almost deserted highway into the city. Progressing slowly, they could clearly see the people below.

Crowds thronged the streets. Some looked up in surprise to see an unrecognised transport. Few, if any, would have known that it was not one of theirs. They believed that the empire's citizens were almost all impoverished subsistence farmers. A conglomerate of wild tribes who only held their noble forces at bay with suicidal fervour. Be'elzar convinced his people that he'd shown the empire mercy by not engaging it in a pointless fight to their death.

The Palace of Be'elzar appeared in the distance, high above the rest of the city, illuminated in a dull red glow. The home of the serpent, Shem thought to himself.

The navigator zoomed his viewers in on a commotion outside a rowdy club ahead. Men were pushing and shoving each other. A smaller group was clearly at a disadvantage to a larger one. A crowd was forming. Shem noticed earlier that there appeared to be no law enforcement presence anywhere. He'd heard that when things got too rowdy, the city security simply carpet bombed a block now and again. He was about to order the navigator to point the viewers forward when something pulled at his heart. He kept watching the situation developing below. His transport was now only 400 cubits from the scene and 250 cubits above it. The Vastar's state of the art screens showed crystal clear zoomed images of the scene beneath them.

The smaller of the two groups below was cornered. Comprising several men, women, a few boys, and a slender girl, they looked to be in a tight spot. The two men at the forefront of both groups talked. After a moment, the leader of the smaller group motioned with his hand. A woman from his group turned and began pulling the slender girl, who had been standing at the rear, forward. Some of the boys kicked her as she was dragged by. None of the men in her group were bothered, except for parting glances and what Shem was sure was laughter. The opposing larger group stood aside as the woman dragging the girl made her way through. She handed the girl over to some scruffy men at the rear. Shem's heart was torn. The girl had been sold, bartered, or exchanged for something. He tried not to think about what a life of misery lay before her. He was about to look away when the pilot excitedly exclaimed.

"Oh look! They're going to burn her!"

To his abject horror, Shem realised that what the pilot said was true. A pile of old heavy transport cushioners was being hauled together by the larger group. Helpful bystanders, eager to watch the coming spectacle, were joining in. A man stood by with a burning torch. The girl was being dragged, frozen in terror, towards the pile of cushioners. Shem stared numbly. By now, their Vastar was right over where the spectacle was taking place.

He was in disbelief. Was this humanity? Was this what it had become?

Somewhere in the distance, Shem heard his voice giving commands. The crew were drawing weapons; their transport descending rapidly. The interior lights flickered to a deep violet. On the outside, it disappeared from plain sight.

"Sir, we shouldn't deviate from the designated course." The navigator's words tried to push through his consciousness.

"You, with me," Shem ordered the co-pilot. The soldier unhesitatingly obeyed. The transport door opened.

They both stepped outside into hell.

Chapter 13

He Who Lifts the Stars

Timnah's life had seemed pointless from the moment she was born until now, her twentieth birthday. Her parents treated her like a bargain sale item that they didn't want but couldn't be returned. Her brothers, uncles, and so called friends had all abused her. At eight years of age, she'd witnessed her first public sacrifice for the Serpent, the god of her people. The screams of the dying and the spectators' sick glee were etched in her mind. Her heart had stopped cold as a priest's eyes had rested on her for too long that first day. In mute terror, she'd prayed to be spared. Some around her had already started to expectantly look her way, but then the day's ceremony ended.

Years later, Timnah had completed another day of chores at home. After she had been abused by her brothers and beaten by her father, she'd slipped outside.

It was the middle of the night, still dark with no dawn in sight. Timnah was only fourteen years of age, yet that evening she wondered why she existed. Why anyone existed; indeed, why anything at all existed. It was all madness. Her family hated her, and she didn't know why. She did all they ordered her to do, but it made no difference. After her nearest brother had abused her, she'd wanted to hate him. To hate all and everything, but she couldn't. She wanted love but had no idea how to find it.

Timnah looked at the sky; through the ever present smog, some stars were glistening. There has to be more than this, she reasoned. Then she had a shocking thought – there has to be more than the Serpent. He cannot be the creator of such beautiful things as the stars. He could not have lifted them into place. Somehow, she knew the stars were not his realm, that they were a place where he was not.

She'd considered running away, but two of her friends had tried that. Their bodies were displayed in the local marketplace for two weeks as a reminder of what happens to children who run away.

Timnah prayed that night looking at the sky, "Who are you who made the stars?" she asked innocently, "I want to know you."

She'd crept back inside and slept; a vivid dream came to her. All around her was water, water as far as the eye could see. Someone was standing next to her. They were looking at the stars with her; they had their arm around her. It was a man, yet all she felt from him was love. It was a very strange dream indeed.

The next day, Timnah's life was back to its usual abuse and drudgery. Her heart was detached from the misery around her. Her refusal to hate made her family look down on her even more. They didn't know what to do with her passivity. Her brothers decided she was the weakest of all her kin; no one wanted her as a wife. They concluded that because she didn't hate, she had no strength. She was hauled around like a spare part. Six years later, her family's old neighbours caught up with them outside the infamous Tamash Club. Land disputes were never ending in the Dark Kingdom and her family had its share.

An argument ensued; her family was at a disadvantage. The old neighbours demanded payment for land they'd never had any legitimate claim to. Her father was reluctant to part with any money, mainly because he didn't have that much. The old neighbours didn't really care about land or the money. They just wanted to look threatening in front of their new neighbours, whose land they had their eye on.

Things had started to get rough, so Timnah's father settled the issue. He gave the neighbours Timnah to end the dispute. Timnah was speechless. Just when she was getting used to the monotony of abuse and chores, she was to be sold to settle family posturing? She knew anything could happen to a traded girl; her life expectancy would be very short indeed. Then, the old neighbour's head of family announced he would burn her, right there, simply for amusement. Her brothers laughed and kicked her as her mother, cursing, dragged her forward to be handed over. Her father didn't even look her way once.

Someone lit a torch, brandishing it before the crowd who erupted into cheering. Two men began tying her wrists behind her back. She looked up to the sky, hoping to see the stars one last time, but there was only smog this far into the city. A strange craft was slowly approaching. For a moment, she thought the authorities might see the fire and bomb the area. But she knew one fire was not enough to get their attention. They usually needed sustained gunfire to even bother to see what was going on. The craft was unlike any she'd seen before. Soon it was almost above them, catching the attention of the few revellers who'd noticed it was not one of their own. Timnah looked at the side of it; their enemy, the Empire of the Son's symbol, was emblazoned on it. That made no sense, but was irrelevant. The two men who'd bound her pulled her towards a metal stand normally used for queue control. The nightclub bouncers had very obligingly lent it to them.

As a child, Timnah had accidentally burnt herself. The pain was excruciating. She wanted a quicker way to die. She looked up again. The melodic humming from the transport passing overhead increased. A single star shone through the fog, right above the strange craft. Timnah remembered her dream from that starry night so long ago. She prayed again, in desperation.

"Whoever you are," she mouthed silently, "please help me!" One of the men in the crowd spotted her lips moving.

"She's praying!" he exclaimed. Raucous laughter broke out.

"Come on, you bitch," someone else yelled, "pray harder." More laughter followed.

Timnah kept looking up. She would die looking at the stars, not at the debased life forms around her called men. Then the strangest thing happened. The transport above them faded and disappeared from plain sight. Many in the crowd also saw this phenomenon. There was a moment of hush and awe.

Moments later, an area slightly above the ground several cubits away distorted. Out of it stepped two men. They were wearing white and gold dress uniforms, as far as Timnah was concerned, they could be angels. Both were tall, muscular, and carried advanced looking weapons. One of the men was particularly striking; he had blue eyes. No one in the Dark Kingdom had blue eyes.

The tall blue-eyed man had a presence about him. He appeared completely calm. Timnah thought she'd never seen such a man; he didn't have any fear at all. She decided he must be an angel. The man walked straight towards the neighbour's head of the family.

"How much do you want for the girl?" he asked, motioning towards her. It didn't sound like a request. Timnah's mind was reeling. He was trying to buy her! The man looked shocked. Someone wanted to buy this worthless piece of flesh? He paused, looking around. Up until now, the crowd surrounding him had been impressed by his machismo.

"A million silver credits," he blurted arrogantly. His bravado was not quite as infectious as he'd hoped. The crowd remained silent. They were not accustomed to challenging any kind of authority.

"I'll give you ten gold credits," the tall blue-eyed man said calmly, holding them out in his hand.

The currencies of the empire and Dark Kingdom were different, but gold was gold whatever stamp was on it. Ten gold Imperial credits was more than two years' income. The neighbour's head of family turned down the offer with a nonchalant wave of his hand. His delusions were quickly shattered.

"Are you refusing my offer?" the tall blue-eyed man spoke, unruffled. His voice carried the air of one who didn't have the slightest doubt that all was to his advantage. He lifted his hand as though to motion to the craft, which all knew was behind him but still invisible.

The full force of his own stupidity hit the arrogant brute. Surely, a craft like that could obliterate the whole area? Their own security transports could and sometimes did. What's more, they couldn't make themselves invisible, and why was an Empire of the Son transport even there? He'd been a soldier in his younger days and knew they were certainly not all peasants and farmers. The whole scenario was too much for him to take in.

"Give me the credits," he blurted.

"Take the girl to the transport," the blue-eyed man ordered the other man accompanying him.

Timnah watched the second man walk calmly towards her, ignoring her captors. He gripped and squeezed the rope that ran from her wrist bindings to the metal pole. It fell apart, sliced by an unseen blade under his ring. He effortlessly hoisted her over his shoulder and began walking back to his transport. His weapon never dropping.

The two men by Timnah were fixated on how her rescuer had so easily cut the rope, and with his unfamiliar weapon. Timnah stared at the receding crowd as she was carried into the transport. In the blink of an eye, she went from the brutish Dark Kingdom to the pristine, high-tech world of the Empire of the Son.

♦♦♦ ﬂ ♦♦♦

Shem was blocking the line of sight to his Vastar from the man he was dealing with. He knew some in the crowd might soon realise it was not as heavily armed as he wanted them to believe.

"Trade complete," he said firmly to the neighbour's head of the family. Handing him the credits, he began walking back to his transport.

As Timnah was carried back to the Vastar, the co-pilot had hesitated to locate the steps. When he'd stepped inside, for a brief moment the transport's outline was in plain sight. It was impressive and sleek, but lacked any heavy armament.

"It hasn't got any weapons!" someone shouted from the crowd. "It's just a diplomatic transport!"

As Shem followed the co-pilot through the Vastar's door, he also hesitated to look for the steps. He quickly guessed their location. But the craft flickered into view for the second time.

"You see!" screamed the same voice.

Someone else shouted, "Kill them!" and the crowd began running madly towards the transport. Shem dived inside; the door instantly slid shut behind him. The pilot immediately performed an emergency take-off. Hails of stones, bricks, the metal pole that Timnah had been tied to, and single rounds of gunfire hit the craft. As they rose higher, they were again invisible. The splatter of automatic disruptor rounds fired blindly at them ran along the underside of the Vastar. None penetrating its titanium armour. They quickly resumed their course.

When they'd first switched on their active camouflage they had vanished from the Dark Kingdom's viewers tracking them. Its traffic controllers had been trying to reestablish contact with them. The pilot had been fobbing them off. He rotated the transmission frequency, broadcasting nonsense. This had bought them a couple of minutes, but now they had to explain their disappearance. Thanks to their camouflage system, the Dark Kingdom would not have known what they'd been doing.

"Empire of the Son transport, you have engaged your active camouflage and deviated from your designated course. You will be taken into custody."

The pilot shouted back at them, "We're taking heavy fire! We took evasive manoeuvres. What's going on? Why are you firing on us? We are on a diplomatic mission. Our active camouflage automatically engages when we are fired on. Please acknowledge."

The pilot disengaged the active camouflage. There was a very long pause as everyone held their breath.

"Acknowledged Empire of the Son transport. Proceed on your designated course. Revise altitude to 350 cubits."

"Acknowledged," replied the pilot, "thank you." The others looked on in a mixture of relief and awe at the pilot.

"Nice," said the navigator. The crew watched the rearview display of what was going on behind them. Gunfire was still spraying wildly at them from the Tamash Club, now hopelessly out of range. Anyone who had anything from a peashooter to a heavy projectile weapon was firing in their general direction. Suddenly, the whole area erupted in a massive fireball. Silence filled the darkened cabin. Eventually, the navigator spoke up.

"I think that's what they call crowd control around here."

Two Dark Kingdom Razbar Interceptors appeared, flying alongside them to escort them for the rest of the way.

◆◆◆ ⚑ ◆◆◆

Timnah stared silently at the rearview display. None of her family could have possibly survived; the blast radius was huge. She remembered her brother's mocking laughs, her cursing mother and her father, who didn't even look back. Where were they now? She turned her gaze and looked forward through the cabin's large panoramic window. Below her was the whole city; ahead, the Palace of Be'elzar loomed ever closer, wrapped in an ominous red hue. Timnah never liked heights and had never flown before.

Timnah tried to place her thoughts. Fifteen minutes ago, she was being dragged around like a slave on her family's drinking night out. Ten minutes ago, she was sold to settle a dispute that was nothing more than posturing. Five minutes ago, she was about to be burned for amusement. Now she was flying in a plush Empire of the Son transport. Soldiers in exotic uniforms surrounded her. And she appeared to be heading straight for the Palace of Be'elzar. The most dreaded place on earth.

The smooth motion of the craft made her nauseous. Timnah almost fell forwards out of the chair; she couldn't steady herself. Her bindings, although cut from the pole, still held her wrists together. One of the men caught her arm and removed her bindings. She looked into his eyes and wondered what new fate awaited her. In her kingdom, no men ever came from western lands to choose a girl and take them away to happiness.

"How are we going to explain our new addition?" asked the man who had carried Timnah onto the strange, foreign transport.

"They don't know where she got on," remarked the other who sat next to her.

"Sure," said the man flying the transport, "but that won't stop them from using one unreported passenger as an excuse to throw a party."

"How long until we reach the palace?" asked the blue-eyed man.

"About fifteen minutes, sir."

"Slow down a fraction," he ordered, looking across at the two Razbars flying alongside them. "Buy me a couple more minutes before we reach the palace. Act hesitant and polite every time you receive a course instruction. Get them to repeat their instructions. That shouldn't be so hard for them to understand after we nearly got shot down." He grinned at the man flying the transport.

Timnah's mind was spinning; had she heard right? She'd been rescued from certain death and now she was actually going to the palace of Be'elzar! She wondered if she preferred being burned alive after all. Stories of what happened to girls who went there abounded. No one was certain of the details except for one undeniable fact: none of them ever returned. Perhaps this was all some cruel twist? An especially tortuous death for rejecting the serpent when she was younger? Maybe she would even be the main showcase girl sacrificed every year in the Temple of the Serpent! Timnah shuddered.

The blue-eyed man spoke to her.

"My name is Shem, don't worry, you are safe for now." Timnah understood him. His accent was a little peculiar, but the earth had only one language from the beginning. 'For now' was still somewhat perturbing. She preferred you are safe without any 'for now' tagged on. But it was definitely better than watching flames lick up a pile of transport cushioners towards her restrained body.

"Listen carefully, you have to do exactly as I say and without any hesitation." Timnah gazed at Shem in silent wonder.

"What's your name?" he asked.

"Timnah," she barely whispered.

"Timnah," he spoke softly but firmly, "follow me." There was a tension in his voice. He led her into the rear passenger cabin that every Vastar executive transport had. Designed for transporting VIPs, the cabin was a compact but lavish hotel room. Complete with a small double bed and minute en-suite bathroom. Timnah was not surprised; a bedroom. Shem looked distracted and hesitated for a second but then looked straight at her.

"Please take your tunic off," he said.

Without thinking, Timnah unfastened her tunic's shoulder straps. It fell to the ground. She was completely naked. Underwear was an unnecessary annoyance to the various men who frequently abused her. So this was it, she thought. This Shem wanted some selfish pleasure before his arrival at the palace, and then he would dump her. Or maybe, if she did well, he would keep her. Timnah did the only thing she knew; she turned and walked towards the bed.

"Timnah, no!" Shem's voice was almost choking. She turned to look at him; he was almost crying.

"The shower, now!" he rasped, gesturing to the tiny bathroom, pointlessly holding out a small towel.

Timnah was bewildered. She'd been sold for nothing, ransomed, rescued, and then asked to remove her clothes. Most men never asked. She'd complied and headed towards the nearest bed, but this Shem had almost started crying. Was he really that upset because she hadn't washed? Perhaps the Empire of the Son was stranger than she thought?

Timnah's mind went completely blank.

◆◆◆　ᚱ　◆◆◆

Shem fought to hold back the tears. "The shower, Timnah," he said again, still absurdly holding out the towel. He hadn't expected her to be naked underneath the tunic. Timnah stood motionless. Shem realised that she was unable to process what was happening. He abandoned the towel and dragged her to the shower. Punching the auto buttons for a quick wash, shampoo, and perfume, he held Timnah firmly in place. The shower burst into life. Hot water mixed with harmless soap shot from all directions above and around, drenching Timnah. She stood motionless, staring at Shem. He looked back at her beautiful pale brown eyes, gazing vacantly from her gently tanned face. Shampooed water hit her head; she barely blinked, more rinses, then tepid water. Timnah was in shock. Shem realised this was not good at all. He needed her to be alert for what was coming next.

"Timnah," Shem looked into her eyes. "Timnah!" he said more forcefully. "I'm taking you home with me to the Empire of the Son, to the Land of the Ancients." Timnah had never heard of the Land of the Ancients. "You will be safe there; I don't have time to explain, but we have a very important mission to complete first. Please try to concentrate and do everything I say, or we will all die."

◆◆◆ ⚑ ◆◆◆

The blowers began drying Timnah's hair. She wondered at the device that had just washed, shampooed, and dried her hair in barely one minute. Her cousins would have loved such an invention, but only to override its settings and scald their hated brothers. Somewhere in the recesses of her mind, she heard the word "die."

Die. The word was familiar; it was a word she'd heard and seen enacted all her life. She gasped as perfume sprayed out from the remaining unused nozzles in the shower, saturating her senses.

"Shem," she pleaded weakly. Shem pulled her from the shower, ignoring her nakedness. The man flying the transport shouted from the main cabin.

"Fewer than seven minutes, sir."

"Navigator!" yelled Shem. A man rushed into the cabin. He looked in shock at Timnah but understood immediately why he'd been called. He ran to a small closet. Timnah watched him as he began flinging clothes out onto the bed.

"These, and these," he shouted at Shem. "She can be a maid," he exclaimed, "a maid to the idol."

"Perfect," shouted Shem. "Perfect!"

A maid to an idol? What! Timnah's mind reeled again. Did that mean she was going to be sacrificed after all? Shem had said he was taking her home. Timnah tried to hold on.

Clothes were being pulled onto her, women's. The empire had male and female VIPs, so the wardrobe was stocked with both to avoid embarrassment. A long white robe, a sash, simple gold jewellery. The navigator pushed her down onto a chair. Holding her head in a vice like grip, he applied make-up to her bewildered face. Shem was tying soft leather sandals to her feet. Her toes were not painted; they would just have to give that one and her short nails a miss. He yelled for the other man piloting the craft.

He rushed in and gasped, staring at the scene before him. "We're almost there, sir."

"Give her a shot of ephadrenalyne." Timnah watched the man frantically unwrap something from a small compartment. He turned to her and stuck it in her neck before she could react. Her senses cleared, sharpening dramatically.

"Clear up the mess," Shem ordered both men. They began throwing everything back into the closet where Timnah's new set of clothes had come from. Somehow forcing it shut, they locked it, left the key in the door, and tumbled back into the main cabin.

Shem quickly followed, ushering a transformed Timnah behind him. Her robes were a bit too big, but a few clasps helped and gave them a loose kind of religious appearance.

"Listen," Shem said to Timnah, "three things and three things only. This is all you need to do. First, never speak out loud at all. Your accent will give you away. Second, you are now a maid to an idol of a god in our cargo hold. When we arrive at the palace and take it out, attend to it as though it were the only thing of any worth to you in the whole world. Clean it, polish it, hold it as though you were protecting it with your very life. Do you understand?"

"Yes," Timnah mumbled, her mind racing as the full effects of the ephadrenalyne took hold.

"And lastly, ignore what anyone may tell you to do except for me or my men. I mean, totally ignore – do you understand?"

"Yes," Timnah spoke a little more strongly.

"No talking, Timnah, none at all, not even to us." Timnah nodded as she eyed up close the intricate gold inlay in Shem's white leather uniform. She wondered if everyone in the Empire of the Son wore such nice clothes.

Chapter 14

Be'elzar's End

*S*hem swallowed hard. They'd begun their final approach to Be'elzar's Palace, rising to meet their landing spot. It wasn't the eerie red glow around it that caught his attention; this had been visible from miles out. It wasn't the size of it. Compared to Nahron's palace, it wasn't spectacular at all, although it was still the largest structure in the city. What bothered Shem was the proliferation of statues of the serpent.

Everywhere on the concourses and walkways below, and at almost every juncture, was a statue of the serpent – the object of the Dark Kingdom's worship. They were now flying over the segregated district of the ruling classes. Here, the streets were less crowded. The layout was better. The highways were busier than the almost empty ones in the outer districts.

This cocoon was the Dark Kingdom's paradise. A place where the few who lived there could delude themselves that they lived in a civilised society. Rumour had it in the empire that no human sacrifices were ever chosen from this district. Even disgraced officials had the choice of prison or a dignified death.

The blackness of the atmosphere around them was palpable.

"This is an evil place," the co-pilot complained. Quite something, coming from a man hardly known for a pious lifestyle.

"VIP landing in one minute," a female voice intoned from the command console. The lights in the craft brightened. A fresh scent filled the cabin, and soft ambient music began playing. It was almost comical. The pilot looked round, raising his eyebrows and slowly shaking his head.

"Next time turn that thing off," he said to the navigator, who was laughing to himself.

They all sat waiting as the craft landed in a large hangar lit with a mixture of red and dull orange lights.

"What is it with these people and lighting?" moaned the co-pilot. Three lines of soldiers, Dark Kingdom Elite Guards, stood ready to meet them. In front of them stood another man in plain clothes.

"Ragzan, head of palace security," the navigator spoke quietly, "he's a nice guy." Both pilots chuckled.

"I hope they buy our last minute maid to the god," he added. No one chuckled this time.

◆◆◆ ⚑ ◆◆◆

Shem motioned to his men. They all came to attention as the transport's side door unlocked and slid open.

Ragzan stood facing them with an angry smile. He didn't like any of this one bit. He was sure his master had made a profound mistake in welcoming personnel from the empire into his lands. "Welcome to the great Kingdom of Light, ambassadors of the south."

Shem bowed slightly and walked down the ramp; the others followed.

"We bring a special gift to your most noble majesty, ruler of all the Da..." Shem caught himself, "...Domain of the Kingdom of Light." 'Dark Kingdom' wouldn't go down well as a description for the Kingdom of Light in Be'elzar's palace. The navigator bit his lip, realising what Shem had almost said.

The two pilots noticed that the Elite Guards all followed Shem with their eyes. Here, right before them, was their enemy's mythical valiant hero.

"And where is your gift?" Ragzan spoke in a level voice, laced with sarcasm. "Would you like us to assist you in finding it?" Shem bowed again. He had known all along that Ragzan would be a problem.

"Our gift to His Majesty is stored carefully away from mere human hands." An appeal to divinity usually worked even if it evoked only a staged response. Shem looked briefly at Timnah, holding his lips tightly together to remind her to keep silent. "The gift is here," he said as he walked to the Vastar's underside storage compartment.

The door panel opened silently downwards on its hinges, revealing an idol laid on its side. The idol was crouched down on one knee. Covered in transparent black netting, it only just fitted into the compartment. Timnah walked quickly forward as though concerned for the idol's well being. Shem was impressed.

"A god on its side," Ragzan chuckled, "I hope he was comfortable." A momentary look of panic crossed the navigator's face. No one noticed except the co-pilot, who met it with a forced glare.

Shem ignored Ragzan's remark. With his men's help and Timnah's feigned aid, he removed the idol. He stood it upright but left it under the net.

"Please allow us to keep the sacred gift covered until we are in the presence of the one to whom it is dedicated." Ragzan barely tolerated Shem's words, but being able to see through the netting calmed him a little. Timnah convincingly tended to a couple of places where the netting had come away from the base of the idol.

"Perhaps a resonance lifter to carry the gift?" Shem looked at Ragzan. He agreed. Moments later, two Elite Guards appeared with a small platform. They carefully lifted the idol onto its low, flat base. It was much heavier than they had expected.

"Solid obsidian," remarked Shem, answering their curiosity.

Ragzan wasn't finished yet.

"You agreed to only bring yourself and three crew members. When you passed the city limits, our life signs scanners detected five aboard. I nearly ordered you shot down," he paused for effect. "And I see there are indeed five of you."

"Yes," Shem answered without wavering. "There was a misunderstanding about the maid before we left." He gestured to Timnah. "Our priests insisted she remain with the gift while it was in transit in order to protect its sanctity." Shem's whole reply was utter garbage and his men knew it. Ragzan didn't like it either. But he could not object without getting in the way of his master receiving homage from Nahron. Besides, the oddly dressed, waif-like maid hardly looked like a trained assassin. Ragzan was uncomfortable; he was suspicious of anything and everything.

"Scan the transport," he ordered the two men who had lifted the idol onto the small resonance platform, "all of it." His voice was vicious.

Shem's mind was racing. Life sign scanners – they had those now too!? He realised that if they'd not picked up Timnah, their whole mission would have been exposed by now. Both pilots and the navigator were having exactly the same thoughts. Shem's eyes met theirs; suddenly, his compassion in rescuing an unknown girl didn't seem so foolish after all.

Ragzan's men searched the ship. Apart from a very messy wardrobe in the VIP cabin, which they didn't report, nothing caught their attention. So far, the plan was working.

◆◆◆ ⚐ ◆◆◆

Timnah walked out of the landing bay following Shem, his three men, Ragzan and their escort. They walked along a vast, black, gleaming marble hallway. Marginally brighter than where they'd just come from. The permanent gloom was all nicely in keeping with the doctrine of the serpent being the ruler of the world. Be'elzar always met dignitaries at night, never in pleasant daylight.

Timnah had to keep reminding herself that she wasn't dreaming.

As she walked along, Timnah caught sight of a reflection of herself. She had to look twice. It looked like someone from a telecast film staring back at her, not her usual scrawny self.

Along the side of the hall sat statues of gods on thrones in half-human and half-animal form. At the end of the hall loomed a huge statue of a serpent, coiled around a pole reaching up to the dark, vaulted ceiling. It glared down at all who walked under it. Timnah looked up. The hall's oppression was tangible. But her refusal to hate all her life had done something to her. It had given her strength. She glared back at the serpent. "You are not my god," she mouthed to it in silence. Its eyes seemed to inflame with rage as she passed by. She kept looking forward and following Shem. Why on earth was the Empire of the Son giving a gift to the evil King Be'elzar?

Soon they came to a magnificent dark wooden door. The Elite Guards stopped and stood well back. The two senior commanders and Ragzan also stopped. None of them were too keen to approach the door.

"Weapons please." Shem and his men handed over their ornamental but working pistols to Ragzan. They would make little difference in any conflict inside the palace. "Your men will wait here." Ragzan was giving orders now. "Only you," he motioned to Shem, then hesitated, "and the maid may proceed." He pulled a cord on the wall.

Shortly after, the doors opened slowly. Two sallow skinned, grey haired priests stood waiting inside a darkened corridor. Accompanying them were two priestly guards. Timnah shuddered; the priests' eyes held a special hollow blackness. She imagined them sacrificing hundreds of begging victims at the public sacrifices.

"Welcome, son of Noah," one of the priests sneered, looking at Shem. "Like your father, you are brave to stand alone," he mocked, emphasising the word alone. Shem held his tongue. The priest, clearly disappointed at a lack of response, led them on into the darkness. Shem walked behind him, guiding the resonance lifter with the idol on it in front of him.

Timnah bravely followed.

Ragzan waited outside. He tried not to impose himself in every audience Be'elzar held. He knew this would only shorten his life as it had his predecessor's. He was also worried. If he entered the throne room, Shem's men might try something away from his watch, despite the Elite Guards. He knew they must be Empire of the Son Royal Guards. It was absurd to keep thirty of his best soldiers outside the door to watch over three unarmed Royal Guards. But he wasn't comfortable leaving Shem alone in the throne room with Be'elzar and a few priests either. He couldn't figure it out. What could Shem possibly do? Kill Be'elzar and then be killed? Even if he successfully overpowered all four priests in the throne room, how would he then get out? The throne room was over two hundred and fifty cubits up. There was no way to climb down outside. Where would Shem go? What would be achieved? In the worst case scenario even if Be'elzar was killed, he would simply be replaced. The Dark Kingdom's defences would be as impregnable as ever. Ragzan hated it. Something was very wrong, but he had no idea what.

Timnah and Shem entered the throne room, a large but not vast hall lit with an ugly golden hue. On the throne sat none other than Be'elzar, the half mad ruler of the Dark Kingdom. A row of skulls set in marble at its base formed a neat semi circle at his feet, well worn from being walked on so often. Some were of children.

The solid dark wooden doors at the end of the corridor closed silently behind them. Timnah looked around in both fascination and dread. Shem positioned the idol in front of Be'elzar's macabre throne.

Be'elzar stood up. He barely glanced at the idol; Timnah was irrelevant. It was Shem he wanted to meet. Shem, son of the Ancients and hero of the northern provinces. Shem who'd shot down so many of his best pilots, led many a secret mission and foiled many too. Why had Nahron sent Shem? Perhaps he wanted him dead; perhaps he was too popular? Be'elzar understood that. But he wouldn't do Nahron any favours. Nor would he mock such a significant gesture if it helped him. He reasoned there had to be more to Shem's visit than a simple gift and gesture of contrition.

"Welcome, Shem, son of Noah."

"It's an honour to meet you," Shem spoke softly back, consoling himself. It was an honour to meet Be'elzar because he had the privilege of soon ridding the world of him.

"I bring a gift from His Imperial Majesty Nahron, ruler of all the lands of the Empire of the Son."

"Not all of them," Be'elzar smiled, derangedly satisfied. He referred to the Land of the Ancients, hoping to provoke a response from Shem.

"Indeed," Shem bowed slightly, treating the comment as though it were a proverb of wisdom.

"Remove the veil," Shem spoke to Timnah without looking at her. Timnah stared blankly for a second, bowed her head and then sprang to life. She carefully pulled back the netting from the idol, delicately folding it. Its handiwork was impressive.

"Solid obsidian," remarked Shem. The priests looked on with mild appreciation but were not that impressed.

Be'elzar was about to continue to see if he could recruit Shem in exchange for a worthless promise of immunity. Shem reached out his hand and touched the nose of the idol. He pulled it slightly. A previously unnoticed layer of obsidian paint crumbled away from the idol's nose to its feet.

The idol illuminated with thousands of tiny sparkling stars. "Solid obsidian, interlaid with diamonds," Shem spoke solemnly. Timnah did her best not to look surprised and knelt facing the idol in feigned adoration. Shem couldn't help but notice her outstanding performance.

This time the priests were impressed. Be'elzar had also never seen anything like it. His face was alight with delight; it was a gift of truly remarkable craftsmanship. Even the progressively flaking cover was far beyond his kingdom's technology. But, embedding so many diamonds in the obsidian and making them sparkle – he began to doubt Ragzan. Maybe Nahron really had sent a gift to pay him homage.

"We should pay homage," Shem said, echoing Be'elzar's thoughts. "To the gift of contrition given by Nahron, in recognition of your greatness." Shem turned and looked straight at Timnah.

"You are dismissed," he said, "wait outside." Timnah turned and began walking back to the closed door. One of the priests who'd opened it earlier seemed about to object to her leaving, but Shem sternly met his eye. Timnah ignored him and walked right round him. The priest saw something in Shem's eyes that unnerved him. Shaken, he followed Timnah and opened the door, unable to understand his weakness. He returned, bewildered, to his position by the throne.

Shem turned, bowed to Be'elzar, and knelt down on one knee facing the left of the idol, which itself faced the throne. It was still on the small resonance platform, which had now come to rest on the floor.

The two priests stood either side of the idol, their heads partially bowed in uncertain homage. The priestly guards stood in similar positions either side of the throne. Everyone was less than six cubits from the idol.

"There's more," said Shem. "The scent of the gods," he whispered, touching the underside of the idol's nose. "The opiate of the gardens of the Great Palace."

The guards tensed. But Shem remained in place right next to the idol. His chest rose and fell as he appeared to breathe in the scent through his nose, while his mouth remained shut.

Be'elzar breathed in the sweet perfume. "Indeed," he said, his words immediately slurring. Very quickly, the priests and priestly guards sank to the floor. Be'elzar slumped forward on his throne. They all swooned into unconsciousness.

Shem, still on one knee, yanked down a tube from inside his ceremonial cap and took two deep breaths. His nose had been carefully blocked when he was still at the Royal Guard medical facility. His chest movement was faked breathing; he'd rehearsed it many times. He held his breath again as the tiny oxygen supply in his cap was used up. The opiate began to dissipate. Shem had seconds to act before his knockout gas was neutralised by the air around. He inserted his fingers into three hidden crevices on the underside of the tiny box the idol held. The lid popped open. Shem took out a handful of small vials. Each had a needle at the end. He rushed to insert them into the neck of every unconscious person, including Be'elzar. He started with the two priestly guards. This would buy him about five or six minutes.

As Shem ran from one unconscious person to another, the idol popped in half, opening from top to bottom. A man collapsed out of it. He fell to the floor, breathing through a tube and wearing nothing but a dark grey skin-tight jumpsuit. Shem turned, took a different, larger vial and pushed it into the man's neck, who then convulsed slightly. The stimulant reactivated his artificially chemically relaxed muscles.

"Wake up, Stalman!" Shem shook him. "Come on, this is it; it's for real this time."

Stalman had practised it all many times before. He had done full dummy runs, drugs to relax his muscles, drugs to sleep. A strict pre-mission diet and a small solution to solve toilet problems. Everything had been rehearsed over and over. Stalman staggered around as Shem began pulling Be'elzar's clothes off, throwing them at him.

Stalman was not a soldier; he wasn't a relative of Nahron; he hadn't been a hero of any kind; he wasn't even a public official. In fact, he'd been a painter and decorator. Even so, he had one quality that pro-pelled him to Nahron's attention. After an in-depth search of every cit-izen's picture in the whole empire, Stalman had one thing going for him. He looked remarkably like Be'elzar, was the same height and sim-ilar build. A few facial operations later and he was identical. A year of relentless coaching, another operation and his voice was almost indis-tinguishable from Be'elzar's. He knew more of Be'elzar than anyone else – except Be'elzar's mother, who'd been secretly poisoned to avoid jeopardising the mission.

Shem anaesthetised Be'elzar again. He and Stalman tipped the idol onto its side, pushing Be'elzar, now only wearing underwear, into it. He didn't fit too well. They managed to close it, re-illuminate the diamond lights that had gone off, and stand it back upright.

Stalman began frantically putting Be'elzar's clothes on. In less than a minute, he was the king and took his place on the throne.

Shem jumped back and reactivated the idol's smoke emitter. It let out a harmless, pleasantly scented yellow vapour containing a neutral-ising stimulant. The guards and priests stirred, alarmed by their struggle to wake. They were relieved, if confused, to see all as it had been before.

Stalman sat on the throne. "Ah, the opiates of the Great Palace. "Nahron is too generous," he crooned. "His god, a masterpiece of craftsmanship; obsidian and diamonds." He went silent as though in reflection, something Be'elzar did often, "But not one for our home."

The priests listened as who they thought was Be'elzar paused and then spoke again.

"Our gods have welcomed his god today. But I must be true to our gods," Stalman declared, repeating set pieces from some of Be'elzar's famous speeches.

"I return this god to your master with thanks, knowing that greater gifts will be exchanged." This was the perfect snub. Be'elzar would have almost certainly said the same himself. An act of appreciation, but then a declaration that it wasn't quite enough.

No amount of contrition from someone who'd not bowed to him would have ever been enough for Be'elzar. In this regard, he was exactly the same as Nahron. There was no equal either of them could tolerate, even if they ruled the other half of the world.

Shem acted suitably aghast, looking down. He froze in shock. Tiny flakes of obsidian paint, hardly visible in the dim light of the throne room, trailed from the idol to the throne. Stalman had inadvertently tramped them there on his feet. In their training runs, they'd never rehearsed with the crumbling paint. Shem stood up, slightly abruptly, to distract the priests and their guards. Stalman also noticed the paint. He added a few unexpected uhm's and ah's to distract the guards and priests, hoping they wouldn't notice the floor. The dim light helped a lot.

Shem quickly reactivated the resonance lifter. Then, he took the idol back to the throne room's great door. The smug priests let him out with looks of disdain. Those outside peered curiously in as Shem came out, pushing the idol in front of him. Stalman walked up behind him; all the Elite Guards and Ragzan immediately bowed.

"Safe passage is granted to you from my lands," he spoke clearly, making sure Ragzan heard and sounding just like Be'elzar. "I await Nahron's next and more valuable gift," he added with gravity and disdain.

Ragzan was relieved, almost amused. He smirked at Shem. "Your gift is not received?" he asked mockingly.

Shem tried to look as much a combination of noble and perplexed as possible. "His Majesty has been most gracious," he said, motioning to his men and Timnah to follow him. He bowed again in the direction of Stalman, as did his men and Timnah. Stalman turned and walked back into the throne room. The priests followed, closing the doors.

Ragzan eyed Timnah, "Perhaps she's failed in her duty?" He walked uncomfortably close to her. Shem was worried. Stalman didn't know who Timnah was. No appeals back to him could save her without risking the mission. Even if Stalman had known, it would be out of character for him to care about Ragzan getting a worthless idol's maid.

Shem decided not to cross Ragzan but rather to buy time. "Perhaps," he replied coolly. He acted as though he was weighing up something.

"Perhaps..." he said again after an even longer pause as they continued walking back the way they had come. "You could offer something valuable in exchange for our devoted maid?"

The co-pilot and navigator listened, worried a last-minute conflict might develop. But they were also curious. Could Shem outdo the pilot's earlier performance by spinning a complete yarn to save their lives?

Ragzan was a little taken aback; he hadn't considered that the girl might really be from the empire's great temple. He'd thought the whole visit a publicity stunt. Things still didn't add up for him. Sending Shem had shown that Nahron had taken every risk in the book. Perhaps the rejected idol really was valuable, maybe even its maid too?

Ragzan said nothing for a while; he couldn't think of a suitable offer off the top of his head. Soon, they all entered the hangar. He seemed to be about to say something when Shem deliberately spoke right before he did.

"Well, I would gladly take one of your temple maids in exchange," he said, sounding serious. "But you keep sacrificing them. Try and save me one for next time." Shem shut down the conversation. Ragzan was left with nothing to offer. He gave up, annoyed, although pleased that his master had rejected Nahron's gift. He smiled to himself. Sometimes polite rebuttals were more satisfying than insulting brutish ones.

Shem and his men carefully placed the idol back in the Vastar's hold and motioned Timnah inside the cabin. Shem turned, saluted Ragzan, and his by now snickering men, closed the door and breathed a sigh of relief. He held his forefinger over his lips and lightly tapped his ear. His men nodded; even Timnah grasped enough to realise what he was indicating. Ragzan might have placed listening devices in their transport.

They took off slowly, flying over the city back the way they came. The pilot talked calmly to the Kingdom route controllers. The huge crater from their earlier encounter at the Club was still burning. No one paid much attention to it except Timnah. She stared silently, wondering again if her family had walked far enough to survive the blast. The Navigator checked for eavesdropping bugs. He found none but activated the cabin's internal jammer anyway.

"Do you think they'll really let us go?" asked the pilot once he believed it was safe to talk. He'd never heard of a failed diplomatic mission to the Dark Kingdom in which there wasn't an accident on the way back.

"They should do," said Shem, "Be'elzar made it clear that we have safe passage." Shem hesitated to use Stalman's name in case the navigator's quick check had missed something.

Then Shem remembered the life sign detectors on the city perimeter. The navigator also had the same thought.

"The detectors," he whispered in Shem's ear, "how are we going to pass them with six people on board!?"

Timnah heard what he said. She carefully counted everyone present; there were five. She checked again, starting with herself just in case she'd forgotten to count herself. There were still only five people present. That was weird.

"We'll have to make a run for it as soon as we pass them," Shem whispered. The two pilots put their ears right next to him. "And use the alternative route home."

"What about Stalman?" the navigator continued the whispered conversation.

"He will have plenty of time to escape," Shem answered hopefully. "If he's blown, they'd be firing on us by now, and every transport in the whole Dark Kingdom would be on our tail."

They all stopped whispering and looked at Timnah. She was quietly counting and unobtrusively pointing a finger at each one of them in turn.

"Who is Stalman?" asked Timnah.

They all laughed, realising how confused she must be. Shem reached over and momentarily put his hand on hers. "Timnah," he smiled, "don't worry, I'll explain later."

Timnah had never felt a man touch her with warmth and affection. She didn't know what to do with it.

♦♦♦   ╠   ♦♦♦

The more Ragzan thought about things, the more they didn't make any sense. What on earth was the Empire of the Son up to? Why did they send, of all people, Shem? He realised Shem was the great anaesthetic to all suspicions. But his visit had achieved nothing and never could have. Curious, he questioned the priestly guards. Their story was very worrying indeed. They'd all lost consciousness! He could scarcely believe it; why hadn't Be'elzar called him in to brief him, or at least to gloat? He'd also heard that Be'elzar had been coughing a little. He wasn't his usual self and had retired early, with instructions not to be disturbed.

Ragzan decided to see his master immediately. He was close enough to Be'elzar to visit him personally if he had a good enough reason. The great doors to the throne room were locked. Be'elzar's quarters were only accessible by going through them. That was unusual. Ragzan had them quietly forced open. He rushed to the royal quarters. He knocked gently but firmly on the private lounge door. He waited impatiently for an answer, but none came. He knocked again and entered anyway; to his great relief, he saw Be'elzar outside on the balcony reading.

Stalman turned to him and smiled, "My faithful servant, is it urgent?" Ragzan couldn't put his finger on it; something wasn't right.

"Err, yes, my lord, the recent visit has left me perplexed; I have, err, concerns for your health." He started to think that Shem may have administered a slow-acting poison to Be'elzar.

"Ah no, not at all," Stalman replied, "it was those opiates from the gardens of the Great Palace. The gardener Floren must have worked very hard to produce such exquisite plants."

"Floren?" Ragzan was confused.

"Of course," Stalman said, calm but unsettled. "Shem mentioned the gardener there was called Floren." Ragzan noticed that Be'elzar's voice was different for a moment, slightly trembling. Ragzan had a flash of panic. He looked at his master's hand by his ring finger. There was the usual, distinctive discolouration. He relaxed. Perhaps the stress of the visit was clouding even his judgment.

Ragzan thought hard. A solid obsidian statue, four men and a girl came in and the same went out. Perhaps the opiates did slightly change one's voice for a while.

"Please forgive me, my master," he bowed, "it has been a most unusual and challenging day."

"Indeed," replied Stalman, "you are dismissed." Ragzan stared. Be'elzar had never said, 'you are dismissed.' He always said, 'that will be all.' Ragzan looked around the room; nothing seemed out of place, only Be'elzar. He politely left.

By the time he was halfway to his quarters, he got a message from the city limits scanning control centre. The Empire of the Son's transport had passed by on schedule and on course but registered six life signs aboard instead of five. The transport had then activated its camouflage and disappeared. It had not been relocated. What were his instructions?

Six life forms? That didn't make any sense, but Ragzan knew something was terribly wrong. He began running back to the royal quarters, gathering Elite Guards as he went.

◆◆◆ ▷ ◆◆◆

Stalman heard the approaching commotion. "Time to fly," he quipped. He pulled off Be'elzar's royal robes, leaving only his dark grey, skin-tight suit he'd worn all day. The private royal quarters' doors, which he'd double-locked, were being smashed open.

"Wow, they're quick," he remarked to a small idol on the balcony, patting its head. He leapt off into the night. His wingsuit deployed immediately. He flew like a diving hawk, down and away from Be'elzar's palace, into the ruling class's district of the city. He deployed his black chute and glided towards the Park of Victory, closed as always for the night. A bag with a suit of clothes and false ID awaited him there. Splashing down in the middle of the park's large shallow lake, he recovered a bag of clothes, a fake beard and accessories from the shallow water. All carefully hidden under an overhanging tree. He took off his wingsuit, wrapped it and his chute in the bag, along with two lead weights that were already in the bag. Then he threw it all back into the lake.

Ragzan and his men raced into Be'elzar's quarters, but there was no Be'elzar, only a pile of clothes. Instinctively, they rushed to the balcony. The drop was immense, more than two hundred and fifty cubits, no rope, nothing; where was he?

Stalman headed north, the opposite of where anyone would expect him to flee. He crossed the city limits before dawn. After that, his chances of being tracked were practically zero.

♦♦♦  ♦♦♦

Shem emerged from his Vastar to cheering crowds. He, his three men and Timnah safely made it to the Tigris Battle Group HQ. They had escaped by flying north-west into the Dark Kingdom's sparsely populated hinterlands. There were no pursuit craft in that area; they had all been rushed south to rescue their kidnapped king. Then, they turned and headed down through the Pazgon mountains, safely crossing the empire's border by dawn. Shem had gone from hero of the border regions to hero of the empire.

Sindain was delighted. Nahron was full of glee.

The mission was an unremitting success. Even Stalman crossed the border through the mountains of Pazgon a few days later. An agent met and escorted him the final leg of the way. He too was now a hero. Timnah was granted full citizenship. No one questioned why Shem had picked her up. It was assumed he'd done so because the Dark Kingdom's scanners had detected five people on their Vastar when they entered the city. But Shem and his men had not found out about the scanners until they'd arrived at the palace. Which was after they'd rescued Timnah. No one wanted to solve that puzzle. They were too focused on the mission's success.

♦♦♦  ♦♦♦

The ruthless and mighty Be'elzar, butcher of thousands, fell from the idol that had so fooled him. Humiliated, he realised he was wearing only his underwear. He'd no idea where he was or what was going on. The last thing he remembered was seeing Shem kneeling in prayer before an idol. A gift of contrition to him from Nahron. He angrily shouted threats and demanded obedience from the strange faces around him. In reply, he received only mockery. Then he recognised Empire of the Son insignia on uniforms. The reality began to set in. Somehow he'd been captured. Had his lands been overrun? He didn't know. He was strapped to a trolley and wheeled into one of Sindain's dimly lit interrogation chambers.

"Just like being back at home," crooned a guard.

"I demand an audience with Nahron," Be'elzar angrily spat the words out.

"I do apologise," said Sindain, accompanying him, "that's only for important people."

It was the ultimate insult to Be'elzar. He'd taken lives just for show. Yet, here he was now being treated like a worthless slave. Be'elzar angrily pulled at his restraints; it was futile.

"Perhaps we should sacrifice him now?" a nearby official laughed. Be'elzar looked around in terror.

A doctor stood nearby next to a table full of medical apparatus. Be'elzar stared closer; the doctor was holding a syringe full of yellowish liquid and smiling.

"A few questions, please, your majesty," he said. "This will help loosen your tongue." The needle sank painfully deep into Be'elzar's arm. He descended into a nightmare of fear and dread. The serum stripped away his arrogance. He betrayed secrets about his kingdom's defences a thousand captured soldiers could not have done.

"That's the problem with autocratic leaders," Sindain joked as the proceedings stretched into their second hour. "They know too much."

Chapter 15

The Brokenness of Men

*T*imnah rushed into the hallway. She'd heard the main door being opened and assumed it was Noah returning from a day at the Ark. A place which, after only a few days in his home, she'd yet to visit. It was not Noah.

Before Timnah stood a man. He was handsome and well-built, but his face was tear-stained. He looked exhausted and undernourished. Timnah saw something else, something she knew only too well. The man was broken. She knew what that did to a person. After only a few days among emotionally whole people, it was a shock to see someone so broken. The Dark Kingdom was full of broken people.

The man stared at her; she stared at him. He was unsure what to do with her.

"Here, let me help you," her strange accent took him by surprise. She gently held him by the arm, led him to the living room and sat him down. Timnah quickly brought a drink, fetched a bowl of warm water, knelt down and began washing his feet.

◆◆◆   ⚑   ◆◆◆

Ham had no idea who the girl was. His recent fling with Sashina and long, lonely walk home had temporarily cut him off from his family and the world.

He tried to piece together what was going on. A strange, slender girl met him at his own door. She acted as though she'd lived there all her life. Then, she took him inside like a long-lost brother. More than that, one look into her eyes and he was sure she understood his pain. It was as though she knew exactly what he'd been through. The girl continued washing his feet; she gently looked up at him. Their eyes met again; she smiled softly. Tears welled up in Ham's eyes.

"It's alright," she said, "everything's going to be fine."

After a short while, Ham managed to compose himself.

"Who are you? What's your name?" he gently asked the girl.

"Timnah," she replied, blushing, "Shem rescued me from Be'elzar's kingdom." Ham had no knowledge of the mission.

"I'm Ham," he said with some degree of resignation.

"I thought you were," she replied, "we've been praying for you." Timnah blushed again and looked down. Silence followed; eventually, she finished washing his feet. "We have prayers soon," she added.

Ham was numb. Family prayers, that was something he hadn't attended for a while. He cleaned himself up a bit. Soon he was outside by the altar at the bottom of the main lawn. His parents, Nadina and Japheth, were already there. Adatenesis was not. No one knew quite what to say to him. No one dared to ask about Sashina.

"Hello," he said quietly. Everyone looked round in surprise. Ham's eyes were glistening in the light of the setting sun. He stepped forward, kneeling at the altar. One by one, the others knelt around him.

Timnah was the last to kneel; she was right beside him.

◆◆◆　ᚦ　◆◆◆

Emzara held her beloved eldest son in her arms. Tears fell down her cheeks.

"This madness has to end," she whispered, "it has to end. Adatenesis cannot keep breaking your heart. I will talk to your father."

"No," murmured Japheth, "I'll be fine, he won't listen anyway. He will not accept a divorce, not now of all times. Who will listen to him about the catastrophe if I get divorced? I'm fine. Marriage is for life."

"Yes, my son. Marriage is for life, not death," Emzara spoke with great kindness yet firmness. "You are not fine, and that your father must accept. The last time I checked, few are paying attention anyway. We probably have only a few months until the time, if that."

Emzara's own words surprised her. She went to help with the evening meal's preparation; more servants had left recently. Their friends scoffing at them for working for the fool with the giant boat was more than most of them could bear. The high murder rate meant there were always other job vacancies, even in the Land of the Ancients.

◆◆◆　ᚦ　◆◆◆

Japheth tried to focus, 'We probably have only a few months until the time if that.' That's what his mother had said. The words seemed unreal. The world would end in a few months? Surely it was only a warning, not the real thing? Japheth wondered why people couldn't see their headlong descent into evil. It seemed the more they plunged into sin, the more self righteous they became. The crowds who'd come recently to see the Ark and hear Noah preach had become increasingly rowdy. Sometimes their barrage of insults caused his father to stop preaching. Yet Japheth found himself asking the same question over and over. Was society really that bad? People still went to temples. They still made sacrifices. They still gave offerings. They still got married. Surely, there was still hope?

Then there was Adatenesis. She was his wife; he didn't want her parents left behind. He would speak to them again, explain everything; surely this time they would listen? He wanted to talk with Adatenesis about it all, to pray with her, to get her advice, but of course she wasn't there. She almost never was.

Japheth stood up again, trying to pull himself together. It was hard to stay focused when he felt so broken all the time, but there was work to be done. He had to find out what Nahron was planning against the Land of the Ancients, especially the timing. There was only one person well trained and skilled enough to accompany him, Nadina.

When he thought of her, Japheth just sat down again.

Nadina.

He remembered the day they'd first met; she'd been young and full of life. They were the first of either of their two families to meet. He'd been hunting early one morning in some woodlands far from anywhere when she'd shot past him. She was fleeing a large wild cat. Japheth killed it with his bow. He preferred hunting with a bow rather than a projectile weapon.

He found her a few minutes later in a clearing. She was holding out a knife, facing the direction of the now-dead animal. There was no fear in her eyes, only determination, unusual for such a young woman. He was struck by her beauty. Her dark eyes and even darker hair accentuated her unusually mildly pale skin. After a few pleasantries, she visibly relaxed. Nadina was soon reeling off a cascade of goals, family history, ideas, and opinions. Whoever she was, Japheth concluded she was a very smart and ambitious young woman.

"What are you doing so far out in the hinterlands?" he asked.

"Exploring," she replied, as though it was a brainless question. The concept of caution didn't seem to exist in her mind.

"Do your parents know you're so far from home?" Japheth seriously doubted they did.

"They know I like exploring," she'd replied flatly.

He decided he liked her.

Japheth offered Nadina some food; she gladly took it. They sat and talked for another hour. His eyes kept catching hers. The depth of beauty in them was captivating; they were alive with all the wonders of life.

Nadina told Japheth how her family had moved to the Land of the Ancients and dwelt by the border where she'd been born. She proudly added that she was almost twenty-one years old. She explained that her parents had more recently relocated further into the lands. It transpired they were no more than fifteen miles from where Japheth lived at Noah's.

Japheth listened patiently to her chatter. Nadina's family had physically moved to the Land of the Ancients. But Japheth soon realised they hadn't spiritually left the empire. Nadina was oblivious to anything about her Creator. She only knew the official religious stories of Nahron's regime. Since most of these had no depth, her faith, or lack of it, also had no depth. In fact, listening to her, Japheth soon realised that it didn't have much latitude either. His heart was pulled with compassion. Here was this utterly vivacious girl. Extremely attractive, smart, and based on the speed at which she'd first run past him, remarkably physically fit. But she could only imagine a glittering career in the empire's service.

Soon, the cool of the day was upon them. Nadina questioned Japheth about many things. She was particularly curious about his family's rejection of the empire's religion.

"So you don't think Nahron is half divine or that the priests in the Great Temple are genuine?"

Japheth thought of a thousand answers, but then said something unexpected.

"Do you want to come on a trip with me?"

Nadina's eyes lit up, then she frowned a little, studying him carefully. Japheth knew that at almost twenty-one she couldn't be dumb to the ways of men. She looked like she was aching to say yes but wasn't sure. He hoped she'd realised by now that he had no evil intentions. Surely she would say yes?

"I have a flying transport," Japheth tried a little harder, "you can have a go at piloting it if you want."

"No way," she laughed.

Japheth stood up, "Well, I'll give you the co-ordinates then; you can walk; I'm flying." He sauntered off.

Nadina was soon beside him. Fifteen minutes later, they reached a clearing. Before them sat Japheth's transport, the Kestrel. It ran on combustible fuel, ethanol, and used air lift technology to fly. With fixed wings and moveable canards, it was like nothing Nadina had ever seen. It had been designed in the last days of Tubal Cain, the pioneer of all metalwork. He and his students had pushed technology so far forward that the world was unrecognisable, even from a couple of centuries earlier.

The craft was awesomely sleek. It was a two-seat racer. Japheth and Shem had modified it to seat three. Nadina walked silently up to it. Her fingertips slid tenderly over every smoothed rivet. She turned and looked deeply into Japheth's eyes.

"Let's go," she whispered.

They took off with a roar. The nozzles on the underside rotated as they ascended. The craft accelerated at an unbelievable rate. Nadina gasped in a combination of shock and awe. Japheth turned the craft sharply to the left, then right. She screamed, but her laughter told him she loved it. He looked at her. What a truly beautiful girl, he thought. He caught himself; she was barely twenty-one, and he was approaching his second century.

"Where are we going?" she shouted above the roar of the engines. Japheth grinned broadly, shouting back, "Somewhere like nowhere else on Earth."

They set down near the Forbidden Gate. Half an hour later, Nadina was praying, giving her heart and life to her Creator. The angel, the Tree, glimpses of the Garden beyond, they all crushed every lie she'd ever heard. On the journey back, she was subdued. Silently, she stared out the Kestrel's cockpit at the forests racing by beneath them. Later that evening, Japheth set the Kestrel down by his parents' home. Nadina went with him and stayed the night as a guest.

The family meal table was extra busy that evening. They'd sat together, talked together, recounted the day's adventures together, and laughed together. Everything had seemed so right.

That was many years ago.

Almost an hour passed; Japheth was still sat gazing out of the window, although by now it was completely dark. He recalled the games he and Nadina used to play. On and on the memories rolled until he remembered that cruel day when she'd left for the City of Light. That empty day she stopped coming round and the fifteen years of void it left in his life. Then he met Adatenesis; they fell in love, or so he thought, and now all she did was live an absent life. One foot in the empire and one foot in the Land of the Ancients, except that more recently it was more like one toe. Tears filled Japheth's eyes; where was Adatenesis now? She was his wife. He never knew when he would see her next. He still couldn't stand up.

Japheth absently gazed at the reflection of the living room in the window. He began to think about Nadina again. Why was every memory of her so vivid?

A little while later, Emzara returned to find Japheth still sitting by the window. She was surprised; far from the tears of earlier, he now had a smile on his face.

"Japheth?" she asked, but she knew. There was only one person who made Japheth smile like that.

Chapter 16

The Beautiful Curse

*A*riana frowned at herself. "Beautiful," she thought, looking in the mirror. Absolutely beautiful, and that was exactly the problem. She was too beautiful.

Her beauty had been a problem from as far back as she could remember. Instead of helping her, it had been more like a curse. From her youth, all she recalled was a long line of suitors. They wanted her only for her green eyes and perfect figure. But they couldn't even spell her name right. As time passed, things got worse. Her mother realised that her daughter's beauty had potential. Not potential for her well-being, or happy marriage, but for the family's social advancement. She decided that Ariana must marry sooner rather than later. Her father, Mandarus, mutely consented.

Her mother worked hard to find a husband for her, someone who would propel the family up the social ladder. Their family came from the borderlands of the Land of the Ancients. In the latter days of what was then Salfar's reign, this ruled out any chance of social advancement. Ariana's beauty was outstanding. But her lineage limited her to being anything other than a star mistress. For marriage, her mother would have to find her some middle ranking relative. And this is exactly what she did.

Ariana's mother found Talmeon and Nahron. The two best available nobodies among their relatives at the time. Ariana was given the choice of either.

Talmeon was the more pleasant of the two, although not at all handsome. Nahron was much better looking, but Ariana decided from the moment she met him that she didn't like him. She understood he was capable of doing absolutely anything if he thought he could get away with it. As young as she was, Ariana knew one thing for sure. Kindness was the one quality needed in a relationship, and Nahron was devoid of any of it. Ariana chose Talmeon, more from companionship rather than love. Talmeon nobly declined. He knew he couldn't live with someone whom he adored but who did not love him at all, or even find him attractive. She hadn't seen him since.

Nahron, assuming that Ariana had become his by default, duly went to visit his bride to be. Unfortunately, the city boy from Vastar knew little of the dangers of the countryside. He'd almost gotten himself eaten by a raptor that had roamed into the grounds of her parents' home. Ariana saved Nahron's life that day. While holding the hungry creature at bay with a disruptor, she got his word that he would never marry her. Nahron's visit had been to give her a handwritten list. It promised the many ways he would love her and be a good husband. His first encounter with a raptor and potential death unnerved him. His first experience of complete rejection, while his heart had made such a rare attempt at being open, cut much deeper.

After that day, Nahron was never the same. He hadn't exactly been a shining specimen of humanity before. But, from then on, Ariana saw another man emerge. Broken but also harder, even cruel.

Nahron subsequently made a deal with Ariana's mother that her daughter would never marry. And so she never had. If Nahron couldn't have her, he was determined neither would anyone else.

After Nahron came to power, he turned Ariana into a religious icon. He gave her the title Chaste Maid devoted to the Son. Her father, Mandarus, was made High Priest of the Great Temple. It was all a giant publicity stunt. Nahron pretending to be a godly man seeking purity, chastity and sincere faith. Nothing could be further from the truth. Ariana doubted Nahron could even spell the word chastity; the only faith he had was in himself, and truth was nowhere in sight.

Of course, Nahron could have forcibly married Ariana after he became emperor. But the irony was that he'd marketed her too well as the Chaste Maid. The public would have been outraged at his taking her as his wife. Even his brutal regime couldn't survive that. Nahron was amoral and selfish, but he was no fool. He hadn't got to where he was by not understanding politics and the power of public opinion.

Ariana woke up early that day with an unusual sense of expectancy. It was true, it was a big day, a really big day. A Victory Parade was planned for some men who'd helped bring about the fall of the Dark Kingdom. Not only that but the main hero, a man called Shem, was none other than a citizen from the Land of the Ancients. Ariana had always wanted to meet someone from there. But she knew she would have no chance to talk with this famous Shem. After all, what did she expect? She was a puppet and a prisoner. She lay awake watching the dawn, trying to remember what it was like to be free, truly free.

Her attendants arrived early. They meticulously prepared her for the day's events. Her role was simple: to be transported to the outer platform of the Great Temple. There she would wait hidden among some columns. Then, at the appointed time, she would step out into the view of the crowds and place five wreaths on five men. She would wave to everyone, then step back into the shadows again. That was it.

Ariana told herself the day was going to be just like any other. Only the briefest contact with those outside her small circle. She would have a fleeting panoramic glimpse of the outside world, but nothing to do with it. Her heart wasn't agreeing with her head at all. Her heart was racing with excitement, and she had no idea why.

After she was suitably made up for her appearance, Ariana had the strongest desire to go and pray. She knelt by her favourite altar in the quiet gardens of the grounds of her only home, the Great Temple.

The air seemed charged with a presence she'd not known before, yet she felt at peace. The words that started to leave her lips surprised her.

"Oh rulers of the heavens..." she'd barely started, and the atmosphere around her tangibly changed. Her mind raced. What was happening? Was she having a vision or something? Ariana continued praying.

"Rulers of the heavens, guide my steps today, show me the true path," her voice was full of desperation. Something didn't fit; who exactly was she supposed to address her prayers to anyway? She was never quite sure. The words that fell from her lips next were definitely not the ones she'd so often rehearsed.

"Oh Ruler of the heavens..." she decided to go straight to the top. Something inside her quit striving. She began crying quietly, "Friend of Enoch, deliver me from all this madness." She became bolder and more direct, "And get me out of here, get me out of this wretched place." She realised how much she hated being a prisoner in the most beautiful and serene place in the city. "Take me away from Nahron, help me to be completely free."

Ariana had very little idea, if any, as to what praying these things could mean practically. Yet somehow they felt right. Far from feeling condemned or rejected, she felt empowered. She reasoned that she had either blown everything with her arrogance, or maybe she was on the right track. After all, how could any god want her locked away in a giant sham temple all her life?

Ariana thought about the Ancient, the man called Shem. The one at the heart of the mission to bring down Be'elzar. She carried on praying.

"And this man, this man, this Ancient who will be here in the city today, please, please let me speak to him."

The very idea seemed beyond absurd. Nahron had every mouse hole locked down in the Great Temple. On every trip out of it, his Royal Guards watched her. They ensured she never met or spoke to anyone. Ariana had the ridiculous idea that her prayers were answered. She remained still for a while, basking in the residue of the atmosphere that had been around her.

Ariana's attendants came to tell her it was time to leave. They were horrified to find her face tear-stained and her makeup running. In a frenzy, they washed her and reapplied her makeup. They begged her not to cry again. They knew they'd lose their heads if she was anything less than perfect.

◆◆◆   🏳   ◆◆◆

Ariana's Royal Guard escort arrived uncharacteristically early. She'd expected a short flight over the temple's vast grounds to its outer platform. There was some confusion between the pilot and whoever he was communicating with about where to drop her off. Eventually, it all settled down, and they set off.

It was refreshing to get to see the city from the perspective of the transport's cabin windows. From the air, it looked as beautiful as ever. Parks and small lakes were everywhere. Shining tower blocks filled the sky. Each unique in colour and design. Soon, they touched down on the Monument of Enoch's central platform. After suitably covering her face, Ariana was led out. Her transport was a nondescript civilian one specifically chosen to not attract attention.

Ariana was mildly surprised. Her morning brief had not mentioned a visit to the Monument of Enoch. She was expecting to go to the Great Temple's outer platform. Perhaps Nahron had changed his mind? His ways always had a reason, she reminded herself.

Her escorting Royal Guards placed the accompanying five wreaths against the base of a nearby column. They still seemed unsure about what was going on. After some puzzled looks and chats on their communicators, they disappeared. That was really odd; Ariana realised she was completely on her own.

She remained hidden among the large marble columns of the monument around her. Ariana waited patiently for her next instructions; none came. She could have asked any Palatine Guard stationed outside the base of the monument for help. They would have fallen over themselves to attend to her. She decided to do nothing, enjoying the freedom that the absence of minders in a public place brought. And besides, she thought, what did she have to do? Place five wreaths around the necks of five men. That didn't sound too hard. She waited, and waited.

The crowds grew and grew. This really is a big day, thought Ariana; no paid crowds were needed for this event. She wondered vaguely where Prebius was, the man who usually organised such things. He was always hovering around on these types of occasions. She liked him. He was a busybody sort of fellow, obsessed with detail. But good at his job. He was one of the few men in the world she was permitted to casually talk to.

After an hour, the crowds on the concourse filled every available square cubit. It soon became clear to Ariana that something had gone very wrong with the day's arrangements. She smiled and took a deep, long breath. Leaning against a column, she enjoyed its cool marble on her bare back. Was this what true freedom was really like, she wondered? Nothing to do and no one to answer to? No posture to maintain, no need to keep waving and smiling at people who adored her but whom she would never meet? It felt good.

Chapter 17

Victory Parade

$\mathscr{S}$hem stepped out of the ceremonial Vastar Executive transport. He walked down its short, extending ramp waving at all around him. The heaving crowds of the City of Light were cheering wildly. A whole week had passed since his mission to kidnap King Be'elzar from the Dark Kingdom. With a little help from a variety of drugs, Be'elzar had been successfully interrogated. He'd given the empire's special forces enough information to locate and raid some secret command centres. After that, it was all downhill. The Dark Kingdom's defences fell one by one. Knowledge of their power sources, access codes, and vulnerabilities all helped. Nahron's technicians found flaws in the Dark Kingdom's detection grids. The empire's active camouflage systems became impervious to their scanners once again. The Empire of the Son didn't even have to launch a full scale invasion to secure their surrender.

Nahron had the Palace of Be'elzar carpet bombed. The sight of their great palace, now a smouldering ruin, was too much for even leaders like Ragzan's to bear. They fled to the Pazgon mountains. The rank and file of the army simply surrendered.

Nahron immediately opened up all of the Empire of the Son's airwaves to the conquered lands. For many, it was too much to take in; the realisation of the extent of their deceptions was beyond belief. The infamous prison and labour camps were opened. Hordes tried to migrate across the empire's borders. Instead of stopping them, Nahron offered rewards to those who stayed. Homes, jobs and all kinds of luxuries. He sent the newly freed masses commodities of little value. Things that had been hard to come by in the old Dark Kingdom. The early arrival of these freebies encouraged many to stay where they were. He also announced a celebratory moratorium on all taxation. The population fell in love with him. The story of the kidnap of Be'elzar was told and retold on every telecast, in every café and in every home.

Nahron was a hero; Shem was too, and heroes needed a Victory Parade.

139

Shem surveyed the scene before him. Vast crowds waving and cheering. He'd been dropped at the far end of the Concourse of Heroes. His parade route was simple. It consisted of walking, riding, then climbing steps, all in a single straight line. He would walk from where he was along the Concourse of Heroes. This would lead him to the front of the mythical Ascension of Enoch monument. From there, he would give a short speech. Then passing through its columns, he would walk through it and come out at the back. There he would meet the three Royal Guards who'd accompanied him on the mission and Stalman. They would ride in three chariots along the main mall to the foot of the Great Temple's outer platform. Lastly, they would ascend the 220 steps to the top of the platform. There, none other than the Emperor Nahron himself would be waiting to greet them.

Shem had no illusions about Nahron, but he was pleased to be there. He believed his fame could only boost his father's message.

Shem began walking slowly, waving to his left and right. He shook hands with his men from the Tigris Battle Group who were lining the concourse. He'd been a hero to them before; now he was like a god. Some had even begun to believe there might be more to him. Perhaps a divine quality? They sought something that would lead them beyond the showmanship religion of Nahron. Could Shem, the son of an Ancient, be the one to give them what they wanted?

♦♦♦   ⌂   ♦♦♦

Prebius was beyond frantic. This kind of mistake could only mean one of two things. The death penalty or worse – banishment to the penal island of Joktan, where life was death.

He was responsible for all the arrangements of the Victory Parade. He'd done this kind of thing many times before without a hitch. Today, something had gone badly wrong.

The general plan had been simple. Shem was to land in a ceremonial Vastar at the Concourse of Heroes. Then, walk down it paying respects to the personnel they'd shipped in from the Tigris Battle Group. That bit was simple. He would give a very short pre-scripted speech in front of the monument. It didn't matter what the content was. Nahron always had the sound systems garble the words from such speeches. That way, the people never really knew what was being said.

Just in case it wasn't completely flattering about their emperor.

After his speech, Shem would walk through the monuments' columns to the back. There he would meet the Royal Guards from his mission and Stalman, Be'elzar's double. They would all ride in three chariots along the 2000 cubit stretch of the Grand Mall. Right up to the Great Temple's outer platform, ascend its steps and bow before their Emperor Nahron. He would then publicly thank them and give each of them a medal. Following this, the High Priest Mandarus would pray a blessing over them. Then the highlight of the whole day would follow. Ariana, Chaste Maid of the Son, who almost never appeared in public, would step out from the columns and place wreaths around each one of the heroes' necks.

Necks. The thought made Prebius sick. The worst possible thing had happened. The more he thought about it, the more he knew it was his assistant Flixus. He'd just had a worrying message from one of the Great Temple's valets. Shem's three men and Stalman were stood like lemons at the bottom of the steps to the outer platform of the Great Temple. Nahron, Mandarus, and a group of dignitaries were waiting at the top. Looking down at them in bemusement. Now this Prebius could handle. He'd had a couple of close shaves before and got through them without anyone noticing.

Shem's men and Stalman could stay where they were; in fact, they would have to. Getting any of them back to the Monument of Enoch was out of the question. What could they do, jog down the mall, meet Shem and then ride straight back up it again? That would look ridiculous. If there was one thing Prebius hated, it was anything he organised looking ridiculous. The four men would wait for Shem, then, as planned, climb up the platform's steps with him to meet the emperor. That part was fixable.

The same valet had heard something else from some very concerned Palatine Guards. In between the columns of Enoch's monument stood none other than Ariana, Chaste Maid of the Son. She was completely alone, with five wreaths stacked neatly at her feet. How on earth she had been dropped off there, instead of at the Great Temple, Prebius had absolutely no idea.

Prebius tried to imagine all the ways he would like to kill his assistant Flixus. Instead, he found himself thinking of all the places where he could flee to and hide. He concluded that the remote Pazgon mountains of the old Dark Kingdom were probably his best chance. Nevertheless, he still thought there might be a way to save the day and maybe even his life.

Prebius quickly set off to walk the 250 cubits from where he was to Enoch's monument. He decided to try and implement his solution to the problem.

Prebius looked for his pass. It was missing from his pocket. He couldn't talk his way past the soldiers from the Tigris region to get to the monument, or Shem. None of them recognised him. He was stuck. He tried his communicator. That didn't work either; a message said his ID had been blocked. Flixus had thought of everything.

Prebius watched hopelessly as Shem began walking along the Concourse of Heroes. He knew what would happen when Shem arrived at the Monument of Enoch. It was unthinkable. Prebius slipped quietly away into the crowd.

♦♦♦   ☚   ♦♦♦

Shem stood at the front of the Monument of Enoch. He gave a very short speech, knowing full well that no one would understand any-thing. He raised and lowered his voice while pointing at the sky as though to say thanks to the Creator. Some thought he was thanking Enoch; others realised he was acknowledging the Creator. Most didn't care. Either way, they all cheered non-stop throughout the whole speech.

Shem finished his speech. He turned and began to walk a few paces towards the inner columns, ready to head through. A woman unexpectedly stepped out from the shadows. She was holding a wreath and looked like she was about to say something but never spoke.

Shem's deep blue eyes met Ariana's green eyes, and time stood still.

♦♦♦   ☚   ♦♦♦

The crowds were becoming excited. A ceremonial Vastar transport appeared in the sky. Ariana's heart was racing at the mere sight of it. She peered out from the columns of the Monument of Enoch where she was waiting. The transport set down at the far end of the Concourse of

Heroes. Someone stepped out of it wearing the white and gold dress uniform of the Air Force. She couldn't see who it was; they were too far away. The crowds were cheering and clapping. The figure began walking in her direction. Ariana felt weak and excited. She knew it had to be Shem, but why was he on his own? Where were the other four men?

At the back of the monument, three chariots with horses and stable boys waited patiently. Ariana was confused, three chariots for two people, and she couldn't drive a chariot herself. What was going on?

For a moment, Shem disappeared from view; Palatine Guards blocked her line of sight. He reappeared. Ariana quickly slipped further back into the long shadows between the columns. Shem arrived and gave a very short speech that was completely indiscernible. Ariana was used to that. More clapping and cheering followed. Shem turned and began to walk past her to make his way through the columns towards the rear porticoes.

Ariana took a deep breath. "Well, I'm not going to just stand here like the statue," she said to herself. She stepped out from the shadows. Extending a wreath in her hands, she got ready to speak her scripted words. 'Welcome honoured Hero of the Empire.'

Ariana's throat went dry. Her tongue stuck to the roof of her mouth. The wreath remained locked in the grip of her outstretched hand. She wondered how long it would be before she could speak. But then realised that even if she could, she had no idea what to say. She didn't remember a single word from her six word greeting.

◆◆◆   ⚑   ◆◆◆

Shem looked at Ariana. Previously, he'd not been at all interested in all the talk of the Chaste Maid. He'd assumed it was nothing more than another one of Nahron's publicity stunts. Everyone knew her father Mandarus' past as a provincial garbage administrator. Although it always got changed to collector. Pictures of her existed everywhere. But they were so doctored she just looked like any other unreal model selling toothpaste.

The woman who stood before Shem was not at all what he'd expected. In fact, he wasn't supposed to meet anyone except the guards from his mission and Stalman there. He definitely wasn't expecting to see Ariana. For some reason, he thought his mother would like Ariana. What that had to do with anything going on right now, he couldn't fathom. For a brief moment he saw himself alone with her on his father's vessel, alone as though they were...

Shem struggled to focus. Ariana was beautiful, really beautiful. Her eyes had an innocence and light that he'd only seen in one other person, Nadina, when she was young and before she'd travelled to the City of Light. When he looked into them he knew that her heart looked for the Creator, possibly knew Him already in some way.

Shem composed himself. Ariana looked to be in a state of total shock. He was quite pleased, making the Chaste Maid of the Son speechless was something he would have to tell Japheth about as soon as he got home. He was about to speak when again he had the over-whelming sense that Ariana belonged to him, that she was not supposed to be the Temple's Chaste Maid at all. A sudden and inexplicable sense of foreboding came over him for her. He knew he had to take her far away from there, rescue her like he had Timnah.

Shem had no idea how any of that could possibly work but he knew he had an appointment with the emperor and that was one appointment he had to keep. He took stock of the situation. Ariana had five wreaths in her hands but his men and Stalman were not there. Clearly someone had messed up the arrangements, and why was she at the Monument of Enoch? Surely she was supposed to be at the Great Temple?

He smiled warmly at Ariana, "Thank you," he said prizing the wreath out of her hand, "would you like a ride home?"

Ariana stared wide eyed at him. Shem realised she was probably used to withering flattery and blustering sycophantic drivel but 'would you like a ride home' was unlikely to be in the repartee of her usual admirers. He also noticed that Ariana appeared to have lost all sense of occasion.

Shem smiled again very slightly raising his right eyebrow. Ariana blushed the deepest red he could remember seeing any girl blush in his entire life. She was rooted to the spot and had not yet managed to speak a single word. He took her by the hand and led her out from the shadows of the columns to the nearest chariot. Stepping effortlessly into it he gallantly pulled her up beside him.

The crowds saw Ariana and went completely wild. Screaming,

cheering, yelling, they didn't know what to do with themselves.

◆◆◆   🏳   ◆◆◆

The deafening roar reached Nahron and those at the Great Temple 2000 cubits away. Nahron was disturbed, surely Shem was not that popular?

After several minutes and the cheering only getting louder a single chariot appeared in the distance. The crowds had gone completely mad and then Nahron saw why. His blood ran cold, his rage knew no bounds, his mind raced as he tried to decide there and then how many hundreds, if not thousands to execute. There in the approaching chariot was none other than Ariana, beside her was Shem. They were holding hands and waving to the crowd.

Trembling, Nahron looked carefully around. Mandarus' face was one of complete utter shock and disbelief; he was gaping, his mouth wide open. Clearly whatever had gone on was not his doing. The attendant priests, guards and accompanying dignitaries were also all staring in bewildered wonder. Prebius, thought Nahron. Prebius had planned this whole day in meticulous detail with him. Where was he? Prebius was nowhere to be seen.

As hard as his rage tried to drive him Nahron could not imagine Prebius ever doing anything like this either in error or deliberately. He stayed calm and decided that there must be a plot against him. He carefully looked around again and this time saw Flixus. In a single moment Nahron understood everything. This was not some great plot, it was the work of a small minded ladder climbing fool.

Flixus had made the fatal error of not putting himself out of Nahron's line of sight. His face had none of the look of disbelief that those around him had, in fact he was smiling. Nahron looked across at Sindain, who himself was looking more bewildered than everyone else put together. His face went white when he saw Nahron looking at him. Nahron frowned slightly and shook his head slowly as though to say, "I know it's not you," and then looked deliberately towards Flixus.

By now Flixus was grinning from ear to ear at the sight of Shem and Ariana in the same chariot. Sindain followed Nahron's line of sight. He caught sight of Flixus whose expression told him everything. Sindain looked back at Nahron, nodding knowingly at him.

Flixus was choking on his own blood in a quiet storeroom in the Great Temple before Shem had even reached the top of the steps where he was to meet Nahron.

♦♦♦ ⮃ ♦♦♦

Ariana had never known anything like it. The chariot ride was a dream, cheering adoring crowds, a hero at her side constantly steadying her with his strong hand. Even the horses played up to the occasion with sudden stops, neighing, tossing their heads and prancing. Ariana knew that if there was ever a time to speak to Shem it was now before they arrived at the Great Temple.

"I want to go to the Land of the Ancients," she shouted, competing with the din of the crowd.

"What!?" shouted Shem.

She turned and yelled as loud as she could right in his ear, "I want to go to the Land of the Ancients."

Shem looked surprised although not as much as she expected. He shouted back into her ear.

"I promise I will take you, but not today."

The crowd went even wilder as though the two of them were lovers telling secrets in each other's ear.

♦♦♦ ⮃ ♦♦♦

Shem and Ariana arrived at the bottom of the outer sacrificial platform of the Great Temple. Shem helped Ariana down from the chariot graciously motioning her to go first. His waiting men looked bemused as Ariana reached back into the chariot for their wreaths and placed one on each of them. The crowd never stopped cheering. To see Ariana at all let alone doing something like putting wreaths on brave soldiers was more than most had seen her do in a lifetime. To see her in a chariot with Shem, recently proclaimed Hero of the Empire was beyond all their wildest expectations.

The group began the long ascent up the 220 steps. Trumpets sounded along with a variety of gongs and drums, none of which could be distinguished above the noise of the crowd who by now had broken through the guide ropes further back and were rushing up the mall towards the Great Temple.

A fresh line of Palatine Guards, several men deep was rapidly forming at the bottom of the temple steps. Ariana reached the top first and bowed on one knee before Nahron. He appreciated the gesture although it had never been in the original script. Mandarus, still wondering how his daughter had ended up in a chariot with Shem also bowed even though he was behind Nahron. This set off a chain reaction as all those around bowed too. No one was going to be caught out not bowing to Nahron. Nahron thought that perhaps everything wasn't going to be quite the public relations disaster he'd imagined after all.

Shem reached the top of the steps, bowed on one knee and with his head well down took off his wreath and held it up with one hand towards Nahron, not even looking up. Shem's men and Stalman all followed suit. They all remained bowed until Nahron, humbly ignoring the offered wreaths tapped Shem on the shoulder and motioned for him to rise. Nahron pinned medals on each man, Shem first.

"It is an honour," Shem carefully mouthed the words because of the din of the crowd. He briefly met the emperor's eye. Down the long tunnel to Nahron's soul Shem caught sight of a very lonely man, a man who had no friends and who knew no love. A man who was always afraid of something and yet unremittingly self seeking.

Nahron glimpsed into Shem's eyes, what he saw shook him. There was no fear there, no hatred, neither was there gloating in the cheering crowds. In Shem Nahron saw a man who appeared to need nothing, a man who was content. He quickly looked away.

Ariana had repositioned herself where she guessed she should have been standing all along.

"A great day," spoke Nahron to the crowds who were a little more subdued by now. He looked around, those on the platform all nodded. No one said anything except Shem.

"A great day indeed my lord, and a pleasure and an honour for me to be here with you to celebrate the success of your great plan to rid the world of the evil of the Dark Kingdom." Shem clearly emphasised the words 'your great plan.'

Nahron smiled and nodded in appreciation. He was very glad Shem was the son of an Ancient with no political ambition because he would surely make a very popular emperor.

Chapter 18

Captivity

*F*ar away in the hinterlands of the Ancients. Another hero was having a far more sedentary day than his fellow soldiers manning the Victory Parade in the City of Light.

The home of Noah was not what Mavron had expected. Outwardly anyone could see that it was beautiful. The grounds, spread over several acres, were exceptional. Perfect lawns, towering trees of every variety, and endless flower beds. Two lakes and a couple of streams, crossed by quaint bridges, were set among them. Even so, it was not the outward beauty that perplexed Mavron. It was the atmosphere, especially in the large and sprawling home. When he regained consciousness and realised where he was, he'd been sure it would be a mad house. A place full of strange practices and a constant stream of hype and religious gibberish. Nothing could be further from the truth.

First of all, there was the pervading sense of peace. Mavron couldn't quite get over it. Every time he woke up and every time he slept, he felt at peace. Why, he had no idea. Here he was, a captive and a badly injured one at that. His head frequently hurt, although it was getting better. His leg had been twisted when he fell out of his Tactan. Sometimes that hurt so much he could barely put any weight on it. So why did he feel so at peace?

Second, there was the ever present humour. Emzara, Noah's wife, cleaned his head wound every day. After only three days of observing her, he decided that Noah was the most fortunate man in the history of the world. Emzara was beautiful, patient, clearly very smart and best of all, she had a subtle and very dry sense of humour. Of all the women he'd ever known, Mavron couldn't think of one that was even half of what she was. Whenever she touched his brow he felt genuinely loved, a feeling he'd not known for as long as he could remember. One day while tenderly removing his bandage she'd quipped about it being a weight off his mind. Noah had been nearby and said something similar about her hair; soon they were both laughing. After they left the room Mavron was reduced to tears. He hadn't cried in over a hundred years.

Here he was watching a husband and wife joke and tease each other. Yet all he could do was fight the pain of the loss of a life with love in it. He'd forgotten that such a life could exist.

After only a week at Noah's, he started to like it there. The pervading tranquillity was intoxicating. Back in the Royal Guard HQ, everyone was always in some kind of agitated state. If they weren't complaining about mismanagement from above, then they were abusing those beneath them.

Japheth had come and questioned him, not harshly but skilfully. At first, Mavron had stuck to the usual name, rank, and number. Japheth eventually told him what their concerns were.

Apparently, Nahron had a plan, code-named Time Zero. Its purpose was to completely overrun the Land of the Ancients. To lay innumerable military bridges along the entire length of the Pishon. To send over the river everything military, flying and ground hugging. To saturate the entire land with man and machine from along the whole of the western border.

Mavron went quiet and looked at Japheth for a long time. He didn't care any more. He'd been captured and failed in his mission. Only disgrace awaited him back home. He was a commander in the Royal Guards. How had he been captured by the son of an Ancient, a crazy one at that, and a solitary girl who'd twice escaped him? More than that, he felt like he belonged at Noah's. He found himself wanting to stay, to leave all the madness of the empire and the capital behind.

"I have no idea what you're talking about," Mavron spoke plainly. "I am here to escort Talmeon, cousin of the emperor and chief science advisor. He wishes to consult the House of Methuselah about a dream."

"Methuselah is dead," said Japheth dispassionately.

"So my mission was pointless," Mavron sighed.

"Not necessarily, we are all the family of Methuselah. My father's counsel and replies would be little different from his. What were the questions about?" Japheth realised that Mavron wasn't holding back any more.

"His divine majesty," Mavron's voice was full of sarcasm, "has been troubled by repeated vivid dreams. In them, the entire world is covered by water."

"It gets worse." Mavron's tone also got noticeably drier. "Apparently, in these dreams there isn't anyone left alive in the whole world

149

for him to rule over." He paused for effect, "So that's why he has sent his cousin to these lands. To find out what the dreams mean."

Japheth stared at Mavron, then got up quietly and left. Mavron saw that Japheth believed that Nahron's dreams were linked to Noah's prophecy. He, however, was yet to be convinced. End of world scenarios had abounded ever since he was a child. He'd always thought that after retiring from the Guards, he would announce the end of the world. Arrange meetings to give further details, and then take offerings. He noticed that many preachers had done this many times over. Their prophecies never came to anything, but their income and reputations somehow remained intact.

Several days earlier, Mavron had worked out his location. He planned to escape and find Talmeon. Unfortunately, he couldn't walk more than twenty cubits without considerable pain. Moreover, every time he sharply moved his head, it felt like someone was hitting it with a bridge support. He understood his chances of reaching the border were impractically low.

Mavron also realised that escaping meant going to find Talmeon and returning with him to the exact same place he would have just left. Nevertheless, he'd decided to flee as soon as he felt up to it.

Two things happened that changed his mind. It was now the second week of his captivity and coincidentally the Seventh Day of the week. A traditional day of rest and religious services. Noah invited Mavron to attend a time of prayer with him at an altar in a secluded spot in the gardens. Mavron's condition was rapidly improving, so he decided that he would go along, pretend to want to stay a bit longer at the end, then abscond.

They knelt to pray; Mavron's leg still hurt so much when he tried putting all his weight on it that he quickly abandoned any idea of escaping. He relaxed, enjoying the fresh warm air and listened to Noah's prayers. Mavron was confused. The prayers were real, from the heart. It was as though Noah was simply talking to the Creator. How could anyone do that? He'd heard plenty of showy prayers in his time but none like this. He listened, mesmerised. Noah prayed sincere prayers for his own family, the healing of Mavron's wounds, for the empire and even the emperor. Mavron was bewildered. Why was Noah praying for him and the emperor? Were they not his enemies?

Mavron decided to stop fighting. He'd been fighting all his life and where had it got him? Nowhere. In some undefinable way, Mavron gave up being a Royal Guard that day. He let Noah's prayers wash over him; he decided he wanted only peace in his life from now on.

A warm, reassuring presence settled around him. Mavron wanted to stay in that moment for ever. Deep in the recesses of his heart, Mavron knew he was in the presence of the Creator. He'd always assumed there would be feelings of guilt, shame, and condemnation.

Surprisingly, Mavron felt only one thing. Acceptance. At the end of the prayer time, he was completely unnerved. He felt weak. He'd been trained to withstand days of interrogation without food and water. Yet here he was, surrendering the will to fight like a child.

Mavron began to slowly accept that Noah was not a madman. But if Noah was not a madman and was building a boat because he claimed the Creator had told him the whole world was about to be destroyed. Then there was only one rational but equally insane conclusion. Maybe the world really was going to be destroyed. After all, even the emperor had been experiencing dreams that matched Noah's claims. Although why any kind of god would bother to speak to someone like Nahron, Mavron couldn't fathom.

Noah finished his prayers; he turned and looked at Mavron.

"You're my guest now," he said, "I forgive you for what you tried to do to our friend. You're not our prisoner any more. If you want, we can take you and your Tactan back to Nahron's Gate."

Mavron laughed to himself. An hour ago, he would have accepted. Then have whoever returned him arrested. But things had changed.

"Thank you," he replied. Unsure how to explain his feelings. "But right now I'm enjoying your hospitality." Noah smiled.

The second reason occurred later that afternoon. Mavron was sitting in the warm sunlight down at the bottom of the main lawn in the shade of some trees. He'd been at Noah's, also known as the household of Methuselah, for two weeks and had no idea where Talmeon or his men were. He had no communicator to contact the empire. Even if he did, it wouldn't work so far into the Land of the Ancients. Talmeon was supposed to be visiting Methuselah's household. He should have arrived, even if he'd taken the slowest land route, at least ten days ago. Mavron could only speculate as to what might have happened to him and his men. Perhaps the mission got cancelled? His eyes rested on the distant hills. How peaceful everything was.

Mavron began to doze again. The frequent headaches had stopped, as long as he didn't move his head too suddenly, it didn't hurt. His leg was much better, although he still had to be careful with it. Memories of centuries gone by floated into his mind. He remembered the time before Salfar's reign, hundreds of years long past.

Things had been different then. People were different. At first, he couldn't quite put his finger on it. The more he thought about it, the more he realised, no one cared about anything except themselves anymore. He remembered when he was young that there were a few kind people here and there. Now, there didn't seem to be any. Well, none except for here at Noah's. He realised that was what he liked so much about Noah and his family, even about Japheth who'd kidnapped him. They were kind.

He wanted to find the girl. The one he'd captured and would have tortured. Although technically he was now her captive. He didn't even know her name. He wanted to tell her that he was sorry, really sorry. He wanted to do something for her, anything. He couldn't imagine what. Mavron longed in his heart to be kind to her, to someone, to anyone. Tears filled his eyes, and he wondered at what was happening to himself. Why did he feel like this?

After a while, he became aware that someone was standing before him, yet he couldn't see them. The garden was quiet; a stillness had come over the birds nearby. He didn't know what to do or say, but he knew the man was waiting. Patiently waiting. Waiting for him to finally say yes.

Mavron tried to speak, his voice slightly trembling. He couldn't remember any prayers from his childhood. Nothing that Noah had recently prayed came to mind either. He struggled to sit forward and lowered his head. It was the best he could do with his wounded leg; kneeling was out of the question. He didn't know why, but he remembered a sacrifice he'd seen. Not any of the ones Noah had made, but one he'd seen as a young man hundreds of years ago. Startled, he realised that this same unseen man, this same presence, had been there. He'd seen a lamb slaughtered. Mavron remembered that he'd faced the same questions then that were coming to his heart now. He saw himself clearly. Horrified, he realised that he'd said no.

Mavron Jared Targemah knew that from this moment on there was no going back. He murmured, "Yes," weeping softly. "Yes," his words gained strength. It was as though his yes was the answer to every question that the unseen person was asking him, and there were many. Was he sorry for his many sins? Was he willing to change? Was he willing to believe? The last question came to him. Was he willing to change his allegiance?

Mavron answered with great conviction, "Yes."

A deep peace enveloped him as all that he had been felt washed away. He'd made his choice. This time he had said yes to his Maker.

Again he fell into a light sleep. The sound of the breeze rustling through the cooling trees was soothing. An hour passed. Mavron stirred, glancing casually at the distant treeline beyond the garden.

Some small sapling trees on a far hill appeared to be moving. They were a long way off; some were darker than others. Mavron was a trained Royal Guard. He might be recuperating from a serious injury, half-dozing and having a spiritual awakening. But, when something didn't fit, it soon caught his attention. He looked harder.

Figures? They were figures! Men walking, stumbling might be a better description. He pressed his call bell button; it chimed quietly in the house. Timnah heard it. Perhaps Mavron needed another drink; she would get it in a few minutes. It chimed again. Emzara also heard it and thought perhaps he was hungry. It chimed again and didn't stop; over and over again it chimed. They ran outside.

In the distance, five men were stumbling towards the home. One was limping and being supported by another. They were all filthy, their clothing ripped, stained with mud and blood. Makeshift bandages covered the arms of two of them. All had dishevelled beards and hair matted with green slime and dirt.

Mavron hoisted himself onto his one good leg. He leaned on his crutches and struggled forwards.

"Elon," he shouted, "Zahar."

"Sir, sir!" Elon called, "sir!" and collapsed. Cavilah picked him up and dragged him to Mavron. Timnah ran forward to help.

"Call Noah and the others," Emzara ordered Timnah.

The five men were in a terrible state. Filthy, hungry, wounded, exhausted, but on an emotional high. Mavron felt as though his whole world was tilting and he was sliding off the edge. But the edge was not the nightmare scenarios he'd faced so many times before in battle and on missions. This was different; it was the kind of edge you wanted to slide off like a child into a pool. One of exhilaration. His men were safe, Talmeon too! The man called Cavilah was with them? They'd been in the wilderness for how long? By Eden, what had happened!

♦♦♦ ⚑ ♦♦♦

Talmeon had never felt so almost dead but alive. The sight of civilisation and friendly faces was a great relief. But, what in heaven's name was Mavron doing at Noah's? He had no idea, but he realised that he was going to live after all.

For two weeks they'd trekked through the hinterlands of the Land of the Ancients. No transports, no hotels, no royal pampering because he was the emperor's cousin. The wild animals weren't interested in any of that, only what they might taste like. Cavilah's knowledge had saved them innumerable times. He also had no doubt that if his team were not Royal Guards, then they would have all been dead by the end of the second day. Survival skills, combat training against wild animals and reptiles, had all proven essential. They'd even trapped and eaten a disgusting tasting baby stegosaurus. He was also convinced that the ground had shaken at least twice in the last week. That was unheard of. He would have to confirm it with his assistant Bezek when he returned to the capital.

That evening was a blur of food, medicines, stories, and possibly the deepest sleep he'd ever had in his entire life.

♦♦♦ ⚑ ♦♦♦

Nahron. Mavron quietly huffed at the mention of his name. He listened to his men and Talmeon discuss their survival tales. Wouldn't it be nice if Nahron didn't exist, he thought to himself.

Mavron decided that there was no way he was going back to the capital.

Chapter 19

The Day of Revelations

After the Victory Parade had ended and the ceremony was complete, a great banquet was held the next day. Mandarus excused himself, priests didn't have to attend banquets. He went to look for Ariana in the Gardens of Solace, her favourite place in the temple grounds.

He caught sight of her in the distance through the vines and creepers of a trellis. She was placing her left hand on her right hand, then repeatedly lifting it off again. Occasionally, she would grip her right upper arm with her left hand and then let go of it. Puzzled, Mandarus watched her for several minutes. She had the most dreamy, happy expression he'd seen on her for a long time. He soon realised what she was doing.

Ariana was re-enacting Shem placing his hand on hers in the chariot from the previous day. Mandarus walked slowly up to his daughter, standing right in front of her. Ariana was oblivious to his presence.

"Ariana," he spoke softly. She looked up in surprise, clearly disappointed that her dream world was not real. "Nahron will not tolerate anyone else in your heart, let alone your arms." Ariana frowned slightly, smiling at the same time. Did he know what she was thinking?

"Father I want to..." she started enthusiastically, but her words trailed off. She looked down, tears filling her eyes.

"I know," Mandarus said, sitting by her, "I know."

"My precious Ariana," he whispered, because he never knew who was listening, even in the temple grounds, "I will get you out of this prison."

His words shocked him more than they did Ariana. "I will seek the Son on your behalf. Three days from now is the third five hundred year anniversary of Cain's revelations. It's the Day of Revelations."

Ariana was numb. She wasn't sure if she believed in any of that Day of Revelations stuff any more. It was a monumental religious occasion, occurring once every five hundred years. Its purpose was to celebrate the Ancient Cain's revelation of who the promised Son was.

The very Son who'd been promised to the betrayed Eve and after whom the whole empire was named.

The books of Cain claimed that Cain learned of the promised Son's identity but could not reveal it. Only a great future priest would be given that privilege. And only on a 500th anniversary of his revelation. To some, it was merely a clever ploy. A way for Cain to elevate himself while at the same time leaving his reputation intact. He'd died without saying who it was. Subsequent priests claimed to know. But, each time, the supposed saviour was identified, they'd turned out to be a dud, either a less than glorious man or mute idol.

"Thank you, Father," was all Ariana could say in reply to Mandarus' excited offer.

◆◆◆ ⌀ ◆◆◆

The Day of Revelations finally arrived. When he entered the Great Temple that morning, Mandarus sincerely believed he would get the revelation of who the Son was. More than that, he would somehow elicit his help to free Ariana. He'd started a partial fast forty days earlier. In the final seven days running up to the ceremony, he had completely fasted except for drinking water. For the last three days, he decided that he wouldn't even drink. He was determined to get the revelation, to be the greatest priest ever known.

Nahron had previously told him, that in the late afternoon of the Day of Revelations, that he would make a series of special announcements. He wanted Mandarus to be at his side when he did. Mandarus thought little of these announcements. He was content to have the morning and midday to himself.

He performed the sacred washing ritual. Bravely resisting the urge to lick the water that splashed on his lips. He went through the Doors of Holiness into the inner sanctuary of the Great Temple. His fellow priests and attendants escorted him up to the doors but went no further.

Mandarus had memorised all the prayers of Cain, intending to pray every one of them and a few more besides. He fully expected to be favoured by the gods for his meticulous preparations. Then there was his unfailing commitment to his fast. His very godly way of life. There were no prostitutes in the Great Temple. He had thrown them all out to disappear with the remnants of Salfar's old and corrupt regime. He took a humble salary. Lived a frugal lifestyle. Diligently cared for his daughter Ariana. And as if that wasn't enough, he meticulously studied the ancient texts, even though he didn't have a clue what most of them were on about.

Surely, if there ever was a priest who qualified for this revelation, it was he. Today he would see the power of the gods. He would be elevated into their realm and understand secrets hidden for centuries. His heart pulled him on in his imaginations. He would even find out who the promised Son of Eve would be!

Mandarus' thoughts ran wild as he heard the great doors of the inner sanctum closing solidly behind him. Then, in accordance with ancient tradition, they were barred and bolted. There would be no interruptions for such a sacred ceremony. The temple attendants would have fought to keep even the emperor out at such a time. They too wanted the revelation of who the Son was.

The inside of the sanctum was dark, lit only by candles. The high ceilings and stone pillars cast long shadows and created areas of deep darkness. Mandarus made his way slowly past the idols that lined the steps up to the high altar. Their eyes gleamed at him, some in anger, some in mockery. Mandarus felt afraid, vulnerable, but he carried on. He carefully fitted the golden token of Cain into its holder on the altar and lit the sacred candle. That was it; the ceremony had begun. Taking several steps back, he knelt down. Looking up into the darkness behind the altar, he began reciting his perfectly memorised prayers. The atmosphere around him was unusually dim despite the proliferation of candles. A coldness filled his body, but he persevered.

An hour later, Mandarus was weary; he felt like giving up. He was sure the idols around were mocking him. Then he heard himself say, "I will not be denied." This was not in the sacred prayers. For a moment he wondered if he had insulted the gods, but still he didn't give up.

Something in the air around him began to change. Mandarus felt it clearly. If he'd described it later, sceptics would say it was merely his feelings or imagination. But something most certainly had changed. He kept praying his prayers, yet the atmosphere around him was not at all what he'd expected. The air was still; there was not a sound inside the vast chamber. No sound could possibly get in from the outside either; the huge granite blocks of the walls made sure of that. Not a single candle flickered, but he was sure, as sure as he had seen the great waterfall of the great western sea, that what he felt was real. It shocked him. There was only one word for it – turmoil. The silent atmosphere of the inner sanctum was in turmoil.

Absolute turmoil.

Mandarus could hear the slightest rustle of his robes. Yet it was as though he stood under a torrent of water and in a great wind at the same time. He imagined he heard screams from another realm. Unknown creatures engaged in a fierce battle, and clearly losing it. It lasted only for a short while; then there were new presences. Ones he'd never known before and to whom he was not at all accustomed. Beings of incomparable strength and majesty. How he knew these things he did not know, but they felt more real to him than the granite blocks beneath his feet. The sanctum became still again, now holding a very different atmosphere. Mandarus glanced around. The idols had lost their fore-boding. The menace had gone from the reflections in their eyes. He waited, not sure what to do next.

Mandarus began praying again. Reciting more of the words from the prayers of Cain, but they'd completely lost their appeal. They felt empty and worthless. His words trailed off; what was he to do now? He whispered, "Help me," although he knew not to whom. Again he said, "I will not be denied." His words now carried a weight of their own; they were propelled from his heart by a strength that he did not know he had.

"I will not be denied," he spoke again fiercely, "What is the truth?" His voice broke on that last phrase. Mandarus began praying fervently in abandon. Nothing mattered. He'd already deviated from the sacred prayers, crossed the forbidden lines of ceremony. He'd fasted, he'd prayed, he wanted answers. He felt that after everything he'd studied, he still knew absolutely nothing. He thought of Ariana. His heart was torn. What would become of her now after the parade? He prayed like he never knew it was possible to pray. Deep from within his heart came the question that he'd always wanted to know the answer to.

"Who are you? Who are you! Show me!" he cried out. As if from nowhere, thoughts of various idols and gods flashed through his mind in rapid succession. Each one extinguished as an absurdity when he saw something contradictory about it. Mandarus grew more exasper-ated.

"Show yourself to me! You who lifts the Heavens!" he cried out.

He was really scaring himself now. He began crying; he was sure he'd gone too far, blown the whole thing yet his heart wanted more. Mandarus could find no more words to say. He knelt, sobbing in despair.

After a while, Mandarus began to see things about himself. He saw his selfishness. His pride. His indifference. His sins of the flesh – long gone but still awaiting judgement. His laziness. His hard work, but only for himself. Mandarus was broken. The cascade of his failures and imperfections poured over and over him until he could stand it no more. Lying face down on the cold granite, he lost all hope for himself. But before he died and left this wretched world, he still wanted to know one thing. He clenched his fists and whispered from the depths of his soul, "But who are you?"

Silence. Nothing. An unexpected peace settled on Mandarus for a while. He lay motionless; there was nothing more he could do. He realised for the first time he had seen himself as he truly was. A broken and lost man in an overconfident, gradually perishing shell.

Then there was something quite out of place, the distant sound of a horse. Mandarus wondered what on earth a horse would be doing inside the temple courts and how he could hear it in the inner sanctum. A few moments later there was another distant sound, that of an approaching crowd. That made no sense either. A dusty mist slowly filled the altar area, the noise of the crowd grew louder. Horses again, this time neighing, galloping. There were also men, shouting. Mandarus looked up, he began to see people, great crowds of people heaving and pushing. Soldiers in unrecognisable uniforms were frantically riding up and down the perimeter of the crowd. Beating and forcing it back. Foot soldiers appeared out of the mist. The crowds surged forward and grew. The shouts of the crowd were confusing; most were full of hatred, a few with grief. Their speech was unrecognisable apart from a few vaguely familiar words. A procession was coming towards him. Mandarus looked to see what all the commotion was about. The soldiers struggling to restrain the heaving masses were well organised and brutal. Mandarus kept trying to place their emblems, but they were unfamiliar. They had primitive weapons. They must be from the past, he thought, but this didn't fit. The people he could see were dressed strangely too. Some were poor, some rich. As the procession came closer, he was sure he could see men who were priests.

The mist cleared. A shocking sight met Mandarus' eyes. A man with completely black skin staggered past him carrying a huge piece of wood. The crowd ignored this man as did the soldiers. How on earth could anyone be so completely black! He also noticed some of the soldiers had strangely pale skin. This was only the beginning.

Behind the black man was a sight Mandarus found deeply disconcerting, even by the standards of his own violent world. Another man appeared, his body severely lacerated and bleeding, his face a mask of blood. It looked as though parts of his beard had been ripped out, taking his flesh with it. The man came closer. Mandarus backed away. He couldn't make sense of anything. A condemned man, a criminal – was this a warning of his own fate for his many sins?

In the vision, the man kept coming towards him, and Mandarus could not get away. The man was carrying a huge piece of wood. As the man came close, he stumbled and fell to his knees. Mandarus was aghast. He knelt to help him; it seemed the right thing to do. He saw the man's face much closer this time.

Mandarus looked right at him.

He asked the question again, this time trembling, "Who are you?"

The man looked up at him and Mandarus saw right into his eyes. He saw galaxies being formed, the earth being created. He saw one man and then a woman. He saw Eden, laughter, fun, adventure. Then everything changed. There was a being of immense pride and utter heartlessness. Darkness fell. Mandarus saw pain and deep, deep disappointment in the man's eyes, a broken heart but above all he saw love. Love beyond all comprehension. A love that broke the already broken Mandarus. He wanted to renounce everything he'd ever said, done and thought. Absolutely everything looked utterly worthless. He knew none of it had been done with this kind of love. From somewhere in his soul he asked the question again, "Who are you?" but this time he knew the answer.

Mandarus knew he was looking into the face of the Creator, and He was the promised Son.

Chapter 20

Special Announcements

*N*ahron arrived at the Great Temple for his Day of Revelation's special announcements. Mandarus was nowhere to be found; the temple attendants were all missing too. After much searching, his Royal Guards found some priests. They learned from them that Mandarus was locked in the inner sanctum. The guards tried to coerce them to go in and get Mandarus out. They flatly refused unless Mandarus gave them a signal from inside first. Nothing could make them acquiesce. Eventually, two were persuaded with great tact by a Royal Guard commander. They went in and brought Mandarus out. He had to be carried. He was in a terrible state, gibbering all kinds of nonsense; no one understood a word he said. Nahron met him.

"Mandarus, what's going on?" he asked for a brief moment, genuinely concerned. He didn't expect anything to come of Mandarus' ceremony. But the sight of him was so shocking that Nahron really did wonder what was wrong. Mandarus looked him squarely in the face and appeared to partially come to his senses.

"Nahron, my dear cousin from Vastar." That was a pretty unusual address. But Nahron swallowed it, waiting to hear what had put Mandarus into such an awful state.

"Nahron," he repeated again, still skipping any formalities, "everything we believe is a lie." He stuttered a bit and then repeated, "It's a lie, a total lie," and began hysterically crying. Nahron and those around stared in disbelief. One of the priests who had brought him out bravely spoke up.

"I think he's had some kind of breakdown, my lord," he hesitated. "Perhaps it's the several weeks' fasting and not drinking for the last three days?" Nahron turned to look at the priest.

"Not drinking for three whole days!"

"Yes, my lord," the priest replied, hastily adding, "none of us recommended that."

Nahron rolled his eyes, "Get him a doctor," he said wearily. He paused, "And bring Ariana to me."

Two senior temple attendants quickly disappeared to find her.

◆◆◆   ⚑   ◆◆◆

"Special announcements," mused Japheth. "Nahron loves his special announcements and today's the Day of Revelations. So what's it this time? More housing for the poor, more artistic funding. More taxes. More workers to be sent to the Dark Kingdom to make up for their lack of skills? More revelations, perhaps?"

Japheth put his feet up watching the telecast in mild anticipation. Nahron appeared on the screen. He was not in the Great Palace; he was in the Temple. "Aha, the Great Temple," he said, turning to Shem, sitting in a lounge chair next to him. "Isn't that where your girlfriend lives?" Shem took a swipe at Japheth's head but missed. Shem was on three months' leave after the fall of the Dark Kingdom, or hero leave, as his older brother kept calling it.

Japheth had left Noah's and the recuperating guests there earlier that day to meet Shem. He was still on his way home from the capital after the victory parade. They were in one of the increasing number of abandoned houses just inside the borders of their lands. From there, they could pick up telecast signals from the empire. Both were curious to see what Nahron would have to say on the famous Day of Revelations.

Nahron started his speech. He began by espousing the various qualities needed to come closer to the gods and the truth. Mandarus was conspicuously absent.

"So where's the garbage boy?" quipped Japheth, "shouldn't he have opened in prayer?" Nahron rambled on. The camera panned to his right, resting on Ariana. She looked as though she knew as much about what the emperor was going to say as anyone else.

When Shem saw Ariana, he sat bolt upright. Something wasn't right. Where was Mandarus? Why was Ariana by the emperor's side? He felt distinctly uncomfortable.

Nahron moved on to the great victory over the Dark Kingdom and the ridding of the world of deviant religion.

"Oops," chimed Japheth, "deviant religion – isn't that us?"

Shem kept waiting for another glimpse of Ariana. He was trying to figure out why she stood by Nahron and not by her conspicuously absent father.

"The Dark Kingdom has shown us the results of a conflict of views," Nahron went on. "A clash between the need for order and harmony, and the need to fully understand one another."

Both of them wondered where this was going. Where was the need to understand anything about the religion of Be'elzar? It was outright evil from head to toe. To their surprise, Nahron began espousing some things about the Dark Kingdom. He claimed they had misinterpreted lost truths but brought fresh revelations to those who served in the Great Temple.

"What!" Japheth couldn't believe his ears, "Mandarus got a revelation from Be'elzar, you must be joking."

Nahron finally got to the point. "Today, I want to share a monumental discovery. It comes from both revelation and a closer examination of ancient texts." Shem rolled his eyes.

"And from recent archaeological research," Nahron continued.

"That was a mouthful," said Japheth, "clearly this is going to be one huge pile of..." he stopped speaking as Nahron's words continued to drift through the room.

"Many have been asking for centuries, who is the Son? The promised Son of Eve, where is he? I have the answer; it has been with us all along. Cain revealed it before his death, but it was not understood." Nahron paused.

"The serpent is the Son."

Shem and Japheth gaped. Nahron carried on speaking, but they heard none of his ensuing words.

"The serpent is the long awaited Son?" Japheth spoke, repeating the words mechanically in utter disbelief.

Shem said nothing for a while, then answered softly, "What Father said is true; it will be this year."

Nahron's speech was by no means over; Shem and Japheth began paying attention again.

"To complete the harmony of our two faiths, which my divinely guided rule has united, I announce today. On the coming Seventh Day, I will take the Holy Sister of the Temple of the Serpent and the Chaste Maid of the Son as my sacred wives."

Shem's mind momentarily went blank. The words circled around his head as he tried to comprehend them. By this time in three days,

Ariana would be married to Nahron! The camera panned across to Ariana; she had collapsed in shock.

Nahron looked around, "And already, a sign! The divine confirmation of our new path of this great bringing together of all the peoples of the Earth."

"Moreover," Nahron continued, Japheth wondered what more there could be, "all our lands will be free from the errors of the past. A glorious new age of perfect harmony, light, and order will prevail."

Shem stood up.

"That means only one thing and one thing alone..." Shem ignored Japheth's commentary. "Where's Nadina?" he interrupted, his voice trembling.

"I don't know," Japheth replied, wondering what that had to do with anything. "I guess she's at home, her parents went on some trip to the capital; that much I know."

"Call her," Shem ordered his older brother as though he were one of his men in the Tigris Battle Group. He began walking towards the door, "and get your stuff."

"Shem?" Japheth called after him, beginning to realise what must be going through his brother's mind. "You're not seriously going to..." His voice trailed off as he thought of what he would do if Nadina were in the same situation as Ariana.

Shem disappeared through the door, then quickly reappeared. "And get that Tactan from home," he ordered, "and don't let any of the visitors see you."

"Shem!" Japheth complained. "Do you think I was born yesterday?" He stood to follow his younger brother. "By Eden, the harmonising of all religions, what on earth?! How can the serpent be the Son?!"

◆◆◆ ｵ ◆◆◆

Nadina hadn't taken a transport home; she'd walked, run and frequently stumbled. It was late evening before she fell through the door of her parent's empty home. The previous few days had been a combination of a dream and a nightmare. After Mavron's kidnap, Nadina had returned home. Deep inside the Land of the Ancients where she was safe from the empire. She'd had no choice but to lay low; her picture was registered on all the security scanners in the Havilah region. Soon afterwards, Talmeon and Mavron's men had unexpectedly shown up at Noah's. Emzara had called Nadina back over and asked her to help out.

The new arrivals were all sick in one way or another, some injured. Emzara also sent word that the commander, called Mavron, whom Nadina had escaped from and then captured, had changed. Rumour had it that he'd become a believer and wanted to see her to apologise. Nadina dutifully went; she got on surprisingly well with him. What was not surprising was how well she got on with Japheth. Especially since Japheth's wife Adatenesis was, as usual, absent.

The wounded men and curious Talmeon asked many questions and had plenty of stories to tell. The truth soon came out. All but one were from borderland families of the Ancients. One had even met Noah's deceased father, Lamech. He had been given a prophecy by him, which appeared to have been fulfilled.

This was all well and good, but the combination of family members in Noah's grand home was what messed things up. Noah and Emzara spent their time sitting and talking with Talmeon. Ham and Timnah were inseparable while they talked to some of the others. Shem was absent, so Nadina and Japheth sat, talked, and answered questions together. It would have all been perfect if it weren't so perfect. She and Japheth always seemed to know when to speak. They never interrupted each other. They naturally understood and finished each other's sentences. They spent almost all the time sitting next to one another. Talmeon and his men assumed they were married; only Mavron knew they were not. By the end of the second day, Nadina had lost all track of reality. Each day was a day with Japheth. Answering one question with him filled her with bliss. Bliss until Adatenesis arrived on the third day. Japheth had stood up to warmly greet his beautiful wife with a hug and tender kiss. Nadina watched as Adatenesis pressed her body right up to Japheth's and then looked at her. The walls came crashing in. Nadina had politely excused herself after the next meal and fled home.

"Never again!" she fumed to herself, "never again. It doesn't work, it can't work, it's impossible. I can't keep doing this!" she protested.

"It's not fair! Change me, take me away from here, do something! I can't see Japheth any more. I can't. He's married!" Her composure began to crack.

For a mad moment, Nadina thought she could abandon it all. Be like a daughter of the empire, be his mistress. Turn away from all sense of right and wrong and finally have him in her arms – at least now and again. Not that she believed for one moment he would agree, but the thought was overwhelming. She stood still, entertaining wild and intoxicating thoughts, until a deep sadness settled over her. She sighed and sat down, resting her back against her living quarters' door.

"He's married," she murmured repeatedly. "He's married. Oh Creator, why is he married?" she got louder. "And she doesn't love him properly like I would!" she shouted angrily, standing up again.

"After ten years she won't even live with him and I've loved him all my life!!" Nadina screamed at the top of her voice. She grabbed the pendant Japheth had given her the day they'd met, meaning to hurl it against the wall, but she couldn't. Instead, she held it close, kissing it repeatedly, quietly sobbing. Slowly sliding back down to the floor next to her bed, she lay there for a while. The comfort of the bed seemed wrong.

Sobbing quietly, Nadina pleaded through her tears, "Please do something. Please, please do something." She had never meant any prayer more in her whole life. Wearily climbing onto her bed, she fell into the deep sleep of emotional exhaustion.

Nadina awoke to her communicator's quiet beeping. It was mid morning; she'd slept over ten hours. Japheth was calling from within signal range of the empire's network by the border. It connected via Nadina's parents' specially fitted landline. A great expense – courtesy of the empire.

"Nadina, coming to get you this afternoon, collect your stuff, go to the pick-up point." His voice was urgent. Her stuff? The code word for another mission. So soon, why? She heard him speak Shem's name in the background.

"I can't come this time," Nadina weakly replied. There was a long pause.

"Haven't you seen the news?" Japheth asked.

"What news?" Nadina mumbled, still in the surreal world of the previous evening, surprised that Japheth didn't know what had happened to her.

"I'll tell you when we get there; we're really busy with some modifications." Her communicator went quiet.

How bad could it be? They were busy modifying what? Nadina stumbled into the empty kitchen, flicking the telecast receiver on. It was already set to the news channel. Nahron was speaking. Across the bottom of the screen, the headlines flashed along in running text. 'New revelation. The Serpent is the Son!'

Nadina swayed in shock. The serpent is the Son? What on earth! A thousand thoughts rushed into her mind. Then, she saw the second headline: 'Glorious Emperor Nahron to marry the Chaste Maid.' She knew immediately why Japheth had called her.

"Another mission with my Japheth," she laughed out loud to herself. "I pray for deliverance from him, and you send me on another mission with him. Perfect."

Sometimes Nadina really wondered if the Creator listened to even a single word she said. She decided life was absurd. The sooner you accepted this, the easier everything became. She went to collect a few things from her quarters. When she came back down, the telecast was showing Nahron speaking mid-sentence.

"...the harmonisation of all deviant religion." The words fell smoothly from his lips. But, Nadina knew exactly what Nahron meant by harmonisation. He meant annihilation.

By Eden, she thought, it is this year. Noah was right.

Later that day, Shem landed discreetly behind a hill near Nadina's parent's in Mavron's captured Tactan. Nadina threw in her equipment and climbed in after it. Japheth was frantically doing something on the scanners; he didn't look up.

"Where on earth are we going in this?" she yelled while Shem ran the resonators straight up to full power as they shot into the sky.

"Oh, you know Nadina," he winked at her, "just clothes shopping."

Nadina laughed, having no idea what he meant. She buckled herself into the co-pilot's seat and caught Shem's eye. The warmth in his heart strengthened her.

"Thank you," she worded silently. A peace settled on her, "So what's the deal this time?" she asked out loud, unsure whether she was speaking to her Creator or Shem.

Chapter 21

The Wedding

Ariana regained consciousness in her quarters. Mandarus sat at her side. Unfortunately, she was not dreaming.

"Father, what happened to you this morning?" she asked.

"I saw the Creator," he said, tears welling up in his eyes.

"The Creator!?" Ariana was incredulous.

"Yes," he said, "there's only one God, the Creator. I'm at peace with Him." He paused, "Ariana, everything we have believed is a lie."

"You mean the serpent really is the Son of Eve?" she asked, wide-eyed.

"No, no," he laughed, dismissing this with a wave of his hand. "How can it be? That's rubbish. I mean everything we've heard about the other gods and idols."

"The sacrifices? Doesn't paying for a sacrifice cleanse you?" asked Ariana, temporarily forgetting her present world and all its madness.

"Paying for nothing cleanses you," sighed Mandarus. "The sacrifices point to our, in fact all mankind's condition. One so serious that only the shedding of blood can free us from it."

"So what are we actually supposed to do?" Ariana wondered if she'd spent her whole life heading in the wrong direction.

"You trust and have faith that what the Creator is promising through the sacrifice is enough. You accept that after you believe you are accepted. And..." Mandarus hesitated unsure if what he was about to say next was entirely correct or even humanly possible, "...after you genuinely repent of all that you've done wrong."

Ariana looked at her father. She realised that this was a never ending and impossible task. You could genuinely repent and then become proud that you'd genuinely repented. In which case, you had to repent of your new problem with pride.

"Although, no one can genuinely repent," Mandarus said solemnly. "The more you focus on your imperfections, the more you exalt them."

168

Ariana realised that if you honestly examined yourself long enough, there was only ever one outcome: absolute despair. All of a sudden, she wanted Shem to hold her, comfort her, and explain these things to her. Then she remembered Nahron, and the reality of her broken world came flooding back.

"Father," Ariana said again, her tone changing. Mandarus knew what was coming next.

"You cannot," he said, "you simply cannot."

"But how will I avoid it? He's declared it for this Seventh Day?"

Mandarus held his daughter's hand. "I will find a way," he said. "I will find a way."

◆◆◆ ⌇ ◆◆◆

The following day, Mandarus sought an urgent audience with Nahron at the palace. Nahron agreed, unsure what to expect. Pleas for Ariana? Outrage at his revelation? He was quite pleased with how he'd tied up several loose ends by making the serpent the missing Son. Polls suggested the masses were happy about it too. The old Dark Kingdom were delighted to keep the serpent but keen to drop the human sacrifices part. The result of Be'elzar's 'misinterpretations.'

Mandarus came in hurriedly; he didn't look right. Nahron sighed; what an inconvenience it would be if he had to get rid of him.

"My lord," blurted Mandarus, "I am very unhappy."

"Really?" Nahron was almost getting used to this new direct approach. "Is it something I've done?"

"Yes," said Mandarus, with shocking boldness. "You have given my daughter the greatest honour in all the empire, your hand in marriage. Yet, you have not asked me to officiate at the ceremony."

For a moment, Nahron was completely lost for words.

"Forgive me, my dear friend," he crooned, "you were unwell."

"Ah yes," sighed Mandarus as though remembering a time he'd broken a window as a child. "The fasting and then not drinking made me delirious. I recall saying things to your majesty that I profoundly regret." Mandarus did regret saying them to Nahron. But he hadn't changed his mind one bit about their truth.

"Well," said Nahron, gauging the public relations impact. "Of course you can officiate at the ceremony." He was sure that the sight of the great high priest Mandarus happily marrying off his daughter could only be a good thing.

"I look forward to receiving your brief. I hope it won't be too involved?" he looked disparagingly at Mandarus. The last thing Nahron wanted was a long and tedious wedding ceremony.

"Not at all," replied Mandarus, acting as though in agreement, "although I ask only one small favour. The wedding for the Holy Sister of the Temple of the Serpent, can that be put off for another day? It's just that I want to make the day special for Ariana."

"Of course," said Nahron. The Holy Sister from the Temple of the Serpent in Be'elzar's old realm had never existed. It was merely an additional pretext for marrying Ariana. Any hapless girl with a northern accent would be recruited for the role. Then sent off to a life of solitude, except for occasional pointless public appearances.

"Thank you, thank you," blurted Mandarus, "I promise a short and very special service. Holy prayers in the inner sanctum. Then a public blessing and vows in the inner courtyard shortly after."

"Excellent," smiled Nahron, "excellent."

Mandarus bowed and left.

How convenient, thought Nahron, how very convenient.

◆◆◆ ʁ ◆◆◆

Ariana didn't sleep the night before the wedding. She'd hardly slept the three nights before that, either. The very idea of sleep was absurd. She had only one consuming thought. How to escape the temple and reach the Land of the Ancients? The last remaining place in the world free from Nahron's control. Shem had promised to take her there. But she was starting to wonder if these were nothing more than empty words from a mad day of cheering crowds and mixed-up emotions. She remembered from her youth that men often made lots of promises when they first met a beautiful woman. And even if Shem had meant what he'd said, how on earth was he going to fulfil it? She had less than twelve hours to flee. It all seemed so hopeless.

◆◆◆ ʁ ◆◆◆

The Seventh Day arrived and not soon enough for Nahron. He

landed on the Great Temple outer platform in his Iridium transport a whole hour early. Eager for nothing except his own gratification. The service was to be at midday. Security was very tight. It was to be a private service. Not all the citizens of the empire were pleased to hear that their Chaste Maid was being married off. Nahron wasn't really that bothered about the event for its PR value, which was questionable. It was all about him finally getting the woman he'd always wanted – Ariana. With Prebius missing since the parade, all the arrangements were left to Mandarus.

The Royal Guard Corps handled the security for what was, in effect, an imperial visit to the Great Temple. Their secondary focus was simple: to ensure that Ariana didn't leave the building.

Mandarus wandered aimlessly around his quarters in despair. The wedding ceremony was now under an hour away. Against all his hopes and prayers, Nahron had arrived, and not only that but early too. Mandarus had a vague plan, but it was incomplete. He went over it a hundred times, but every outcome was the same. Ariana still married Nahron, and Nahron had him executed shortly after.

After greeting Nahron with great forced enthusiasm, Mandarus returned to his quarters. He walked woodenly into his ceremonial dressing room and began to robe up. The door chime rang. Who now? Ariana again?

Mandarus had left his only daughter moments earlier, weeping in terror in her quarters. Her despairing attendants were there trying to save their lives. Applying waterproof make-up to her face to cover her crying. They lathered on the thickest layers of foundation and eye liner ever seen on a woman. Profusely dousing her eyes with whitening drops and throwing on her the heaviest veil one could imagine for a bride. Some of them had already called their relatives to say their last goodbyes. Mandarus despairingly pressed the accept button on the nearest wall; his quarter's main door opened. A female voice greeted him.

"The robes you requested from the tailors of Pishon have arrived; thank the gods, just in time." The voice was level, calm, and completely unfamiliar.

Mandarus searched his mind through the haze of the last few days. He'd neither requested nor needed any robes for the ceremony from the Pishon Valley. He turned, curious to see who'd brought these things he'd not asked for.

A strikingly beautiful, dark-haired woman stood before him. She held several brightly coloured priestly garments. The robes immediately caught his attention. Their quality was exceptional. He knew they must have been made long before the preceding two days.

Two Royal Guards stood accompanying the woman, both looking unsure of the situation. The temple was not their usual territory; they knew little of its ways. Their wedding security brief was simple. Keep the emperor safe and don't let Ariana out of the temple. The trouble was with the unspoken parts. Things like not hindering the ceremony, which meant guessing their way through quite a lot. Mandarus' mind raced; something in his heart urged him to accept the robes.

"Aha, at last," he said, "I thought they wouldn't be here in time and I would have to use something plainer. Please, come in."

"Thank you," the woman nodded to the Royal Guards. Mandarus waved them away with his hand, quickly pressing the door close button.

The woman stepped forward, handing him a bundle of robes.

"Put them on," she said. It was not a request.

"Who?..."

"We don't have time," she interrupted firmly, "do everything I say and your daughter will be free."

"Free! What? What shall I do?" Mandarus asked desperately.

"We will take care of everything," the woman answered, "Go into the sanctum with Nahron. Pray your prayers and then come out. Five minutes is enough. You don't need to stay in there hoping the world will end sooner than Noah, son of Lamech, has predicted."

"Noah!? But..." Mandarus didn't know where to start. The woman ignored him and carried on talking.

"There will be an additional guest at the wedding, a cleric. Do you understand?" Her tone was very firm.

"How will I..." Mandarus stuttered before she interrupted him again.

"I am now master of ceremonies; act like it's so. I will introduce the guests to you. The sooner you come out before the start of the service, the better. Don't try to communicate with your daughter. The usual lip-readers will be present among the guards.

"I also have a new wedding outfit for Ariana. You will be extremely shocked when you see it. You have to trust me on this. Her clothing is an essential part of our plan. Make sure you do not appear surprised when you see her."

The woman finished dressing in a very ornate, priestly styled garment and turned to face him. Her eyes met his; they were a strong deep dark brown, full of fire and energy. They reminded Mandarus of the eyes of the man in his vision. He was taken aback. The woman faintly smiled and quickly walked out.

Mandarus was bewildered, full of wild hope but also exceedingly afraid. Who – how could anyone pull off any kind of stunt in the presence of so many Royal Guards? Surely it was certain suicide! He hurriedly finished putting on the new robes. They were of a finer quality than anything made in the empire.

"The Land of the Ancients," he whispered softly to himself. Mandarus found hope.

◆◆◆ 🏳 ◆◆◆

Nadina walked calmly to the Great Temple's inner courtyard. The paltry few guests Nahron had invited would arrive in ten minutes. Not being recognised was a major concern. There were no scanners inside the temple grounds. However, one of the Royal Guards Corps might recognise her from her academy days. They would have to be from the secret training wing and very unlikely to have been assigned to the wedding. Mavron could have been one exception, but he was safe at Noah's. The wild card was Sindain. She knew he would be there; she needed him to arrive soon, but not yet. Nadina knew that he would arrive at the very last moment; he always did.

Craspus, the city governor, bumbled into the courtyard, overweight and sweating. He was an enigma; his stay in power had outlasted all of Salfar's reign and continued from the start of Nahron's until now. He was an icon. Yet, he had done nothing noteworthy in his entire career – which was the reason why he'd lasted so long.

Nahron had notified the Royal Guard commander of his invited guests. Three more cronies arrived and, except for Sindain, no more were expected. Nadina solemnly welcomed them all. The Royal Guards assumed she was one of Mandarus' temple attendants. The attendants thought she was part of Nahron's security entourage with a ceremonial role. Delivering Mandarus' priestly garments had been her passport to the temple.

Another guest arrived who was not on Nahron's list. The lady of ceremonies welcomed him as though it were a foregone conclusion that he would be there. Cleric Japhene, who was also carrying some weird oversized musical instrument. Nadina walked him through to the other waiting guests.

"Cleric Japhene, he isn't on any citizen list from Nahron's Gate?" the Royal Guard commander politely questioned the lady of ceremonies.

"Of course not," Nadina replied icily. "He lives on the eastern side of Nahron's Gate. He will be playing the marriage anthem."

"Ah," the commander backed off. He knew those in the Land of the Ancients weren't on any Imperial citizen list. Furthermore, he hadn't the faintest idea what she was talking about with regard to the music and wasn't going to ask.

Sindain arrived. Nadina slipped out of sight, occupying herself folding some robes she'd laid in odd places. No one had a clue what she was doing and weren't interested in finding out.

Nahron talked idly with his guests. Cleric Japhene had bowed to him from a polite distance and stood respectfully to one side. Nahron was informed a cleric from the Land of the Ancients was present; he was surprised but pleased. Mandarus really was making an effort.

Sindain fidgeted impatiently. All the guests knew that the safest thing to do was to completely avoid him. That was except for Cleric Japhene. Apparently, he didn't know who Sindain was, so he politely introduced himself. The cleric stepped forward to meet Sindain. Taking a very deep breath, he bit into the small compressed gaseous capsule inside his mouth. Then he exhaled with a fixed smile, straight into Sindain's face. Sindain involuntarily drew his breath in – a nervous reaction to the gas. He tried to step back but immediately felt light headed. The cleric warmly shook his hand, squeezing it firmly. Some-thing pierced his hand from underneath the ring of the cleric's middle finger. He realised in an instant what was going on, but the gas left him momentarily unable to speak. His whole arm clenched in excruciating pain as the serum ran straight to his nervous system. He looked like he wanted to say something but collapsed.

Cleric Japhene was shocked. As all turned to see what had happened, he looked up frantically for help. He gently lowered Sindain to the ground. Holding the back of his head and piercing his neck with a syringe from another ring. Sindain slipped deeper into unconsciousness.

"He's collapsed," gasped the cleric. Sindain's vital signs were checked; he appeared to be fine. Perhaps he was exhausted; maybe it was a mild stroke; no one knew. He was sent to the emperor's Iridium transport on the outer platform to be thoroughly checked in its tiny medical bay. Nahron was deeply concerned, not for Sindain but for what he would do without him. The accompanying doctor advised Nahron that it was probably just exhaustion. It wasn't the first time he'd collapsed recently.

Nahron overruled him and had Sindain sent off to the palace clinic. "Don't release him without my express permission," he ordered.

The lady of ceremonies, whose name no one knew, slipped back into the inner courtyard entrance.

"Only one more guest on the list," she informed the guards stationed there, "he must be late."

"Yes, ma'am," they replied, clueless.

Mandarus appeared from the direction of his quarters; he looked nervous. Ariana appeared at the same time from hers. Beautifully made up but shockingly seductively dressed. Even Nahron was uncomfortable with her appearance. Mandarus really was making a big effort but perhaps had overdone it a bit. Every Royal Guard stared at her.

Nahron looked at all of Ariana's form, which wasn't difficult to see in the euphemism of a wedding dress she was wearing. His eyes met hers through her veil; all he saw in them was fear and despair. He could think of nothing else he would rather see. He hoped Mandarus would indeed keep the service short.

"Let us begin," Mandarus said, his voice quivering. He clumsily read an introduction to the wedding, praised Nahron, then recited a prayer. Everyone bowed their heads. He finished quickly. Most guests, unsure whether to say amen or remain silent, half-grunted. Cleric Japhene boldly amen-ed as though he knew exactly what was going on.

Mandarus welcomed all, made vague statements about the union's blessings, and then invited Nahron to the inner sanctum.

Ariana stood waiting in petrified isolation. She had been told to stand by the steps to the great stone Altar of Acceptance. She wondered if she preferred being sacrificed on it to marrying Nahron. When delivering her new wedding outfit earlier, Nadina couldn't tell her that what she thought was the worst day of her life might turn just turn out to be the best.

Mandarus and Nahron went inside the inner sanctum; the stone doors closed behind them. No sound from outside could enter the gloomy world of the Empire of the Sons' idols.

Japheth began fiddling with his musical instrument, preparing to play it. The Royal Guards relaxed a little; their emperor was safe inside the inner sanctum. They all stared at Ariana, who was dressed barely any differently from a backstreet stripper.

Nadina discreetly pressed the signal button on her communicator.

An Imperial transport landed on the outer platform. The door opened. None other than Shem, Hero of the Empire, stepped out in full ceremonial white and gold uniform. The Royal Guards nearby were surprised. Saluting them, he marched briskly past them to the inner courtyard entrance. Nadina rushed out to greet him. Feigning great annoyance, she motioned for the nearby guards to follow her.

"You're late, Hero of the Empire," she scathed, "the emperor has already entered holy prayers."

Shem looked duly shocked. "Which way do I go?" he apologised. Nadina motioned to the guards to show him. "Quickly," she ordered, "before the emperor comes out." They hurriedly ushered Shem into the courtyard without question.

"Let's get that out of the way before the Iridium returns," she told the nearby Royal Guard commander, who was surprised to see Shem arrive. Nadina calmly walked off to move the transport. It rose slowly from the platform, went out of sight behind a wall, then disappeared.

◆◆◆ ⚑ ◆◆◆

Shem was hurriedly escorted into the courtyard. He glanced around, his expression full of remorse for being late. He nodded politely at the other guests, including Cleric Japhene, who nodded back.

Cleric Japhene, aka Japheth, walked ceremoniously forward. He began playing some unbearable mournful tune on his musical instrument. The guests and temple attendants didn't know what to do except solemnly stare. The temple attendants assumed the racket was Nahron's choosing. He was famous for having no musical taste whatsoever. Nahron's guests assumed it was all Mandarus' choosing and represented something spiritual. The Royal Guards were doing their best not to burst out laughing.

◆◆◆   ⚑   ◆◆◆

The commander of the Royal Guards in charge of the wedding's security was an alert man. Unlike his men, he wasn't imagining removing the few remaining clothes that Ariana was wearing, or laughing at the cleric's abysmal music. He was doing his job.

His job was to consider unlikely things. So he did: If Shem and Cleric Japhene were both from the Land of the Ancients and nodded in acknowledgement of one another. Why didn't they stand together? Then there was Sindain's collapse when he met Cleric Japhene. On its own, also insignificant. An unfortunate coincidence, overwork, lack of sleep, something like that. He explored further. Guests not on a pre-arranged list. Mandarus had invited them, or had he? Again, on its own, not surprising. The wedding had been all very last minute. Two separate parties rushing arrangements and neither side really knowing what the other was doing. He explored a little more. An Imperial Vastar landing, of all places, on the Temple outer platform. Something about the transport hadn't seemed quite right. And Shem, a famous Ancient at the wedding? Had he and Ariana not been seen famously holding hands at the Victory Parade? Where was the lady of ceremonies? Why had she decided to move Shem's transport instead of asking any nearby guard to do it? Moreover, how did she know how to operate a Vastar and why hadn't she returned? He pondered the transport further. Why was Shem flying an Imperial transport without an attendant pilot? Was it a coincidence he arrived only after Sindain fainted and Nahron went into the inner sanctum? His thoughts were in no particular order. He carried on. Why was Nahron in a place where only priests ever went, conveniently cut off from everything outside? Most of all, why was Cleric Japhene playing such awful music? The commander could hardly hear himself think above the racket. Each item on the list was insignificant on its

177

own. But when combined together, he realised he might be facing an unthinkable situation.

His orders were to keep Ariana from leaving the temple. Mandarus was all for the wedding, or was he? The commander thought of his own daughter. Were there any circumstances in which he would like her to marry Nahron? Definitely not! He rearranged his thoughts and came up with an impressive scenario.

Mandarus did not want his daughter to marry Nahron, so he'd arranged to have her kidnapped. The protagonists were the Cleric Japhene, Shem, and the unnamed lady of ceremonies – who none of the temple staff actually appeared to know. The getaway vehicle was the Vastar, which the lady of ceremonies had recently flown off in. Doubtless hovering nearby with its active camouflage engaged. This particular point really irked him. He'd written a special report about this very possibility. Active camouflage was brand new technology. The Dark Kingdom had never developed it. It was only available on Tactan's, which Royal Guards exclusively flew, and Vastar's, which again only Royal Guards and a handful of carefully vetted civilian pilots could fly. The result was that no Imperial protocols existed on how to counter it. He'd written about this vulnerability, but his bosses had ignored him. Next, Cleric Japhene's instrument was to drown out the hidden transport's humming. Mandarus had taken Nahron into the inner sanctum so he wouldn't see Shem, who arrived only after they entered it. Oh, and he almost forgot. Cleric Japhene had somehow knocked out Sindain to prevent him from seeing Shem too. Then there was Ariana and her scanty clothing. The perfect distraction for his men.

The commander was quite pleased with himself. He contemplated taking up writing thrillers. His eyes wandered across the courtyard. Ariana's head was bowed. She looked up and saw Shem arriving and gasped. Her face revealed a look of joy and the one thing that the commander did not want to see – hope. The commander realised his scenario might not be just a potential novel after all. At that moment, the cleric pulled a lever on his musical instrument. A large canister thunked out from its main horn. It flew in the direction of the highest concentration of guards, who didn't see it coming. Yellow smoke exploded in every direction. Shem and the cleric crouched down on one knee, pulling tiny masks down from under their caps over their faces. Simultaneously, the two small piles of bulky robes that the lady of ceremonies had left nearby exploded. Small canisters blew out in all directions, spewing yellow smoke. The smoke immediately obscured the guests and nearest guards. The commander raised his weapon to shoot, but acquiring a target was impossible. The risk of accidentally shooting Ariana or Craspus was out of the question.

"Gas," he yelled as if any of his men hadn't already realised.

The commander took a deep breath before the smoke reached him. He sprinted into the melee to try and rescue the obvious target. He glimpsed Shem running towards Ariana who, like all guests and guards, was doubled over coughing. Shem crashed into her, flinging her over his shoulder as he ran up the steps of the stone altar. The commander pursued him, wondering what Shem intended to do when he got to the top. He was also concerned that with all the smoke he couldn't see where the cleric had gone.

Shem jumped onto the altar table, leaping straight across the middle of it. A doorway appeared in mid-air opposite him, out of the pursuing commander's line of sight. Shem dived into it. The commander kept desperately running. He saw the outline of the missing transport that the lady of ceremonies had absconded in.

Cleric Japhene appeared through the smoke behind him. Grabbing the commander's collar, he threw him backwards to the ground. The helpless commander watched the cleric jump over him and dive into the transport. It rose, turned, and disappeared from plain sight.

Ariana, Chaste Maid devoted to the Son and bride of Nahron, the half divine emperor, was gone. The whole operation took less than fourteen seconds.

◆◆◆ ⌐ ◆◆◆

The few Royal Guards who glimpsed the transport through their coughing and smoke fired blindly at it. The transport momentarily reappeared higher up. It fired sixteen large smoke canisters in all directions. Some exploded mid-air, further obscuring it from sight. Some bounced around on the ground, spewing out yet more thick yellow smoke. By this point, the acrid yellow smoke had completely enveloped the entire inner courtyard. No one could see a thing.

The commander, thrown backwards off the altar steps by Japheth, had landed roughly but unhurt. Coughing violently, he stumbled back across the courtyard and out of the smoke. He issued an alert for a Mark IV Vastar Executive transport with its active camouflage engaged to be stopped at any cost, but not destroyed. All available resources were to be deployed. This was a Level 8 security alert. He took the bold step of issuing a Code 47 for the entire capital. He knew that if he didn't recapture Ariana, then he and many of his relatives near and far were all as good as dead.

Chapter 22

Hidden

*V*ery few in the empire understand how the new active camouflage systems work. Although ingenious, the technology is really very straightforward. Exactly the same as a chameleon.

Miniature cameras are embedded all over a transport's main body. They send images to a super processor. The processor organises them, feeding them to a mosaic of tiny screens. These screens cover the entirety of the transport. They display what is on the opposite side of the transport. It works from any angle. In this manner, a transport becomes invisible to the naked eye. Like a chameleon, it is indistinguishable from what is around it.

The system even works on the special glass of the cabin windows. These become opaque from the outside when the system is activated. Yet, they remain transparent from the inside.

The genius of the system is not in the screens or the cameras. It is in the programming that processes the images from all the cameras. Then assembles them as one cohesive image, matching perspective, brightness, colour saturation, and so forth.

The system does, however, have its limitations. A transport's outline is faintly visible while moving. However, when stationary, either in the air or on the ground, it is almost impossible to see.

◆◆◆　▷　◆◆◆

Ariana was still heavily coughing but beginning to grasp what had just happened. She was desperately wondering what on earth would become of her father. Shem had taken over flying the transport and Nadina simply didn't have time to talk. Japheth held Ariana firmly, spraying a colourless, sweet smelling gas into her mouth. She heaved as though to cough again but then relaxed.

They were flying just above rooftops and in between tower blocks. Aggressively changing course. Japheth took the navigator's seat, eyeing various screens and operating the transport's scanners.

"Looks like they're launching everything they've got," he warned.

"Plan A?" asked Nadina.

"Why not?" said Shem. "Let's visit the palace."

The transport shot towards the Great Palace. The plan was to access the palace grounds through a rear service gate. Hovering just above and merging with any ground transport accessing the site. They couldn't fly high across the palace's perimeter. Its security grid would alert everyone for miles around to their intrusion. But if they could enter undetected at ground level, once inside it was very unlikely that anyone would find them, or even think to look for them there. The palace was the last place on earth anyone would expect them to hide.

They hovered and waited. Soon, a noisy trundling dumpster approached the nearby palace service gate. The driver was blissfully unaware of their presence. Shem manoeuvred them right up behind it.

Nadina transmitted the palace's rear service gate access codes, unchanged since her years at the academy. They swung silently open. The dumpster driver, mildly surprised that he was let through without identification, carried on.

The last thing the Imperial Palace control centre staff were paying attention to was dumpsters entering their back gates. They were fixated with yelling on their secure channels about Ariana's kidnap, and the search for a fleeing Vastar with its active camouflage engaged.

Once inside, Shem set the transport down against a plain grey wall. Japheth altered the image projectors.

"There you go," he laughed, still visibly tense, "now we're a garbage truck." The tiny screens on their transport projected an image of an old decrepit garbage truck. The screens that covered the parts of their transport that didn't fit inside the perimeter of the image displayed a dull grey. Exactly matching the wall behind it. Nadina powered down the resonators and switched to batteries. They sat and waited.

Ariana stared at Shem. "What about my father?" she asked.

Shem explained that Mandarus was likely stepping out from the inner sanctum as they spoke. But was hopefully not going to be held responsible for the rescue.

◆◆◆ ☞ ◆◆◆

Shem was right. Mandarus reluctantly finished his prayers. He'd hardly any idea what he had said, and Nahron certainly hadn't been listening to a word.

"This way, your majesty," he mechanically instructed the emperor. Disappointed that some divine fireball had not consumed them in the inner sanctum. Mandarus slowly swung the heavy stone doors of the inner sanctum open. He began coughing violently.

Nahron looked out in horror. He immediately had the presence of mind to retreat back inside to avoid the smoke. Grabbing an ornamental cloth, he held it over his nose and mouth and made his way outside. Guests and temple attendants were on their knees coughing. Royal Guards were running around. Some coughing, some with masks on and shouting instructions to each other.

The commander came running towards Nahron, holding out an emergency mask. He took it and fastened it to his face.

"What's going on?" Nahron demanded. The look of terror and hesitation in the commander's expression told him everything.

"They've got Ariana, your majesty," he said. "But we're getting her back," he added desperately.

Nahron looked icily at him and then at the scene around him.

The commander blindly hoping the blame might fall on Sindain and not him continued. "Word is that Sindain remembers the cleric sticking something into his hand."

Nahron turned to look at Mandarus. It was highly unlikely he'd planned or been capable of planning any of it.

"And who are 'they?' " Nahron asked the petrified commander.

"Shem took her, my lord," he said, "it was Shem."

The words hit Nahron like a sledge hammer, the humiliation, the embarrassment, the rage. "Continue with your duties," he instructed the commander. His voice devoid of all emotion. "Bring her to me, dead or alive."

"Yes, my lord," the commander quickly departed. Thankful that at least he'd been spared summary execution. As heartless as Nahron was, he was no fool. He knew he needed experienced commanders alive in a time of crisis, not dead. He would have all the relevant parties executed later. The commander knew this and was already planning his faked death and disappearance. Ideally to the remote Pazgon mountains.

Nahron boarded his returned Iridium transport and went to see Sindain.

Sindain was enraged at being kept in the hospital. The doctor was between a rock and a hard place. Letting him out was disobeying the emperor's direct orders. Keeping him was holding the empire's most feared intelligence chief against his will.

The doctor was palpably relieved to see Nahron. He immediately blurted out that he'd kept Sindain in the hospital exactly as ordered. Nahron waved him away. Sindain was glaring at Nahron. Nahron was his emperor, but this was no time for pleasantries.

"They have openly mocked us, my lord," he seethed.

"Indeed," Nahron was dispassionate as he uttered the words Sindain had been hoping to hear for a long time.

"The time has come, and now we have a perfect pretext," Nahron paused. "I am almost thankful," he chuckled.

Sindain smiled a very wicked smile.

◆◆◆　 ⴑ 　◆◆◆

The entire military of the great City of Light was on full alert. Every soldier and all security personnel there were engaged to find Shem's transport. The trouble was they couldn't find it. All the latest Mark IV Vastar transports in the city were accounted for. Indeed, all those in the whole empire had been quickly located and accounted for. There were only fifty of the latest model ever built. Twenty-two of them had never left the factory; the rest were used by provincial governors. Talmeon's was known to have been destroyed, so no one could figure out where Shem had got his. Nevertheless, it had been seen at the wedding, so they kept looking.

Bezek, Talmeon's junior assistant, like all surveillance personnel, was assigned to find the transport. It was pretty certain that it had not yet left the city. This was because nothing had left the city since the commander at the wedding had issued a Level 8 security alert and Code 47 lockdown. The city's perimeter detection system was as near perfect as it was possible to get. A legacy of years of uncertainty in the long wars against the old Dark Kingdom. Everyone knew Shem was somewhere within the city limits, but where? The City of Light was a very big place indeed. It comprised more than 12 million inhabitants and a few million transports. Even so, the city scanners had not detected the resonance signature of a Vastar Mark IV transport. It was a complete

184

mystery.

Security analysts and Sindain were crowded into the dimly lit city operations centre. They were all looking intently at the vast array of tracking screens. They couldn't find the resonator wake from Shem's transport exiting the temple grounds. It seemed his yellow smoke did far more than make people cough. Something in it masked the fumes that came from the converters that fed the resonators in all transports. It was these light fumes that made transports uniquely traceable, at least for a short period of time. Shem had clearly turned straight into the city's busiest skyway, but no one had a clue when or where he'd left it. Bezek was studying data with several other assistants. Suddenly, he leapt out of his seat with such a shout that some guards dived to the floor, drawing their weapons.

"I've got it!" he exclaimed.

"Where, where!" demanded a nearby supervisor.

"No!" he cried, "I've no idea where they are yet, but I know what they're doing!" Sindain walked calmly over.

"What is it that they are doing that we can't find them?" His voice carried an unusual mixture of curiosity and threat.

Bezek composed himself, pausing briefly for effect. "They are double mimicking," he declared, enjoying the hushed awe that settled on the room.

"And what exactly is double mimicking?" Sindain asked, unashamed that he had no idea.

"Well, they don't really have a Vastar Mark IV Executive Trans-port," he announced proudly. "That's why they are all accounted for. Because they are all accounted for. They have something else using our camouflage technology to look like a Vastar. Even to create the faint outline of a Vastar. But it's not really a Vastar Mark IV at all."

Sindain was impressed but also disappointed. "So, they could be flying anything with active camouflage?" he said dryly. "But it's not a genuine Mark IV Vastar?"

"Erm, yes, my lord," Bezek replied, remembering to whom he was speaking. He adopted a more conciliatory tone.

Sindain looked at him. "Find that modified transport. You will be honoured by the emperor himself. I patiently await your report."

Bezek began to wonder if stratospheric career jumps were the best way to get the most out of life after all. Another analyst joined the

185

discussion.

"They must have had access to a lot of technical resources to modify a transport that well. The kind of resources only a government would have access to?"

"The Dark Kingdom," Sindain complained. As if Be'elzar's death wasn't torturous enough. "They must have got it from there somehow, after the collapse. All those weapons and technology lying around." He continued, "Talmeon's Vastar was detected, tracked and shot down by them. They understood how our active camouflage works." This was something of a revelation to many present.

"The Dark Kingdom could track Vastar Mark IVs with their active camouflage on?" asked a specialist, perturbed.

"Yes," replied Sindain flatly, "they were managing to do a lot of things that's why we had to send..." his voice trailed off. He was going to mention Shem but decided not to. Everyone remained silent.

Bezek broke the silence, "Maybe they're flying something like a modified Razbar?"

"Ahh!" the Royal Guard commander from the wedding sounded as though someone had stood on his toes with heavy boots.

"When Shem first stepped out of the Vastar, well, the transport," he corrected himself, "I thought I saw a momentary distortion of double tail fins at the back of the craft and it reminded me of a Tactan but because they are so similar in every way except for their tail fins I dismissed it as my imagination and, and..." his words trailed off as he wondered if he'd just inadvertently admitted responsibility for the entire kidnap.

"And you didn't expect the hero of the empire to arrive at the emperor's wedding in a Tactan? With its active camouflage modified to disguise it as a Vastar to kidnap the Chaste Maid," Sindain helpfully explained.

The commander's face had a look of deep gratitude. Sindain continued, "No more than I expected a cleric from the Land of Ancients to knock me out with a poisoned ring."

"Fellow citizens," Sindain moved to stand in the middle of the room, the dimmed light casting eerie shadows across his face. He spoke gravely, "We have a very cunning enemy, more dangerous than the Dark Kingdom ever was. We have to hunt them down and destroy them. All of them." He paused and then said again, "All of them."

Everyone in the room wondered exactly what he meant by that. Were they going to try and do what the 12th Legion had failed to do? A few gulped. It was unthinkable.

♦♦♦   ⚑   ♦♦♦

"So, we're disguised as a garbage truck?" asked Ariana in disbelief.

"Yes," replied Nadina, "no one is looking for a garbage truck parked in the waste disposal area of the Great Palace. They're looking for a sleek Vastar Mark IV transport attempting to flee the city."

Ariana looked around inside, "This is very different to the Vastar I went to the parade in. It doesn't look much like a standard VIP transport at all; the panels, the décor, the shape, it's all so utilitarian." There was a hint of disdain in her voice.

"Absolutely," Shem joined in, "it's a Tactan."

Ariana's eyes widened, "A Tactan!?" She knew what a Tactan was. The empire's fastest, best protected, and most advanced military transport. A command and control vehicle. Only senior Royal Guards and top level military commanders had access to them. "How on earth did you get your hands on it?"

"Someone owed me a favour," Shem grinned, his piercing blue eyes meeting hers. Ariana was falling more in love with him every time he spoke, laughed, or did almost anything. Nadina found it slightly nauseating but smiled to herself. She thought about how she sometimes was around Japheth.

"Well, we still have to get out of here and back home," Shem spoke out loud to himself, baiting Ariana's ignorance.

"How do we do that?" Ariana wasn't a pilot, but she knew the distance from the City of Light to the Land of the Ancients was a very long way. If everyone between here and there was looking for them, it would be extremely hard to get there undetected.

"We're going the long way," quipped Japheth.

"The long way?" Ariana looked bemused.

"Yes," winked Shem, "we don't go east; we go west."

Ariana frowned. She was getting used to his perpetual mild teasing.

"You're going to fly all the way around the whole world!"

"Of course," chimed in Japheth, "in one of these, it will only take about five or six days."

"Five or six days of continuous flying! What will we eat?" Ariana looked dismayed.

"Nadina brought some sandwiches, didn't you?" enquired Shem.

"Actually, I forgot them," she apologised solemnly.

Ariana noticed they were all developing bigger and bigger grins. Japheth finally spoke up.

"Truthfully," he said, unable to stop grinning, "we don't need to fly all the way around the world. Just to the western sea, then south, and circle right round to the eastern shore and back into our lands."

"But transports don't work in the Land of the Ancients," protested Ariana, wondering if they were still joking.

"So I've heard," said Shem. "Actually, they do. But, only as long as their batteries last. From what I've heard, the batteries on these new Tactans would get more than halfway across our lands." This little baby will take us right home; in fact, its already been there. All we have to do is pick up enough altitude while we are out at sea before we enter the flux over our lands."

"So the empire can now fly across your lands with impunity?" Ariana badly needed to be reassured that she wouldn't soon be recaptured in some violent raid.

"Not really," Shem reassured her. "The troop carriers like the Vandeon can barely go twenty miles; they're way too heavy to fly far on batteries. Ordinary Vastars could possibly get a third of the way, advanced Mark IVs almost the whole way. The main thing that prevents any incursion is the memory of the 12th Legion. Almost no Imperial pilot will fly into the Land of the Ancients even on a peaceful mission. Most of them will create a malfunction near the border and claim it was something outside of their control. And suppose they did fly in. They still can't get home. Their batteries wouldn't last long enough for the round trip.

"They would need to set down and recharge for several hours, and where could they do that? The empire doesn't have any charging stations in our lands. In fact, they don't have anything. The few thousands of people who still live there only use combustible fuel powered craft. Why mess about with converters and charging? Only a handful of tourist spots have recharging facilities."

"I have a racer that runs on combustible fuel," chipped in Japheth. His smile rapidly faded when he saw Nadina's pained expression. The memory of their first trip was too real, with Ariana and Shem sitting next to each other in a transport for the first time.

"Great," said Ariana, now suitably convinced, "so what are we waiting for?"

"Weeds," said Nadina. "Lots of them. But not until this time tomorrow. So sit tight and don't even think about a walk in the gardens."

Sitting tight was certainly the best way of describing spending a night in a Tactan. Unlike Vastars, they have no reclining seats, no cabin with a bed, no mini ensuite, and no kitchenette. But they do have lots of displays which, after looking at them for several hours, become very boring. None of them slept much. Shem kept a careful eye on the scanners to make sure no one stumbled upon them. They ran the essential systems on batteries in passive mode so as not to make any noise or emit any fumes.

Japheth remained in the pilot's seat, staying as alert as possible in case they needed to make a quick getaway. Ariana questioned Nadina at great length about the Land of the Ancients. Fortunately, Tactans, designed for extended missions, do have a small toilet in the back.

The next day, as Nadina predicted, the weekly waste from the palace gardens was collected. Three heavy loaders set off lumbering through the western gates. Heading out towards the southern parkland areas of the city beyond which were the city waste sites.

Everyone held their breath. Shem switched the camouflage mode from static to active. Then, he manoeuvred the Tactan onto the back of the last heavy loader. As they'd hoped, the city was now obsessed with the kidnapped Chaste Maid. Staff at the palace grates were about as interested in doing their job as working unpaid for three years. They didn't even bother to look up as the heavy loaders rumbled past. The gatekeepers were supposed to check for anything of value hidden in the garden waste. But not today. They were all glued to their telescreens. Each one keenly followed every pointless news update about their missing Maid.

The driver of the last heavy loader couldn't figure out why his recently serviced resonators weren't pulling so well. He wanted to hurry up and get to the waste disposal site and watch further news updates on the search.

For three hours they trundled along near deserted roads. Passing two poorly manned checkpoints at the city limits, they came to the countryside. The loaders entered the main waste disposal site. All three drivers parked up without unloading. They immediately ran into the staff building to watch the latest news. Shem, realising that straining the last ebbs from the batteries of the Tactan would make too much noise, powered up the converters. It lifted invisibly into the air and flew off towards the coast, skimming the fields and forests as it went. No one nearby noticed a thing.

"So much for their lockdown," remarked Japheth.

"Fleeing commanders need to leave their own back doors open," Shem answered.

"True," said Nadina.

They all knew the wedding rescue would leave a lot of people desperate to flee Nahron's wrath.

Faster and faster the Tactan went until it shot over the coast and out to sea. As the land receded rapidly behind them, Shem avidly checked the scanners; nothing. There were no Imperial craft on their tail. Doubtless, they were all hovering like flies along the eastern routes to the Land of the Ancients.

They'd made it. They had escaped.

"Is it safe to fly so far out to sea?" Ariana anxiously stared at the endless expanse of water beneath them.

"Why not?" laughed Shem, the stress of the last few days finally wearing off.

Ariana took a good look at him. Here he was, Shem, Hero of the Empire – the man from that memorable parade who'd said he would come back for her, and he did. She found herself smiling uncontrollably at him. He had the same problem with her.

Below them, the clear emerald blue hues of the waves on the sea sparkled in the sunlight as they raced along. For the first time in her whole life, Ariana Elam Asshur felt completely free.

Chapter 23

Warmth

*M*avron knew something was up. The servants were all frantically chattering among themselves. News had come to him a few days earlier that the Dark Kingdom had fallen. Thanks mainly to Shem and some brilliant secret mission. He'd been looking forward to meeting him, but then Shem was unexpectedly held up. Nadina then disappeared, and soon after so did Japheth. Mavron had started to really enjoy Nadina's company; they had a lot in common. He heard there had been a Victory Parade. That wasn't surprising. Nahron cashed in on every self–aggrandising opportunity that came his way. And if none did, he simply made them up. What Mavron really wanted to know more about was the most recent rumour, that Ariana had been kidnapped from the Great Temple at her very own wedding ceremony! At first, he assumed it must have been Nahron. Sometimes he did things like that to twist public opinion, but the more he thought about it, the less sense it made.

Something happened that evening which answered all his ques-tions. As Mavron sat on the terrazzo of Noah's home, discussing with Talmeon the various religious versions of the past. A Tactan, running on its last batteries, landed on the impeccably manicured lawn.

"Shem, Japheth!" Emzara yelled, running out of the house undoubtedly relieved about something. Clearly, she knew exactly where they'd been. Talmeon was shocked, a Tactan – in the Land of the Ancients! He half expected Nahron to step out and order them all executed. Mavron wasn't surprised at all; he recognised the ID on the fuselage; it was the one he'd been kidnapped in. Nevertheless, that was nothing compared to what they all saw next. Out stepped Shem, Japheth, Nadina and finally, wearing the skimpiest outfit Mavron and Talmeon thought they'd ever seen, none other than Ariana, Chaste Maid devoted to the Son.

"Talmeon!" Ariana gasped, "What are you doing here?"

"What am I doing here?" Talmeon laughed.

Ariana walked briskly towards him, hugged him, then looked sol-emnly into his eyes. Shem stared worriedly at the two of them.

Japheth elbowed his younger brother. "Oh well," he said, grinning, "don't worry, we can always go out next week and rescue someone else. How many is that now, two? You know what they say, third time..."

Shem sharply elbowed Japheth before he could finish his sentence. His older brother impressively faked being severely winded.

"Thank you," Ariana said quietly to Talmeon, "thank you." No one had the slightest idea what she was talking about.

The guards were all speechless – Ariana, here in the Land of the Ancients! Did the emperor know? Evidently not. Emzara was also speechless, but for different reasons.

"Sorry, Mother," Shem spoke sheepishly. Well aware of Ariana's almost non-existent clothing underneath a spare military jacket found inside the Tactan.

"Ah yes, Shem decided it was an essential part of the mission," Japheth quipped. His younger brother just rolled his eyes.

"Guests?" Shem looked around at Talmeon and his men. "You haven't been feeding them very well, have you?" He laughed out loud at his own joke.

Mavron and his men decided that they liked this Shem. They'd all heard so much about him.

Timnah was thrilled to see Shem; without hesitation, she ran towards him and hugged him. A tear filled the corner of Shem's eye; he looked across at his mother; she nodded and smiled.

Japheth noticed Ham had been standing next to Timnah with his arm openly around her. "Hmm, finally got a decent girlfriend, eh?" Sometimes Japheth's humour was truly merciless. Emzara glared at him in static disbelief.

Ham blushed terribly, struggling for a reply. Shem was about to rescue his youngest brother when Japheth pushed his shoulder and plunged in again. "Well, at least he got her a decent set of clothes."

Shem looked at Japheth like he couldn't quite believe him sometimes. There was no pretending about anything with Japheth. His candour was always from a good heart, but something about him was changing. It was as though beneath it all he was angry and the only way he expressed it was in his biting humour. Emzara soon appeared with more suitable clothing.

Nadina was the last to step down from the transport. She looked drained but elated; they'd succeeded against impossible odds. Her eyes met Japheth's as he watched her climb down the few steps from the cabin. She quickly looked away. Japheth seemed to lose some of his sparkle and turned to talk with his father, who'd recently come out of the house.

Nadina looked around, no Adatenesis or her son. "Typical," she said to herself. She caught Mavron's eye. He was smiling at her. His face was radiant. Nadina walked calmly over to him and looked with a fake pained expression at his bandaged head.

"Hello," she spoke softly and warmly, "how's your head coming along?" She frowned, looking at the scar and swelling, now noticeably less than before.

"Much better," Mavron chuckled. "I see things more clearly now." There was something in his tone that wasn't joking. "You went on a little trip in my Tactan, I see?"

Nadina knelt on the floor beside his chair. "Yeah," she smiled, "it came in handy."

"How's that then?" Mavron wanted to hear how his master had been so completely humiliated. An hour later, Nadina was still telling Mavron about the rescue and her life story. She had him laughing constantly at her tales from the Royal Guard Academy. Elon, Zahar, and Malael were listening too. Chuckling at the familiar idiosyncrasies of being a Royal Guard.

Japheth stood nearby, busy but watching. He noticed how close Nadina seemed to Mavron; it bothered him. Where was Adatenesis? Why wasn't she here to meet her husband after the most dangerous mission of his life? True, she didn't know where he'd been, but that was because she hadn't been there for him to tell her in the first place. It irritated him that she was absent from their home yet again.

♦♦♦　↰　♦♦♦

Cavilah surveyed the scene before him. The happy family of the Ancient Noah, Royal Guards, Ariana the famous Chaste Maid, Talmeon the emperor's cousin. A girl rescued from the Dark Kingdom, oh, and himself, a spy turned tour guide. What a truly bizarre mixture.

After stuffing themselves earlier, Elon the pilot and Zahar the co-pilot had already started tucking into the evening meal. They still had plenty of weight to gain after their arduous trek.

Cavilah took it all in, his mind wandering back to his own happy times. He missed his wife and son. He wished they were here with him now. He knew they would have liked this life. He missed his men too, his friends in Nahron's Gate; they looked to him for leadership and guidance. They always called him boss. He'd never demanded it. They did it from respect. Not respect for his physical strength or how clever he'd been at keeping them safe from the empire but because he cared for them. He told them the truth and never let them down. He wondered how they were managing without him.

Out of the corner of his eye, Cavilah saw an altar at the bottom of the huge lawn, hidden away among some trees. He walked down to it, unnoticed by all except Mavron. He knelt to pray.

The sound of distant talking and laughter floated down the lawn in the cool of the day. Time drifted aimlessly. Cavilah remembered his wife. The pain was deep; he often thought he was over it, but it still surfaced from time to time. She'd left him, only to be hurt and abused, but afterwards she'd never returned. It seemed that the more he'd loved her, the more she'd turned away. For the first time in his life, Cavilah understood why. She couldn't cope with his love. It had been too much for her. All she'd known before was rough and selfish men, especially in her own family.

At first, his wife had been overwhelmed by his charm and kindness. They'd enjoyed every waking moment together, but then the fear had crept in. She'd retreated from him, secretly terrified that one day he would stop loving her. So she'd gone back to familiar ground, to shallow relationships, to being abused. Bizarrely, she was more secure being mistreated than loved. Cavilah's heart had been utterly broken. There had been thousands of things he wanted to share with her. Things he saw, things he thought, things he did, but she was out of reach. He didn't even know if she was still alive.

After a while and much to Cavilah's surprise, Mavron hobbled down beside him.

"So, you're Sindain's brother?" It was an unusual way to begin a conversation, but Mavron didn't want to go all round the houses. There was a silence as both men watched the trees around them swaying gently in the evening breeze. Cavilah said nothing in reply, so Mavron carried on.

"Thanks for saving my men."

"You're welcome," said Cavilah. They remained quiet a little while longer, Cavilah kneeling and Mavron sitting on a wooden stool taken there a few days earlier for him.

"Nahron is evil," Mavron announced sombrely.

"So was Be'elzar," Cavilah replied. These somewhat obvious revelations seemed to level things out between them.

"I was a preacher once," said Cavilah. Mavron wanted to say he was surprised, but he wasn't. Sindain's missing brother had been public enemy number one for a long time. Knowing his past was part of every Royal Guard's brief.

"I wanted to be a preacher," said Mavron. Now Cavilah was genuinely surprised.

"A preacher to a Royal Guard?" he chuckled.

"Speak for yourself," said Mavron. They both remained side by side for another ten minutes, neither speaking. A warmth was in the air. Neither of them wanted to lose it. Mavron broke the silence.

"These are good people."

"I know," said Cavilah, "they're not going to stand a chance against Nahron. We have to do something."

"Do something?" Mavron laughed, "against the whole of the empire?"

Even as he spoke, he had an idea. Only an idea, but it was something.

◆◆◆   ⮂   ◆◆◆

Talmeon and his guards had eaten and slept well. Their various minor injuries were much improved. He'd seen enough of life and almost death in the last two weeks to not care less about the fact that Ariana was at Noah's. But he knew he had to get back to the capital. He had to report to Nahron that a man called Noah had apparently heard from the Creator about a huge flood. The details of which exactly matched his disturbing dreams.

By midday, all were up and about. Talmeon had asked to see the Ark, and naturally his guards were going with him. Mavron, no longer a servant of the empire in his heart, agreed. He was content to feign obedience to Talmeon for as long as it suited him. Cavilah had never seen the Ark except in local telecasts. Timnah hadn't been yet either. Shem couldn't wait to take Ariana; the two of them were inseparable. Emzara and Noah grew tired of having to say everything several times to get their attention. A couple of visitors from Nahron's Gate had mentioned to Noah's workers that Mandarus was still alive and well in the Great Temple. This put Ariana more at ease about her father for the time being.

Even before Ariana's rescue, the tourists had stopped coming to visit the Ark except privately, which now meant very few indeed. Noah could only speculate. The New Eden Council must have warned off the tour operators. It made little difference now. After the wedding débâcle, no one from the empire dared to even mention the Ark except in derision, let alone visit it.

Several more of Noah's workers had slipped away from the building site upon being paid the previous week. Now Noah needed all his sons to help him complete the work.

An hour later, they were all on their way to the Ark in what had been an abandoned, broken-down tourist transport. Shem had come across it a few months earlier and easily repaired it. It had been specifically built for the long journey from Nahron's Gate to the Ark. The batteries in such transports took a long time to charge, usually a whole day. However, once they were full, they could travel many miles. On this occasion only a few miles with fifteen passengers and their picnics on board.

The journey took just over an hour; everyone was on board except Nadina, who'd finally gone home. Noah and Emzara noticed that she had been acting very strangely. She kept mentioning she was going home, but never actually did until right before the transport left for the Ark. Even Japheth's wife, Adatenesis, had finally appeared with her son, Vindad. She agreed to come along, although she'd been several times before. The transport's atmosphere felt like a seaside holiday. Talmeon wondered why he'd spent his life on serious pursuits when he could have had this much fun every day. The guards were happily singing thanks to Mavron's extensive repertoire of ancient marching songs.

As they trundled along, Timnah looked around. So this is the Land of the Ancients, she thought. Heavily wooded and sparsely populated. The few dwellings they passed looked abandoned. Timnah peered towards the rim of some hills they were approaching. As they ascended, a huge structure began to appear from behind the rim. The transport trundled on towards the ridge and through a narrow gap. Timnah stared in ever increasing wonder. A massive wooden vessel loomed closer and closer. One by one, as each person in the transport saw it, they fell silent.

"This is not the work of a madman," muttered Elon.

Ariana was in awe. "By the heavens," she breathed, and was lost for words.

The others all gazed in wonder. Even Shem and Japheth, who had not been there for a while, were struck again by its magnitude.

The Ark was indeed massive. A staggering three hundred cubits long, fifty cubits wide, and the main body at least thirty cubits high. At the front was a tall wind catcher; at the back, a large but fixed rudder.

Timnah knew nothing of boats. She'd only seen the sea in pictures. But she could imagine this huge vessel riding the great waves of the deep. However, even to her untrained mind, there was one problem. They were hundreds of miles from the coast and atop the high plain that Noah lived on. Moreover, the boat was nestled in a small basin with even higher hills around it. How on earth was it ever going to have anything to float on?

They came through the gap in the hills, stopping at a huge construction site almost empty of workers. A handful of men were seen moving things about. Most wore the type of caps that were clearly intended to hide their faces. A precaution against unexpected visitors. They were all in dire need of the generous wages. Working for Noah had become more than just a joke or an embarrassment. Even for those in severe debt, it had become a risk.

Ham got very animated. "Come on, let's go round," he beckoned to the guests. Timnah's hand was in his as he marched boldly forwards towards the front of the towering vessel.

Shem and Ariana – who in her ordinary clothing was no longer recognisable as the famous Chaste Maid – were last out of the vehicle. They were barely able to let go of each other. Mavron drily asked if they wanted a resonance platform with a couch on it. Japheth laughed out loud; the other Royal Guards chuckled. Noah and Emzara smiled and went to see how their few remaining workers were doing.

Japheth walked hand in hand with Adatenesis, her son Vindad

chattering excitedly along beside them.

◆◆◆   ⚑   ◆◆◆

Cavilah trailed quietly at the back of the group. He left the procession and began climbing the steep slope on the east side of the hills surrounding the Ark. The sight of the Ark and its sheer immensity had a profound effect on him. Memories of his days as a preacher, days long gone, came back to him.

He reached the top of the line of hills surrounding the basin's east side and stood on a small plateau. He'd not been to the Land of the Ancients for more than a hundred years. It had been much more heavily populated then. The area looked vaguely familiar. Strewn around him were stone ruins, what looked like an old altar and other structures long disused. He walked slowly to the middle of a circle of broken columns in front of the tumbled down altar.

Suddenly, Cavilah realised where he was. He sank down to his knees and closed his eyes. "Oh my," he murmured, "it was here, right here." The crowds came back to him, the bustle of people all around. His wife was there, startlingly beautiful; her unusual pale eyes had captured his heart from the moment they'd first met. As soon as he saw her, he knew she would be his forever.

The familiar voice of a long dead preacher filled his ears, the message, the challenge and then the appeal. He saw himself walking forward. His wife had been in the same group of people who'd knelt there responding to the appeal and putting their faith in their Creator on that distant day. They'd chosen to believe the sacrifices, to live for Him. It had been a warm sunny day, a very sweet day. Cavilah had found himself talking to the beautiful girl who'd knelt beside him and from that day on they'd been inseparable. They'd married soon after, but only a few years later they were apart.

"Why am I here, Lord?" he whispered, "why did you bring me here, was it only for me to have my heart broken again? I saved those men and this is my reward?" Cavilah felt nothing except the warmth of the sun on his back. In the distance, the voices of the few workers and sounds of their machinery floated up the hill.

Cavilah was confused. He also heard shouting and the noise of a great crowd. Children crying in fear, adults arguing, fighting. There was another sound too, unfamiliar, like that of a great waterfall yet all around. He felt disorientated and grasped a nearby broken column. What was going on? He heard voices again, familiar voices but full of desperation and pleading.

"Boss, boss, what's going on?"

Startled, Cavilah opened his eyes expecting to see his men, but they were not there. All around him was peaceful and calm. The sun shone gently. The grass was its usual verdant green. The distant sound of hammering drifted up from the Ark. He walked quickly down the hill. He knew he had to get back to his men.

◆◆◆ ⚑ ◆◆◆

There was a lot of empty space on board the Ark. Ham showed his guests all three decks and animatedly explained the different areas. Places for animals, people, their own cabins on the upper deck. The ventilation system, water supplies, stores, everything. Talmeon was impressed. Mavron and his men knew order and efficiency when they saw it. The Ark was a masterpiece of engineering, but as time wore on, the questions went in all directions except two. Finally, Zahar spoke up and asked both of them.

"So when will this catastrophe happen, and who are the people that will come on board?"

The group had come out onto the Ark's top. From there, they could just see over the basin's hills and across the area beyond. The great emptiness of the Ark seemed to compete with the equal vast emptiness of the landscape around it.

They all fell silent; Ham stared quietly at the deck.

"The time," he hesitated, "no one knows the time yet, but it will be soon." He paused, "very soon. Perhaps only a few months."

"The people? There are not many," he said with regret, "in fact, so far only our immediate family and two friends."

No one said anything. Zahar looked like he might say something else but didn't. Ham answered his unspoken question for him.

"And the animals, the Creator promised He would send them."

Ariana looked up and down the length of the Ark. At the bow, the far end from where they stood, the huge wind catcher stretched into the sky before her. Behind her, the low-slung apex roof of the stern cabin merged into the fixed rudder that ran all the way down to the underbelly of the giant vessel. It all seemed completely mad and yet she felt as though she belonged there. Perhaps it was only because Shem was there beside her, but no – it was more than that. Deep in her heart, she had a burning conviction; without thinking, she spoke out loud.

"This is my home."

The others looked round in surprise; something in Ariana's voice took them all slightly aback. She let go of Shem's hand and stepped forward. Japheth looked very deliberately at his brother's hand she'd let go of, raising his eyebrows and staring straight at him with a slight smirk. Shem scowled back but couldn't keep himself from grinning.

"This is my home," Ariana said again, emphatically.

"Amen," said Ham.

"Mine too," added Timnah quietly.

"It's all of our home," spoke Japheth with conviction. He looked at Adatenesis, who smiled warmly but said nothing. Vindad was in a world of his own, gazing at the wind catcher, trying to imagine what kind of force it would take to turn a vessel this big.

Mavron was quiet. "Yes," he said, "this is the work of the Creator." His men nodded in agreement.

Talmeon said nothing. He couldn't help but wonder what would happen to everyone if Nahron came on board.

Below decks, Noah paid his workers their extra bonuses for the last working day of the week. They seemed unusually grateful. Emzara watched them walk away down the ramp; each carrying their bag, which seemed a little more full than normal.

"They're not coming back," she said with a finality that made Noah realise it was true.

Cavilah appeared at the bottom of the ramp.

"Are you going to look around?" asked Emzara.

"No," said Cavilah, "I've seen enough already. This is not the work of a madman; this is a rescue vessel for all mankind."

Noah sighed and nodded wearily, "Or for as many as will come on board."

Chapter 24

The Kiss

$\mathcal{N}$adina decided that life was too cruel. She'd helped rescue Ariana, so now Shem had his dream girl. He'd proposed to her the very same night they arrived from the City of Light. Ham had gone off the rails about as far as it was possible to go, yet now he was blessed with Timnah. No one knew which of them had proposed. Certainly, it wasn't Timnah. That was against all the customs of the Dark Kingdom, but rumour was that neither had Ham. He was too hesitant after all he'd been through. It seemed that Emzara had suggested that the two of them have their wedding at the same time as Shem and Ariana. They both readily agreed. As upset as she was, Nadina couldn't help but smile. Emzara certainly had a way when it came to getting things done. The weddings were taking place in two hours. They were going to be a simple affair. It was the day after they'd visited the Ark, and all the guests had agreed to stay. Even Cavilah had reluctantly put off returning to Nahron's Gate out of respect for all of them. He'd also promised to do a little acting for the proceedings.

Nadina had ruefully returned to Noah's for the occasion. She knew it would be a touching and moving ceremony. First of all for Timnah, a girl who'd grown up knowing only abuse and pain and who would marry Ham. Nadina thought about Ham; he'd always been warm-hearted. She had always liked him. She liked all the family, but Ham was the most gentle yet also the most vulnerable. She wasn't sure, but she thought that Ham's relationship with his father wasn't all that it should be. There was a wall between them that Nadina couldn't understand.

Then there was Ariana, Chaste Maid devoted to the Son, although that absurd title was irrelevant now. She too, like Timnah, had been a slave all her life. A slave to her own beauty and to Nahron's ambition. Nadina didn't dare imagine what would have happened to Ariana if she'd really ended up marrying Nahron.

None of this was what made Nadina find life too cruel. What she thought was cruel was that at almost twenty-one years of age she'd met

Japheth. Fallen madly in love with him and briefly enjoyed his company. Then, for the next fifteen years, she was exiled to the City of Light because of her parents' work. Picked after being talent spotted at an athletics event, she'd become the only female Royal Guard trainee in the history of the empire. She'd lived through years of intense training and shallow relationships. These brought her fleeting physical pleasure but left her heart wounded and empty.

Ariana hadn't recognised Nadina from the palace garden where they'd met all those years before. That moment had been a turning point in her life. Nadina had got herself back together but only to live a new life of torment. She'd returned to the Land of the Ancients with her parents and found out that Japheth was married. Married to a vacuous beauty who spent most of her time in Isis while Japheth spent most of his time upset. She was pathetically spending every waking moment wondering when she would next see him. Only to experience disbelief each time she did and was reminded that he was married with both a wife and a stepson.

All of this had been barely tolerable. But now new boundaries had been passed and the pressure was overwhelming. She had begged her Creator never to see Japheth again. But the next day, she was summoned to rescue Ariana with him. Working with him, seeing him, talking with him, it was all too much for her, and yet even that wasn't the end. Finally, the unthinkable had happened. Neither of them knew how.

That morning, she and Japheth had done some routine maintenance on the captured Tactan. They never knew when they might need it again, so they kept it in flight-ready condition. They'd been alone for about twenty minutes. She'd finished restocking some items in the cabin. Japheth was checking the underbelly for damage from the wedding. Nadina came down the steps and stood with Japheth looking at the front right dorsal fin. There was a row of three small projectile indentations in it.

"That's it, all done," Japheth had said, tapping the fin, "these are nothing to worry about."

As he thanked her for her help, he said, "See you at the weddings," then, for no reason, he went to kiss her on the cheek.

Nadina had looked up, surprised, and moved unexpectedly slightly to one side, misjudging which cheek he would kiss her on. Their lips met. She remained motionless. Japheth didn't move either. The kiss was soft and gentle. Each one waited for the other to step away first. Neither did.

They were still kissing without moving a full five seconds later. It was as though moving their lips would admit they were going too far. But the kiss itself was acceptable since it was accidental. The fact that neither of them had ended it yet was conveniently ignored.

Japheth slowly took his lips off hers. Nadina was gazing straight up into his eyes. He looked like he would say something. But, he squeezed her fingertips gently, repeating softly, "See you at the weddings." He turned and walked away.

Nadina decided that this was the end of all ends. Purely for the family, she stayed for the weddings.

♦♦♦  ♦♦♦

The weddings went well. Cavilah had everyone in stitches with his speech. Mavron, his men and Talmeon had not had so much fun in ages. Adatenesis was thrilled to help with both brides' last minute dresses and flowers. Vindad didn't stop talking even through the vows.

Emzara noticed that Japheth and Nadina never looked at each other. Not even once during the whole preparations. In fact, they pointedly avoided each other. Something was very wrong, and she knew it. None of Japheth's usual jokes were forthcoming. His wedding ceremony speech for Shem and Ham was lifeless. Shem, as captivated as he was with Ariana, was deeply concerned. He observed that Japheth had crossed a line. He no longer appeared to even have the strength to smile properly.

Ham, while unaware of the nature of his brother's problems, realised that he was reaching a breaking point. He decided to try and talk to him after the service.

Adatenesis was concerned too. She decided she and Japheth needed a little break away together. That was her usual solution to everything.

Noah preached a powerful message which was a little too long. Then he turned to face the setting sun in the direction of the distant Forbidden Gate. He lifted his hands and started praying a long, moving prayer. Thanking the Creator for His goodness in providing all of his sons with such beautiful wives. At this point, Nadina, who was sitting unobtrusively at the back, began quietly sobbing.

Surely Japheth's father knew the sorrows of his own eldest son?

♦♦♦   ᚕ   ♦♦♦

Mavron's trained eye missed nothing. He'd noticed days ago that you could power a hundred heavy transports with the feelings that ran between Japheth and Nadina. He moved along to sit next to her. Putting his arm around her, he gently caressed the side of her head with his hand. She didn't object, leaning into his chest and weeping silently. Noah carried on praying at full speed and volume, facing away from them all in a world of his own.

Mavron felt Nadina's tears soak his shirt and wondered at what had become of him. From a man who'd served the emperor without remorse, he now felt only compassion. He desperately wanted to keep Nadina safe. The woman who'd kidnapped him, almost killed him, in fact. Yet here she was weeping into his chest, soaking his black shirt. He wanted her tears to run through his heart and to unconditionally love her for the rest of his life. She held him tightly back.

♦♦♦   ᚕ   ♦♦♦

Noah had gone quiet. Cavilah, being a former preacher himself, was sure he had overdone his message and prayers by quite a bit. Several minutes passed as Noah remained motionless, facing the setting sun. Everyone waited in polite but increasing anticipation for him to turn around and finish his blessing. The tempting scents of the food were already wafting out from the kitchens.

Eventually, Noah turned around. He was ashen faced.

"Seven days," he said, his voice quivering. "It will be seven days," he sat down, shaking.

Everyone was shocked. No one had expected it to be that soon.

♦♦♦   ᚕ   ♦♦♦

Nadina decided that this latest turn of events was in fact ideal. She was not as surprised as she thought she would have been. Everyone had seen it coming for some time. There were no people left who cared about the message any more. She was glad too. Japheth could get on the Ark with Adatenesis. And she would go home and die, ending both their misery.

◆◆◆   ⊱   ◆◆◆

Talmeon announced his imminent departure for the City of Light. Mavron and his men prepared to take him. Shem returned Mavron's Tactan, with a few jokes about minding the step by the side door.

Talmeon had heard the backstory about the Tactan and Mavron. After years of service in the empire under Nahron, he'd learned one thing. Keep your nose out of everything that doesn't directly concern you. Talmeon cared only that Mavron and his men were safe and that they would escort him home in the morning. As for having seen and met Ariana, Talmeon decided that none of them had done that. To have anything to do with such an emotive topic was definitely not smart. He knew Mavron and his men could be executed even for talking to Ariana. So, they all decided to stay silent about her.

Chapter 25

New Orders

The Countdown – Seven Days

$\mathcal{E}$arly the next day, while the newlyweds were still asleep in their quarters. Nadina, in tears, said an emotional goodbye to Mavron as he boarded the Tactan with his three men and Talmeon.

"You have to come back," she insisted.

"I will," he promised out of earshot of Talmeon, "and you'll still be here?"

"Of course," she answered, but he knew something was amiss by the tone of her voice.

"Thank you," Mavron said, looking into her eyes.

"What for?" she asked, slightly incredulous.

"For bringing me here."

Nadina smiled at him, "You're welcome," she said and laughed a little, "just mind your head in future." Mavron looked at her, smiled, then frowned.

"You're not intending to be here when I get back, are you?" He spoke softly. Nadina was unnerved. Mavron read her like a book. She replied by mimicking his earlier frown, pretending to be both amused and puzzled.

"Goodbye," she said softly, tenderly kissing his cheek. Mavron took the back seat in the Tactan, praying quietly. He carried her pain in his heart; he felt her torment in his soul. He pleaded silently for her. He realised he truly loved her, the girl who'd made a fool of him, evaded his capture, and then escaped. He really cared about her. How strange life could be.

Elon lifted the Tactan into the air, it accelerated away towards Nahron's Gate.

♦♦♦   ☞   ♦♦♦

Nadina watched Mavron's Tactan disappear in the distance. Then headed for her parents' home. She indicated to those at Noah's that she was going home and implied she would return shortly. Nadina detached herself from everyone around but remained chirpy as if all was well. Noah reminded her of the obvious. That failing to return before the deadline meant only one thing, certain death. She didn't need anyone to remind her about that.

Nadina's plan was simple. She would stay out of the way until the world ended and therefore be put out of her misery. The thought of living on a vessel even as large as the Ark with Japheth around was more than she could bear. Wasn't this all supposed to be the Creator's judgement on the world for its sin? She didn't intend to start off building a new world as Japheth's mistress. She collected the few belongings she'd brought earlier and walked away into the morning mist. Japheth was still in his quarters with Adatenesis.

Nadina didn't use a transport. Though it was fifteen miles to her parents' home, she always preferred to walk and took her own paths. By late afternoon she was close when something caught her attention. The faint acrid smell of disruptors drifted through the air. A light breeze was blowing towards her, away from the direction of the house. She froze. Disruptors were standard weapons for use against reptiles. They were very effective, but dangerous reptiles almost never came this close to her home. Something didn't add up.

Nadina carefully put down her bag and activated the movement sensors in her Favicon boots. She stood perfectly still until they were set. She began to walk slowly forward through the trees. The outline of the house appeared through the remnants of the morning mist. Nothing seemed out of order.

All at once, Nadina knew something was very wrong. Her parents' transport was parked alongside the house, but with one big difference. It was facing towards the house. Her father always turned it around and left it facing down the driveway whenever he came home – always. She knew it was a trap. Disruptors used to leave a tell-tale scent, as though a dangerous reptile was around and to explain why no servants were outside. The transport parked up to make everything look normal but parked the wrong way round.

Nadina doubted her parents were even home. In their last argument, they'd openly mocked her faith, then told her that they were going away to the City of Light for three months. When Nadina warned them that the deadline for the catastrophe was possibly much closer, they'd simply scoffed.

Something had been broken between them that day. Not that their relationship had exactly been flying before. Ever since Nadina told them years ago about her visit to the Forbidden Gate, things had been hard. More recently, that gulf had only widened.

Nadina quietly circled the property. She saw a small, poorly placed listening device on the ground. She opened her mouth wide to breathe as quietly as possible and lightly stomped her feet. Carefully taking her communicator from her arm pouch, she went through the menu until she found animal sounds. She played wild boar grunting noises followed by a couple of low whines. Anyone listening would think there was a small boar roaming about nearby.

Nadina stayed well back in the trees. Whoever might be waiting for her would expect her to come down the main driveway. That meant they would be hiding behind the wall that blocked the top of the driveway from the garden. She edged forward as her line of sight moved closer to where the wall stood. Sure enough, in the distance she could see several uniformed men sitting behind the wall. One of them was looking through a hole he'd made right through it. All of them were watching the driveway. But they were not the empire's men; they were security men from Ladan's Council.

"Welcome to the Land of the Ancients," Nadina muttered to herself. These buffoons were nothing to fear. But their presence told her the empire must have realised she was the master of ceremonies at Ariana's abruptly ended wedding.

Nadina backed off slowly. Surely she should return to Noah's? She started to walk back there again. After she was a safe distance away, she allowed herself to start thinking of Japheth. She stopped. There was no way she could go back to Noah's. No matter from what angle she considered it, she told herself it was impossible, even madness. Death was more preferable.

Nadina turned and headed in the direction of her parents' summer chalet. They hadn't used it for years; it was where Nadina stored some of her equipment; there was also food there. It was near to where she'd first met Japheth. It would be a nice place to die.

◆◆◆   ʁ   ◆◆◆

Talmeon had expected to fly straight to the City of Light. Mavron had other ideas. He discreetly let his men know before they left Noah's to set down in Nahron's Gate. When Talmeon realised they were about to land at Nahron's Gate, he politely challenged the pilot. Elon replied with silky civility. Talmeon quickly realised that, whether he was the emperor's cousin or not, the guards took their orders from one person only – Mavron. Who sat quietly behind Talmeon, looking out of the window as if he hadn't heard a word.

After Talmeon's second failed attempt to get a reason from Elon for not flying straight to the capital, Mavron politely entered the conversation.

"We should not risk flying across empire airspace in this previously stolen Tactan. Although hostilities have ceased with the Old Dark Kingdom, some transport ID systems may not be updated."

Mavron's three men looked at each other. They knew he was talking rubbish. Their Tactan would not be shot down. Malael had already classified it as recaptured and set it to broadcast the Imperial ID codes. Nevertheless, they all looked suitably impressed, as if Mavron had shared some great wisdom and just saved all their lives. None of his men were in a hurry to get back to the City of Light.

"I will secure a more suitable Vastar for you as soon as we land in Nahron's Gate," Mavron reassured Talmeon.

Talmeon agreed, wondering if Mavron was right after all. They disembarked at the central security HQ in Nahron's Gate, and Mavron went to look for the station chief. Talmeon set off with his guards for the short walk back to his original hotel.

◆◆◆   ☞   ◆◆◆

Mavron eventually found his way to the station chief's office. The previous officer in charge had inexplicably disappeared, a common occurrence.

"Any palace communiqués for Mavron Jared Targemah?" he asked the arrogant looking new chief. Mildly annoyed, the man worked his way through a few screens. Mavron was not wearing his uniform. The chief assumed he was a nobody, a civilian. Someone contracted to find supplies for the Imperial Palace or something unimportant.

"Yes," his face held an expression of mild surprise and slight concern, "one outstanding, a Level 7." He realised his guest might be more important than he'd thought. He checked the details. "From more than two weeks ago."

The chief looked up at him with smug derision. As if to say that taking that long to answer a Level 7 communiqué was a sure way to bring a rapid end to your career.

"Give me your office for half an hour." Mavron didn't like the new station chief at all; "My clearance is Level 8."

Without asking, Mavron placed his palm on the station chief's ID pad by his telescreen. The screen went blank as everything he'd been working on was disregarded without being saved.

A female voice the new chief had never heard before spoke eloquently from his console, "Royal Guard Corps. Commander Mavron Jared Targemah. Clearance Level 8. Please select the service you require."

The station chief double swallowed and stood up, contorting his face into a smile. Horrified that he hadn't grovelled at Mavron's feet since he arrived. He knew what a Level 8 security clearance meant. Mavron was one of the emperor's Royal Guards; worse than that, he was a commander! He desperately tried not to picture himself struggling with sacks of salt in the mines of Joktan.

Mavron waved him out of the office and sat down at the desk. He called up the Royal Guard HQ. After a while, the Palace Guard commander came on screen. His face had a look of suspicion and incredulity at the same time.

"Mavron?" he asked, "what's been going on, where's Talmeon?"

Mavron casually saluted and took a deep breath. "I got separated from Talmeon and my men. I was captured by a suspect I was trying to apprehend in Nahron's Gate. I'd pursued them because I believed they were a security risk to Talmeon's visit to the Land of the Ancients."

He couldn't quite bring himself to refer to Nadina as 'she'. He paused while the commander at the other end said nothing. He looked genuinely interested in hearing what was coming next.

"I was badly injured and held but eventually released. I met up with Talmeon at the household of Methuselah when he subsequently arrived there. I have now escorted him back here to Nahron's Gate. He is ready to give his report to the emperor."

"You were held and Talmeon subsequently arrived?" The commander was struggling to fit Mavron's story into the paradigm that he was one of the empire's most trusted and capable guards.

"Yes, sir." Mavron knew that at times like this, the less he said, the better.

The commander remained silent as though expecting a much more colourful story, but when Mavron said nothing else, he carried on.

"And the spy Cavilah?"

"We have a spy in the household of Methuselah?" Mavron feigned complete ignorance. Cavilah had left Noah's earlier that day by ground transport. He would have easily crossed the open border unnoticed.

The palace commander seemed to want to say more, but didn't. He sat back and relaxed in his chair as if nothing mattered anyway.

"The emperor will be pleased to hear of your..." he paused, "successful expedition." There was a clear note of sarcasm in his voice. "He looks forward to receiving Talmeon's report in person without delay."

"Talmeon will be with his majesty shortly, by morning at the latest," Mavron answered. "I needed to secure a more suitable transport for him. My Tactan was stolen and recovered. Apparently, Talmeon lost his Vastar in a crash?"

The commander looked as though he wasn't really that interested in transports lost, stolen, or recaptured.

"Are you alone?" the commander pointlessly lowered his voice.

"Yes," Mavron tried to understand the commander's odd question.

"A lot has happened while you were away."

"So I've heard," Mavron was curious and kept his words few.

"His Divine Majesty has ordered the start of preparations for a mission code-named Time Zero." The commander had a gleeful look on his face.

Mavron took a deep breath while trying to appear as dispassionate as possible. So it was true there was a Time Zero mission. This was what Japheth and Nadina had been asking him about. His thoughts turned to Noah's warning, but the palace commander's talking interrupted them.

"Time Zero is the full mobilization of all forces, Imperial and previous Dark Kingdom. The goal is to bring harmony to the last few places not yet under the rule of His Divine Majesty."

Mavron half laughed out loud in derision but managed to make it look like he'd spluttered in surprise, "We're invading the Land of the Ancients!?"

"Well, you just came from there; was there anything you saw that makes you doubt the success of such a venture?"

Mavron thought hard and fast; how could he put them off?

"Er no, but what about the 12th?" he asked with mock concern.

"What about them?" the commander was nonchalant. "That was a long time ago; whatever weapon was used to destroy them is almost certainly no longer functional. Talmeon's Vastar was shot down by the old Dark Kingdom, not any mysterious weapon."

"Your orders are to bring Talmeon here as soon as possible and then to take command of the Pishon Air Battle Group."

Mavron stared, saying nothing. The last thing he was going to do was take command of a battle group and invade Noah's homeland.

The palace commander raised his eyebrows. "Is there a problem?" It wasn't really a question.

"No, sir," answered Mavron, standing calmly to salute as though any hesitation on his part was purely the commander's imagination.

"The emperor's will is first and foremost in my mind at all times," he spoke as though addressing a parade of fellow guards. He'd never meant those words as much as he did right now.

◆◆◆   ☞   ◆◆◆

Zahar, Elon and Malael trailed reluctantly behind Talmeon. The short walk to the hotel was a strange one. They felt as though they were in another world, yet this was their world. The one they'd left earlier that morning wasn't, or was it? They all missed the atmosphere at Noah's, the friendship, even the tasty food. Zahar spoke softly enough to the other two so that Talmeon wouldn't hear.

"I miss that place," he said.

Elon and Malael nodded knowingly. Their eyes scanned the concourse. It was filled with rowdy groups, women at every office door, and stalls selling prophetic trinkets.

"Was it really like this before we left?" asked Malael, bemused. "I thought this town was different."

"Maybe we just didn't notice it," Elon was also unsure.

"Do you think that angel is still at the tree?" Zahar said, unwittingly letting his voice rise.

Talmeon heard him and looked round. "We have to get the message of Noah to the emperor," he said, trying to address their concerns.

The guards said nothing for a while; then Zahar spoke again, quietly this time, "Sure, go ahead, but will he believe it?"

◆◆◆   ↳   ◆◆◆

Mavron met Talmeon and his men at the hotel. He'd made an understanding with his fellow guards while they were still at Noah's. If they didn't want to go back to the capital, he would take care of that on their behalf. They'd all unanimously confirmed that whatever they'd been before no longer applied. They'd seen too much. They'd seen the truth. They were not the emperor's slaves any more.

"I have orders to report to the Pishon Air Battle Group to take command," Mavron informed Talmeon. "A Vastar and pilot are arranged for you. They will be here soon."

"My guards?" enquired Talmeon, looking at Elon, Zahar, and Malael.

"They are required with me," Mavron spoke convincingly. He wasn't really sure what was going on in Talmeon's mind. All Talmeon seemed to want to do was deliver his report to Nahron. "I have arranged a more than competent civilian pilot," he reassured him.

◆◆◆   ↳   ◆◆◆

Talmeon took the long flight back to the City of Light that night, courtesy of the Havilah region governor's Vastar and pilot. The governor was very unhappy about parting with his beloved transport and most trusted pilot.

Talmeon snuggled down into the small but comfortable bed in the VIP cabin of the Vastar. The soft lighting and gentle melodic humming of the resonators soothed his troubled mind. Tomorrow he would see Nahron; more than that, he would be back in the city, the great City of Light and his palatial home. He tried to remember what it was like to be home. The adventures of the last few weeks had taken him through another world. He'd seen the Forbidden Gate, been attacked by a swamp dragon, chased by reptiles, trekked through endless forests and, to top it all, he had seen the Ark. He closed his eyes. The Ark and the family of Noah, how very different they were, how different everything was there.

Before him was a river, perhaps the Pishon; he was not sure; it was flowing steadily. He stood facing a footbridge. On the far side was a man; the man was beckoning him. He looked like Noah. Talmeon decided to wait. He wanted to cross over, but not just yet. The man kept beckoning him. Why is he beckoning me so much? thought Talmeon. Doesn't he know that I want to cross, but that I will come over when I'm ready?

The river rose higher. Talmeon realised it would soon wash over the bridge, but still he decided to wait a little longer. The thought came to him: why would he wait and do nothing when he could plainly see that if he kept procrastinating he would lose the opportunity to cross? Eventually, the waters engulfed the bridge completely, washing it away. The man on the other side disappeared. Talmeon became distraught. He began to realise that he was dreaming, but even in his dream he knew he had made a terrible mistake.

Talmeon fought to wake up. He decided to get up and abandon sleep for the rest of the long journey. He switched on the VIP cabin viewer using the remote control by the bed. It displayed the view in front of the Vastar; they were high in the sky approaching the City of Light. So soon? The early morning sun shone brilliantly from behind the hundreds of tower blocks before them. Lighting each one with a golden glow. Something caught Talmeon's attention. He looked down and couldn't believe his eyes. The streets were filled with masses of heaving water. The flood had already started! He had to get home and warn his family! He shouted at the pilot to fly straight to his house. The pilot immediately put the Vastar into a steep dive. They headed right for his house but they were approaching it far too fast. The house loomed closer and closer, the sun shining blindingly through the windscreen straight at them. They were going to crash! Out of nowhere Talmeon realised something wasn't right. They'd flown west from the Land of the Ancients in the east. The sun could not possibly be rising in front of them. Just before the pilot smashed the Vastar into his house, he realised he was still dreaming.

Talmeon got up trembling. This time he made sure he was awake. He was. He'd only slept an hour. It was still completely dark outside; they had more than six hours to go before reaching the city. He poured himself a glass of water and sat on the edge of the bed in the subdued cabin light.

The ambience and comfort of the small cabin were reassuring, but Talmeon couldn't get the dreams off his mind. He thought about the man on the other side of the river. What did he want? Slowly, Talmeon began to understand. He was going to lie back down and sleep, but he decided not to put it off any longer.

In the dim stillness of the Vastar's luxury cabin, Talmeon stood up, turned around, and straightened the bed sheets. He knelt down against the side of the bed and said the only words in prayer he knew.

"A sacrifice to save us all, to cover our sins, an innocent life to carry our guilt." He stopped and considered carefully what he was about to say next. "A sacrifice to save me," he whispered and put the palm of his hand to his face and fingers to his forehead. In his mind's eye, he saw a lamb being slaughtered; he didn't really know what that meant, but he felt a profound peace.

Talmeon climbed back into the bed and fell into a deep sleep. This time he heard his daughter's voice, "Daddy, Daddy, am I going to die?" He knew he had to tell her what he had seen.

The sleek Imperial Vastar raced smoothly across the great expanse of the darkened Empire of the Son.

By early morning, Talmeon was making his way through the outer courts of the Great Imperial Palace. He hoped his cousin would listen.

Chapter 26

Take Counsel

The Countdown – Six Days

*M*avron rose early, sending a message to his commander at the Imperial Palace. He told him he would go straight to the Pishon Battle Group HQ, pretending to be eager to take up his position there. He knew Talmeon would have already arrived safely in the City of Light, so there was no need for him to be there. He then let the Pishon Battle Group HQ know that he'd be at the Imperial Palace for a few days. On urgent business with the emperor. He figured that this would keep him from being reported absent for a while.

Taking the Tactan and his men, Mavron returned to Noah's. He spent the rest of the day helping Shem, Ham, and Japheth finish loading the Ark. Nadina was worryingly absent. Shem reassured Mavron that she must be at her parents' home nearby, doubtless trying to persuade them to return to the Ark with her.

◆◆◆   ᛈ   ◆◆◆

The news of Shem rescuing Ariana was something that Noah knew would be impossible to keep secret. Servants, eager for payouts could never have resisted disclosing such monumental information. Soon, the news that Ariana was at his home was everywhere.

The Council of the Land of the Ancients simply could not stomach the rescue from any perspective. Rebuttals and apologies were quickly sent to the Imperial Palace. However, no immediate punitive action was taken against Noah and his household. There were two main reasons for this.

First, the Council had no capable military force. Only low-grade security staff who occasionally ventured out to arrest citizens for minor crimes. The strong family network of the Land of the Ancients kept crime to a relative minimum. Moreover, no one was the least bit interested in raiding Methuselah's household with Royal Guards there.

Second, Shem was still very popular in the border regions, and the emperor was not. The Council were reluctant to risk the disfavour of

216

the nearby provincial governors. After Ariana's abduction, things changed. But they still maintained that the best course was to do nothing, leaving the whole thing up to the empire. That was at least until they were informed of Noah's announcement about the timing of the end of the world. This crossed a red line, their religious red line. For the fourth time that year, Noah was summoned to the Council.

A late evening emergency session had been convened in New Eden to bring about an end to his ravings. Noah's announcement was bringing their lands and the Council into disrepute. News of it had gone across the empire airwaves. Saturating the masses with more information about Methuselah's family. As if, after Ariana's kidnap, they didn't know enough about them already. A documentary on one of the main news channels was being prepared. It was due to air on prime-time telecasts the day after the supposed catastrophe was due to take place.

◆◆◆   ☙   ◆◆◆

Noah walked calmly into the council chamber of the Elders of the Land of the Ancients. He didn't have to be there. He'd decided to attend. He hoped to persuade some old friends to join him on the Ark.

Familiar faces were all around: family, friends, even some co-workers from the early days of the Ark. At the front sat Ladan, the aged and respected chairman of the Council for several hundred years. Inside the chamber, a single line of grand chairs formed a large semi-circle. All slightly elevated above the rest of the floor level. The chairs faced inwards to a small, circular area. Delineated by colourful floor tiles.

Noah saw a modest wooden chair in the centre of the colourfully tiled area. So this was it. He was going to sit on a plain wooden chair while the elders looked down on him from their little thrones. Noah laughed. All his life, the elders had tried to belittle him. To assert authority over the most precious gift his Creator had given him. His free will. Their demands were always dressed up in the usual litany of nonsense. Everything from 'obedience brings freedom' to 'if you serve the Creator, you will always do what we say.' 'We' invariably meant the Chairman.

The truth be known, he was tired of them. Tired of their self-righteous posturing and asinine appeals to their supposed higher status. They were always right, even when they were blatantly contradicting

217

themselves. Sometimes, he thought he preferred the empire's cronies. Their selfish ambition was more straightforward than these religious hypocrites.

Ladan was standing, trying to look as important and grave as possible. Noah waved to him.

The council members cringed as Noah strolled into the chamber. He sat casually on the humble wooden chair.

"Where's my cap?" he asked. Few, if any, got the joke. Ladan maintained his composure and began his address. Noah wondered how people went from normal, to being like Ladan. The embodiment of an endless religious farce.

"The Council has been summoned to address the charges," he said solemnly.

"The accused..." Noah waved around, smiling at all present. Ladan lost his composure momentarily. "The accused is present here to answer the serious accusations brought against him by none other than myself, and all the Council members present."

Wow, thought Noah, that was a very long winded way of saying we don't like what you're doing.

Ladan continued, "The charge is disobeying the Council of the Elders of the Land of the Ancients. Before we begin..."

Here goes, thought Noah. The trick questions designed to make you guilty, whether the charges were comprehensible or not.

"Before we begin," Ladan repeated himself for effect. "Noah, son of Lamech, do you accept the Council as it sits now and its authority as the Ancient Council of Elders of the Land of the Ancients?"

"Yes," said Noah. Ladan looked disappointed but carried on. "Do you accept that all authority is from the Creator?"

Aha, there it was. It was like watching paint dry. It didn't really matter what the actual issue was; sooner or later, it always came back to the same thing. Authority. In other words, you have to do what we say. What they said, why they said it, and even if it was barely legal, let alone morally right, was never addressed. It was one thing and one thing only all the time. Authority.

Noah had learned this lesson at a young age. If a religious leader had no basis for their assertions, they would simply demand compliance based on their authority. It was the great catch-all. Authority covered absolutely everything from immorality to endorsing outright megalomania. The oddest thing was that people preferred mindless obedience. They consistently chose it over thinking for themselves and making informed choices.

Noah stood up, irritated. "Yes, I accept that all authority is from the Creator. I also accept that all gravity is from the Creator, too."

He sat down. The implications of what Noah said took several moments to sink in; for some of the Council members, it never did.

Ladan wasn't sure what to do with such logic, so he simply launched back into his demands. "But we forbid you..."

"Gravity forbids me to step off a steep hill into a ravine," interrupted Noah. "But if I want to cross the ravine, I build a bridge and defy gravity. Am I defying the Creator since all gravity is from Him?"

This was way beyond the intellectual capabilities of most of the Council. Almost all had been chosen for their subservience. Euphemistically called 'commitment to the vision.' Not for their mental acuity or moral fibre. Most people who faced the Council either acquiesced or railed against it. Noah did neither. He simply informed them that he didn't accept the extent of their authority. Nor the way they were attempting to apply it. Not that authority itself hadn't originally been created by the Creator for a purpose.

Ladan ignored everything Noah said and repeated the accusations. He called his witnesses. They tediously reasserted the basic crime: Noah wasn't doing as he was told.

Noah said nothing. He waited for them to tire themselves out. Then, he hoped he'd get a chance to defend himself.

Eventually, weary of Noah's polite silence, Ladan decided to skip reasoning. He moved on to direct threats.

"Since you won't accept the Council's authority, I must pass judgment on you."

At this point, Ladan's sidekick jumped up as though in genuine concern.

"Brother Noah, son of Lamech. Free yourself from the bondage of your striving against the leaders the Creator has ordained. Only then will your heart be free. Sow a seed for enlightenment to the Council temple and you will reap a blessing. Both you and your family will find the breakthrough you are looking for." He sat down to murmurs of approval from the other Council members.

Noah was temporarily lost for words. How did one counter such plummeting descent into absurdity? Where did one even begin to try and prise open the mind of an idiot who'd lost all connection with reality? Here was an ordained Council member suggesting that enlightenment came from giving offerings. Not a knowledge of the ancient texts. Following a council headed by a man whose salary was treated like it was a state secret. Whose bonuses were unmentionable. And who everyone knew had three mistresses. Noah started to get angry.

Something pulled at Noah's heart to watch his words. He stood up slowly, looking around. It dawned on him that he was no longer in the company of old friends. He was in the company of the enemy.

Ladan spoke before Noah could. "Noah, you have announced divine judgement in only five days from now. Not only on these lands but on those of all the empire too and therefore," he paused, "on the emperor." The rest of the Council visibly stiffened in apprehension. "Do you renounce your warning of judgement?"

Noah realised he could talk his way out. Ask for a chance to reconsider his position. Buy a little time and promise to return after the deadline. Clearly, none of the Council believed in it for a moment.

In the Land of the Ancients, senior family members could reconsider a charge against them. This was a common practice. When they eventually acquiesced, it gave the impression they'd thought it through. That the accused had seen their folly and accepted the Council's wisdom. Noah had never been one to acquiesce to anything. He felt anger rising in his veins. These imbeciles had not only deceived themselves but all those under them too. People like them were the main reason the world had fallen into its pitiful state.

Noah felt a strong urge to sit down but remained standing.

"You wish to speak, brother Noah?" Ladan gleefully egged him on. He'd known Noah long enough to see that he was seething.

"Do I wish to speak?" Noah spoke harshly. "Why should I bother? By this time next week, you and your godless emperor will all be bloated corpses, floating on the sea. It will wipe out your hypocrisy, lies, thievery, fornication, and adultery. And, above all," Noah shouted, "your abject stupidity."

"Do you think there is no Creator? Do you think that you will live forever and never face judgement? Do you think that you will not answer for your deceptions? Do you think that He who lifts the heavens is blind? Blind like that fool in the City of Light, your half divine clown who thinks the serpent is the Son."

The Council was deathly silent.

"I think we have heard enough," Ladan broke the silence. "Noah son of Lamech you have insulted his divine majesty Nahron our..."

"Divine majesty!" exclaimed Noah. "Have you lost your mind! He's an administrator from Vastar and his priest is a garbage boy."

"As I said, you have insulted our benevolent emperor. I order you to be detained," Ladan somehow maintained his composure.

"Detained?" Noah looked around, realising he might have gone way too far.

Four burly council guards dragged Noah, shouting, from the chamber.

◆◆◆ ☡ ◆◆◆

Emzara was heading home after a long and perplexing day. It was two whole days after Noah's announcement at the weddings. Nobody had wanted to listen to warnings of the impending end of the world.

News of Noah's apocalyptic announcement had travelled fast. Their household servants had repeated everything. Their motives may have been derision, but Emzara didn't mind. That the warning was spread far and wide was exactly what she and Noah wanted.

Emzara had spent the entire day visiting many different friends in several homes. All were direct descendants of Enoch, some close relatives of Methuselah.

Many pretended to be out. A few answered their doors but were too busy for visitors. Very uncharacteristic for the Land of the Ancients. Especially towards those like Emzara, who were from the family of Methuselah. If there was any name that commanded respect in the region, it was that one.

Emzara hadn't been so naïve as to expect everyone she visited to accompany her home that evening with a packed bag. But she had hoped for some polite interest. The few close friends who'd invited her in looked blankly at her as she talked about the catastrophe. She might as well have been discussing some sale in a curtain shop. They'd all smiled politely and, in reply, talked about nothing in particular.

As the day had drawn to a close, Emzara had felt pulled in her heart to go home and pray. Her husband was strongly on her mind, but she wanted to visit one last person. Someone on the opposite side of her home to the others. Emzara had not seen her for many years. She reasoned that the long absence would make her visit more special. It was a woman she'd grown up with. A friend who had been enthusiastic to learn more about the times of the beginning and the ways of the Creator.

The visit turned out to be the hardest of all. Her friend had opened the door after some considerable time just as Emzara was about to give up and leave. Yet she did not welcome her in. She had that blank expression so common among those who'd chosen to blindly follow the Council. She'd heard all about Noah's announcement. Everyone had.

"Emzara, your husband's prophecy is not in line with the vision of the elders," she repeated like a child's wind-up toy.

"But it's the word of the Creator," Emzara politely insisted. "Consider how society has morally collapsed, the recent changes in the weather, the ground shaking and..." she hesitated, "and everyone knows the Council is corrupt. The head of the Council, Ladan himself, has at least three mistresses. He doesn't even bother to hide it any more."

Her friend stared vacantly. "Ladan may have his imperfections, but we are obedient," she said, "so the Creator will bless us."

Emzara struggled to know where to begin in answering such absurdities.

"Please consider," said Emzara in increasing desperation. "What if what my husband says is true? What is there to lose in giving it some prayerful consideration? Come to the Ark for the Seventh Day. If nothing happens, then you will know for sure that we are wrong."

A slight hesitancy flickered in her friend's eyes as she considered the logic of Emzara's suggestion.

"Remember when we were young?" Emzara pleaded, "The temples were very different then, were they not?"

The woman smiled faintly for a moment, then looked oddly past her. Her smile rapidly faded.

"Thank you for taking the time to visit me," she announced politely, "but I'm enjoying my freedom." She promptly closed the door in Emzara's face.

Emzara stood aghast. She stared at the ornately carved oak door of her friend's home. Now nothing more than a tastefully engraved prison entrance.

"Enjoying my freedom," Emzara repeated to herself. Freedom to abandon all moral discernment. To throw money without end into the coffers of one show after another. To follow men who were even less accountable than local government officials. To supposedly rest in the Creator's presence and yet ignore everything He had to say.

Emzara walked slowly back to her transport. A tear slid softly down her cheek.

"Why don't they listen, Lord?" she pleaded silently. "Why?" No answer came; rather, she was surprised that the same question was asked back to her.

"Why won't they listen?" Emzara felt the overwhelming sadness of her Creator's heart. His own children turned away from Him. Their hearts hardened against His love because of their unremitting self-seeking.

Emzara struggled with her loneliness, all the friends she'd grown up with had disowned her. Then it dawned on her, the Creator missed a lot more than the small handful of friends she did. He missed multiplied millions of His sons and daughters. She sat down in her transport, tears filling her eyes. The atmosphere was so tender that she hesitated to speak.

Finally, she said, "I'm your friend and I love you. I'm not leaving you." A great warmth filled the air around her, yet the impression came strongly to drive away immediately. Emzara started up the resonators and watched as the battery bars rose to only a tenth. Barely enough to make it home. Again the impression came, "Go, now!" She turned the transport around. In the distance, the lights of three transports approached from the opposite direction. Emzara had only one thought.

Betrayed.

She wasn't going to visit any more friends. So be it, she thought; if you choose death, death is what you will have.

She accelerated quickly away into the dusk.

Chapter 27

The Portion of Enoch

The Countdown – Five Days

$\mathcal{N}$ahron's face interrupted the midday news. The disappearance, location, and recapture of Ariana had been headlines for several days. But it was becoming increasingly obvious that she was not in the City of Light. Eventually, the rumours were confirmed. Ariana was indeed in the Land of the Ancients with the treacherous hero Shem, son of the madman Noah.

Public speculation shifted to how the divine emperor, whose divinity had not prevented the kidnapping, was going to exact punishment on those deviant people.

Before Ariana's kidnap, no one cared about the Land of the Ancients. Noah's boat had featured in a couple of provincial documentaries. But it attracted little real attention outside the Havilah region. The City of Light had enough quacks and false prophets to keep everyone entertained. After the kidnap, everyone knew where the Land of the Ancients was, and Noah was a household name.

Mavron sat watching the news programme with his three men in his Tactan. The first thing that morning they'd gone to meet Cavilah at an agreed rendezvous point, but he'd not appeared. Soon after, they went to Nadina's to try and find her, but she was not there either. Only some local security personnel were present. They'd ventured out hoping to find Nadina and arrest her. Mavron had feigned arriving for the same reason and ordered them away. He'd made sure they departed then returned to Noah's. But, Noah still hadn't returned from a Council meeting the previous evening. Mavron and his men promptly set out again to look for him.

After a fruitless search, they decided to top up their Tactan's batteries. They moved out of the flux and crossed the Pishon, setting down to recharge and plan their next move.

"Faithful citizens of the Empire and of the Kingdom of Light." Nahron's laconic voice filled the cabin from a small display. He was careful to identify his new subjects by the familiar names. "Today I have good news. Our allies in the east have captured the madman and criminal Noah. He will be brought to the capital to face trial for treason."

"What!" Zahar was the first to digest what had actually been said. "They've got Noah! How?"

Mavron calmly took it all in. He knew Noah should not have gone to the Council meeting. Especially after all that had happened recently. But, he also understood that Noah wanted to give his old friends a last chance. Friends he'd known for hundreds of years.

The news programme was very obliging. Text beneath Nahron's image revealed that Noah was being held in New Eden's Council HQ. Elon met Mavron's eye. There was no time to waste. They aborted the recharge and raced to New Eden.

New Eden was the capital of the Land of the Ancients. An old town, grandly named for its position. It sits near where the great river of Eden first divides into one of its four main tributaries: the Pishon.

Nahron's speech continued in the background. "I know these deviations have greatly concerned you all. But, with a happy heart, I can tell you that soon all our lands shall be completely one."

The signal began to break up as they crossed the border back into the flux, so none of them caught that last phrase.

◆◆◆   ⊱   ◆◆◆

Elon landed the Tactan right in New Eden's town square opposite the Council Headquarters. Zahar and Malael stepped out in full combat gear, holding heavy duty weapons. The local security personnel on guard outside the building all drew back in surprise. No one dared so much as raise a hand for an explanation, let alone object.

Mavron, walked straight past the guards. He marched up to the main reception desk.

"Where is the prisoner?" he demanded. "Why isn't he ready!"

The pretty girl at reception was speechless.

"Well?" Mavron's impressive bulk and height left little room for pleasantries. The girl had never seen anyone in Imperial combat uniform this far inside the Land of the Ancients.

"Err," she hurriedly called the building's security chief. Her hands quaked as she eyed the two men outside with their weapons, standing next to a frightening looking transport. Like most people, she had never seen a Tactan before. They were quite rare, much bigger than they appeared in pictures and incredibly sleek. Its long cannons and launchers protruded ominously from its fuselage. The neutral flecked grey colour scheme made it look especially lethal.

The Council security chief soon appeared looking very confused. He eyed Mavron up and down and then saw the Tactan outside. An Imperial military transport in the Land of the Ancients! He was shocked.

"Ah," he gestured, nervously twitching. "We err, understood that you would be here later for the err," he hesitated as Mavron stared him down. "The err, photo shoot with Councillor Ladan?" His voice trailed off to a whimper.

Not one to miss a chance to promote his new allegiance to the empire, Ladan had agreed to a live press event later that afternoon. He planned to ceremonially hand Noah over, with a contingent of his own security personnel lined up in the background.

"Do I look like I care about photo shoots?" Mavron stepped slightly towards him. The chief stepped back and gulped. His daughter, the receptionist, sharply drew in her breath with a small shriek.

"There's been a change of plan. Emperor's orders." Mavron had the kind of demeanour that suggested even the slightest flicker of resistance would result in instant death. "Take me to the prisoner now."

The chief, too terrified to think straight, pathetically squeaked, "Come this way."

Moments later, Mavron marched out of the building with Noah, hands still bound but feet unshackled. He walked him to the Tactan's side door. Zahar impressively pushed him in, holding down the back of his head. The Tactan rapidly lifted into the air and shot off at a frightening speed. Moments later, Ladan arrived in his ground transport, all dressed up for the afternoon. He'd planned to gloat over Noah for a few hours before the handover ceremony.

"What were you thinking!" Mavron reprimanded Noah as they raced away. "Why did you come back?"

"For six hundred years those people were my brothers. How was I to know that they would sell me out to the empire?" Noah was pained in his voice. Mavron said nothing in reply.

Soon they reached a rendezvous point further east where they met Shem and Japheth in the Kestrel. Noah climbed in and Mavron reassured them that he would see them again soon. He had to collect some supplies before his superiors learned of his defection and his ID was blocked. He needed to act quickly.

Mavron had taken an inventory of the various equipment Noah had loaded onto the Ark. It was an impressive list and obviously very carefully thought through. If the world was ending, why not take every conceivable piece of useful technology aboard the Ark? With all the hoped for passengers that had not shown up, there certainly wasn't a lack of space for supplies. However, there were still some valuable additions that Noah could not get. Mavron knew just where to get them.

♦♦♦   ⌫   ♦♦♦

Cavilah stepped discreetly into the great temple of Isis. The evening service was in full swing. He slipped through the crowd, finding a darkened seating area at the back. Sitting down he looked all around.

Nothing much had changed. The band was as impressive as ever; the quality of lighting and sound was second to none. People of every age were around him, singing.

Cavilah had seen it all before. He knew that despite the range of personalities, they would all have one thing in common. Wilful gullibility and unswerving blind commitment to whatever the temple promised them. Which was why they were all there in the first place. To get what they wanted. The singing quietened a bit. After a soothing song, everyone took their seats.

He knew what was coming next.

"You have all cheated me, you have consumed the portion of Enoch..." The priest at the front shuffled about, head down. He appeared almost sad, even though what he was saying would qualify him for a sizeable portion of the income of everyone present.

Without remorse, he expounded his favourite passage from the Book of Enoch. He took it completely out of context. Deftly ignored who it was written to. Then declared it was an eternal principle because it was from before Enoch's ascension. There were lots of other things in the Book of Enoch from prior to the ascension. However, since these didn't line his pockets, he completely failed to mention them.

"It's not really about the money," the priest shamelessly continued, "it's about the heart." The offering buckets were immediately passed round.

Cavilah had seen it all before. These priests were the lover-boys of the religious world. They seduced new converts with promises of great blessings, without any accompanying lifestyle changes. Their sincerity was corrupted and replaced with greed. Their souls were filled with the desire to receive only the abundance of their own wants. The route to which was always more donations.

Cavilah sighed; he wasn't angry anymore because he knew it was what the people wanted to hear.

People were always ready to give it another try each new passing Seventh Day. They played an endless lottery which, unlike the lotteries of the empire, they could never win.

Cavilah was there to look for his men. "If anything goes wrong and the empire comes for you, hide in plain sight," he'd told them. "Go to crowded places and blend in. I will find you. Find another town and mix with the crowds." He scanned all four thousand people present using his miniature ocular viewer. His men weren't there.

Cavilah left before the main message started. He didn't know if he could stand listening to another gifted communicator this side of eternity. It still pained him to watch their deceptions.

On the way out of the door, he was comforted by a familiar presence. "A sacrifice to save us all," he whispered to himself. His confidence was not in the temple; it was in his Creator and His promises. He knew they were not the same. He went out into the night to look for his lost sheep.

Cavilah went north from Isis. He searched for his men for three days but found no sign of them. Their houses were empty. Their apartments too. Their usual haunts were devoid of even a single one of them. He couldn't help but think perhaps he'd trained them a little too well. Obviously, they were not hiding in plain sight; they must have really found some remote place. He knew the empire would use his image from the Forbidden Gate to track down all his contacts. As soon as the empire moved in on one of them, the rest would have all melted away. But where? He'd been to both rendezvous points and there was no sign of them. Not even a broken twig to suggest anyone had been near those places for months.

Cavilah made his way to the woodlands north of Isis. He badly needed rest and sleep. It was a bit of a nowhere place. Few ventured there except to visit their holiday chalets, which were empty for most of the year. He had a log of when the chalets were used and, more importantly, when they were not. Cavilah let himself into one of his favourites and settled down. He watched the news about Noah's arrest and then mysterious disappearance. The reports told of unidentified Royal Guards collecting him and then vanishing. He smiled. "Well done, Mavron," he said out loud even though no one else was present. Those buffoons at the Council could be taken for anything.

That late evening of the third day brought with it something more sinister. Cavilah heard the deep melodic hum of heavy transports. Perhaps he'd been recognised in Isis and they were searching for him? That seemed unlikely. As the night progressed, the flyovers increased. He realised what was going on. The empire was gathering its forces for something big. But they were flying over sparsely populated areas to hide their activities. By the middle of the night there was a never ending procession of Vandeons and Seekers overhead. Interspersed with Vastars, the occasional Tactan and a variety of auxiliary craft. He'd never seen so many flying transports in all his life. The sight was both awe inspiring and frightening. He knew it meant only one thing.

He decided to skip his much needed sleep and set off through the woodlands back towards Nahron's Gate. Now more desperate than ever to find his men.

Chapter 28

The Rise of the Preacher

The Countdown – Four Days

*A*deep rumbling woke the inhabitants of the western lands of the Empire of the Son early on the fourth day of the week. Once again, the ground was shaking, but this time objects and buildings also vibrated. It only lasted a couple of minutes but caused great consternation. Times were changing. Their divine emperor had demonstrated that he was not as divine as claimed. His bride had been kidnapped from right under his nose. The Dark Kingdom had fallen, a great victory for the empire but by the hand of a man from the Land of the Ancients. No less the son of a madman who had predicted the world was going to end in a mere three days. Some people were starting to have second thoughts. Crowds were roaming the streets instead of going to work. Something had to be done. Nahron already had it covered. Mandarus was going to give a speech. Everything would be explained. The emperor would be solidly re-endorsed and the deviance of the Land of the Ancients would be short lived. Very short lived.

❖❖❖   ⋺   ❖❖❖

Mandarus had prepared his speech with the utmost care. Nahron checked it and approved. His cousin had told him that his daughter would soon be rescued, but Mandarus knew Nahron had other plans. He seriously doubted that he had any chance of seeing Ariana alive again. Moreover, he knew that if Nahron reached her first, she would be as good as dead, not heroically rescued. He also knew that none of this really mattered now.

Mandarus was increasingly convinced that Noah's flood really was coming. He saw that the world had reached a tipping point. Even so, he was determined to give everyone, especially those from the old Dark Kingdom, a final chance.

With great pomp, Mandarus was deposited at the Monument of Enoch. Nahron had decided that the Great Temple, as great as it was, would not do. To quell the crowds, he wanted an appeal to history, to the core of the beliefs of the past.

The great statue of Enoch being carried up into heaven by angels was a well known landmark. Nearly every tourist had their picture taken by it. But few considered what had really happened that day. Or how very different Enoch was from the religious rulers of the present time. Nahron understood this. He wanted the masses to believe that he was the embodiment and continuation of their history. That he was the heir of their spiritual heritage and guardian of the truth. Their ignorance was his fortress.

The cameras were in place and a live feed was being broadcast to the whole world. Even the pleasure islands of the western sea were getting the signal. Nahron knew Mandarus' speech might lack style. But, he trusted him enough to make a live speech to the whole world.

Nahron left the arrangements to Sindain and went to chair a meeting with his generals at the palace. A meeting of the utmost importance and close to his heart.

Mandarus stepped into place. The air was unusually cool, a gentle breeze blew across the platform where he stood at the base of the great statue. Behind him were the same columns that Ariana had waited among on that fateful day of the Victory Parade. He knew he would never see her again in this world. Before him was a heaving mass of people. Concerns about the ground shaking had left many worried.

The first five minutes went as planned. Mandarus read exactly what he had written in his notes. Sindain retired to a nearby Vastar to get some sleep. Since Ariana's kidnap, he'd been awake almost continually. Mandarus plodded on and then turned to the third page. Instead of reading across the lines, he went down the page. Reading prompts he'd ingeniously hidden, blending in with the approved text. And so it started...

Mandarus explained his recent life story. How he was promoted to High Priest. What was remarkable was that he told it like it was and not as though it was all some great divine plan. He recalled the behind-the-scenes talks with media moguls for air time for Nahron's early shows. The ones where they'd used a set as though it was the inside of a humble temple. He talked about how the moguls had been promised promotions if Nahron came to power and how they were now all dead. He didn't say Nahron had them murdered. He simply left it as obvious.

The crowds listened with increasing fascination. No one doubted that what he said was the truth. No one woke up Sindain. Mandarus had not accused anyone of anything wrong. He was just telling the truth and leaving out the gory details. Besides, no one in their right mind would wake up Sindain.

Mandarus began to feel different. Something came over him. The same presences that had accompanied him in his vision filled the air around him. His speech became bolder, his voice stronger. Soon he was thundering out his message like a real preacher. He declared the travesty of the serpent being the Son. He explained from the Book of Enoch how the serpent had stolen the rights of men, not preserved them.

He slammed the arrogance of the first man, Adam, in turning from his Creator. He praised the courage of the first woman, Eve, for unflinchingly identifying the serpent as her deceiver. He dismissed as absurdities the popular gods of the recent past – they were mere men, he declared. And here he reached his crescendo.

"We are all mere men, once great but now fallen, every one of us." His voice boomed throughout the whole world, the conclusion undeniable. Even the emperor was a mere man. A sinful fallen mortal.

"We have forgotten the ways of truth, abandoned them for self-seeking and the love of ourselves. We have filled the world with violence. We have shed innocent blood but have scorned the blood of the innocent sacrifices shed on our behalf."

Everyone knew about the sacrifices. They were a way to remind man of the serious and destructive nature of his sin. Unfortunately, sacrifices had degenerated into nothing more than rituals and excuses to take offerings.

Fifteen minutes later, Mandarus was still going strong. Finally, someone woke Sindain.

◆◆◆  ◆◆◆

A very worried official knocked on the door of the senior staff meeting that Nahron was holding. He didn't wait for a reply; he walked straight in, his legs shaking. Interrupting a senior staff meeting with Nahron was unthinkable. But then the unthinkable was already happening.

"Your Majesty," his voice quivered. "Your servant Sindain

232

urgently requests that you contact him. It is of the utmost importance."

Nahron looked up, annoyed but perplexed. He couldn't think of anything that would warrant an interruption, short of an invasion. But the old Dark Kingdom was gone. Had Ariana been found dead or something? Even that could wait. He arose and went outside, away from the signal blockers in the conference room and onto a nearby balcony. He was handed an encrypted communicator. Sindain's ID had already been dialled.

"How bad can it be, Sindain?"

There was a noticeable pause as Sindain could be heard taking a deep breath. "Your majesty," his voice was full of desperation. Something Nahron had never heard in him before. "Your majesty," he repeated, "Mandarus has betrayed everything we stand for. He has mocked the serpent and blasphemed the Temple! He has declared you a sinful mortal and Noah the spokesperson of the Creator!"

Nahron was stunned. He couldn't believe what he was hearing. Why would Mandarus do such a thing? He'd given Mandarus everything. Taken him from garbage administrator to High Priest and this was how he thanked him? Another thought came to him, how on earth would he put this right? He turned and yelled at the nearest Royal Guards, "Get me my transport now – get it immediately!"

Moments later, Nahron was flying at full speed to the Monument of Enoch in his Iridium transport. He watched Mandarus on the transport's telescreen. Nothing he was saying agreed with anything that Nahron had declared to be true.

The transport rapidly set down and Nahron ordered his guards with him. He strode across the monument's platform towards the back of Mandarus, who was still preaching and unaware of his arrival. When Nahron reached him, he put his arm around his neck. Pulled his head round and dragged him, gagging, towards the altar.

The guards attached Mandarus' voice disperser to Nahron's cheek. Their emperor addressed the world.

"This madness will be brought to its end," he declared angrily. He struggled to sound noble and composed. "The lies of the kidnapper and extortioner Noah have corrupted the minds of too many already. Without the divine union of the Chaste Maid and myself, these imbalances have begun to spread." He took a dagger out from his robes and held it to Mandarus' throat.

"Only a sacrifice of the highest order can bring us freedom and restore the harmony we have lost."

◆◆◆ ⮑ ◆◆◆

Two thousand miles away, in the Land of the Ancients, Ariana, Shem, and Japheth watched the whole proceedings. They had come to Nadina's home to try and find any clues as to where she was. Mavron's recent visit had run off Ladan's men, but there was still no sign of Nadina. Ariana had also started to become increasingly worried about how to bring her father to the Ark. They had barely forty-eight hours and no one had any realistic suggestions. Japheth idly flicked on the telescreen. The signal was strong thanks to Nadina's absent parents' specially fitted landline.

They all stood frozen, watching as Mandarus preached a bolder and bolder message. Ariana was beaming with pride and joy. Shem and Japheth were trying to figure out why Mandarus wasn't already dead.

Then Nahron appeared. He landed in full view of the cameras but behind the unsuspecting Mandarus. His sermon was dramatically ending with, "The Creator's heart is grieved at our wickedness." They and the whole world watched as Mandarus was grabbed and dragged to the nearby sacrificial altar.

Ariana screamed in terror. "No! Father – Shem!" Shem forcibly held her, covering her eyes. Japheth couldn't move; surely not, he stared, dreading what was coming next.

They watched as Mandarus was forced to his knees. Nahron looked up triumphantly. Mandarus, knowing that the voice disperser would pick up his own voice too, waited until Nahron bent back down to kill him and then cried out, "Ariana, I'm at peace, build a better..." He got no further. Enraged, Nahron viciously cut his throat. Ariana collapsed, shaking and sobbing hysterically. Shem had stopped her from watching the screen. But the sounds told her everything.

Nahron lifted the blade high in the air, shouting, "Freedom! Harmony!"

◆◆◆ ⮑ ◆◆◆

There was a silence. The crowds of the City of Light had certainly not expected Mandarus' speech to end this way. Soon there were the beginnings of a noise, indistinct at first. Talking? Complaining? Heckling? It grew louder and louder, rising to a crescendo.

The crowds began to cheer and laugh, and sing, and dance. The roar of it filled the airwaves of the world. Nahron had done it again; he'd given them what they wanted. Their freedom. Freedom to rid themselves of the constraints of the past. From the condemning words of the Ancients' first cruel prophecies.

The ground tremored again for a second time that day. The statue of Enoch fell slowly forwards. Smashing into a thousand pieces onto the platform where Mandarus had been preaching.

"A sign," yelled Nahron, "I have set you free!" The crowds went wild with joy.

Nahron was elated. What at first had seemed like a total disaster had become his moment of greatest victory. He returned to his Iridium transport. The atmosphere in the plush cabin was jubilant. Nahron's guards took the liberty of congratulating him. The pilot broke all protocol to speak to him and tell him he was the greatest ruler the world had ever known.

Nahron leaned back in his soft, deep leather seat. Sindain had joined him. This was it, Nahron decided. The time had come. All of Ladan's sycophantic grovelling had been futile. Nahron didn't just want to rid the world of Noah and his household. He wanted all of the Land of the Ancients overrun. Even the memory of anything that contradicted what he declared to be true was too much for him to tolerate. It all had to go.

Nahron turned and looked at Sindain and spoke the words he'd wanted to say for a long time.

"Execute Time Zero."

Chapter 29

Men of Honour

The Countdown – Three Days

*M*avron wondered how long it would take for his superiors to realise he was missing and to block his ID.

A command went out across the empire. Operation Time Zero was now under way. All air units from the west were to report to their assembly points in the Pishon or Tigris regions. The old Dark Kingdom forces had similar orders. They were to go to rally points along their south-eastern borders.

No one sent a specific order to Mavron. His juniors at the Pishon Air Group were not keen to interrupt his supposed business at the Palace. His superiors at the Palace HQ assumed he was carrying out his duties at the Pishon Battle Group. Mavron's Tactan continued to broadcast its Royal Guard Commander ID. The multitudes of transports filling the skies kept out of its way.

Mavron and his men, after spending the previous day searching for Nadina and rescuing Noah, decided to move on with their plan to collect valuable equipment for the Ark. Two days earlier, they'd stopped at a small Imperial supply depot north of Isis. They'd picked up a lot of gear and taken it back to the Ark. Mavron decided to risk going back for a second and final visit. The skies were full. Every empire transport was converging on the region.

"That's at least the sixtieth Vandeon I've seen in the last hour!" exclaimed Elon, "how many do we even have?"

"More than two thousand," remarked Mavron solemnly as they landed outside the depot. Mavron's ID still worked and he and his men collected a variety of specialist equipment. It was an odd assortment which made no sense to the quartermaster. But questioning a Royal Guard, especially one with Level 8 clearance, was unthinkable.

◆◆◆   ⌐   ◆◆◆

Mavron intended to avoid all contact with the empire. Engage his Tactan's active camouflage and slip back to Noah's. That was until the general order came through for all units to advance.

The silence in their Tactan was palpable. They set down just west of the Pishon in a deserted woodland area. No one knew what to say. How on earth would the Land of the Ancients survive a direct air and ground assault? They knew that the heavy Vandeons would have to drop troops off soon after crossing the border. The Seekers wouldn't get far either, they were designed for air superiority and had minimal batteries. But the new Vastars and lethally armed Tactans, these were the biggest threat. They could get all the way to Noah's without recharging if they maxed out their batteries at the borders. And this was exactly what seemed to be happening at the rally points they'd flown over.

Elon broke the silence, "When you have seen the source of life, do not forsake the opportunity to give life."

"What's that supposed to mean?" asked Zahar.

"We have to stop them," Elon announced as though this particular thought hadn't crossed anyone's mind.

"Are you mad?" gasped Malael. "One Tactan against over two thousand Seekers, Vandeons, and other Tactans. And what about the Dark Kingdom? "After we shoot down all this lot," he waved to the west. "We nip across the border and shoot down Razbars and Meta bombers from the north too." All with four air to air missiles and a few hundred cannon rounds?"

"There must be something we can do," Zahar replied. He didn't know where to begin. The whole idea of doing anything was beyond absurd.

Mavron remained quiet. They all looked at him.

"Sir, is this it? Is this how it ends?" Elon's voice was almost pleading.

"No," said Mavron, "this is how it begins."

◆◆◆  ◆◆◆

The famous Havilah Auto Batteries were much more extensive than most people realised. Their automated command centre was in Havilah, but the defences crossed many regions. They ran along the north eastern borders of the Empire of the Son and the northern borders of the Land of the Ancients. Forking south, they also ran past the High Hills of Havilah. Skirting the eastern border of the empire and facing the western border of the Land of the Ancients. A double precaution in case the old Dark Kingdom overran the Land of the Ancients and invaded the empire by that route. The batteries had been the mainstay of the empire's defences for decades. The north-west of the empire was protected by the natural barrier of the Pazgon mountains.

After the fall of the Dark Kingdom, they had become defunct. But, in his paranoia, Nahron had left them active.

Swarms of military transports were heading to the borders of the Land of the Ancients. They flew at the most economical speed to get the most out of their batteries. Each pilot was keen to let others go in front. The memory of the 12th Legion, although distant, was still strong.

All Imperial and old Dark Kingdom craft transmitted standard ID codes. The Havilah Auto Batteries accepted them. The only way to manually change the centre's recognition parameters was remotely. The battery's fully automated command centre didn't know that the war with the Dark Kingdom had ended. How could it? It was only a machine. The appearance of countless transports in the skies was abnormal. So, it went to a heightened state of alert. Thousands of missiles were automatically loaded into their launchers and primed.

In its new, heightened state, the system's detectors scanned the skies for many miles. It logged the ID and tracked the position of every moving craft. All the empire transports in the sky checked out. They were broadcasting standard Imperial ID. So, the Command Centre's auto-response system remained neutral.

Dark Kingdom Razbars and Meta Bombers approached the northern borders. They were recognised as enemy craft. However, since they were broadcasting the same Imperial ID, they were deemed safe to ignore. The Batteries remained neutral but on heightened alert.

The system had one terminal flaw. It had a fail-safe mechanism. Designed to prevent spoofing it into accepting enemy transports as friendly. The person who'd designed the system was a consultant. He had never been a soldier or flown anything. He had no idea how unpredictable war could be. One day, he'd sat at his desk and created an impressive 'what if' scenario checklist.

The result was a brilliant solution. If any part of the missile batteries received fire from more than three craft broadcasting a friendly ID, the scanners would re-classify all craft broadcasting this ID as hostile. You didn't have to be a genius to see the flaw in the mechanism. Mavron wasn't quite a genius, but he was very smart.

◆◆◆   ⚐   ◆◆◆

The atmosphere in Mavron's Tactan was tense as they approached the Battery Command Centre. The whole place was locked down as it always was. No one worked there; everything was automated. The centre received instructions directly from the Imperial Palace's tactical HQ.

"Active camouflage engaged," Malael's voice was calm. He was a soldier and on a mission.

"Confirmed," Elon answered, concentrating as a Vandeon came right at them without seeing them. He pulled the Tactan sharply out of its way, "Descending to firing point."

"Four targets selected," Zahar stared intently into the targeting scanner.

"All targets locked," confirmed Malael.

"Hold targets," ordered Mavron, "hover over the firing point. Maintain height at thirty cubits."

"Thirty cubits," Elon swallowed hard. That was a little too close for comfort, but he knew they'd have to be that low. They hovered right by the main scanner array.

The Command Centre systems easily detected them even with their active camouflage engaged. It ignored them. They were broadcasting Imperial ID and not firing on it; therefore, they were friendly. They had not engaged their active camouflage so that they could hide from the Command Centre.

"Set detectors at maximum. As soon as we fire, engage the auto evasion system." It seemed just like old times. Mavron's words sounded strangely familiar as Zahar diligently followed his instructions.

There was a tense silence as they waited for Mavron's next command. He looked up through the cockpit into the sky. Watching men and machine fly towards the peaceful Land of the Ancients. He knew they only had one intent: annihilation. He had given the order to fire many times in his long career as a soldier. But, he'd never done it with such conviction or such regret as now.

"Fire!" the words fell heavily from Mavron's lips.

All four of the Tactan's air to air homing missiles shot away. Each raced towards nearby Imperial Vandeons. All the targeted Vandeons' anti-missile systems detected them and instantly activated. For the two nearest, it was not soon enough.

Two missiles hit their targets. They blasted small, but significant, holes in the nearest Vandeons. The active defence systems of the remaining two Vandeons destroyed the other two missiles heading their way. It didn't matter.

"Disengaging camouflage, pausing ID broadcast." Malael spoke from his usual position in the navigator control seat. His voice had lost some of its calm.

All four of the Vandeons' defence systems detected the Tactan. It was firing on them and it was not broadcasting a friendly ID. In less than two seconds, their own much heavier anti–air missiles were launched at it. A piercing alarm went off in the Tactan's main console.

"Engaging camouflage," shouted Malael, "broadcasting neutral ID."

"Dropping heavies," shouted Zahar. The Tactan's only two small ground-penetrating munitions fell freely from the craft. They landed on the small hill covering part of the Command Centre. The first explosive charges in them ripped open the earth. The second ones exploded out of the back of the munitions. They pummelled them deeper into the ground. The final charges detonated; the ground erupted in a spectac-ular explosion.

The Command Centre defence systems activated. It was under attack.

The Tactan's auto evasion system automatically threw the reson-ators to full power. They began to accelerate rapidly away as debris and the shock wave from the penetrators hit them. Unexpected pieces of stone hidden below the innocent looking hill struck the craft. Elon des-perately tried to adjust the yaw of the Tactan as it began to swerve uncontrollably.

"The resonators are out of line," he yelled. The craft began to buck, as if kicked from behind. Alarms blared in the cabin.

"Set us down!" yelled Mavron.

Elon had already made that decision. The Tactan ploughed into the ground. They ended up facing the smoking crater they'd created barely a hundred cubits away. For a brief moment, they all sat staring at it in silence.

The four targeted Vandeons' incoming missiles were not fooled by the sudden ID change. But their systems couldn't track the Tactan after it re-engaged its active camouflage. Therefore their missiles targeted the last known coordinates of what was fired at them. They went straight into the hole blown by the Tactan's ground penetrating munitions.

The Auto Batteries Command Centre defence system had to analyse what to do next.

First of all, it had to identify where the first two heavy ground penetrating munitions had come from. The ones that had blown a harmless but impressive hole on top of the Command Centre. Mavron's Tactan had dropped them, hovering 30 cubits from the surface. Consequently, the system had no incoming trajectory to analyse. So, it couldn't tell where the munitions had come from. A small child could have told it the answer. But it was a machine. It couldn't put two and two together unless it was programmed to.

Secondly, the Centre had to calculate where the missiles fired at it had originated from. This was easy. They'd all been fired from nearby transports broadcasting the Imperial ID code. It did exactly what its smart designer had programmed it to do. It counted three or more transports firing at it, all broadcasting a friendly ID. It reclassified this ID as stolen and the transports broadcasting it as hostile.

Next, it reclassified all transports using the same ID along its grid as hostile too.

♦♦♦ ☞ ♦♦♦

The view from inside the Pishon Air Group Command Vandeon was impressive. The Air Group's Marshal was proud to be part of this monumental occasion. He thought of how impressed his mistress would be. Multitudes of airborne transports were crossing the borders.

"So much for the 12th Legion," he commented to his lieutenant.

Some transports were already several miles over the border and nothing had happened.

He gazed ahead and blinked. Dark lines were rapidly running up from the ground everywhere. Hundreds of them. What was that? Acrid lines of black smoke were running right into the sides of transports.

They were spectacularly exploding. A sharp buzzing filled the peaceful cockpit; there was a very loud bang – and a blinding flash.

Cool air was rushing against the commander's face. He opened his eyes. Below him was a beautiful patchwork of fields interspersed with woodlands. He wondered why he'd never noticed how pretty that was before. He was free falling.

◆◆◆   ⚑   ◆◆◆

The sky was full of fireballs. Plumes of black smoke littered the horizon in every direction. Missiles continuously raced up into the sky.

"Look!" exclaimed Zahar, "they're turning back!" He was right, transports everywhere were turning around and fleeing the border. It was the 12th Legion all over again.

"We have to get out of here," Elon was glad their plan had succeeded but wasn't keen to hang around.

The two pilots looked round. Malael was unhurt, but Mavron seemed dazed.

◆◆◆   ⚑   ◆◆◆

Far away in the Imperial Palace Tactical HQ the emperor's most senior commander faced a dilemma. The Havilah Auto Batteries had started firing on his invasion force. It was treating all Imperial and friendly old Dark Kingdom craft as hostile. His technicians couldn't reprogram the system. They were locked out.

There was only one solution. There was not even time to ask Nahron. He had to act now. He gave the order.

◆◆◆   ⚑   ◆◆◆

Mavron and his men had been on the ground for less than a minute. He was mildly concussed. They began quickly collecting essential supplies. Elon started kicking open the Tactan's deformed side door little by little.

A flashing light caught Malael's attention. He looked at his sensor display and frowned. Mavron saw his expression.

"What is it?" he asked.

"Contacts, extreme distance but moving," he stopped talking for a moment in disbelief. "Moving very fast towards us." His voice rose rapidly in urgency, "We have to go!"

Elon kicked the door much harder, it came right up off its rails.

"Twisters," Mavron looked grave and slightly sad. He thought of Nadina. "Help her get to the Ark," he whispered in prayer. Whooshing sounds filled the air as the Centre launched defensive missiles. Mavron knew it was useless.

"They're targeting the Command Centre! They will get shot down, right?" Zahar tried to reassure himself that Mavron wasn't really praying. But he already knew the answer to his fears from Mavron's expression.

"Land Huggers," Elon called them by their unofficial name. Hypersonic missiles that flew a skewering trajectory, equipped with super high-yield incendiary warheads. The empire's last stand against being overrun by the Dark Kingdom. They'd never been used before.

Mavron looked at his men, "It's been an honour," he said. They realised that if he wasn't running, then there was no chance.

They all stood to attention inside the cabin. "Yes sir," they replied in unison. Saluted and then touched their right hand fingertips to their foreheads.

Elon momentarily thought he heard the sound of air being rapidly compressed.

The whole area around them reached several thousand degrees in less than one second. In the midst of the fireball, a man appeared. He motioned with his hand to Mavron and his three men.

"Come with me, men of honour." They turned and followed him, their bodies already unrecognisable ash.

◆◆◆  ◆◆◆

Commander Mavron Jared Targemah was at peace. All his men were accounted for. They were with him and they were safe now, forever. He'd left no one behind.

◆◆◆  ◆◆◆

The sun's rays streamed through the blinds at Nadina's parent's woodland chalet earlier that morning. They were warm and comforting. What was not warm and comforting was what Nadina's heart was telling her. Something was nagging at her and through all her misery she had to admit that everything was not about her. This was hard. She wanted it to be about her. Hurt people always did and right now she was as hurt as she'd ever been. The same thought kept coming to her again and again: 'Go back to the Ark.'

By the early afternoon she'd somehow found the strength to come out and decided to follow her heart. But only after resolving to visit her parents one last time.

♦♦♦   ⼁⊢   ♦♦♦

Nadina's father slammed the door. He always did. He was that kind of man. When he wasn't in control, he went around the house shouting and slamming doors. Today was a spectacular display of door slamming. He and his wife had returned unexpectedly early from the City of Light. Forcibly sent back might be a more accurate description. He'd heard all kinds of things about Nadina he could hardly believe. He wanted to know what was true and what wasn't.

Nadina's father and mother had been questioned extensively about their daughter. Their interrogators eventually realised that they knew more about Nadina than her own parents. Her father and mother had always been faithful servants of the empire. Passing on as much information about events in the Land of the Ancients as they could. What they hadn't realised was that the biggest source of concern had been right under their noses: Nadina. She had been caught on camera spying on Talmeon in Nahron's Gate and, unbelievably, at Ariana's kidnap. She was now, along with the rest of Noah's family, public enemy number one.

Nadina decided to selectively explain most things, except for the flood warnings. Her father was incensed. Here he was suspected of treason because of his daughter's activities. Yet all she could talk about was a crazy old man's prophecy and an absurd boat high up in the hills. That's when he started slamming doors in earnest. He ranted on and on until he realised that she wasn't going to budge an inch. As a last resort, he threatened her with complete disinheritance.

"Father," Nadina laughed in disbelief and exasperation. "By this time in two days there won't be any inheritances anywhere in the whole world. It will all be gone. Why won't you listen and stop thinking only of the empire?"

Her father was momentarily caught off guard.

Nadina's mother sat nearby watching her favourite religious telecast. She interrupted their arguing to ask for her husband's payment number. A preacher was selling trees to plant in Eden's Gate, an arboretum next to New Eden. The idea was to plant lots of beautiful, rare trees and contribute to restoring the beauty of Eden. It was complete nonsense and very popular.

Nadina groaned in despair, "Mother, the world is ending because of its sin and violence, and you are buying trees for a park!?"

Nadina was still reasoning in full swing with her mother and to no avail when something caught her eye. On the mirror above the kitchen side was a small yellow note. Her parents never left notes anywhere. She did, to herself, but she didn't remember leaving this one. Nadina walked over to it and read it. Her heart froze.

It said, 'I bumped my head and I'm looking for you.' A tear filled Nadina's eye, "Mavron," she gasped quietly. He was nearby and looking for her. Maybe she could find a new life with him? He was over 250 years her senior, quite an age difference but not impossible; after all, he was very fit and healthy.

In an instant, Nadina realised that coming back to her parents had been a complete mistake. While she'd been arguing, something in her heart had kept telling her to leave, to go and pray. All she could think of was that Mavron needed her help. But now the urgency was gone from her heart, replaced with stillness and deep sadness.

Nadina's mother completed the purchase of three trees. These were accompanied by the promise of a special threefold blessing. Her father seemed restless. He acted like he wanted to talk but didn't have anything in particular to say. Her mother's telecast ended. Her father flicked onto the evening news channel to try and hold Nadina's attention.

Nadina was speechless. It wasn't the glorious sanitised version of the empire they were all used to. The broadcast showed transports burning and falling from the sky. Then a clip of a Tactan with its active camouflage switched on. The editors had highlighted its outline. It was dropping ground munitions onto the Havilah Auto Batteries. The few pictures explained everything to Nadina before the commentator did. While she was hidden away in the chalet feeling sorry for herself, there had been an invasion attempt. Mavron had clearly done something to the Havilah Batteries, causing them to fire on Imperial transports. The screen changed, it showed another CCTC image of the same Tactan on the ground near the Command Centre. It was damaged with its active camouflage off. The faint outline of men was still inside. The next picture was of a massive burned out crater shown from the air. It was the Havilah Auto Battery Command Centre.

Nadina sank slowly down into a chair. There had been Mavron – a glimmer of hope and now... she didn't dare think, but the sequence of events on the news left no room for doubt. Now he was dead. She watched the rest of the news programme in a daze. He was definitely dead, heroically dead, but still very much dead. She wanted to cry but couldn't.

"That's it," she said to herself, "I did my best, I came back for Mama and Papa but they're not listening. I could have gone on the Ark with Mavron but not any more. I will see him very soon, and Enoch too."

Even in her sorrow, Nadina observed that her father looked increasingly agitated. He had tried to peep through the living room curtains twice without her noticing. It didn't take her long to realise what was happening.

She maintained a sad demeanour and announced wearily, "I'm going up to my quarters." Nadina looked across at her mother watching the telecast; she didn't even look up. Her father gave her an empty smile.

You made your choices long ago, she thought sadly as she climbed the stairs. Nadina collected a few things, slipped out of a window, skimmed down the wall, and jogged across the lawn. She headed back towards the summer chalet.

Chapter 30

𝒫𝑜𝑜𝓇 𝒞𝒽𝑜𝒾𝒸𝑒𝓈

The Countdown – Two Days

𝒮indain sat silently in the chair. The emperor was reading something and hadn't looked up when he'd come in. He'd motioned him to sit down with a casual wave of his hand. Two Royal Guards were stationed inside the door. It was almost imperceptible, but they were unsettled.

Nahron's private quarters were opulent. Yet Sindain couldn't help but think of how opulence had done nothing to stave off the recent series of débâcles.

Nahron stopped reading and looked up. "I'm beginning to question your commitment." His voice was level and smooth. He looked squarely at Sindain.

Sindain thought of a hundred hurried answers but held his tongue. Nahron continued.

"First of all, my bride is kidnapped from under my nose. Second, Noah is captured but then escapes. Third, our anti-air batteries fire on our own Air Force. Bringing down more than half of it."

Sindain looked down and took a deep breath. He could have objected outright. The kidnap was sort of his domain because it happened in the city. But it was really the Royal Guard's responsibility. They were in charge at the wedding. They were the emperor's own soldiers and received their orders exclusively through the palace commander. Sindain vaguely wondered why he wasn't at the meeting.

Being blamed for Noah's escape from custody in New Eden was completely unfair. No one in the empire had any jurisdiction in the Land of the Ancients. Again, it was rogue Royal Guards that had whisked Noah away. The same could be said of the Havilah Auto Battery fiasco. He had no role in designing the batteries. He remembered objecting to their lack of testing when they first went operational. He recalled how his objection was drowned out by the Tigris Battle Group commander. His cousin had won the contract to build the batteries. And again, their sabotage was the work of rogue Royal Guards, not any members of his own security services.

"My lord, many unexpected events have attempted to discolour your glorious reign. However, I would like you to know that my commitment has not waned. It is as unswerving as ever, both to you and to all that you stand for."

Sindain didn't know how else to put it. Adding 'unexpected' into his affirmation was the best he could do to try and say that none of it was really his fault.

Nahron appeared unmoved. "Then perhaps your competence needs to be re-examined?"

Sindain was speechless. Surely Nahron understood things better than that? Royal Guards, flaws in things he'd not designed, and unoccupied lands were not his responsibility. He waited an appropriate amount of time and then replied.

"Thank you for your advice, my master," he bowed his head slightly even though he was already seated. "I will avail myself of all that I can to make sure these kinds of things do not happen again."

Sindain paused.

"Would you like me to take personal command of the Royal Guards to make sure that this level of treachery is not repeated?" He spoke smoothly and in an even tone, but his anger seeped through.

The Royal Guards at the doorway noticeably stiffened.

Nahron's thin lips faintly smiled. He was impressed. This was what he liked about Sindain. He was ruthless, and when he got into a fix, he didn't look for a way out. He always went deeper in.

"Perhaps a few more... safeguards will suffice," Nahron laughed at his own pun. "My dear cousin Talmeon will be with us shortly. In his role as Chief Scientist, he will publicly explain to the people the débâcle with the Havilah batteries. He will attribute it to mistakes made by poorly trained airmen from the old Dark Kingdom."

Sindain wanted to roll his eyes. There wasn't a living soul in the whole empire who didn't know that yesterday's catastrophe was the result of rogue Royal Guards exploiting a weakness in the battery's systems. The CCTC of them pulling off the whole thing had gone viral. For the first time in his life he began to wonder why he served Nahron.

◆◆◆   ⌐   ◆◆◆

Talmeon had decided as soon as he got back to the city that it was futile to hide anything from Nahron. On the morning of his return, he visited his cousin and told him all about Shem and Ariana. Not that Nahron didn't know everything already. Noah's servants had gossiped with abandon. Talmeon reminded Nahron that he'd been nearly dead when he arrived at Noah's. And in no condition to mount a rescue or flee with Ariana. Also, it was impossible for him to contact the empire so far inside the Land of the Ancients. He gave the impression that he was subtly coerced by his four Royal Guards. Who'd recently and conveniently disappeared, adding credence to his sanitised version of events. He also feigned complete ignorance of who Cavilah was.

Despite all this, Talmeon had, in polite but clear words, told Nahron that his dreams matched the disaster foretold by Noah and should be taken seriously.

"I do take them seriously, very seriously," Nahron had said, giving nothing away. "I intend to do something about it. But tell me," he continued, "how can someone who so completely disagrees with all I say and whose son mocks me, be a carrier of the truth?" It seemed Nahron was mystified as to why, if Noah was a true prophet, he was not in complete agreement with him.

And with that, Talmeon had been dismissed. After all the geniality that had been between them before he'd gone to the Land of the Ancients, Talmeon had expected more. But he got nothing.

By the fourth day after his arrival Talmeon really began to wonder if he should do something. He'd seen the news. Noah had been apprehended then escaped. Surely that was a bad omen for Nahron? His divinity had certainly been plummeting recently. Talmeon started to plan going back to the Land of the Ancients. That was until he watched Mandarus' speech and especially how it ended. There was no way he was going to fall foul of his cousin and meet an end like that. The next day, there was the disaster at the border with the Air Force. Talmeon realised he must leave, but how?

As if in answer to his indecision he was summoned to the palace the following day. Nahron required his presence immediately. Talmeon wondered what it was this time.

♦♦♦   ⊢   ♦♦♦

Talmeon and Sindain sat in silence trying to digest what they had just heard. The official reason for the border defeat would be the previous Dark Kingdom personnel's inexperience. Sindain already knew this. Talmeon, who was going to have to give the speech to explain it all, was less than mildly surprised. That was not what was hard to digest.

Nahron had ordered full conscription in all regions surrounding the Pishon and Tigris. He was sending an army of more than two million men on foot across the border into the Land of the Ancients. Everyone who'd ever served was being called up, every reservist and anyone in any security role too. They would cross the border in two days' time at every available crossing point to completely overwhelm the Land of the Ancients. Whilst challenging from some perspectives, this also wasn't what was hard to digest.

What was hard to digest was Nahron's take on the apocalyptic warnings of Noah. He actually believed them. He also believed that his own dreams were real portents of doom. They had become more vivid recently. He believed that they really were from the Creator.

Sindain tried to take this in. Nahron believed in a literal single Creator, not the multitude of deities and the serpent he publicly espoused.

Talmeon was confused for other reasons. If Nahron believed his dreams were real and valid warnings, why was he not running to the Ark instead of planning a second invasion? An invasion one whole day after the predicted warning was supposed to come to pass!

"Don't you see," Nahron explained, "the Creator is trying to threaten me. He has grown jealous of my power and wants it back for Himself. He knows that soon we will discover the genetic mystery of ageing and reverse the curse of Eden. We will return to our godlike state."

Sindain, despite years of managing his expressions to appear innocent, was staring open mouthed at Nahron. Talmeon was looking at him like an exhibit in a zoo. Neither of them could find a single word to say. Nahron became convinced his brilliance was overwhelming them; he continued with his monologue.

"Noah and his household are the last few people who really follow the Creator," he smiled as though he had achieved this all by himself.

"The Creator knows that when He loses them, He loses everything. He will have no way back into mankind because no one will believe His word any more. The promised Son will never come. Everything will become completely mine, and I will finally be free."

"I will have my day of freedom," Nahron's voice changed. A strange and terrible presence filled the room.

Talmeon wished he'd stayed at Noah's. Sindain inexplicably started thinking of all the people he'd had murdered. They both struggled to speak.

Eventually Sindain found some words, "Your majesty I would never have believed that anyone was capable of the things you have done in your..." he was going to say career but realised he needed to make it more divine, so he changed it to, "your time on this earth."

"Thank you," Nahron was pleased, but only with himself.

Talmeon's endorsement was a little less flimsy. "My lord, the signature of your handiwork is present throughout all of mankind."

For some reason, Nahron especially liked this compliment.

"Prepare your speech, Talmeon; it will be aired tonight after editing." Nahron wasn't letting anyone make any more live speeches.

"Sindain," Nahron spoke in a genial tone as though they had become close friends and a new epoch of eternal goodwill had begun.

"My lord?" Sindain began to realise that the dream of his life to sit at Nahron's right hand unopposed and rule a united world was perhaps a nightmare after all.

"You may take full command of the Royal Guards. The palace commander has been relieved of his duty." Nahron smiled as though giving a grandchild what they'd always wanted for their birthday.

Sindain had wondered where the palace commander was earlier. He realised that he was already dead. "I am speechless. Thank you, Your Majesty. My eyes have been truly opened today."

They both stood and bowed as Nahron dismissed them with a wave.

Chapter 31

Two of Every Kind

The Countdown – One Day

$\mathcal{T}$he seventh day had arrived. It was a warm, calm and sunny day. A gentle breeze rustled the stillness of the air. All was peaceful.

Noah had brought the last of their essential possessions with them to the Ark early that morning. Timnah wandered idly around the ring of small hills immediately surrounding the Ark. She ran her hands over the rocks and through the leaves. Pausing at the many stone ruins atop the hills overlooking the construction site, she wondered if any of it would be recognisable when they returned.

Timnah loved the countryside; every quiet glade was a paradise, an Eden created just for her. Her Dark Kingdom home had been nothing but a stinking urban sprawl. She'd not known anything of nature as a child. She leaned against a tumbled-down wall overlooking the hills leading west to Havilah. Something was moving in the under-growth nearby. Timnah frowned. Ham had warned her to be very careful with unknown creatures, especially reptiles. She reassured her-self that nothing bad would come so close to the Ark.

Suddenly, two reptiles stepped out from the foliage, whining at her. They were almost as big as she was. Clearly frightened, they came and stood next to her, muzzling up to her. "Aww," said Timnah, noti-cing how they each had a very impressive long set of teeth and large jaws.

I'll take these to Ham, she decided; he likes reptiles. As Timnah led the creatures through the ruins, she began to play a little game of hide and seek. She ducked behind a broken column; the reptiles ran after her in fright that they'd lost her. Soon she got bolder and ran faster. They ran after her faster too. Timnah decided to run down the hill to the construction site and surprise her husband.

Ham was having a relaxing morning double-checking the outer hull of the Ark for extruding dowel pegs. There were none. The whole Ark was built of a laminate of three layers of mortise and tenon wooden planks. All joined with wooden dowel pegs set through two layers at a time. When pitch had been applied to the wood, it soaked into the exposed end of the dowel pegs. They then expanded, sealing every joint extremely tight. This design made the Ark practically indestructible. It was nothing like a clinker-built wooden-framed vessel. If built like that, the Ark would fall apart almost as soon as it was floated.

Ham heard a noise and looked up. He couldn't believe his eyes. Timnah was running at full speed down the nearest hill, shouting, "Ham, Ham!" and being chased by two baby raptors.

"Japheth!" he yelled at the top of his voice. "Disruptor!"

Japheth shot out of a nearby cabin like a missile from the Havilah Auto Batteries. Brandishing a disruptor, he saw Timnah and began running straight towards her. He set the disruptor to severe stun – he didn't want to miss and kill her by accident.

Inexplicably, Timnah stopped running. She laughed and waved at Ham. The two raptors caught up with Timnah. She turned and began petting them while they muzzled her neck and shoulders. She was giggling.

Japheth, still running, slowed to a stop as he approached Timnah and stared in disbelief. Ham looked on wide-eyed. A roar from behind him nearly caused him to jump back out of his skin for the second time. Two young wild cats came trembling towards him, looking pleadingly at him. Japheth raised his disruptor again but realised something was different. Ham cautiously walked towards Timnah while Japheth kept an eye on the cats.

"Hey baby, look," she said, "aren't they cute?"

"Yes, dear," Ham raised an eyebrow, "let's take them somewhere safe."

By now, the rest of the household inside the Ark had come out to see what the commotion was about. Noah pointed excitedly past Ham and Japheth towards the gap in the hills.

"They're here," he shouted in great excitement. "The Creator has sent them; they're here!"

More sounds filled the air. A great procession of creatures worked their way up through the gap in the hills surrounding the Ark.

There were streams of them, all in a hurry. Moving quickly as though a predator was trailing them. Yet many of them were usually each other's predators.

Noah had constructed stalls for the animals several months before. He'd expected them to come in stages over a period of time, but they never did. Their absence only added to the derision of the few tourists who were still visiting the Ark at that time. Some tourists had even brought their own unwanted pets. Placing them in the empty stalls during the Ark tours to further mock Noah.

The arriving animals and reptiles were all in pairs and agitated. They were keen to be herded to their stalls inside the Ark as though something told them it was the only safe place to be. The birds didn't wait; they flew straight in and up to the top deck, perching in pairs in their cages.

Only different kinds, not breeds, of each land-breathing animal, bird and reptile arrived. The empire had become fascinated with pets and had bred innumerable species. But none of these fancy domestic breeds appeared. Only those that most closely resembled their original created kind had come. Young, healthy, rich in DNA and ready to diverge into thousands of different new species of their kind.

The rise in popularity of the Ark had brought a wave of mocking documentaries. They all made a point of deriding the expected presence of reptiles on board. Experts had proven that barely a handful would be able to fit inside. Scoffers imagined only the oldest and biggest reptiles would board. Noah had answered the question of large reptiles in a Channel 12 interview. He explained that only younger, healthier, smaller, and more manageable reptiles were expected.

Far from taking several days to load all the animals and reptiles, it took only a few hours. Curiously, none of them seemed to have an appetite, and few, if any, were thirsty.

◆◆◆   ⚑   ◆◆◆

Adatenesis had stood by her husband throughout the last week. A lot of unusual things had happened, but she was determined to give her son the best. Of course, she loved her husband Japheth and respected his family. Without a doubt, the arrival of the animals earlier would be a sign to unbelievers everywhere. She believed in the Creator and was stirred by Noah's message. But when faced with choices about her son's education, she had to be practical.

"I'm going back to Isis," Adatenesis informed Japheth. "Vindad has an important event at the school this evening. I don't want him to miss it. I will be back tomorrow."

"What!" Japheth was speechless.

"Don't worry," Adatenesis smiled warmly, kissing him softly on the lips, "we'll sort something out." She turned and walked to her battery-powered transport.

For years, Japheth had gone through the endless torment of trying to explain things to his wife. She would talk, make vague reassuring comments and then do nothing – or the very opposite of what he'd asked. Conversations lasted for hours, some even resulted in temporary separations. This time, Japheth was determined to make things abundantly clear. There was no way Adatenesis could leave the Ark and return safely on the eighth day after Noah's seven day warning. He began to look for the words to say, but something held him back. He couldn't speak. He knew deep inside that this time his words would be even more futile than they'd been on all previous occasions.

Japheth had known Adatenesis for years. He knew in the final analysis that she always did exactly the same thing – whatever she wanted. All the reasoning, begging and tears in the world never changed her. She was an enigma, a beautiful, charming and intelligent woman. Soft, warm and tender in so many ways, but if anything contradicted her choices. She was like a stone fortress, impenetrable and immovable. Japheth watched his wife walk away.

As Adatenesis' transport receded into the distance, Ham appeared. He looked quizzically at Japheth.

"Where's she going, Japth? Picking something up from home and coming straight back?"

"No," Japheth said numbly.

"No? But she'll be back by sundown, right?" Ham had known about Adatenesis and her ways for years, but this took even him by surprise. He looked at Japheth and didn't dare ask any more questions. Surely she would come back before the end of the day? The Creator had told his father at the weddings that after seven more days the flood would begin. A day ended with sundown. That could only mean one thing. This very evening was when it would begin.

Chapter 32

The Angel

Far away in the lowlands of the distant western province of Assyria, several thousand miles from the land of Havilah. A man lay relaxing on a grassy hillside. It was early morning. He looked forward to another perfect day; the sun was rising, and the first day of the week had begun. In the east, the Seventh Day was still drawing to a close.

The man was glad the Seventh Day was out of the way. He didn't like Seventh Days. He already had everything he wanted, so why complicate life with religion? His wife and child were inside their tasteful country home a couple of miles away. His mistress was already on her way to a nearby town to choose an outfit for their next encounter that evening. He looked at the beauty all around him. The hills that formed the skyline caught the rising sun. Their trees, illuminated with a pleasant hue, swayed gently in the breeze. Everything was perfect. What more could he need?

A bright light appeared in the sky. The man was startled. It was brighter than anything he'd ever seen. Descending rapidly, it stopped about a hundred cubits above the tree line. His heart froze; it looked like a man. His whole form throbbed with light. He had huge, gently resonating wings.

An angel! The man's mind was reeling. He was seeing an angel with his naked eye!

The angel plunged his sword into the earth. With one effortless sweep of his wings, he shot forward and out of sight. Ploughing a huge furrow in the ground as he went. Incalculable volumes of water exploded from the rift the he was creating, shooting high into the sky.

In an instant, the man understood that this creature could encircle the whole globe. The water being released would easily submerge many towns and cities. He died under a colossal wall of water before he could have his next thought.

♦♦♦ ⊨ ♦♦♦

The man's daughter put down her copy of the Book of Enoch. She had prayed the simple prayer that she always prayed from her heart. To be real before her Maker, to accept His love and to trust in Him and Him alone for her cleansing from all wrongdoing. She loved her home, but today the bond to it in her heart had been gently, almost imperceptibly broken. It wasn't her home anymore. Now, even at the age of only eleven, she'd seen it for what it was. A place of utter self-seeking. Her father was away too often. Her mother was devoted only to her appearance and many inexplicable disappearances.

Her little brother had died tragically two years before. Bizarrely, she thought her parents were actually pleased to have one less child to care for. He'd been a cute boy of only five when he'd died. She missed him and missed the way they knelt by their beds and prayed together at evening time. The way that their distant Auntie Nadina had taught them to do. Auntie Nadina was also the person who'd given her the book of Enoch she'd been reading. Her parents had been polite when Auntie Nadina visited but scoffed when she'd left. "Stupid Ancient," they'd said. The girl remembered the venom and loathing in their voices. She wondered why her parents would hate their only relative who believed. Standing up, she walked to the bedroom where her mother was applying make-up to her eyelids. Her mother glanced irritably at her then looked away.

"Goodbye, mother," the girl spoke sadly but calmly, "I'm so sorry that you have not believed."

The woman looked around, surprised. Her child sounded like an adult. She paused for a moment as though considering something, then shrugged her shoulders and carried on applying her make-up.

The wall of water hit the house, crushing it like a blade of grass under a rolling boulder. The little girl felt nothing; a man was holding her hand, she was ascending. In the distance, she saw a realm of light, indescribably beautiful in every way. It reminded her of the stories of the perfect garden. The one beyond the Forbidden Gate that Auntie Nadina had told her and her little brother about. Across the land, she could see a city, so beautiful that it was actually shining with light. It made her memory of the City of Light seem like a disappointing birthday present.

The man stopped. The girl noticed he had wings which were made of wafer thin layers of diamonds. Rather than flapping, they resonated and he only had to move them a little to travel very quickly. They stopped at the edge of the border of the land; the angel motioned towards the city.

"Enoch lives there," he said, "and that is your home." He started to lead her away, "But you cannot go there yet, the way is not open."

They both descended through the earth into a realm of peace and beauty, but it was dim compared to the city she'd observed. She saw her brother waiting for her, he was waving. She waved back.

"When can we move into our home?" the little girl asked the angel. The angel looked at her and smiled.

"When the Son is revealed," he replied.

Chapter 33

Day of Freedom
The Countdown – Day Zero

*T*he family of Noah was not experiencing its most glorious moment. They'd spent most of the day loading every last conceivable necessity onto the Ark while looking over their shoulders to see if anyone else was coming to join them. No one did. Everyone sincerely believed that Cavilah would, but he was nowhere in sight.

Japheth eventually appeared from his cabin. He looked terrible. He tramped about performing minor tasks in a depressed daze. His father could not speak to him. His mother found no words with which to console him. Shem was clueless where to even start. Everyone knew that Adatenesis had left for a school event for her son. Absurdly promising to return the next day.

The day drew to a close. The sun began to set. It was now a whole seven days since Noah's warning at the weddings. They all stood at the ramp door of the Ark. Waiting for neighbours, family, Adatenesis, Cavilah, Nadina, anyone. Emzara could not stop praying, but for some reason, Noah started to find it annoying.

"Where is Nadina?" Shem kept asking over and over again in bewilderment. "What's happened to her? Surely she wasn't with Mavron when he died?"

Ariana deeply missed her father. The horror of his death live on a telecast had numbed everything between her and Shem.

Noah was trying to be authoritative and take command. But he only ended up falling out with Ham, who ignored everything he said.

The only person who seemed to be really composed was Timnah. An unexpected bastion of inner strength and serenity. Years of abuse and solitude had taught her one thing. When your world is falling apart, there is still Him who lifts the stars. Timnah loved her Creator, whom she had never seen. She knew all the madness of this life had never been His original plan for the world.

The ground trembled again; this time it was different. The tremoring became more severe and didn't stop. The sky, already darkening from the sun setting half an hour earlier, went very dark. They all stood in the doorway at the top of the ramp looking up to see why. An ominous swirling mist filled the sky.

"No stars!" gasped Ham, "where are the stars?" The coldness in the air increased.

In the distance, a strange sound could be heard. Like thousands of small creatures running towards them. Shem and Ham drew their disruptors, setting them to maximum. But through the gloom beyond the reach of the Ark's powerful lights, they could see nothing. Ham looked up as flecks of water began to fall from the sky.

"Something is dripping," he said.

"Dripping?" Noah stepped forward, "From what?" They all gazed upwards.

"From the heavens," said Timnah in wonder. The dripping quickly got heavier. The unfamiliar sound of the drops on the ground finally reached them. They all stepped back into the doorway of the Ark. Soon, water was falling in a torrent of heavy drops from the sky.

"A flood from the sky?" Ariana asked, incredulous, forgetting her pain. "How is that possible?"

Japheth slowly sank to his knees as the rain began to pour through the huge door. The increasing blackness outside perfectly described how he felt inside. His wife, faced with the choice of him or her son's school event. Had simply left once again, choosing anything to do with the society she lived in rather than him. It was impossible to care anymore. She'd made her final choice and was gone. All he could think of was the day he'd met Nadina. Her laughter, her smile, everything about her, especially their recent kiss.

The world was ending and where was she? He knew full well where she was. She was hiding somewhere to avoid him. In the madness of it all she would die like Adatenesis in this terrible flood. Japheth looked up again at the lashing rain. His composure broke. He collapsed to the floor.

"Nadina, Nadina!" Japheth sobbed, pathetically lying on the deck.

◆◆◆ ☙ ◆◆◆

Nadina was still locked away in her parent's holiday chalet. She felt the ground shake again, her mind was in turmoil. She'd died a thousand deaths in the last few days what difference would another one make? Kissing Japheth was the very last straw. There was no way she was going on the Ark with Japheth and Adatenesis.

She knew she would die if she didn't go to the Ark. She would go to her Creator, like Enoch, like Methuselah, like all those before her who'd believed. Methuselah. Once again her thoughts troubled her; hadn't Methuselah told her she would be a leader of new peoples? How could she be a leader of anything if she was dead and in Paradise with him?

Nadina sat with her head down, cross-legged in the middle of the floor. She hadn't bothered switching any lights on. The wind outside was the loudest she'd ever heard. The water lashing against the windows created enough noise to drown out a thousand heavy transports. Whatever it was that Noah predicted had clearly started. Nadina was numb; soon she would be dead. She hoped it would be quick.

Once again the thought came to her to return to the Ark. She dismissed it as an absurdity. How could she possibly swim to the Ark now? And the Creator was asking her to do something even more impossible than that. To live in a confined space with Japheth. She couldn't even marry Mavron now that he was dead.

Nadina clutched the pendant Japheth had given her that eternal day they'd first met. She held it to her lips; something outside crashed in the wind. She imagined a huge wave approaching and decided the end must be near. She hugged the pendant and began to kiss it, whispering, "My Japheth," over and over to herself. She could think of no better way to die than with his name on her lips.

The whole cabin shook. Everything outside flashed white, followed very quickly by another immense crashing sound. Nadina closed her eyes in preparation. Tears gently rolled down her cheeks onto the pendant.

She'd made her choice. Here she would stay with the man she loved in her heart. She would do the right thing.

◆◆◆ ⚐ ◆◆◆

Noah didn't know what to do. He'd imagined praying together as a family, singing hymns, welcoming last-minute arrivals. His family congratulating him and thanking him. And what did he have? Distress, no friends, strife, his eldest son calling out the name of a woman he wasn't married to. Ham showing him little, if any, respect. His own wife crying all the time instead of being strong.

When he tried to take Emzara by the arm, she'd cried out, "I told you, you should have listened! Who is there now to care about your son's divorce? Where are they?" she sobbed. "Where are they – show them to me, son of Lamech, show them to me!"

Noah was distraught. He'd obeyed the Creator; why was this happening? His world felt like it was caving in. For decades he'd done all he knew how to obey the Creator, to build a righteous family and the Ark. Now his family, even his own wife, was blaming him because others hadn't listened. His mind flashed back to the day he'd spoken to Adatenesis about her refusal to dwell with Japheth. He realised how he had ignored the obvious. How he chose to have a family without the stigma of divorce but fractured spiritually. And now what did he have? Emzara was right. Where were all those people who would come because Japheth didn't divorce Adatenesis? And where was Nadina? He realised he loved her more than his long absent daughters.

Noah leaned heavily against the Ark's ramp's door frame, the rain masking his tears. "Oh Creator of the heavens, forgive me. Have I built an ark to save mankind and filled it with nothing except my own self-righteousness?" He thought about his drinking. A deep sadness overwhelmed him. This day of vindication and supposed victory was turning into a nightmare. One from which there seemed to be no escape except in the dark swirling waters of his own predicted flood.

◆◆◆ ☞ ◆◆◆

Nadina's parent's chalet illuminated with a brilliant white light. A man stood right in front of her. She fell backwards across the floor.

The man looked resolutely into her eyes and spoke with a voice that sounded like the shout of a crowd. It was utterly compelling.

"NADINA TIRAS JAVAN, RUN!"

Nadina stared at him, completely bewildered.

A thousand thoughts raced through her mind. None made any sense. The angel stood glaring at her. Nadina abandoned thinking. She jumped up, pulling on her Favicon boots. The straps automatically fastened themselves tight around her feet and ankles. Attaching the boot's arm controller, she set them to extreme assistance mode.

Flinging on her black leather utility jacket and cap, she ran straight at the front door. Kicking it open, she expected to meet an incoming wave, but there was none. Nadina leapt out over the balustraded porch, looking up in wonder. Water was pouring from the sky! The stars were obscured. The moon was barely visible through a dark swirling mass that looked like smoke from a fire.

If there was one thing Nadina Tiras Javan could do, it was run. The men at the Royal Guard Academy had all assumed she would be easily outrun in training simulations. She never was. Every single one of them had learned that the hard way, some several times over.

Nadina ran forward into the darkness down the path to the road, but saw only water swirling beneath her. She abandoned that route and ran up the hill.

"Run on the hills, not the lower roads," she warned herself out loud. In training she'd been taught to stay focused by talking to herself. The muddy ground made running much harder. She could hear more water flowing along the road below. It was beginning to flood over.

She paced herself; sixteen miles to go. All in the dark, over hills and through dangerous woodland. The angel had said run not walk, so she did. Nadina practically sprinted the first two miles. The moon briefly shone through the dark swirling mass in the sky. Trees loomed ahead, eyes peered at her through the foliage. Was it a large reptile or a small animal? She drew her knife from her leg holster and kept running straight towards it. Surprised, the creature hesitated then stepped out to meet her. It was large. Very large and quick, not another raptor – a young agile stegosaurus.

"I don't have time for this," Nadina shouted, running full on towards the hungry reptile. Suddenly, the whole sky went bright white again. A distorted line of light struck the ground between the two of them. Followed immediately by the loudest crashing sound in the sky she'd ever heard. The creature jumped back in terror; he'd been shot with a disruptor years before, but this was something else. Its fright was its death sentence. While it hesitated, Nadina dived under it, sliding across the mud on her back. She ripped open its belly with her titan knife, rolled back up onto her feet and sprinted on into the woodland. More white flashes and crashing sounds followed, the creature was not pursuing. Nadina came out through the other side of the small woods. Emerging onto a ridge leading west, she ran purposefully along it.

The ridge was uneven with numerous difficult jumps and rocky stones. She leapt at each one. Her boots did the rest automatically. Sensing rate of ascent and descent, their cushioners reacted every time her feet hit the ground. Absorbing the impact and bouncing back, they gave that tiny but important spring for each next step. The inner sole levellers adjusted for off-balance missteps. Sensors measured lactic acid build-up in her leg muscles. Compensating against hypoxia by injecting hypoxa–mataline. A top-secret Royal Guard chelated oxygen serum.

"I was never going to hand these boots back anyway," Nadina gasped, remembering her old, moody supply officer from the Academy.

Eight miles later, Nadina was flagging and only a little over halfway. The rain, the mud, the darkness, the uneven ground—it was exhausting. She stumbled and fell. Nadina punched the manual stimulant override button on her arm controller. Short needles flooded her ankle arteries with concentrated caffeine and tauratin. Soon she was up and running again. The rain was heavy on her clothing, but her jacket wick'd away the water. She drank the last of the super-hydrated water from her jacket's emergency supply.

"So cold!" she exclaimed perplexed. The rain was icy, stinging her face like a thousand needles. Her boot's arm readout told her she still had six miles to go. Nadina badly wanted to rest, to walk, but she remembered the angel. She didn't know how much further she could run on this surface. She could hardly see a thing and the ground was getting more and more slippery. Her boots' mini auto spikes were compensating, but it was barely enough. In the very far distance, she saw the faint silhouette of the cluster of hills where the Ark was. Were there already valleys of turbulent water between here and there? Was she already too late? The thought was unbearable.

"Japheth," she sobbed, dropping his pendant she'd been holding in her hand. She stopped to pick it up but couldn't find it.

"Japheth!" she cried out loud at the top of her voice. Now she had nothing of his.

"Give me strength," she pleaded, but only felt more exhausted than ever. She changed what she was saying.

"I am the leader of a new people," Nadina shouted, still running. "I am a daughter of Noah," she cried, leaping across a six-cubit gulley.

"I will reach the Ark," she gritted her teeth, yelling fiercely.

Mortal fear assaulted her mind, threatening that she was already too late. A thousand voices screamed at her to give up, but then she felt the presence of the angel again. He was not visible, but she knew he was there. There was nothing to see except the driving rain and dark, billowing clouds overwhelming the landscape, but she imagined him clearing a path before her, cutting through hordes of evil creatures.

The last valley before the hills surrounding the Ark was not flooded. The swirling waters had created a temporary blockage at one end, sparing it a little longer from the fate of the rest of the nearby valleys. The final stretch was all uphill. Her legs were numb, her chest ached, her face was stinging from the icy rain, and her clothing soaked right through.

Nadina Tiras Javan was beyond exhaustion but somehow still running faster than most people ever could even on level ground at any time in their entire life.

♦♦♦ 🏳 ♦♦♦

Ariana was shivering, unable to stand the cold. Emzara was hugging herself to keep warm, half praying and crying inconsolably.

Shem wanted to look for Nadina, but leaving the Ark, not to mention Ariana, was unthinkable.

Timnah stepped forward onto the ramp, looking into the darkness. She turned and looked at Ham.

"We have to find her," she shouted through the din of the rain. "Nadina is near, I know it." Timnah took a step further out into the lashing rain. Ham looked at his wife in disbelief. Timnah, the frail slave girl from the Dark Kingdom, was suggesting they go out in this torrent of water falling from the sky!?

Timnah began walking down the ramp into the gloom. The water soaked right through her clothing, leaving it clinging to her skin. In that moment, she looked more beautiful than any time Ham had ever seen her. He wondered if he had already held her in his arms for the last time and not known it.

"Ham!" Noah shouted desperately through the downpour. "The ramp has to be lifted soon or it will be too late!" He pointed towards the end of the ramp. It was true, water and mud were swirling over the bottom of it. They would not be able to raise it if it became trapped in the mud.

Timnah was purposefully wading through the knee-deep water, heading towards the nearest hill.

Ham looked at his wife, then at his father. He didn't care anymore. "You have your wine!" he shouted angrily. "You don't need a useless son, and where are my sisters? You got them married off young enough, didn't you!" he yelled. "Yes, married and drowning – that really makes us look good as a family!" Ham stepped out into the pouring water, down the ramp and after Timnah.

Noah was pale and visibly shaken. Shem stared in shock. Ham had sworn at his father. Shem realised there was something about his father that Ham knew which he didn't. Ham waded after Timnah, clambering up the nearest hill. They both peered into the darkness. A white flash illuminated the sky as another crashing sound filled the air. Ham ignored it; this had been happening for more than two hours now, but nothing actually came of it. They stood hand in hand in the darkness, unsure where to search.

Another sound filled the air; it was the roar of the Kestrel. Impervious to the rain, its combustion-powered thrusters easily overcame the wind and water. Shem hovered near Timnah and Ham.

"Get in!" he yelled. They clambered in and rose up off into the chaotic night sky to find Nadina. The four left at the Ark's door stared after them. They wondered if they were all that would be left of humanity.

◆◆◆ ⌐ ◆◆◆

Nadina was staggering towards the rim of the hills surrounding the Ark. She stared, delirious, at her Favicon display. Only three miles to go, all uphill, in complete darkness and heavy driving rain. She fell to one knee, punching the final stand buttons on her arm controller. Her distress beacon activated. Her boots injected metamorphine and diatrom into her arteries – Royal Guard stimulants. Standing up like a machine, she began running again.

Inside the Kestrel, a beacon proximity alert sounded.

"Nadina's distress beacon!" Ham shouted at the top of his voice through the noise of the engines, falling water, and buffeting winds.

Shem looked over; Ham was right, it was Nadina's own signal, no one else could have it. He turned and began flying towards it, activating the Kestrel's powerful searchlights. For several minutes they saw nothing. Then they saw her! Running like a world-class medium-distance sprinter up a steep hill through heavy mud and driving rain was a figure. It was Nadina. She didn't even look up despite the bright lights.

"Diatrom!" shouted Shem to Ham, "We're going to have to pull her in." Ham nodded; he knew what diatrom was and what it did. They set down on level ground in front of Nadina. She kept on running as though to pass them.

"Nadina!" yelled Timnah, confused, leaping out of the Kestrel into the rain and mud. "Nadina!" Timnah screamed again.

Nadina stopped, staring blankly at Timnah, then at the Kestrel. She swayed, looked confused, and tried to start running again. The first decision anyone made when taking diatrom was the last one they could make until it wore off.

Ham ran forward, catching hold of Nadina. Holding her firmly, he dragged her into the Kestrel. All the while shouting her name to try and break the hold of the drug. Timnah and Ham squeezed Nadina back into the cabin designed for two, modified to tightly fit three and now somehow holding four. They raced back to the Ark. The ceaseless racket of the downpour drowned out all other sounds except the roar of the engines.

Shem remotely opened the top covering of the Ark, set the Kestrel down inside, and closed it again. Noah had seen the Kestrel's lights and, realising Shem had returned, raced up to the top deck. Ariana followed him; the thought of now losing Shem as well as her father had jolted her out of her grief.

Shem, Ham, and Timnah piled out of the Kestrel, dragging Nadina between them.

"Dad, we've got her," Ham cried breathless, as he met his father coming the other way. The elation of finding Nadina broke the hardness between them from earlier. Ariana passionately hugged Shem. Noah, seeing everyone was safely aboard, went back down to the main door to raise the ramp. Timnah and Ham helped Nadina, taking her further down the corridor to their cabin.

On the lower deck by the ramp door, Japheth sat, head in hands on the floor, his body convulsing with sobs. Emzara had buried her head in his shoulder, holding him. She'd stopped fervently praying. Noah didn't wait to explain anything. He flung the switch to raise the ramp; as he half expected, the motor whined and grated, but the ramp would not rise. The weight of the mud over it was too much for its lifting mechanism to overcome.

Shem came down from the upper deck, seeing the problem, immediately ran down the ramp. He began trying to push the mud away with his hands. It was futile. The swirling waters were only piling more on. Then he had a brilliant idea: hover the Kestrel over the ramp and use its engines to blow the mud away. He ran quickly back up the ramp. But when he reached the top, he noticed Noah, Emzara, and Ham, who had now also come down to help, staring past him. Even Japheth was looking up. Shem turned around. The ramp was rising of its own accord, the rain lashing it clean. There was a firm but gentle interlocking series of thuds as it closed securely into place.

The silence was deafening.

The pouring rain and frequent crashing sounds from the skies were barely audible inside the Ark.

"The Creator has shut us in," breathed Emzara. Japheth stared numbly at the wall of laminated wood before him, fresh tears falling down his cheeks.

"Hey," Ham slapped the back of his brother's shoulder, "your sweetheart is upstairs. We picked her up in the Kestrel."

Japheth stared uncomprehendingly at Ham. At the stairwell, an exhausted and bedraggled Nadina appeared, steadied by Ariana and Timnah. The effects of the diatrom, designed to last only a very short time, had started to wear off. Nadina looked at Japheth's tear-strewn face. Even in her half-drugged, exhausted state, she knew his tears were for her. She leant against a bulkhead, trying to compose herself, took a deep breath and looked slowly all around twice.

"Where is she?" Nadina asked, sounding drunk.

"She's not here," Emzara answered solemnly.

"She was never really here," Shem added.

Emzara nodded thoughtfully, slightly raising an eyebrow as if admitting to herself something she'd known all along. "No, she never was," she agreed quietly.

Noah looked at the floor. Ham said nothing. Timnah watched silently. It was the end of the world, yet what was happening here seemed more significant. The old world and all its futility was passing away. Here a new world was being born.

Japheth was staring with a fixed expression at Nadina. Trying to process everything her presence meant. Everything that the last couple of decades had meant or not meant. He remembered when he'd first met her, the way the sun caught her hair in the woodlands that eternal day. Her determination. Her lack of fear in the presence of danger. Her smile. Her whooping with delight when he took her up in the Kestrel. Her laughter. Her endless chatter, and now?

And now, here she was.

Japheth climbed off his knees and walked slowly over to Nadina. He took her hand like he did the first time they kissed beneath the Tactan.

"Nadina," he spoke hesitantly, exhausted from the most traumatic day of his entire life. His voice was soft and quiet. Nadina had always loved his voice. "Nadina," it was all he could say.

Nadina smiled weakly, wondering if she was dreaming. The elation of the diatrom could not compete with the elation of the reality of what was happening. She rested her head on his shoulder and pulled him close.

"My Japheth," she murmured. "My Japheth."

Chapter 34

What You Leave Behind

The Countdown – Minus One

*A*datenesis had seen the reports of the strange weather coming over from the west. Water from the sky and water from the ground. It sounded very disconcerting, but she knew that news stories always exaggerated things. With all that had happened recently, reliable reports were hard to come by. Nahron's forces were rumoured to be on the move again. She was sure that Japheth would be safe and that the Creator would preserve him from the evil of Nahron. But she couldn't help but wonder why his family had to stay on the Ark provoking the emperor. Surely Noah had got his point across by now? The disaster with the Auto Batteries had shown once again that the Creator should be revered, and the Land of the Ancient's integrity respected.

Evening had fallen. The Seventh Day ended and the start of the eighth day after Noah's warning had begun. Adatenesis looked up at the imposing stone walls and high ceilings of the great Assembly Hall in Isis. It sat securely on the banks of the Pishon. She was gathered there with several hundred other parents. The solid building insulated those inside from the elements outside. Local experts had assured the residents that the weather phenomenon would soon pass. The building was packed. Parents and children sat chattering. The orchestra was warming up. It was going to be a great evening.

Adatenesis was so proud of her son and had always given him the best for his future. Getting him into the select school had been a monumental achievement. She knew others thought she went too far with her focus on education, but she knew it was for the best. After all, one had to be practical. Her only regret was that Japheth was not by her side. She wished he would leave all the things to do with his father's preaching behind to come and join her, but he never had. She considered it a great sacrifice on her part that she had stood by him despite his choices all these years. Of course, he'd already been engaged in building the Ark when they'd met. But it would have been much more romantic if he had abandoned it all for her. She was glad he hadn't started another long pleading conversation with her about the evening's event. She appreciated that. Few men were as patient and under-standing as Japheth.

The ambience of the atmosphere around her was reassuring. Applause began to ripple through the audience. The orchestra began playing. Parents quickly stood, eager to catch a glimpse of their beloved children performing. They were so proud.

◆◆◆   ⚐   ◆◆◆

Reports of bizarre weather had been coming into the City of Light throughout the day. The east had seen torrential downpours of water coming from the sky. The north had too, but neither experienced any-thing like the severity of what happened in the west. The west had experienced a massive and inexplicable flood coming out of a huge fis-sure in the ground. The remote pleasure islands of the western sea were completely out of contact. Rumours were circulating that an angelic being had been seen travelling at great speed, cutting open the ground. There was even a video feed from a couple of military transports that supported the rumour. It had been leaked and gone viral on the central highlands news channels. It was immediately fact-checked as fake.

Telecasts from aerial news transports showed footage of the low-lands of the west covered under a mass of swirling waters. Handfuls of survivors told of huge waves rising as if from nowhere out of the sea. The floodwaters were reportedly heading right for the capital. When they would arrive, no one knew. Many doubted they would rise above the level of the great central plain on which the City of Light stood. However, a few concerned souls were already heading north for the long journey to the Pazgon mountains. Those in the rain-soaked east headed towards the High Hills of Havilah.

Prebius was one of those heading to the Pazgon mountains. After the débâcle of the Victory Parade and Ariana's subsequent kidnap, which was being attributed to him by some commentators, he was already halfway there. Travelling by slow public transport to avoid detection, he was loathing every moment of it. He gazed unhappily out of the window of the lumbering transport. Someone was talking loudly on a communicator.

"Orion is completely submerged," they exclaimed to everyone on the transport, "and Gemini, too!"

271

"My gods," shouted someone else, "what about Aquarian!?"

"They will be next," another man spoke up, "if the water is already going in that direction."

"How many are dead?" another passenger joined the conversation.

"Hundreds of thousands already, maybe millions. The roads there are blocked. The grids are losing power," a veteran had been in contact with some friends still in the service.

"What about us?" asked a concerned passenger, addressing her question to the driver as much as to anyone else.

"Our power absorption is at 65%," the driver informed everyone cheerfully. "The energy lines are still strong here. That's more than enough to maintain a good speed. From here on, it's all uphill to the Pazgon mountains. The waters will never get that high." His confidence was high.

"What if they do?" the passenger replied, her voice quivering.

"Don't be ridiculous, how can the water get that high?" a young man who'd been quiet until now spoke up nonchalantly.

"Well, how can it cover Orion then?" she retorted. "Isn't this what that preacher with the boat said would happen?"

The young man flew into a rage. "Don't start bringing religion into this," he riled. "Why do some people think everything is about religion!"

"I was just asking," the accused woman answered sharply.

"Well, keep your views to yourself," the man said angrily, forcing his views on everyone else. After that, no one cared to speak much.

Prebius kept his head down. The converters on the public transport started to faintly whine. He knew only too well what that meant. They were losing their energy supply. Moments later, the resonators died as the transport ground to a halt. The driver was pulling levers and pushing the start switch, but nothing was happening.

"We've lost our energy supply," he said, confused. "The power line has disappeared. How is that possible?" A stunned silence filled the bus. "We're going to have to walk," all his optimism had fled.

"Walk!" someone cried, "It's a day's journey by road. Walking will take more than a week!"

Prebius was first off. It was raining moderately. He noticed the ground was very damp.

Soon everyone else was off the transport, some already walking.

He looked across a nearby field. A path led directly across it, meeting the road they were travelling on further up.

"I think that way's quicker," he spoke out loud to no one in particular. Soon everyone from the transport was tramping across the field and through the rain as Prebius fumbled with his bag. He waited until they were a good fifty cubits away, then slipped back into the transport. He switched off the power line blocker he'd purchased prior to leaving the City of Light. The transport's converters hummed back to life, its resonators quickly followed. He placed a small, priceless Iridium power surger into the transport's auxiliary power socket. While the Victory Parade was in full swing, he'd stolen several from the one place on earth where they were stored. The transport's power absorption surged to 100%. Prebius hit the accelerator. The large, now-empty public transport raced forward around a bend. It passed its former passengers still crossing the field, went over a hill and out of sight. They screamed and yelled abuse.

Prebius was very pleased with himself. Without the weight of all the other passengers and with the added help of his power surger he knew he would reach the mountains much quicker and that none of the previous passengers would. For a brief moment, Prebius had the strange feeling that someone stood beside him asking him why he'd done that. He dismissed the notion, smiling smugly.

Prebius raced along the almost deserted roads, ignoring all calls and waves for help. He joined the main arterial speed route to the north. Relaxing, he set the velocity control. Then, he switched on the passenger telescreen above his head. The documentary about the madman Noah was playing. Its signal coming from the new Altereon telecast station high up in the Pazgon mountains. There was more than enough backup power there to broadcast for at least another week. He laughed as the commentator parodied Noah's warning that the whole world would be covered in water.

"Fool," he scoffed to himself, "there's no way the water can get as high as the mountains of Pazgon."

◆◆◆ ⏎ ◆◆◆

Cavilah had been searching Nahron's Gate and its surrounding area for days. But he hadn't been able to find any of his men. He knew they would not let themselves be press-ganged into the empire's reservists for the assault. That was irrelevant now anyway. He also wanted to get back to the Ark but was beginning to wonder if that would be possible either.

The skies had been pouring down huge volumes of water. The river Pishon had burst its banks. Most of Nahron's Gate was under several cubits of water. Cavilah had the presence of mind to get to the eastern side of the Pishon before it overflowed. He very reluctantly decided that since he could not find his men anywhere, he would go back to the Ark. He began to make his way eastwards with hundreds of others along the ridges of the Valley of Shadow. The bottom of the valley was already a river in its own right.

The skies had been grey all day. New flashes of light, followed by immense crashing sounds, terrified most refugees. The sun briefly appeared and talk spread rapidly that the catastrophe was over. Cavilah wasn't so sure. The new rivers in the valleys were rising, fed by unchanging sources. He seriously doubted that Noah was so wrong that this cataclysm could be survived by climbing a hill.

Towards the end of the first day after the water had started falling, Cavilah noticed something odd. None of the people around him had changed. Their arrogance and mockery of any suggestion that Noah's prediction was true, was not waning. If anything, the more the waters rose, the angrier the people became. Angry at Noah, angry at the Creator, angry at the empire for not saving them, and angry at each other. Violence was all around. Bodies littered the routes to the hills. Cavilah openly carried his hunting knife to discourage robbers.

As he climbed a steep path up one of the famous High Hills of Havilah, Cavilah came to a large plateau at the top. He walked to the far end of it and found he could go no further. A ridge overlooked a steep drop beyond the plateau. Below was a seething mass of water. It was a safe distance away. But its vastness and power were terrifying. In the far distance, he could see the hills leading to the hinterlands of the Land of the Ancients. Somewhere beyond that lay Noah's.

Cavilah sombrely realised that without a fully charged flying transport, he would never make it. He turned to look behind him. A sea of people was settling on the gently sloping plateau that led up from the Valley of Shadow. He sat down, unsure what to do next, watching the crowd move around like ants. Small tents were going up. Soothsayers were giving readings and taking donations. Tents for prostitutes were established to his right. Some people were cooking and selling food. Children were running about; a few were fighting. In the distance, hundreds more people were filing up onto the plain. The falling water eased a little and the sun briefly appeared. The crowds began cheering.

"Boss, boss!" Cavilah looked to the left at the sound of familiar voices. His men were there! They were with their wives, girlfriends, and children. A few escort girls had joined them but didn't appear to be there for work. Cavilah's men had taken in anyone who needed help.

"Boss, what's going on?" his old friend Habian was pleading, "what are we to do, how will we get out of this?"

Cavilah stood up, nodded at Habian and faced his men. He waited until they were all seated in the sparse sunlight and paying attention.

"There is no getting out of this. What Noah said is true. I have been to his home. I have seen the Ark." The sun disappeared again.

Some of his men laughed in disbelief, but they respected Cavilah. He had stood with them all these years. They struggled to take it in.

"We mocked him," one said, then after pausing a little, added the unthinkable, "and the Creator. How can we be saved?"

Cavilah felt a deep, interminable sorrow for his men. He stood still, not knowing what to say for a while. Then something came over Cavilah, something that he had not felt for years. He was trembling slightly. The power was upon him.

"Bring me that chest," he motioned to two of his men who'd brought a flat-topped chest full of valuable possessions. His voice was different. They carried it forward; he stepped onto it. The sky began to darken horribly again.

Cavilah bowed his head, "O Creator of all things seen and unseen, please forgive me," he pleaded quietly. "I should never have stopped preaching your word."

Cavilah lifted his head. Multitudes looked up in shock as his voice boomed across the plain.

"Hear the word of the Lord..."

◆◆◆ ☞ ◆◆◆

Cavilah preached with fire and conviction. Everyone on the plain could hear him. Many cried out in sorrow. Some yelled in anger. Others mocked. Some passed around offering bags in his name. Some ignored everything and made use of the cheap prostitutes.

Cavilah preached solidly for half an hour. The atmosphere began to change. Multitudes knelt in sorrow, weeping. His men and their wives and girlfriends knew him well. They knew his story. They knew they had to take his message seriously. He was Cavilah, the boss, the fearless honest preacher of times past.

The crowd began to recognise him from days long gone. "It's the honest preacher," they said. There was only one to remember.

When Cavilah reached the point in his message for the call of repentance, thousands knelt. His men, their families, the escorts. Little children stopped crying. Men stopped fighting. Prostitutes and their clients came out of their tents.

Cavilah led the multitude as they spoke the sacred words. "A sacrifice to save us all, to cover our sins, an innocent life to carry our guilt. A sacrifice to save me."

The sky darkened further, the ground trembled again, the rain returned. Falling heavier and heavier. Cavilah looked down at his men.

"This is it," he said, looking past them into the near distance. A huge swell was heading up the plateau from behind, relentlessly sweeping all in its path.

Cavilah stepped off the chest and knelt down. Everyone around lifted their right hands to their heads. They covered their faces with the palms of their hands, putting their forefingers to their temples. The sign of a true believer.

Cavilah did the same as the screams and sound of the wall of water approached. He thought of his son and of his first wife, that sunny day he'd first met her while listening to a preacher long ago. He thought of his brother and wondered how he would die.

"Open his eyes," he prayed.

♦♦♦   ⌐   ♦♦♦

Cavilah was walking with his men. They were laughing. The brick path they were on wound gently upwards, running alongside a low wall. Further along, he saw a gate, quite narrow. Many people were waiting there as all those travelling up the path passed through it. Cavilah looked at his friends around him as they approached the gate. The men, the women, the children and the girls. They all smiled back.

"We made it," one said to him, "thanks to you, we made it." Others joined in thanking him.

Another voice called out from the other side of the wall.

"Dad, Dad!" Cavilah looked round as he walked through the gate. His son came running to him and hugged him.

"Dad," he whispered in his ear, "Mum is here."

Chapter 35

Complacency

The Countdown Minus Two

*C*haos reigned in the high central plains of the Empire of the Son. The waters had reached the distant hills around the capital. The news was well known. All that remained of the world were the High Hills of Havilah, the Pazgon mountains, and the elevated plain around the City of Light. Unbelievably, the whole of the rest of the planet was now completely submerged. The early sudden torrents of water and huge waves that had swept all in their path had been replaced. Now steadily increasing swells and continuous heavy rain threatened the remnants of humanity. Everyone expected it to stop, but it never did.

Nahron had lost more than half of his Royal Guard to desertion. Most of the rest of his forces were already dead. The dependable energy lines that traversed the globe had weakened. In some cases completely disappeared. Innumerable fleeing transports fell from the skies, taking their occupants to watery graves. The Altereon telecast station transmitter in the Pazgon mountains was still broadcasting. It was airing a documentary about the madman Noah and his absurd warnings of a worldwide flood. The program aired non-stop, as though its mockery of what Noah predicted ensured it could not be true.

◆◆◆　☞　◆◆◆

Nahron sat back in his favourite chair, relaxing in his quarters near the top of the Divine Tower. The tower itself had been sealed off. His two most trusted, experienced Royal Guard pilots were the only ones inside. Outside, on the rain soaked sky platform, sat his Iridium transport. A masterpiece of engineering and luxury. Glistening under the platform's lights, it was like a hybrid of a Vastar and a Tactan, only bigger and faster.

Fully stocked with food, water, and twenty-four Iridium power surgers to feed its batteries, it was ready to go. The craft could easily stay aloft without energy lines for at least three months. Nahron had decided that the mountains of Pazgon would be his final destination.

278

Everyone knew that the waters could never reach that high.

Gazing calmly at the torrents of rain, Nahron wondered if perhaps it was better this way. At least he could make a fresh start. Whatever survivors there were would be easier to manage and mould into his loyal subjects. After the waters reached their peak, he would find the Ark and destroy it. He assumed it had survived the fury of the initial waves. All the known ships of the world had been lost in an early relentless succession of high and brutal waves. Now, the waves were more subdued. He wondered how the Ark was faring. He knew it was in the highlands of the Land of the Ancients. He didn't know exactly how high up its construction site was. Only that it had been high enough to exact perfect derision from all who'd seen or heard about it.

From his vantage point almost at the top of the tower, he could see for many miles around. The swell was encroaching on the parks at the city centre. He calculated that the rate at which the waters were rising gave him one, or even two more peaceful days.

Nahron decided to stretch his legs and watch the melee below. In the distance, he could see crowds ransacking the Great Temple. It was already full of bodies from those killed in the first looting attempt. He refused to allow himself to be concerned. Nahron knew the floodwaters would recede. It was impossible for Noah and his family to stay on the Ark forever. All he had to do was wait out the catastrophe along with them.

He made sure his own thoughts reassured him. Nahron had always been good at that. He felt much better. Resting his hands on the white marble of the tower's balcony, he looked out into the early evening gloom. There was no sign of the sun, only swirling clouds releasing torrents of never ending rain. The inlaid jewels along the top of the wall had been designed to reflect the late rays of the setting sun. They weren't reflecting anything at the moment. He ordered the spotlights on his Iridium transport trained on them. They glistened but without much appeal in the artificial white light.

Nahron carefully placed a glass of the empire's best wine down in front of him. He gazed proudly across the vast city. He had achieved so much, come so far. It was a shame he would have to start over again, but he would. The Creator had made a big mistake challenging him. The wine in his glass gently rippled. Something broke behind him. He looked around, annoyed to see which of his pilots had knocked something over. Neither had. One was talking into his communicator, looking very worried. He quickly ended the call.

Something else fell off a nearby shelf and smashed. The Tower perceptibly swayed, then went still. Both pilots looked around aghast. The Divine Tower was well built, but not designed to withstand the ground shaking beneath it.

Without saying anything, all three of them walked briskly to the Iridium transport.

"Take her up," ordered Nahron, "optimum power-saving settings."

"Yes, my lord," both pilots took their seats, staring intently at their scanners. Trying to see what was happening beneath them. The backup battery power came on automatically; there was no power line to draw on.

"Set a course to the Pazgon Mountains," ordered Nahron. "Take your time."

They flew away from the city above the partially submerged lands of the high central plain. Below were lines of reptiles tramping to higher ground. The creatures appeared to have turned back from an earlier course and ended up being herded by the waters into one huge area. There were tens of thousands of them as far as the eye could see.

The pilot peered into the distance and then at his scanners. A gargantuan plume of grey-white smoke filled the sky. He stared in disbelief. No weapon could make an explosion that big. Something was erupting from below the waters. He changed course to avoid the cloud. Huge waves had been created by the eruption, but they were black, made of silt and mud. The very ground below had broken up and turned to liquid. They were smothering all in their path. He thought of the reptiles they'd recently flown over. Soon, they would all be encased in this sediment, forming one giant graveyard.

More plumes of smoke appeared in the distance. It looked as though the whole world under the waters was coming apart. The pilot couldn't get any clear signal from the Pazgon mountains. He decided that things might be a whole lot worse than he'd first thought. He had to look after himself. What if the mountains of Pazgon were overcrowded or uninhabitable from the rain? They might have to stay aloft until the waters receded. He had no idea how long that would be.

The co-pilot went to the galley, appearing shortly after with three pre-prepared meals. He gave the first to the pilot, the second to Nahron, who was sitting in his private cabin, and the third he kept for himself. The pilot eyed the food on the tray placed on his lap.

"Hey, can you get me some spice for this?" he casually asked his comrade, who was about to sit down.

"Sure," the co-pilot set his tray down on his seat and went back into the galley.

The pilot deftly swapped the identical meals. He stared intently into his scanner as his comrade returned, handing him a spice sachet.

"Thanks," he tucked into his meal. He noticed his comrade kept looking at him while eating what he thought was his own meal.

Halfway through the meal, the co-pilot who'd prepared the food started to look unwell, then went white. He realised what had happened.

"You fool," the pilot laughed at him. The co-pilot clutched his stomach, convulsed, fell to the floor and then locked his knees to his chest. The poison he'd intended for his comrade killed him in seconds. The surviving Royal Guard slowed the transport to almost a stop. He dragged his comrade's body to the side door. Opened it and threw the dead man and his half-eaten poisoned dinner out.

"Less weight and more food," he laughed to himself, sitting back down to finish his meal.

Nahron appeared. "What's going on?" he asked, perturbed.

"He relieved himself of duty, Your Majesty," the pilot answered dryly.

"I see," Nahron smiled, "less weight and more food for us." He decided he would cook his own meals from now on.

Chapter 36

Sindain's Child

The Countdown Minus Three

Things hadn't really worked out for Sindain. He'd expected to be admitted into the Tower of Light. Instead, he was politely turned away by the Royal Guards stationed at the bottom of it. Technically, he'd been promoted to be their commander, but that clearly meant nothing. They all ignored his orders. He could have used his much bigger security apparatus to impose his will on them. But with the world ending, no one was ready to follow orders like that.

Sindain had watched in disbelief from his command centre while hundreds of towns and cities in the lowlands were wiped out on the first day. As the waters deepened, the giant waves diminished and were replaced with steadily rising swells. Sometimes the waters receded a little, sending everyone in their path into mad jubilation. But they always returned, gently submerging town after town until they encroached on the outer limits of the great capital itself.

Refugees were thronging the streets. The rain never stopped. Violence was everywhere. Almost every few cubits lay a dead body. Lunatic priests no longer shouted garbled messages on every corner. The richer slick priests of the bigger temples had all fled. They left their gullible flocks to sow special miracle seeds for their deliverance. They flew away in their luxury transports towards the higher grounds of Havilah or Pazgon. None made it. Their transports had been procured for prestige, not endurance runs on batteries.

Sindain walked briskly through the quieter streets behind the palace. He slipped away from his disintegrating Command Centre. The only unified purpose that remained there was to use the communications networks to find out how far and how fast the waters were moving. He headed into the nearby elite district where his palatial home was. Why had Nahron betrayed him? He was angry and confused; what more could he have done?

He rounded the corner of a street near his home and found it flooded. A nearby river had burst its banks with all the excess rainwater running down from higher up in the city. Debris floated past. Sindain waded gingerly forward, perhaps he could cross it? He never stopped to think why he was going home. Why he wasn't admitting that this was the flood Noah had predicted. Sindain just carried on trying to survive without facing the inevitable – that he would not survive. That he would die with the blood of hundreds of men on his hands. All he wanted to do was get home. He wanted to be where he felt safe.

He heard a cry. It sounded like a child, possibly a girl. The noise of the downpour made it hard to distinguish one sound from another. Suddenly, a little girl swept past him, clinging to a large piece of floating furniture. The girl saw him and called out, lifting her hand towards him. As she did, she lost her grip. She slid out of sight behind the sofa she'd been holding on to. Sindain shouted back, he waded as fast as he could after her. The mass of furniture drifted further away. He dived in after it, frantically shouting. Soon he was pulled along and struggled to stay afloat. At least the water was clear – it was only rain-water from the streets above. Somehow he reached the tangled mass of clutter where he'd last seen the girl and heaved himself on to it. Behind the large sofa was the girl, her head partially submerged. She was kicking pathetically, trying to free herself. Sindain lunged towards her, pulling her up. She was coughing and retching. She didn't even look ten years old.

The floating pile of debris they were on became lodged against a low bridge support. Sindain pulled the child out of the water. He was almost crying. Sindain was more than 500 years old, yet he couldn't remember the last time he had cried. The girl began choking. Desperately, he turned her over, trying to free her airway, but she didn't stop. He thumped her back, but she still couldn't breathe. Her choking was getting weaker. Sindain became frantic, he tried again to free her airway. The child's little fingers wrapped themselves around his fore-finger as if to make one last plea for help, then she went still.

The roar of the rain and overflowing river increased. The sky darkened with the onset of evening and ever more swirling clouds. Sindain turned the girl back over. Her face looked so innocent yet pained, distressed and above all sad. Something in Sindain broke. He sobbed uncontrollably. How many little girls had he deprived of their fathers? In that moment, he hated himself. But when he looked at the body of the little girl, he saw only innocence.

"Why!" he screamed through the driving rain. "Why!" he stood and held her body up to the heavens as though to show the Creator something He didn't know.

"I am the murderer," he yelled, "not her!" The roar of the rain was his only answer. He sank down to the ground. "I am the murderer," he cried again weakly. The body of a woman floated past, barely discernible in the dark, in her hand was a knife. In that moment, Sindain knew and understood everything.

He realised that if the world had carried on and the dead little girl in his arms had grown up, she too would have become like the rest of humanity. Like him. Every thought and intent of her heart only evil. Sindain hung his head in mute realisation of this awful truth. Then another thought came to him. The girl he held had died in her innocence, she was not lost. At least one person from this sin-soaked world was safe. He felt insanely happy; he began to hysterically laugh and cry.

After a while Sindain grew tired; the rain was cold, the sky completely dark. He could hear distant screams as the rising waters steadily engulfed his neighbourhood. Finally, he considered his own impending fate. He knew he wasn't ready to die. He never had been. He thought of his brother Cavilah. The fool of the family. The preacher. He wanted to make things right with him.

"Forgive me, dear brother," he begged over and over until the last of his strength ebbed away.

From somewhere in the very recesses of his soul, Sindain spoke the words again, "Forgive me." But this time not to his brother. He lifted his right hand middle fingers to his forehead and then rested his head on the silent chest of the little girl. The cyanide from his concealed tooth capsule stopped his heart moments later.

◆◆◆   ⌐   ◆◆◆

"Uncle Sindain, is that you?"

◆◆◆   ⌐   ◆◆◆

Talmeon realised he should have flown back to Nahron's Gate and then on to Noah's. He could have used the same Vastar he'd been brought to the City of Light in. The morning before he had been summoned to see Nahron, his pilot had asked permission to return to the Havilah region. Talmeon had considered going with him but he'd hesitated for fear of Nahron. He asked the pilot to wait. He also wanted to see his children, to tell them all about the Ark and what he'd seen.

Later, when Talmeon returned from his visit with Nahron and Sindain, his pilot had gone, taking the Vastar with him. After reports of the flood started coming in, Talmeon realised this was it. He knew he would never get back to the Ark. He went to visit his children for the second time. They were all at his eldest son's for a wedding. In desperation, he tried again to explain the situation to them. He told them about the Ark, the warning, the Forbidden Gate, anything he could think of.

None of them listened, even his wife. Was he accusing them of being unbelievers? How could he suggest such a thing! They were having a wedding soon, a religious service with everything done properly. Was he blind, or what? Had he too become some kind of religious nutcase like Noah? Was he not a scientist, didn't he have any idea how much water it would take to cover the high plains around the City of Light? As for the idea of water covering the whole world, that was beyond absurd.

Only his youngest daughter started to take him seriously after the floodwaters drew closer. They both watched the increasingly sketchy telecasts. News transports showed aerial footage of huge swells engulfing more and more cities across the empire's high central plains. The family wedding went ahead. Neither Talmeon nor his daughter attended.

"Dad?" his daughter asked, losing all the nonchalance of her wild youth. "Am I going to die?" It was strange, millions had already died but until she faced her own death, his daughter had treated it as though it hopefully might never happen.

"Yes, my precious child," Talmeon answered her truthfully. "There will be no survivors."

"But I still have so much to do, I'm only young. Why?" tears filled her eyes.

Talmeon was overwhelmed. Religious question and answer sessions were hardly his speciality, but he knew he had to say something. Normally, any soothing answer would have sufficed but this was different. It was the end of the world and his very own daughter asking him the questions – with whom he soon expected to leave it. The time for shallow explanations was long gone.

Talmeon took a deep breath, "Iona, our lives are a gift. We have the choice of what to do with them but what we choose is what we get to keep."

"What do you mean, father?"

"Well, you see, without us welcoming the Creator's involvement, everything in our lives naturally corrupts. Our bodies eventually corrupt and die; that we all can see. What is overlooked is that unless we choose the Creator's ways, so do our souls, our very characters. This is why the older people get, the more hardened their hearts become. Sooner or later they reach a point where they care about absolutely nothing except themselves. Even their outwardly pleasant behaviour becomes their own hidden self-righteousness. They start to see everything they have, including even the gift of life itself, as their own. And look what this has done, the whole world is full of violence."

Iona thought about that. She had never been violent herself, but many times she'd felt anger that wanted to express itself in violence. She remembered a college friend who'd greatly annoyed her and had met a violent death only the year before. She recalled how happy she was about that. How she enjoyed talking and thinking about her old classmate's demise. Did this mean she loved violence but only lacked the courage to carry it out?

"And secondly, the world around us corrupts us," Talmeon continued, "our kindness is extinguished by its hatred. Do you remember the time you made those cakes for Uncle Faran?"

Iona was still very angry about that fifteen years later. She'd worked particularly hard to prepare some special cakes for a distant visiting uncle. She'd been intently looking forward to him commending her for her efforts. When she presented them to him, holding the hot tray in her gloved hands, he barely glanced at the cakes. He insulted her and her cooking from every angle. She'd wanted to take the hot glass tray and push it right into his face. Uncle Nahron had heard about it later and had him executed by being burned to death in an oven. It was one of the happiest days of her life. Iona had joyfully told all her school friends about it. After that, her teachers were particularly careful to be polite to her.

Iona despaired. The truth was she was still happy about it even now. "Why didn't you tell us these things before, Father? I can't change now, and even if I could, what difference would it make to anything?"

"I didn't know them myself until I went to the Land of the Ancients and saw the Forbidden Gate," Talmeon confessed. "Mankind has reached a tipping point. All our thoughts and plans are utterly selfish. We cannot live forever in this condition. The flood is to save mankind, not to destroy it."

"How will it save us?" Iona wasn't convinced.

"I don't know, but it will certainly stop the violence. Where are the circuses of Zanbar now?"

Iona didn't need to answer that. It was a rhetorical question. The whole western province of Zanbar was submerged. Not a living soul remained alive there to enjoy the violent circuses. Condemned men and women, many guilty of nothing more than someone else's disfavour, were sent to fight to the death against wild reptiles. It had become prime-time viewing on all the telecast channels.

The downpour outside increased. The sound of water flowing nearby could be heard clearly.

Talmeon stood up and walked towards the window. Water was running down the outside of it like a river. Iona followed his line of sight. Madman or not, she realised what Noah had said had come true.

"When I was at Noah's, they didn't pray like most people do," Talmeon said. "They really mean what they say in prayer." He knelt down by the steps facing the large window. The sky outside had no light in it at all.

Iona stood next to him. She had never knelt to pray before and had never prayed sincerely about anything in her whole life.

Talmeon repeated the well known words. "A sacrifice to save us all, to cover our sins, an innocent life to carry our guilt. A sacrifice to save me."

Iona knew these words were from the very beginning of time. What they meant she had absolutely no idea. Why her father was repeating them without having anything to sacrifice she had even less idea, but she decided to pray them too. To really mean them. Why not? Soon she would be dead. Iona knelt down next to her father.

"A sacrifice to save us all, to cover our sins, an innocent life to carry our guilt," she spoke softly as a quiet peace enveloped her soul. Her father gently put his arm around her.

"A sacrifice to save me," she whispered.

It wasn't long before the whole district was underwater.

◆◆◆ ⚑ ◆◆◆

Prebius was elated. He'd made it with the last of the survivors from the great central plains all the way to the mountains of Pazgon. He was already inside the remote town of Altereon.

Refugees were crowding into the streets everywhere. Prebius decided to part with his public transport before it drew too much attention. He hid the six heavy Iridium power surgers he'd stolen. Then he made his way through the busy streets to the upper end of the town.

The distant surge was still far below the town. But the rainwater running down from the peaks above made staying even in Altereon barely tolerable. Prebius decided to make the final ascent to the nearby Pazgon village. The highest inhabited place in the world, and to wait out the catastrophe there. Thousands of others had already made that same decision.

The road to the village was impassable, so all the refugees were filing onto a narrow rocky pathway that also led directly up to it. Frequent fights broke out. Many were unceremoniously pushed off the steep pathway's edge to settle disputes.

Prebius walked slowly behind a large, overweight man. Behind him, he heard a rowdy family pushing and shoving their way forward. He could have carefully stepped aside and let them pass, but he wanted to make sure he got a good spot in the village. The man in front stumbled. Prebius surreptitiously stuck his foot out, catching the man's heel while he was still trying to regain his balance. The man fell over and rolled along the shallow slope, unable to stop himself and then off the steep drop. Prebius acted suitably aghast and carried on a little quicker. He was a survivor, and he intended to remain one.

Why Noah had said the flood was coming didn't interest Prebius in the slightest. He simply intended to stay alive and get on with his life. He looked forward to a world with fewer people in it to annoy him. It would be like the stories from the early times of the Garden. He thought about the Garden for a moment. But quickly decided he had more important things to do than waste his time on religion.

Imperial Vandeons appeared in the sky, a line of six of them. They all bore the crest insignia of the Royal Guard Corps. The crowds climbing the steep walk to Pazgon village began cheering. They were being rescued, resupplied, or something similar. Perhaps the flood had receded in the central plains and they were going to be ferried home?

Prebius was not among those cheering. He was halfway up the path when he saw the Vandeons. He knew they must have availed themselves of some of the remaining Iridium power surgers. The huge craft would have used two each just to get from the City of Light. He also knew that their presence was anything but good. He quickly turned and began trying to force his way back down, but was angrily pushed aside.

"We're going up, you fool, not down," someone kicked him and he almost fell off the same ridge he'd sent the fat man down earlier. He didn't dare look up as the sound of the transports spread out all around. Perhaps they would miss him? He knew they never did.

♦♦♦ ⚑ ♦♦♦

The Royal Guard Commander of the Vandeons waited impatiently until all his craft were in position. They had fifteen minutes of power left, that would have to do.

"Clear a path and secure the area," he ordered. He laughed at the crowds below, "Well done, at least you made it this far."

The Vandeons unleashed their heavy weaponry into the screaming refugees, their bodies ripping apart and exploding. Round after round reduced them to piles of grotesquely mutilated corpses.

The Vandeons set down in a semi-circle right by the only entrance to Pazgon village. The elite troops rapidly disembarked and began systematically entering the nearby houses.

"Shoot the men and keep the women," ordered the commander.

"What about the children?" asked a lieutenant.

"Who cares?" he replied.

The first seven of his men to approach the village were killed stepping on a series of mines. The villagers had already decided they didn't want refugees there.

Resistance was futile, soon the whole village was secure. The commander was pleased. They were safe. The waters would never reach this high. He settled down, taking refuge from the rain inside the village temple. The body of a priest lay near the altar, surrounded by a pile of gold coins. Blood ran down his outstretched arm onto the coins his hand was still clutching. The commander hated priests.

He took a break while his men raped the surviving local women. It had been an exhausting day. The heavy walls of the temple deadened the noise of the rain outside. He was very pleased with himself. Surviving this catastrophe was quite an achievement. He drifted off to sleep.

Something woke him. He had the sensation of moving. He ran outside and looked around in shock; all the buildings of the village were collapsing. The entire hillside had begun to slip and unravel. Like a huge undulating carpet, the whole village slid down towards the town of Altereon, covering it with its own dead and rubble.

The commander looked desperately across at the other mountains. Through the pouring rain, he could see that they too were falling apart and crashing into the waters. He saw two of his own Vandeons take off. He knew it was futile, they would have barely six or seven minutes before their batteries gave out.

He struggled to keep his balance as the ground began to fold over on itself. The cries of his men filled the air. He looked up towards heaven and shook his fist.

"I hate you!" he screamed as he and the whole mountain slid inexorably down into the hungry waters beneath.

◆◆◆   ⊱   ◆◆◆

"Your majesty," Nahron's pilot was trembling. "A distress call has come in from one of our Vandeons already in the mountains of Pazgon." He barely had the strength to speak. "The mountains are... they are collapsing and sliding into the waters!"

His face was white. He looked at Nahron as though he might order them to stop or something.

"Set a new course," Nahron ordered, "The Land of the Ancients."

He knew there was only one way out of this now.

The Earth's Rest

All the foundations of the earth had become unstable. Man's wickedness broke the harmony between him and his home. Pressure was building up inside the earth. Perhaps in His mercy, the Creator sent an angel to cut a furrow around the globe. The earth fractured but was preserved. Men who would never have given a thought to anything except more evil saw the rising waters. Facing the inevitability of their doom, a few may have changed their hearts.

Noah and his family were imperfect like you and me. But their faith gave them favour with their Creator. They made the right choices. Instead of being engulfed in a fragmenting planet, they were delivered.

Huge volumes of water swept across the globe, carrying with it all the broken sediment of a once perfect earth. Billions of creatures were trapped and drowned, some in the very act of eating one another. Without oxygen, they quickly fossilised, some in days, some in hours.

Millions of reptiles were corralled by the floodwaters, leaving fleeing footprints to their vast fossil graveyards. Even the highest mountains of the world have marine fossils set in their peaks. As the sediments compacted and hardened, they serve as a perpetual reminder of a broken world that tried everything. Everything except what its Creator directed.

The way chosen by the first man, the way of the knowledge of good and evil, had brought with it only fear, jealousy and the first murder; which led to all other murders – even the civilised murder of neglect by the eye that chooses not to see.

And God saw that the wickedness of man was
great in the earth, and that every imagination of
the thoughts of his heart was only evil continually.

And the Lord regretted that he had made man on
the earth, and it grieved him at his heart.
And the Lord said, I will destroy man whom I have
created from the face of the earth; both man, and
beast, and the creeping thing, and the fowls of the
air; for I regret that I have made them.

But Noah found grace in the eyes of the Lord.
Genesis 6:5–8

Chapter 37

Emzara and Noah

"You were right, my dear," Emzara lay snuggled next to her faithful husband of more than five hundred years. "You were right, you have preserved mankind."

Being proved right sounded good, but sometimes being right wasn't all it was cut out to be. Noah lived in two worlds. In one, he had a simple life. His beloved wife was all he needed; her love, friendship, and devotion were more than any man could dream of. In the other, the burdens were almost unbearable. He knew he hadn't always handled things right. He'd saved the world, or had he? How many people were on board? Eight. What could the Creator possibly do with eight people? And eight imperfect people at that. Was he supposed to govern all those who would be born after the catastrophe? He didn't even know how to get on with his youngest son, let alone lead a new civilisation.

Noah had won the victory, but he was weary, weary of the fight, weary of the race. He remembered the wine his workers had brewed. How on occasion it had masked the frustration of years of preaching to mocking crowds. They were all dead now, but that didn't help. He recalled his endless problems with the Council. Had they not been his brothers, fellow believers? Evidently not. He thought of all his imperfections, things he had said and done, and not done. He wondered if he had acted differently that there might be more people on board. Even at the last trial, should he have been more respectful? Would it have made any difference? His eyes were heavy, his body longed for rest. Two weeks had passed since the flood began; there was less work to do on board now, but his mind was still not at rest.

Noah got up to close the cabin's air vent. No one had expected it to get so cold outside. After the first day of the flood he'd been very concerned. The air temperature in the stalls of the larger mammals and reptiles had become very cold. This had a strange effect on them – they all went into a deep sleep and stayed asleep. The family had conferred and decided to leave their vents open. The dark forms of mammals and reptiles all sleeping in their stalls on the dim lower deck made it an eerie place to walk through. A whole new world was in slumber until the time of its awakening.

Noah climbed back into the bed. He thought again of all his dead friends and relatives. "They have perished," he murmured to himself as Emzara squeezed warmly up to him in her sleep, "yet I am still alive – why?"

As if in answer to his question, familiar words floated into his mind.

"A sacrifice to save us all, to cover our sins, an innocent life to carry our guilt."

He smiled faintly as he buried his tired face in his pillow. "A sacrifice to save me," he answered quietly. "Yes, I do believe. I most certainly do, and that's the only reason why I'm here."

A warm presence settled on Noah's weary heart. Not a moment of his tiredness, not an ounce of his drained strength, not a single one of his shed tears would ever be forgotten.

They are all recorded.

Chapter 38

Shem

*A*riana gently ran her fingers through Shem's hair. He tenderly caressed her back. They gazed at each other, both smiling.

"I never thought I would marry a zookeeper," Ariana teased.

"Perhaps it's your true calling too? That hippo certainly liked you," Shem prodded her side; Ariana squealed.

They lay still and held each other close for a long time, the motion of the Ark causing mild creaks now and again. After two weeks, they stopped hearing them. The warmth of the wooden cabins was snug compared to the bitter cold outside.

The previous day they'd all rushed up to the top deck to open one of the shutters to see a new phenomenon. Innumerable flakes of white ice floating down from the heavens were settling in a white sheen on the face of the waters. A great stillness had descended. Then slowly, the flakes had all melted, disappearing into the deep. Each one had been unique and beautiful.

"Is it a message from the Creator?" Ariana had asked. Like the people of their world, the flakes were without number, and yet all lost. What had been so unique and beautiful was now gone forever.

Ariana decided two things. First, whatever she did would be based on kindness. The one thing absent from the old world was kindness. The only person who'd ever shown her real kindness until Shem was her father. Second, whatever the new world would bring, she would build it only with her husband at her side.

Every moment with Shem turned Ariana's days into fun and laughter. Yet Shem had another side to him, something that others didn't readily notice through all his humour. Something that made him almost indestructible. He had conviction and an unswerving love for the Creator. Ariana knew in her heart that this was his real strength.

This was what made him who he was.

This was why she loved him.

Chapter 39

Ham

"Hey, let's have a break." Timnah kissed Ham gently, pulling him reluctantly out of bed.

"Where are we going?" he mildly objected, smiling at her pale, warm brown eyes.

"To my favourite place, of course, to see the view," she laughed.

Timnah was turning out to be anything but weak. Things between them just got better and better. She soothed Ham's broken heart in so many ways and eased the tensions between him and his father. Ham was in a state of mild perpetual amazement at her inner strength and wise counsel. After one very tense time with his father the previous week, she'd spoken to him soon after in the quiet of their cabin.

"Ham, you cannot let your brokenness lead you," she'd said. The words had stayed with him ever since. Ham stared at her blankly, reliving the moment.

"Are you even listening to me, Ham, son of Noah?" Timnah playfully frowned, dragging him out of the cabin and down the corridor.

That was another thing about her, Ham thought to himself. Three weeks at Noah's, two on the Ark and some decent food and exercise, and she was ridiculously strong. How anyone who looked that frail and slim could be so strong, he had no idea.

They came to the rear of the upper deck where the view looked out behind the Ark. It was their favourite spot. Ham opened the protective shuttering. It was night, the wind had dropped a little. Timnah gasped in delight; the stars had reappeared. It was the first time she'd seen them since coming aboard. Ham stood next to her, putting his arm round her. She looked up and remembered that starlit night from so many years ago, and the even stranger dream accompanying it.

All she could see around her was water.

A man was next to her. He had his arm around her.

All she felt from him was love.

Chapter 40

Japheth

*N*adina's soft lips pressed warmly against Japheth's. In the dimness of their candlelit cabin every part of him that could be was a part of her. Their wedding days past but seemingly only moments ago.

"Nadina," her name fell repeatedly and softly from his lips as he held her like the Creator had made them to be.

"My Japheth," she breathed out, smiling at him in the dark as he came to rest eventually falling asleep in her arms.

After a while, Nadina gently eased herself out of the bed and tip-toed across the cabin to get some water. There was a picture of a beautiful forest fixed to the wall. She smiled. The day she met Japheth in the woodlands came back to her like it was yesterday. She remembered their trip to the Forbidden Gate. How he'd given her the pendant at the end of that eternal day. For all the long and lonely years after that, she'd never let it go. It symbolised not only her love for Japheth but also what she'd seen at the Forbidden Gate. Her only regret was that she'd dropped it while running to the Ark.

Nadina was a little cold. The vents that fed air into the cabins had to be frequently closed because the outside air was so cold. Then they had to be opened again; otherwise, condensation built up everywhere.

Nadina opened her wardrobe to find something warm to put on. She pulled out the first jacket her hands found. It was the one she'd fled to the Ark in, washed and dry. She put it on, idly resting her thumb in the tiny lower left key pocket; something touched the end of it. She pulled it out.

Nadina stared wide-eyed in wonder. It was Japheth's pendant; it had fallen not to the ground but into her pocket. How unlikely was that!

She turned and looked at Japheth's sleeping form on the bed. The dim bedside light silhouetted his toned shoulders. His chest gently rose and fell with his contented sleep. How was it that he was finally hers? That she was even on this vessel? She fastened the pendant back around her neck, holding it up in her hands and gazing at it.

The impossible had become possible. She would never let it go.

Chapter 41

Water, Water Everywhere

𝒩ahron's pilot took the Iridium transport to its maximum height; it didn't help. The soft white flakes that filled the skies interfered with its resonators. They'd used up almost four fully charged Iridium power surgers in less than two weeks. The buffeting winds and violent rain had drained them at an alarming rate. Even so, the transport handled that better than these mysterious pieces of floating ice. Nahron and his pilot desperately hoped to catch sight of land somewhere. But they couldn't see anything through the serene white veil. They had no idea where they were.

It was short-lived; the rain returned after a break of only two hours and the high winds with it. The atmosphere was almost always dark. In some places gargantuan columns of smoke rose from giant fires burning under the sea. They changed course many times to avoid them. Occasionally, the moon and stars or sun appeared, but as comforting as that was, it was of no particular help.

Nahron had thought of killing the pilot and throwing his body out to save weight. However, he realised that even though he could fly the transport on his own, he still needed the pilot. They both had to sleep some time. With either of them dead, the other would soon follow. They hardly spoke. The few words they did exchange were not pleasant. The final straw was when, on the tenth day, the pilot suggested Nahron should have listened to what the preacher Noah said after all. Nahron had snapped, scathing him with a barrage of curses and threats. The pilot simply laughed in reply, deciding that he would kill Nahron as soon as they found land.

The low power warning light came on.

"Pass me another Iridium surger," the pilot's tone was level. They had to co-operate to stay alive.

Nahron opened the safe. The Iridium power surgers were stored in a spring-loaded tube. The standard stock was twenty-four. He pulled out the next one; his heart practically stopped. There were no more behind it. The others were all missing.

"Where are the other surgers!" he demanded frantically of the pilot, assuming it was his doing.

The pilot looked round, confused, "They're in the safe. There should be twenty left in there."

"Well, there's only this one," Nahron hissed holding it in his face.

The pilot came over, looked for himself, and began laughing. Nahron became enraged.

"What are you laughing at?" he demanded.

"Obviously, they have been stolen your majesty," he mocked.

The pilot placed the last new surger in the auxiliary power socket. It was completely flat. He quickly swapped it back.

Nahron couldn't believe it. He'd expected to be able to stay aloft for months. "Who would dare do such a thing?"

"We have about twenty minutes to find land, maybe half an hour if the wind calms." The pilot ignored Nahron's last absurd question and started to take the craft down. The two of them peered out of the panoramic windscreen, looking for anything they could set down on.

The views that had been seen through the transport's windows so many times before were now all history. Cheering crowds, parading troops, the Great Temple, the Palace with its magnificent Divine Tower. None of those could be seen now. Only the faint white crests of the darkened waves below, barely visible through the rain lashing against the windscreen.

They flew in no particular direction for twenty minutes, then the resonators failed. All went silent. The final power reserves automatically stabilised the transport. It turned around slowly, making its final descent.

As they rotated, Nahron let out a shout, "There! What's that?"

The pilot saw nothing. The craft would make one more rotation before landing on the water. He waited; as it turned around again, he saw it too. A huge dark bulk, something effortlessly riding the huge swell.

"My gods!" exclaimed the pilot in disbelief. "The madman's boat!"

"Land on it!" yelled Nahron, "I order you! Land on it!"

"I can't, you fool," he shouted back, "we don't have any power."

The craft splashed down heavily on a rising wave. Emergency buoyancy aids inflated immediately. They were woefully inadequate for the swell, designed only for a soft landing on a calm sea or idyllic lake. The main cabin door divided in two. The bottom part automatically sealed shut while the top folded down. An ingenious design for one in a million scenarios. The first wave sloshed right over the top of the closed bottom half of the door. The water ran straight to one side of the cabin, then down to the lower front end. The craft immediately began to list.

The two of them rushed towards the door. If they had helped each other, they both could have escaped. They could have fired a distress flare or sounded the onboard siren to attract attention. Neither of them thought like that.

In an instant, Nahron adjusted the underside of his middle finger's ring, slapping the pilot's back. A needle beneath it punctured the pilot's clothing and skin. The poison went straight to his muscles. The pilot understood immediately what had happened. The anti-serums were in the medical cupboard. He could have reached them in time, injected himself, and followed Nahron out. But he didn't think like that.

The strong, unarmed combat-trained Royal Guard pilot grabbed Nahron. He flung him across the cabin.

"Goodbye, your majesty," he sneered, pulling out a concealed weapon from his jacket. Nahron desperately lunged back towards him. The pilot shot at him. As he pulled the trigger, the craft tipped. Another wave pushed it to one side. The pilot missed Nahron's chest and hit his thigh. Nahron cried out in pain as he collided with him. The pilot fell backwards, knocking his head on the top of his seat. Dazed as the poison began to take hold, he slid into the water rapidly filling the front of the cabin.

The Iridium transport slowly began to point its nose down into the sea. The water sloshing around the front cabin was now waist-deep. The pilot reached up and clenched his right hand around Nahron's ankle. He knew that when he died, the poison in his muscles would lock his hand solid.

Another wave knocked the transport, sloshing over the divided door again, tipping it even further until it was almost vertical. The weight of the additional water began to drag the transport down.

Nahron manically kicked the dead pilot's hand off his ankle. He desperately pulled himself up and somehow struggled out of the large open side door. He clambered up the canards, using them as steps and onto the back end of the craft. The transport sank yet lower. The side door went below the waterline. With all the air trapped in the back of the main and private rear cabins, it stabilised. Bobbing in the swell like a giant marker buoy from a yacht race Nahron had once fixed. It floated nearer and nearer to the Ark.

Nahron started yelling and shouting into the wind and rain as the massive form of the Ark began to tower over him. The Ark was far bigger than he'd imagined.

"Hey!" he screamed, "Hey!" The voice that only had to utter a word and thousands of lives were ended now cried out unheard into the outer darkness.

Nahron was on all fours. He clung desperately on to some recessed maintenance grab handles on the back of the upended trans-port. Soaked in the driving rain, he shivered in the cold. His leg bled profusely. His white royal robes were ripped and stained with blood.

The darkened bulk of the Ark slowly came closer, appearing to respond to his cries. It gently bumped his Iridium transport. Nudging it back away and slightly knocking it over to one side. The last of the air from the front cabin escaped out through the door. Water rushed in, enough to counteract the buoyancy created by the air trapped in the rear. The transport began to rapidly sink into the sea.

Nahron dived into the water, frantically swimming towards the Ark, still calling out. He was on the leeward side of the giant vessel, shielded from the wind and rain. The waves were much more subdued there. As he struggled through the water, he was careful to adjust his ring shut. It had one remaining hidden vial of poison in it. He never knew when he might need it again.

The Ark was passing him by as the wind and waves pushed it along from behind. He desperately swam towards it, but its wake pushed him away as though the vessel itself was rejecting him.

Nahron's strength began to fail. He struggled to stay afloat without being able to use his wounded leg to kick.

He looked all around to see if there was any other way to survive; there was none.

All he could see was water. Water everywhere. An ocean as far as the eye could see. He knew it was deep. How, he did not know, but he was certain that it was. He also understood that no matter how far he might travel in any direction, the waters would never end.

Then there was the atmosphere over the rolling waves.

Peaceful.

For one brief moment, Nahron was filled with wild hope; he was dreaming!

Then he realised. This time it was real.

♦♦♦   🚤   ♦♦♦

Character List
(without plot spoilers)

Nahron	Emperor of the Empire of the Son.
Talmeon	Cousin of the Emperor Nahron and his senior scientist.
Bezek	Talmeon's usual assistant.
Iona	Talmeon's youngest daughter.
Mandarus	High Priest, distant cousin of Nahron and Talmeon.
Ariana	Daughter of Mandarus.
Prebius	Nahron's event organiser.
Flixus	Prebius' assistant.
Sindain	Head of Nahron's intelligence services.
Cavilah	Citizen of Nahron's Gate.
Mavron	Senior Royal Guard Commander.
Elon	Royal Guard and pilot.
Zahar	Royal Guard and co–pilot.
Malael	Royal Guard and navigator.
Be'elzar	Ruler of the Dark Kingdom (*or Kingdom of Light*).
Ragzan	Head of Dark Kingdom security.
Noah	The man with the boat.
Emzara	Wife of Noah.
Japheth	First born son of Noah.
Adatenesis	Japheth's wife (her son is called Vindad).
Shem	Second born son of Noah.
Ham	Third and youngest son of Noah.
Timnah	Young woman from the Dark Kingdom.
Nadina	Daughter of Imperial officials from the City of Light.
Sashina	Daughter of Imperial officials from Isis.
Ladan	Head of Council Elders in the Land of the Ancients.

www.ingramcontent.com/pod-product-compliance
Lightning Source LLC
Chambersburg PA
CBHW031659170626
46808CB00005B/1528